MATCHBOX

Ashapurna Debi (1909–95), the author of dozens of novels, short-story collections, and children's works, is one of the most significant Bengali writers of the twentieth century. Her best-known novels were the trilogy of *Pratham Pratishruti*, *Subarnalata*, and *Bakulkatha*, which spanned the period from the 'twenties to the 'sixties, and in which she led the way in tackling women's issues. In 1978 she received the Gyanpeeth Award and in 1994 she was chosen a Fellow of the Sahitya Akademi.

Prasenjit Gupta is the author of *A Brown Man and Other Stories*, the children's novel *To the Blue King's Castle*, and a collection of stories translated from Hindi, *Indian Errant: Short Stories by Nirmal Verma*. A former Fulbright scholar, he writes fiction in English and translates fiction and poetry from Hindi and Bengali into English; he was the recipient of a National Endowment for the Arts fellowship for translating the stories in *Matchbox*.

Jhumpa Lahiri is the author of the novel *The Lowland* and three previous works of fiction: *Interpreter of Maladies*, *The Namesake*, and *Unaccustomed Earth*. A recipient of the Pulitzer Prize, a PEN/Hemingway Award, the Frank O'Connor International Short Story Award, and a Guggenheim Fellowship, she was inducted into the American Academy of Arts and Letters in 2012.

ALSO BY PRASENJIT GUPTA

Indian Errant: Short Stories by Nirmal Verma
(Translated from the Hindi)

A Brown Man and Other Stories

To the Blue King's Castle: Adventures in the Underground Forest

MATCHBOX

Stories by

ASHAPURNA DEBI

Translated into a Bengali English
by
PRASENJIT GUPTA

Introduction
by
JHUMPA LAHIRI

hachette INDIA

First published in 2015 by Hachette India
(Registered name: Hachette Book Publishing India Pvt. Ltd)
An Hachette UK company
www.hachetteindia.com

SRD

The story 'Neejer Jonno Shok' was taken from *Bangla Galpa Sankalan* ('A Collection of Bengali Short Stories'), Vol. II, compiled and edited by Asru Kumar Sikdar and Kabita Sinha, Delhi: Sahitya Akademi, 2002

All other stories in this collection were taken from Ashapurna Debi's *Swanirbachita Sreshtha Galpa* ('Self-selected Best Stories'), Calcutta: Model Publishing House, 1988

The translated stories 'Grieving for Oneself' and 'Matchbox' have previously appeared on the website www.parabaas.com

This translation project was supported by the United States National Endowment for the Arts

ISBN 978-93-5195-042-4

Hachette Book Publishing India Pvt. Ltd
4th/5th Floors, Corporate Centre,
Sector 44, Gurgaon 122003, India

Typeset in Gentium 10.5/14.1
by InoSoft Systems Noida

Printed in India by
Manipal Technologies Limited, Manipal

FSC www.fsc.org
MIX
Paper from responsible sources
FSC™ C104740

To the goddess in your home

Contents

Introduction*

Jhumpa Lahiri

Ashapurna Debi, one of the most celebrated, admired, and prolific Bengali writers of the twentieth century, is virtually unknown to readers outside India. Her first short story was published in 1936, when she was twenty-seven years old; in the course of her lifetime she published over one hundred novels and innumerable works of short fiction. Her stories were gathered into dozens of collections and were regularly featured in Bengali literary magazines for over fifty years. She was the recipient of several prestigious awards, including a Gold Medal from Calcutta University in 1963, a Tagore Award in 1966, a Golden Lotus Award from the Indian government in 1976, and the Jnanpith Award – India's most coveted literary prize – also in 1976. In 1994, she was selected as a Fellow by Calcutta's highly distinguished Sahitya Bharati Academy. She held honorary degrees from three Indian universities.

While dizzying in quantity, the bulk of Debi's short stories[1] adheres to a single subject: private life within the homes of Calcutta, the city in which Debi lived most of her life. Her stories mine, with scrupulous

* An excerpt from Jhumpa Lahiri's master's thesis on Ashapurna Debi, completed at Boston University in 1995.

care, commonplace trials and trifles typical to Bengali domestic life, and unearth the sheltered follies and frailties of the city's colossal middle-class population. Although Calcutta's presence – its diversity, adversity, incongruities, and energies – unmistakably shape Debi's imagined world, the stories themselves take place almost exclusively behind drawn curtains and locked doors, inside the city's millions of flats, quarters, bungalows, and other dwellings. It is Debi's tendency to isolate a small spatial unit, such as an apartment, a neighbourhood, or a city block, and to explore in microscopic detail the manner of life identified with that place.[2] To read Ashapurna Debi is to cross the thresholds of Calcutta's inhabitants, to witness intimately their private scenes and struggles, and to encounter life in the city from a distinctly interior perspective.

Another notable feature of Ashapurna Debi's work is the spirit of emotional insurgency in the lives of her characters. Moments of intense confrontation are a trademark of her world; seemingly trivial disputes contain the seeds of enormous, and often disproportionate, conflict in her hands. Her stories expose private clashes between husbands and wives, parents and children, in-laws and brides, servants and residents. The architectural borders of the domestic world create an enclosed arena for Debi to depict the discord commonly at play in the lives of ordinary people, and to reveal the often unspeakable skirmishes which seldom surface beyond the opaque peripheries of the home.

The home itself, as both physical setting and symbolic space, is the most central feature of Ashapurna Debi's stories, and it frequently plays a complex and contradictory role. At times the home represents an adversary, a physical prison, a site of constraint beyond which the truth about a family cannot be disclosed. At other times her stories endorse the home as a haven, a refuge representative of ownership, comfort, and escape, which protects the individual from the danger and disorder rampant in city life. This polarized notion of home, as both prison and sanctuary, provides perpetual grist for Debi's fictional mill; a simultaneous defiance and embrace of private life and space provokes dissent both within and amongst her characters, and informs her tales with a complex dynamic between interior and exterior, secrecy and disclosure, isolation and community, captivity and release.

The significance of private life in Debi's fiction is not only underscored by her consistently domestic settings but also by her painstaking attention to the hidden, internal lives of her characters. An explorer of introspection and sensitivity, she has been described by one Bengali critic as a 'deep-sea diver of human emotions.'[3] In Debi's world, the home's enclosure of the body is analogous to the body's 'enclosure' of inner conscience. For just as a home contains private life, so does a character's outward mien house private thoughts, motives, and feelings. By combining internal monologue with omniscient narrative, and by often shifting points of view within the course of a single story, Debi repeatedly discerns between the internal desires and external actions of her characters. The reader is aware of the stunning and often comic discrepancies that exist between one's public and private behaviour, for Debi is a master at isolating situations that betray that very discrepancy.

The stories are written in a laconic, concentrated, yet whimsical style. Often the time frame occupies little more than two or three hours, and the core of the tale is almost always encapsulated within the first handful of sentences. Deceptively small in scope, these pithy encounters illuminate the private lives of her characters with astonishing lucidity, and reveal domestic nuances and vicissitudes with extraordinary depth and amplitude. Debi's straightforward prose is so unadorned, so agile, that it frequently sounds conversational in tone, but it is at the same time polished, poetic, and graceful. Her narratives maintain a steadfast balance between authorial concern and detachment, between urgency and restraint.

And although there is frequently a bitter strain of confrontation embedded in her work, it is always tempered by a palpable blend of humour, irony, and wit.

Debi's portrayal of realistic subjects in a realistic yet light-hearted manner resembles, to a certain extent, the style of Rabindranath Tagore (1861–1941), who is generally acknowledged to have both created and perfected the medium of the short story in Bengali literature. Like Debi, Tagore's stories are 'about ordinary people's lives and emotions in real social contexts.'[4] Like Tagore, too, Debi's tone is ironic rather than hectoring, her criticism covert rather than explicit.[5] According to Anima Bose, Tagore introduced certain essential features to the genre of Bengali short fiction; each of these elements is manifested in Debi's work:

> . . . One, the form of a short story must be short. Two, although a short story necessarily portrays a part, or a slice of life, the portrayal must have the flavour of the whole. Three, not only is the external aspect of life portrayed in short stories, but the invisible inner life too must form a part of that portrayal. And finally, the essential ingredient of a short story is a particular moment amidst the monotony of routine daily life culled out by the author's own experience and sensitivity.[6]

The third point is of particular importance in understanding Ashapurna Debi. Simply stated, the 'invisible inner life,' as Bose puts it, is Debi's fictional métier; boundaries between domestic life and the exterior world – and the reasons for either observing or transcending such boundaries – are what her stories succeed in locating.

The short story has maintained a rich, diverse, and vital presence in the Bengali literary tradition. Debi wrote for a sophisticated, demanding audience, and throughout her career, her popularity endured the test of time as well as shifts in styles and tastes. Like all writers of genius, Ashapurna Debi's fiction is conspicuously stamped with an inimitable voice and vision, and her masterful variations on the theme of Bengali private life lack comparison amongst either her predecessors or peers.

Debi's Life and Times

Ashapurna Debi's life spans a remarkable succession of changes in Calcutta's social, cultural, and political history. She is a writer who may be classified both before and after India's independence from British rule in 1947, and thus both before and after the nation's turbulent, pervasive struggle for sovereignty, in which Bengalis played a particularly prominent role. Debi also witnessed the implementation of several reforms leading to radical changes in the Bengali social structure, especially in regard to women's lives and roles. During Debi's lifetime, Bengali women of the middle and upper classes went from living in a culturally endorsed system of domestic segregation, known as purdah, to entering both the political field and work-force in the public sector alongside men. It is perhaps her unique vantage point as the product of one distinct historical period, as witness to its erosion, and as participant in a modern, post-colonial age, that endows Debi's fiction with such breadth and complexity.

She was born 8 January 1909, into a conservative middle-class Bengali Hindu family. Discouraged by her grandmother from attending school (for it was considered improper for Bengali girls to do so at the time), Debi learned to read and write from her mother, but apart from this, received no formal education. Her three brothers, on the other hand, attended college. Debi's father was an artist and her mother was a housewife with a strong interest in literature. Together they must have instilled in their daughter a passion for artistic creation at an early age, for by the time she was thirteen, Ashapurna had already published a poem in a children's magazine. While still in her teens she was married – a partnership negotiated by her parents – into another conservative family. Debi conducted her literary career within her own home, in conjunction with her duties as a wife, mother, and member of a traditional Bengali joint family. Her talent for writing was recognized and encouraged throughout her married life by her husband, the late Kalidas Gupta. They had a daughter and one son, Susanta, who serves as her literary executor.

Over the course of the twentieth century, specific incidents in Calcutta's history drastically challenged not only the private lives of its residents, but the collective notion of home. The city has been the repeated site of displacements, disruptions, and natural devastations that have resulted in making shelter, property, and private life increasingly precious and precarious commodities for its inhabitants. Calcutta is a place defined by staggering residential extremes, perhaps more so than any other city in India. As Paul Oliver notes, 'It has fine administrative buildings and museums, large public spaces, light and heavy industry, and many citizens with considerable wealth. It also has for hundreds of thousands of people probably the worst living conditions in the world.'[7]

Since its role as the administrative center for the British East India Company, and as the capital of India until 1912, Calcutta has always attracted enormous numbers of migrants from rural areas.[8] In 1905, Lord Curzon attempted to divide Bengal into West and East Bengal on a Hindu/Muslim basis, claiming administrative convenience as his reason. India's participation in World War II undermined Calcutta's economic life, and between 1943 and 1944, a massive famine killed at least three million people, or roughly four percent of the population at the time. In 1947 India and Pakistan were divided along religious lines; during the process, Calcutta was racked by violent riots and massacres, until Bengal was eventually divided into the political territories of West Bengal and East Pakistan. As a result of Partition, between four and six million refugees poured into India between 1950 and 1956, a quarter of them settling in Calcutta.[9] In 1971, the Pakistani Civil War, which eventually created Bangladesh, resulted in a new flood of refugees amounting to five million more. Still another influx followed the 1977 flood disasters in Bangladesh.

As a result of so many millions of migrants, Calcutta's infrastructure, which is appropriate for two million people, must today support a population of more than four times that number.[10] Approximately one-third of Calcutta's population lives on the streets. Hundreds of thousands live in registered slums or illegal squatter settlements with little sanitation and even less security. There are also those who exist without any physical shelter whatsoever. The arrival of refugees has complicated matters in more ways than one, for in addition to fighting for physical space, the city's residents must also incorporate culturally distinct, dispossessed others who constitute an inescapable presence in daily life.

Ashapurna Debi's stories are rooted firmly in the homes of Calcutta's comfortably sheltered families; her principal characters seldom struggle with the levels of poverty and destitution common to the city's less fortunate population. However, in any analysis of private life, it is crucial to understand the public conditions and circumstances which exist in contrast to the inner domain of home. As Antoine Prost explains, 'Private life makes sense only in relation to public life; its history is first of all the history of its definition.'[11] In Debi's case, the symbolic meaning of space is resonant on a social level as well. Her stories, though almost uniformly interior, are thus insulated from, but not immaterial to, the public sphere. In Debi's stories we see how external pressures determine the actions and attitudes of characters in relation to the outside world. We see how, for the middle class, the claim to private property is a means of both defining and defending oneself from the city's displaced. We see, too, that the physical fact of being at home often has little to do with the psychological luxury of feeling at home. Finally, we see how, even within the material security of home, instability, dislocation, and estrangement remain perpetual threats.

Critical Background

Extremely little has been written in English about Ashapurna Debi's work. This is hardly surprising, given the fact that so little of her work has been translated into English. There have so far been only a half-dozen works in English translation of her work. These books, printed in India, have not been marketed in either the United States or England, and thus have done little in the way of promoting Debi to English audiences.

Much of the critical attention Debi has received in English has been stolid and uninspired. Due to her subject matter, she has been dismissed by many as a domestic writer, one who is narrow in vision and limited in scope. Her novels have been described rather ponderously as being 'concerned with the struggle of well-educated middle-class Bengali women to free themselves from the social chains of male-dominated society.'[12] Rasik Bihari's appraisal of her trilogy[13]? the novels *Pratham Pratisruti* (First Promise), 1964, *Suvarnalata*, 1966, and *Bakul-Katha* (Bakul's Story), 1973?consists of little more than wordy plot summaries and an arbitrary smattering of historical background. This award-winning trilogy has been hailed as being Debi's most significant contribution to Indian literature, yet Bihari makes little effort to describe Debi's artistry, or to probe the content or context of the novels in an inventive way. The result is an underdeveloped essay which does justice neither to the trilogy nor its author.

In a preface to a collection of her stories published in 1988 (the source for most of the following translations), Ashapurna Debi states that the short story is her most beloved form of writing.[14] However, while her novels have received at least some critical acclaim, her short stories have been virtually ignored by literary scholarship. Selections crop up in anthologies here and there, usually with a few cursory words of introduction. Krishna Dutta and Andrew Robinson, editors of the Bengali short-story anthology *Noon in Calcutta*, describe her work as 'pared miniature[s] of domestic Calcutta life.'[15] The editors continue, 'The setting is quotidian, typical of her work, a neighbourhood like any of a thousand congested, shabby, middle-middle-class Calcutta *paras* [neighbourhoods], riddled with social and economic tension, with constant conflict between and inside its human residents.'[16] According to Dutta and Robinson, however, Debi's work lacks the 'political punch' of some of her contemporary writers. Their summary of Debi appears to classify her work as something fundamentally diminutive and detached from the greater body of politically 'relevant' contemporary Bengali literature. Susie Tharu and K. Lalita, editors of the anthology *Women Writing in India*, add that the exclusive confines of Debi's work inhibit the presence of widespread scholarly attention, for they write, 'Obviously a critic trained – or indoctrinated – into the perspectives of the 'mainstream' is not sensitive to the questions, however broad their import, that arise in a woman's world, or appreciative of what is at stake in the struggles and victories that take place within it.'[17]

Another complaint issued by critics is the author's supposed conservatism, especially with regard to women's lives. This charge is further complicated by the fact that Debi's vigilant attention to domestic life has saddled her with an unwarranted reputation as an author writing primarily for and about the concerns of women. Debi herself stated, 'I have thought and written mostly about women because I have seen their helplessness and that is what I know best. Over the years, great clouds of protest have accumulated, unexpressed, in my mind.'[18] Yet Debi's fiction has not been championed by feminist scholars. Indeed, Debi's ostensibly 'feminine' subject matter, coupled with her popularity and exceptional prolifacy, are regarded with such suspicion that Lalita and Tharu go so far as to caution, 'The profile of her career reads so much like that of a writer of popular romances that we must emphasize that she is not one.'[19] They continue:

> Where Ashapurna Debi is concerned . . . the critical dismissal is also the result of the apparently conservative posture her narratives promote. Rebellion, defiance, anger, resentment, and passion are portrayed to evoke our sympathy. But . . . order, somewhat chastened no doubt, is always carefully restored. It is as if, given the scheme of the Ashapurna world, a rebellion that stubbornly insists on its fruits is an escapist dream. . . .[20]

In other words, while Debi depicts systems of oppression – more specifically, oppression towards women – Lalita and Tharu find that these systems, though disputed, are ultimately reconfirmed and accepted by her female characters. I challenge this analysis; I believe that the reconfirmation of traditional values in Debi's stories does not necessarily signify the passive conformity or disempowerment of their female characters, nor the conservatism of the author. In fact, in a number of Debi's stories, the female characters are themselves agents of manipulation, exploitation, and deceit. I wish to emphasize here how the critical reception of Ashapurna Debi suffers from an insistence, by literary critics, to assess her fiction under the rubric of some sort of polemical posture. It appears that feminists are at odds with Debi's alleged conservatism and re-inscription of patriarchal norms, while mainstream critics are thwarted by her parochial concerns.

The dismissal of Ashapurna Debi is not limited to critics of literature. Manisha Roy, a Bengali cultural anthropologist writing in English, has the following to say about Ashapurna Debi's writing:

> [She] writes about the wives of upper-class and upper middle-class homes who are always exploited both physically and emotionally by men. . . . Ashapurna Debi's novels, which emphasize the glory of conjugal love in an urban setting, are frequently given to brides

> as wedding presents. They have attractive jackets, often with illustrations of a demure wife touching the feet of her husband to show respect.[21]

While Roy writes as an anthropologist and not as a literary critic, her analysis of Debi's work is inaccurate. As any reader of Ashapurna Debi is aware, she does not write only about housewives, nor are those housewives always exploited or subjugated by men, nor does her work blindly glorify the institution of conjugal love. Debi writes about men as well as women; exploitation is not meted out according to one's gender, and the institution of marriage is one of several social traditions that Debi continuously interrogates. Debi is a subtle and fiercely intelligent author, and her work demands like attributes from her reader. Roy's comments, which disregard totally the value of Debi as a creative writer, and focus instead on the superficial attributes of the books' pretty covers, exemplify the way in which Debi's fiction has been relegated by most scholars to the status of popular culture rather than appreciated as a product of the literary imagination.

Perhaps an interesting comparison to consider at this point is between Ashapurna Debi and a fellow Bengali woman writer, Mahasweta Debi (b. 1926).[22] An author, journalist, activist, and anthropologist, Mahasweta Debi's typically cynical, politically charged fiction has been taken under the wing of what is known in critical circles as subaltern studies, most notably by the critical theorist and translator Gayatri Chakravarti Spivak. Both translations and theoretical interpretations of Mahasweta Debi's work are featured in Spivak's book *In Other Worlds*,[23] now considered a seminal text in feminist, poststructuralist, and postcolonial critical discourse. Mahasweta Debi is also the sole woman writer featured in an anthology of Bengali short stories translated into English by Kalpana Bardhan, *Of Women, Outcastes, Peasants, and Rebels*, a collection designed, in Bardhan's words, to introduce Western readers to Bengali literature 'interrelated [by] forms and mechanisms of oppression at various levels of society.'[24]

Mahasweta Debi's work, linked to such theoretical hotbeds as gender, ethnicity, caste, and class, fits conveniently into contemporary academic agendas and their pursuit of multicultural, 'socially' based texts. As Tharu and Lalita confirm, 'Throughout Mahasweta Debi's varied fiction, women's subjugation is portrayed as linked to the oppressions of caste and class. . . . In the best of her writing, she quite brilliantly, and with resonance, explores the articulation of class, caste, and gender in the specific situations she depicts.'[25] Bardhan notes that Mahasweta herself has 'described her writing of fiction as inseparable from her work as an investigative journalist and editor of a 'people's' magazine.'[26]

While Mahasweta Debi's politically informed writings lend themselves to current trends in literary and cultural studies, Ashapurna Debi's relatively insular fictional world occupies a more remote, less 'relevant' position within much of today's critical framework, especially as it relates to the discovery and reading of non-Western writers. As a result, Ashapurna Debi's work runs the risk not only of being misunderstood as a dubious representative of 'third-world feminism' but also of being exiled to the ancillary realm of regional literature.

The existing attitude towards Ashapurna Debi stands in need of revision and expansion. Rather than dismissing her work as domestic, conservative, or anti-feminist, it must be appreciated, first, as an example of artistic creation. It must also be esteemed as a rich and intelligently realized portrait of private life in one of the world's most incomprehensible cities. Moreover, just as Mahasweta Debi's writing is appreciated for its resistance and rebellion on a public and political level, so must Ashapurna Debi's be read as exemplary of insurgency on the private, domestic level. Much of

Debi's work charts the disintegration of traditional values and the way in which public change affects and alters private life. As Anima Bose puts it: 'Ashapurna is indeed a rebel: a rebel against the fetters of customs, against time-worn prejudices, against meaningless traditions hugged by society, against the indignities heaped upon women by men, by women themselves and by the social order as a whole.'[27]

In Debi's work, domesticity constitutes the very means by which resistance and a struggle towards reform are articulated. The characters' relationships to physical space are representative, on a concrete level, of an individual's relationship to liberty, both personal and public. The home serves as a locus for dramatizing not only constraints placed upon women, but upon men, children, the elderly, servants, and even the homeless. While culturally specific and bound to a restricted sense of place, Debi's stories resonate beyond both architectural and national borders. If substantially translated and carefully studied, Ashapurna Debi's fiction will not only contribute to the study of modern Bengali literature but will also serve as an invaluable source, to English readers, for understanding Bengali private life in the twentieth century.

Domesticity and Literature

A good deal of attention has been paid by scholars to the subject of domesticity in Western literature. The home has been interpreted as a series of wide-ranging metaphors: as extensions of characters' personalities, as sites of confinement or escape, as wombs of spiritual regeneration, and as physical representations of an irretrievable past. One seminal analysis of domesticity in literature is Gaston Bachelard's *The Poetics of Space*, first published in French in 1958. Bachelard's book is a phenomenological inquiry focused on the home, its interior features, and its relationship to the outside world.

He explores the home as a physical representation of intimacy, and investigates the impact of human habitation on architectural form as well as the impact of concrete space upon its inhabitants.

Bachelard describes his project as 'topophilia' – a celebration of place, and of interior spaces in particular. According to Bachelard, the home shelters the unconscious, and is thus the site of our innermost, private being. The home provides a crucial refuge for the dreamer; it is a physical sanctuary in which the imagination can flourish. Bachelard's study incorporates literary analysis, modern psychology, and even zoology as he isolates both man-made structures and natural objects that constitute a universal vocabulary of space. According to John Stilgoe, one of Bachelard's primary contributions is to reveal how 'setting is more than scene in works of art, that it is often the armature around which the work revolves.'[28] Bachelard's innovative perspective revamped and contributed significantly to new interpretations of interiority in literature.

While Bachelard's study, although supplemented by literary examples, remains primarily a theoretical investigation, Philippa Tristam, in her book *Living Space in Fact and Fiction*, draws explicit attention to the relationship between the home and fiction. Both, in her opinion, are 'small worlds defined against, but also reflecting, larger ones.'[29] According to Tristam, an inherent connection exists between the contents of a home and the material for fiction. She explains, 'Most of life, after all, is spent within four walls, and the space they define, the objects that fill them, the prospects on which they open, inevitably influence and express our consciousness.'[30] Tristam's book focuses specifically on the British novel and its developing awareness of interior space. Beginning with Samuel Richardson, whom she considers 'the first writer of fiction to be really interested in living space,'[31] she traces the responsiveness of such novelists as Dickens, Thackeray, Trollope, and others to the social, psychological, and physical dimensions of homes.

Another study which addresses the growing celebration of private life and its influence in Western art and literature appears in Witold Rybczynski's *Home*. Rybczynski, an architect, locates a historical connection between the obsession with domestic life and the emergence of the European bourgeoisie; he cites John Lukacs, author of *The Bourgeois Interior*, as saying: 'Domesticity, privacy, comfort, the concept of home and the family; these are, literally, principal achievements of the Bourgeois age.'[32] Rybczynski traces shifts in the notion of private life from the middle ages – when the home served as a public meeting place and thus offered virtually no privacy to its inhabitants – to the seventeenth century, when people began no longer to live and work in the same building. As a result, Rybczynski observes, the home became a place exclusively of residence, which created a clearer separation between public and private worlds.

Rybczynski explains that the growth of private life in seventeenth-century Europe had a distinct impact on the art and literature of the period. He points to Dutch painters Emanuel de Witte and Jan Vermeer as examples of artists who pioneered a genre of painting glorifying deliberately domestic, interior scenes, rich in seemingly insignificant detail and emblematic of the private, everyday world.

Rybczynski regards the domestic novel – another artistic product of the seventeenth century – as the literary counterpart to Dutch interior painting. He singles out the novels of Jane Austen (1775–1817), and describes her work as follows:

> An Austen novel is a tour de force, at least by modern standards. Nothing extraordinary happens – no murders, escapades, or disasters. Instead of adventure or melodrama we read about the prosaic daily comedy of family life. . . . Austen chose to stay strictly within the limits of the everyday, not because her talent was small, but because her imagination did not require a broader canvas.[33]

Rybczynski's celebration of Austen's interior art stands outside the circle of a good deal of Austen criticism, especially what was written during the writer's lifetime. Resistant to conventional approaches to techniques of narrative and structure, her idiosyncratic work was chided, by generations of critics, as insignificant, claustrophobic, and domestic. While never lacking a loyal following of readers, and staunchly defended by such writers as Sir Walter Scott, even by the end of the nineteenth century, Austen 'appeared narrow and provincial, interesting enough as a period writer, a historian of manners, but limited in culture and intellect, unlearned and without a declared seriousness of aim.'[34] Coventry Patmore rejected Austen as a "surface' writer, 'as small as she is perfect."[35] Her reputation as a literary miniaturist is curiously echoed by Austen herself who, in a letter of 1816, describes her imaginative workspace as a 'little bit (two inches wide) of ivory.'[36] In 1914 Ezra Pound, in a comparison between Austen and Stendhal, charged that 'a book about a dull, stupid, hemmed-in sort of life, by a person who has lived it, will never be as interesting as the work of some author who has comprehended many men's manners and seen many grades and conditions of existence.'[37] It was not until 1939 that Mary Lascelles wrote the first serious study devoted to Austen's artistic achievement.

By now the reasons for considering Austen's critical reputation should be apparent in light of my study of Ashapurna Debi. While a full-blown comparison between Austen and Debi is not my intention, it is impossible to ignore certain fundamental similarities between both the artistic devices and critical perceptions of the two writers. Like Austen, Debi is endangered by such descriptive labels as limited, insulated and confined. As a result, although they are separated by centuries, circumstances, and cultures, both writers may be summarily classified as parochial – Austen in regard to the world of Regency manners, Debi to that of Bengali domestic life. My reading of certain contemporary critics of Austen, especially those who address her interiority, has enabled me to articulate a corresponding critical appreciation of Debi's short stories. Meenakshi Mukherjee, for example, notes that 'the survival and development of the private individual in a very close knit society that affords little solitude seems to be one of the underlying concerns of Jane Austen's fiction.'[38] Mukherjee's observation of Austen is central in the context of Debi's conception of private life as well.

While critics like Bachelard, Tristam, and Rybczynski analyze a celebration of private life in literature, an opposing view exists that interprets the home as a site of oppression and constraint, especially in relation to women's lives. Perhaps the most comprehensive investigation of this idea was made by Susan Gilbert and Sandra Gubar in *The Madwoman in the Attic* (1979), a book which attempts to draw attention to nineteenth-century women's literature in light of its interiority. According to Gilbert and Gubar, women's literature of this period is characterized by 'recurrent images of enclosure and escape.' They observe a contrast between 'frozen landscapes and fiery interiors' – a contrast between the public and private worlds, between docility and subordination, and between psychological oppression and the emotional release of madness. The authors argue that the social position of the woman writer was one of fundamental confinement; she was enclosed within the architecture of a patriarchal society, both in life and art, by a male-dominated society as well as by male-inscribed definitions of literary production and value.

Gilbert and Gubar point to metaphors of physical discomfort manifested in women's writing and the thematic concern with spatial constriction in writers such as Jane Austen, George Eliot, Emily Bronte, and Emily Dickinson. Claustrophobic rage is expressed by enacting rebellious escapes, by explosive moments of violence, and by mad doubles. All forms of resistance are representative, the authors maintain, of an anger repressed until it can no longer be contained; this containment is underscored by the traditional relegation of women's lives to the domestic sphere. As a result, the home becomes the primary symbol of female imprisonment. The authors write:

> Imagery of entrapment expresses the woman writer's sense that she has been dispossessed precisely because she is so thoroughly possessed.... Literally confined to the house, figuratively confined to a single 'place,' enclosed in parlors and encased in texts, imprisoned in kitchens and enshrined in stanzas, women artists naturally found themselves describing dark interiors and confusing their sense that they were house-bound with their rebellion against being duty bound.[39]

While Gilbert and Gubar raise several important questions about the significance of interiority in fiction, their project is restricted to the parameters of a specifically feminist poetics. As a result of isolating what they interpret as the oppressive constraints of obligatory domesticity for women, they pay little attention to the historical function of the private home as a locus of resistance to public forces of exploitation, repression, and greed.[40] Gilbert and Gubar distinguish between male and female experiences of spatial enclosure, insisting that while male images of imprisonment are metaphysical and metaphorical, women's experience with boundaries are social and actual.[41] Not surprisingly, they contrast Bachelard's description of felicitous space with the decidedly claustrophobic imagery of domestic life they find inherent in women's writing:

Clearly, for Bachelard the protective asylum of the house is closely associated with its maternal features, and to this extent he is following the work done on dream symbolism by Freud and on female inner space by Erikson. It seems clear too, however, that such symbolism must inevitably have very different implications for male critics and for female authors.[42]

Consequently, Gilbert and Gubar's study draws a distinction not only between gendered nineteenth century experiences of privacy, but between contemporary notions of the 'masculine' domain of criticism versus 'feminine' creativity.

In the twentieth century, the home continues to redefine and renegotiate the articulation of private life. Advances in communication, such as the radio, telephone, and television, as well as in mobilization, have not only exerted a tremendous impact upon the domestic sphere, but have served to attenuate the division between public and private life. Sociologists have argued that 'the individual in a modern society is typically conscious of a sharp dichotomization between the world of his private life and the world of large public institutions to which he relates in a variety of roles.'[43] As a result, the modern individual is forced perpetually to shift between highly discrepant and often contradictory social contexts. In their book *The Homeless Mind: Modernization and Consciousness*, Peter Berger, Brigitte Berger, and Hansfried Kellner determine that while the home functions as a compensation for the discontents brought about by drastically modern, urban society, and as a shelter from the threat of anonymity, private life may itself be a region of extreme disorder. The reason for this, according to the authors, is twofold: first, in the private sphere, '"repressed" irrational forces are allowed to come to the fore.'[44] Second, modern private life lacks any institutional medium capable of organizing or structuring human activity. The territory of the modern home, the authors maintain, provides the individual with an increased and overwhelming latitude when it comes to designing his own particular private life. Consequently, the private sphere becomes an area of unparalleled liberty and anxiety for the individual. Whatever compensations the private sphere provides are usually experienced as fragile, possibly artificial and essentially unreliable.[45]

Not only can the modern home exacerbate a sense of private

disquietude, but it can also be the source of alienation within a communal setting. Chiara Saraceno explains that modern life has witnessed a revolution in technological innovations, in the acquisition of new needs, in transformations in consumptive patterns, and in the rejection of old duties, all of which revise the boundaries between public and private life. The progressive modernization of the family, coupled with the discontinuity of experiences, models, and values between generations, contribute, in the author's opinion, to severe and unprecedented conflicts within the domestic sphere. Saraceno writes:

> Symbol par excellence of private family life in the twentieth century, the home – its ownership, its internal organization, the roles and rights that it delineates – is the scene of often angry interaction and struggle among the various actors involved.[46]

While technological developments have allowed greater privacy in the home for family activities, Saraceno finds that a further consequence of contemporary domestic life is an increased demarcation of each person's space, and of each family activity, within the home itself. As a result, individuals dwelling under a common roof may encounter a paradoxically increased sense of separation from one another.

Several of these critical insights are beneficial when reading a writer as committed to representing domesticity and private life as is Ashapurna Debi. However, it is a mistake to assume that Debi can be defined by such interpretations, or to rely too heavily on any one critical perspective. Each of the arguments I have touched on stems from an exclusively Western critical and cultural perspective. This would not necessarily be a problem, were it not for the fact that these arguments incorporate, and are dependent upon, historically specific details, none of which are directly related to an understanding of contemporary Bengali private life, which has its own set of determining factors, priorities, and consequences. Unfortunately, no comprehensive study exists in English which explores the subject of Bengali domesticity, apart from studies limited to anthropological, sociological, or demographic ends. Articles about third-world housing tend to focus on rural or lower-class dwellings rather than the homes of the urban middle class. Meredith Borthwick's *The Changing Role of Women in Bengal, 1849–1905*[47] is an excellent resource for understanding domestic life and the female experience in Bengali culture, but her insights are limited historically, and are thus not wholly sufficient for appraising twentieth-century private life. While Borthwick's book is useful for understanding many of the norms underlying traditional Bengali society, Debi's short stories, though sensitive to traditional expectations, are beyond the scope of Borthwick's study. Confronted with this scarcity of critical sources, I have had to exercise vigilance and discrimination regarding the critics and theorists I have read in relation to Ashapurna Debi, filtering out what seems impertinent while accommodating and assimilating what is germane.

The Home and the World in Ashapurna Debi

A sense of interiority is central to Ashapurna Debi's work. Necessary to an appreciation of what makes her fiction interior is an acknowledgment of the complex ways in which privacy is conceived and manifested. First, one must consider the physical settings themselves, almost all of which are some sort of private space, most often one's home. The next thing to bear in mind is Debi's use of interior narrative – private monologues, indirect discourse, and asides – which constantly point to the concealed thoughts of her characters and enable the reader to distinguish between what they are feeling and doing in any given situation. The third aspect of Debi's interiority is her subject matter, for Debi's stories are typically about private moments, describing private actions and decisions, and centering around private objects, such as letters, or semi-private spaces, such as mail-boxes, balconies, and windowsills. Most significantly, Debi's stories confront private or otherwise masked emotions: suspicion, rumour, shame, and fear. At the same time, the presence and pressures of the outside world, and the power that society wields over inner life, is one of Debi's most recurring themes. As Tristam puts it, '[T]he house presents both the self to society and society to the self, as a reflection of social priorities on the one hand, as an escape from them on the other.'[48]

While always set in private places, Debi's stories describe little in terms of furniture or decoration. Her homes amount to more or less generic walls defining space, with equally generic windows, doors, balconies, stairways, passageways, kitchens, and bedrooms. Nevertheless, she is quick to seize upon the significance of those windows and doors, and the way in which these standard architectural features create boundaries, means of escape, defences, or enclosures. In Debi's work, the reader is constantly aware of the presence of four walls, both by the disposition of her characters and by the intimate dynamics between them. Her description of the home is suggestive rather than particular, atmospheric rather than visual. Again, in Tristam's words, the writer 'tends to sense, rather than see, domestic environments, registering the definition of space and not its detail.'[49] Despite the rare description of interior space, a vivid sense of location is a central and recurrent sensation for Debi's readers. This spatial texture is not created by objects, but rather by Debi's sensitivity to the minutiae of emotions, actions, and gestures at play within her characters.

The home is a site of both protection and constriction, isolation and involvement, intimacy and estrangement, vulnerability and defence. In Debi's stories, the acute juxtaposition of the inner world with the public geography of streets, offices, and shops reflects a dynamic intersection between community and private life. However, while the confluence between inner and outer worlds informs her stories, the central conflicts and resolutions always occur in an interior setting.

Debi's work reflects a psychology which is culturally determined. Private life may be the one thing that succeeds in setting not only individuals, but entire cultures, apart. The fact that Debi writes about Bengali homes may therefore seem especially at odds with Western domestic values and norms. Nevertheless, the architectural confines of her fictional world reflect a universal psychology. As Bettina Knapp reminds us, 'Within its walls, columns, ceilings, chimneys, windows, turrets, or other structural elements, an edifice may be looked upon as a world in itself – a microcosm – an expression of a preexistent form that may be apprehended on a personal and temporal as well as a transpersonal and atemporal level. As such, it may be considered archetypal.'[50]

Translator's Note

The question I am most often asked about my translations relates to a choice all translators must make: how closely to follow the original text. The relative merits of the 'literal' translation (closely following the original) and the 'creative' translation (less committed to fidelity, for the sake of linguistic smoothness and polish) have been debated through the centuries, and each option – and others between those two poles – has its pluses and minuses, its critics and its champions. My note here merely seeks briefly to state my reasons for choosing to stay very close to the original and to offer a few examples of how I've done so in this collection.

I write and translate in the context of the United States, the global center of linguistic and cultural power. Translating in this U.S. and, more generally, Western context, I try to resist the powerful urge to translate into a smooth U.S. (or other Western) English that would place this very Bengali literature in a Western linguistic mode and literary framework. A smooth translation, in facilitating readability for the Western reader, would gloss over differences in linguistic and literary style between Bengali and English, and thus erase, I believe, much of what makes this literature Bengali.[51] Of course, some measure of this 'Bengaliness' is lost in the very act of translation, in separating the literature from its language, but my hope is to minimize that loss, to preserve as much of what is Bengali about it as possible. And this includes the features of language – idioms and metaphors, the use of tense, the kinship terms – that make Bengali Bengali.

My commitment, to put it bluntly, is more to the writer's language than to the reader's. I have tried, however, not to Bengalify the English to the point where it becomes awkward and hard to read. It's a fine line to walk: between the attractions (for an open-minded and sensitive reader) of a somewhat Bengali English on the one hand, and, on the other, the dangers of using language that is simply too unwieldy and graceless to sustain interest; and in the end only the reader can tell how well the translator has succeeded for that particular reader. By preserving the phrase, metaphors, and linguistic constructions of Bengali in my English, I have tried to arrive at a hybrid language for these stories that, while it is a modern, colloquial idiom, is influenced, subtly or markedly, by the Bengali, and thus conveys – in an engaging way, I hope – some of the flavor of the original language and culture. I hope the reader will understand my reasons for translating as I do; and I trust that in trying to honor the Bengali language I have not done a disservice to the Bengali writer.

In translating idioms, I have sought wherever possible to use a literal version. Where clarity would have suffered, I have introduced some slight explication, perhaps an added word or phrase. Where this has not been possible, I have provided a footnote, as I have in other places where it seemed necessary to the reading of the text. Kinship terms, items of food or clothing, and other such words have been listed in a glossary.

I've tried as far as possible to avoid using turns of phrase that are familiar to English readers: when I read a story in translation that contains a cliché or an idiom or metaphor common in English, it immediately jolts me out of the story and starts me wondering what the original phrase might have been. More importantly, I find that being introduced to the riches of other cultures' metaphors is one of great pleasures of translation and of reading translations. Here are some examples that may indicate how I've been able to stay close to the original in some places, and how I've had to stray a little in others.

I have translated 'ghor kora' quite literally as 'making house' (in the story 'Foolhardy'), with the belief that the context is sufficient to make the meaning clear.

I have used the literal 'neither will seven maunds of oil be burnt, nor will Radha dance' ('Shadowsun') with the footnote 'that is, an impossible condition won't be met, and the desired result won't be achieved' and an entry for 'maund' in the glossary.

In rendering the idiom 'matha kata jaoa' – literally, to have one's head be cut off, meaning to be greatly ashamed or disgraced – I have added an explanation: 'Her rudeness leaves me headless, the shame of it' ('Shadowsun').

For 'para mathaye korey tola' – literally, to lift the neighborhood upon one's head, meaning to raise a hue and cry – I could not satisfactorily preserve the 'head' and convey the meaning of the expression, and so I have said 'churns up the entire neighbourhood' ('Grief').

I have rendered the expression 'tiki dekha jaye na' – literally, the 'tiki' (a tuft of hair at the back of the head) cannot be seen, meaning there's no sign of the person – as 'the tips of their mustaches couldn't be seen' ('To Be Unable to Be Able') in order to avoid having to explain 'tiki' within the idiom. (I have, in other words, translated the hair to an antipodal position on the head.)

I have coined compound words, such as for 'opomanahoto', wounded by insult ('Glass Beads Diamonds'), where I have 'insult-wounded' (similar in construction to the English word 'windblown').

Phrases such as 'eight–nine years,' meaning eight or nine years, are common in Bengali, and I have left them that way.

Another example of the way I have tried to reflect the original language is in the matter of tense. Often Bengali stories use tense more fluidly than English stories do; in places in these stories, for example, present tense is used to indicate a permanent state of things, and past tense for the current action. Elsewhere, a fluidity of tense provides a sense of continuity, of the past within the present. I have preserved some of these moments; in others, I've smoothed out the tenses, as otherwise the transitions seemed overly awkward in English.

Comma splices are common in these stories; I've preserved them in most places, for example, 'Aroti's mother is astonished, stupefied, she stays quiet for a minute or so, then says . . .' ('Entering the Underworld').

In Bengali, words may be repeated in ways not often encountered in English prose, for example, 'Then at least this terrible dramatic moment would never have manifested itself in this drama' ('First and Last'). I've preserved this feature of the original.

I have generally not translated kinship terms, except when they have occurred in a bunch: 'Mother-in-law, brother-in-law, sisters-in-law, their husbands, nephews–nieces' ('Glass Beads Diamonds'), where the exact terms were not as important, it seemed to me, as an immediate sense of a multiplicity of relatives and their degree of connection.

For the stories, I have followed the Indian conventions for English spelling and punctuation, such as in the use of single and double quotes and the placement of other punctuation marks within quotes and without.

Finally, in rendering Bengali names into English, I have used, perhaps controversially, what might seem like an old-fashioned approach reminiscent of colonial times. My spelling is meant to reflect the current Bengali pronunciation of the name as opposed to its transliteration into English from its pronunciation in Sanskrit or Hindi. Thus, I have Obinash instead of Avinash, Poddolota instead of Padmalata,[52] to give a better sense of how the name is pronounced in Bengali. I do provide the Sanskrit- and Hindi-based equivalents in the glossary.[53]

Acknowledgements

First of all I must acknowledge the gracious support of Ashapurna Debi's son, Susanta Gupta. He was most kind and considerate in granting me the rights to translate these stories and in his responses to my many requests.

My heartfelt thanks go to Jhumpa Lahiri for so generously agreeing to provide the introduction to this collection of stories.

These translations would not have been possible without the considerable help of my mother, Pratima Gupta, and my wife, Subhasree Sen Gupta, both of whom devoted a great deal of time and effort to this project. My deep gratitude goes also to my teachers and fellow translators who have helped me in so many ways over the years.

I greatly appreciate the work of my friend and editor Devapriya Roy, as I do her continued support and her valuable insights.

These translations were supported by a fellowship from the National Endowment for the Arts and by a grant under the Arts and Humanities Initiative of the University of Iowa. I am deeply grateful for both these awards.

Wealth

ঐশ্বর্য

Oishorjo[1]

Srikumar descended the stairs and walked across the courtyard, and the air filled with the scent of expensive cologne. Wearing a panjabi of glossy addhi cotton frilled by hand, the pleats of his dhuti – of the finest quality, and also hand-frilled – skimming the ground, expensive leather Grecians on his feet, silver-cased walking-stick in his hand, walking rapidly, Srikumar went out.

He goes out every day.

He's been going for eighteen years.

Even if the world turns upside down, Srikumar's routine won't change. Rules are not broken, there's no change in his dress or style. Maybe he's never even considered it.

Ever since he was twenty-five, he's been putting in his attendance at the same place, exactly at the same time, dressed exactly the same way.

Of course the clock can tell the time of his return too. Eight to ten in the evenings – these two hours.

Where he goes – that is not unknown, certainly, but unspoken.

Everyone knows it, but no one says it clearly, out loud.

They don't say it – perhaps to preserve the honour of the master of the house, or perhaps the mistress's! But does Oporna live in the world of such traditional honour–dishonour? Can one stand on the ground here and stretch out a hand and touch her?

And Abha's tried, too – to treat her with disrespect!

Abha, wife of Srikumar's younger brother Shukumar, sat at one end of the courtyard preparing her paan. As soon as her bhashur went out, she raised her eyebrows and smirked at her husband's cousin, Nonda, sitting in front of her. Her manner suggested, 'You saw that, didn't you? I am right in what I say, aren't I?'

Nonda put a hand to her cheek and feigned a wordless astonishment that could have been put into words thus, 'O Ma, really, so it's true! Even now – at this age – ah!'

Nonda has come to this house after a long time.

While her mama and mami were alive, she used to come and go frequently; as a niece widowed young, she was treated affectionately. But now her cousins had no great desire to bring her over or treat her with affection: 'Come, dear Lokkhi – and now go, you pest!' was the general feeling. So, Nonda, too, no longer felt the same urge to visit.

Still, this time she had decided to come.

Of course, not even for an hour after she arrives does she let herself be considered newly arrived; it doesn't take long for a woman as restless and garrulous as Nonda to make a place for herself.

Right away she delivers a caustic comment to her cousins' wives: 'Don't they say, "Brother's rice is in the pot, but sister-in-law serves it out"? *That's* certainly true. Really, you blessed wives! You couldn't ask after your poor cousin even once? You've kept both my brothers completely tied to your anchols, haven't you? Not once, not even by mistake – '

Her brothers have sat down to eat, and she swoops down on them. She laughs softly, sharply. 'So, gentlemen, you couldn't ask after your poor cousin, not even to find out if she's alive or dead? How can anyone turn their relatives into strangers this way? Chhi chhi. If I come to visit your house for a couple of days, how much of your food will I eat up? Nothing more than a handful of atop rice once a day.'

Srikumar says, laughing, 'That – that atop thing, that's what's hard to get nowadays. We'll ask you here with great affection, and then should we starve you to death?'

'Oh, sir, if you really want to treat someone with affection, you can feed them rutis made of grass and still do it, understand?'

'Is that so?' Srikumar, easily amused, laughs out loud, *ha, ha.* 'Then should I go and see if I can gather some grass or straw for you?'

Nonda takes out a small silver snuff-box from its hiding-place in her chemise and places a pinch of perfumed jorda in her mouth, then turns to the younger Shukumar for arbitration: 'Did you see, Shuku-da, did you see that? Isn't that a classic insult? He says he'll feed me grass!'

Shukumar's nature is the exact opposite of his elder brother's. His manner is solemn, his mode of speech that of a wise man, his dress and style that of the master of a household. This sort of unwarranted liveliness, such laughter and taunting – ! Besides, having recently been initiated by his guru and given a mantra to recite, he's become even more grave, more reserved.

He does sit down to eat with his dada in the same courtyard, but not next to him. The fact is, he's a pure vegetarian, whereas Srikumar cannot lift a handful of rice to his mouth unless there's some fish involved. Once Shukumar washes his hands – after casting a glance of utter aversion and contempt at his dada's plate, arranged with abundant helpings of flesh – and sits down to eat, he doesn't take any part in the conversation until he rises to wash his hands again. So he doesn't answer his cousin's question.

'Ah! I see that his wife isn't happy with just tying the man to her anchol, she's made him deaf and mute as well!' Nonda leaves, laughing.

Over there, sitting in the kitchen, Abha is sputtering inside, an eggplant in hot oil. For one thing, she can't stand this garrulousness in women, and on top of that, to mock Shukumar's manner, rituals, and devotion this way!

She looks at her older sister-in-law, Oporna, and says with some annoyance, 'Really, Didi, she'll never grow up, will she? Still craving that same indulgence! It burns me up to see it. Always the same old habits!'

The cast of Oporna's lips is so strange, it always seems as though a thin smile might break out at the corners of her mouth, and that smile is one of irony.

Let the cast of her lips be what it may, but it seems to Abha that when Oporna answers, that smile appears distinctly on her lips. But no, she speaks in an easy manner. 'Whose habits ever change, Chhoto Bou? If they did, the Shastros would be proved false.'

Abha says to herself, 'Well, you can certainly say that, what other choice do you have!'

This is, however, the history of only the first day of Nonda's visit. Now ten days or so have passed – and some magician's trick has given rise to an intimate friendship between this brazen cousin and courteous Abha – who is at least eight years younger than Nonda. But let her be the junior in age – surely she's the senior in position? That's why the balance, one feels, is all right.

There's no end to the laughing, joking, whispering, buzzing complaints between them. Most often they get together to eat their paan and crack their betel nuts. Nonda eats so much paan that it won't do unless she sits down with her paan box five or seven times a day. And Chhoto Bou isn't lazy about this either. Today, too, she's sat down to make her paan, and Nonda has sat down with her betel-splitter, legs stretched out. A faint fragrance in both their mouths. It's a good thing no one else caught the loaded glance that passed between them as soon as Srikumar stepped out.

It seems a huge relief for Abha to have found someone of like mind, with whom she can spend a few minutes laughing about the exploits of her brother-in-law.

Even if she can complain a little to her husband about her bhashur, she can't really make jokes with him. And the two housemaids are so stupid they miss all hints and signs. The mere word 'Boro-babu' evokes a surge of devotion in them. But the only one at home who will not even drink water before his two-hour prayer ritual, twice a day, who always takes a Gonga-bath, who strictly avoids women during his fasts – mention his name, and everyone turns into a sulky aunt! Because he grumbles a little about neatness, about the cleanliness of the utensils. Keeping himself well turned out is not his only concern – like it is his brother's!

And apart from that – is there only one reason for Abha's burning anger?

Oporna?

That special cast of Oporna's lips? Why cannot Abha look directly at her? Why does standing in front of Oporna make her feel somehow smaller, and – yes, nothing's hidden from the mind – inferior?

People could have mocked Oporna – but it seems as though Oporna's the one always mocking them, with that sharp instrument, her invisible smile.

A woman who should have sunk into the earth with this black mark of fortune – but not even the faintest smudge of that black ink appears on Oporna's face! Would it not make anyone burn to see this?

What source of contentment keeps Oporna always so pleased?

As she thinks about this, Abha grows restless and unhappy. Why,

Oporna, do you think no one understands your husband's qualities? Are all the world's people so naïve? But yes – no one announces the fact publicly, just to keep your honour intact.

Anyway, at least she's found a listener after so long, on whom to unload some of her venom. Even though sometimes Abha feels her bile rising, burning, when she sees her cousin's childish excesses, still, she can endure it, if only because she doesn't have to defer to her cousin.

Nonda sets down her betel-splitter and opens the little silver snuff-box. 'Ei Bou, do you want some?'

'O Baba!' Abha is afraid. 'There was such a row after I had some the other day! But let me have a little bit. Hope I don't get another scolding from your brother!'

'Ish, a scolding indeed.' Nonda carefully puts the box away close to her heart and pouts. 'You watch, I'll get you hooked on this jorda and get my brother to make you a golden box for it, and only *then* will I leave.'

'That'll be the day – ,' Abha says and stops.

Oporna's coming.

Maybe she has found some time off after supervising the Brahmin cook's activities.

'Ei je, Boro Bou,' Nonda bubbles up. 'Are you done at last? Baba! If you're always rotting in the kitchen, why bother to keep a Brahmin? Why, doesn't he know how to cook?'

'Why shouldn't he? It's my bad habit.' Oporna laughs a little and turns towards the staircase.

She spends the next few hours upstairs, with her books and such. She'll come down again at ten at night. Srikumar will return, the boys' tutor will leave, Shukumar will finish his prayer rituals, the bustle around dinner will begin at that time.

Sudden lightning flashes in the glance between the two companions. Is there a touch of intrigue to this lightning?

Nonda breathes out a disappointed sigh and asks in a sorrowful manner: 'Now what will you do upstairs, Bou?'

Abha lowers her head and searches for who knows what in her paan box.

Oporna is quiet for a second before answering her sister-in-law's question. 'What's there to do – I'll count the beams and lintels.'

'Yes, that's more or less all there is. What kind of common sense is this, babu, can't Kumar-da stay home even one evening?'

Maybe that invisible smile isn't invisible any more, but how can Abha lift her eyes to look! So she keeps searching for the masala.

'Maybe you're seeing this for the first time, Thakurjhi?'

Oporna asks the question like an utter innocent.

Nonda drags a smile onto her embarrassed face and says, 'Oh, leave those old matters aside. In their youth people go out to talk with their friends. But now, it's a matter of age, after all, and there are many duties to be done in the household. Look, for instance – you're paying a lot of money for a tutor for the boys – maybe there's money enough, but still Ma Lokkhi shouldn't be disrespected this way. Helping the boys with their studies in the evening instead, now that would save a lot of money.'

It's as though Oporna's walking down the street and suddenly finds the moon in her hands. She says with great enthusiasm, 'O Ma, that's true, Thakurjhi! I never noticed what a lot of money that was! Wait, I'm going to fix it today.'

'O Ma! Don't mention my name, will you?'

'Are you crazy, would I ever do that?'

It's as though Nonda has suddenly become a little girl; she says coyly, ingratiatingly: 'So, it's never called off, even if the world turns upside down? – But where does Kumar-da go every day?'

'O Ma, you don't know even that? Oh, dear fate! What have you done since you came here? He has a rendezvous!'

Abha's groping for cardamom in her paan box doesn't end. It

won't, not as long as Oporna is there. Abha knows for sure: the radiance of that sharp blade, the keen edge of her lips, has blazed up in every line of Oporna's face.

Nonda still drips honey: 'Let the jokes be, tell me the truth, Bou.'

'I'm telling you the truth, Thakurjhi! Why, has your Dada grown old? Look at him carefully some day. I often think – if he were someone else's husband I'd swoon just to look at him.'

'Will you listen to that – ,' says Nonda, and is quiet, astonished. Even she, loud-tongued though she is, suddenly cannot find any words.

As soon as Oporna goes upstairs, Abha lifts her head and says scornfully: 'You saw that, didn't you, Nonda-di? Didn't I tell you? She'd rather break than bend.'

'I can see that. In the evenings I see her laying out her husband's white panjabi, his frilled dhuti, his shoes, his walking-stick, his cologne, his talcum powder – all with her own hands!'

'Look at the evening's arrangements, you'll think he's going out on some royal mission. And what is it – her husband will go to a Bai's house to hear her sing! What can I say, Nonda-di, if it were me, I might have put a rope around my neck twice every day, morning and evening!'

Whether it's possible to put a rope around her neck in the evening after having once done it in the morning – Nonda doesn't question that, she only says, 'Blessed woman!'

Blessed indeed! At dinnertime that night on the courtyard, of her own volition Oporna mentions Nonda's point to her husband. And quite solemnly too! She says, 'Look, tell the tutor not to come from tomorrow.'

'The tutor? What, why?' Srikumar is startled.

'A large chunk of the household money is lost that way, for no reason – you could do that job yourself!'

'I?' Nonplussed, Srikumar says, 'I'll teach the boys? What sort of notion is that? Who said that?'

'I'm saying it.' Oporna moves the milk-bowl closer to his plate. 'Why, what's so surprising about it? You passed your B.A. too, at one time.'

Srikumar is astonished, agitated. 'Do I still remember all of that? Ba!'

'You don't?' Oporna sounds utterly crestfallen. 'Then there's no choice! I thought maybe you could help with saving some of the household expenses.'

Now Srikumar feels this is all a joke. Because it is he who bears all the expenses of the household. That is his principle.

Oporna's jests are delivered in this manner, cool, quiet, solemn. And over there, Abha slides the jar of sugar into the room from outside, and Nonda sinks into the earth.

Shukumar, meanwhile, is silent. He has washed his hands and sat down to eat, so there's no way he can even say 'ha' or 'hm'.

At night, they sit side-by-side on the bed, legs dangling.

Srikumar turns his wife's head slightly towards himself and says: 'Why try so hard to make me a household worker?'

'It's a good thing. Who pays any attention to someone who doesn't work?'

'Even if no one else pays any attention, as long as one person does, that's enough.'

'Ba! Why should she pay any attention either? What need does she have? With the humiliation of it – '

'What, what did you say?' Srikumar is startled. 'What were you going to say?'

'Nothing, now move, let me lie down.'

Srikumar moves aside to make room. After staying quiet a minute or so, he calls out in a grave voice: 'Oporna!'

He doesn't dare to lay his hand on her body, he lays it on her head.

'Oporna!'

'Unh!'

'Do you truly feel humiliated, Oporna? Then why didn't you let me know earlier? I've tried for so long to give up the intoxication of habit – you're the one who laughs away such things! You dress me up and send me off! Why do you do it? Why such indulgence?'

'Oh, what a fuss!' Oporna abandons her pretense of sleep and sits up. Her invisible instrument peers from the corners of her lips. She says, 'Why do I do it? O Ma! "Kindness towards your fellow creatures" – is there such a saying in the Bengali language, or is there not?'

'Kindness? Oh!' Srikumar says in a hurt manner. 'So it is your kindness towards me that – '

'No, I simply can't deal with you any more, I can see that! Are you merely a "creature" to me? Say Shib[2] instead. The kindness is towards that *other* poor soul. That "lonely-swallow-forever-seeking-your-shelter" of yours – and all the other nice things – say them, can't you? I don't remember them all. She sits and sits, and watches the road, all in the hope of seeing you – ?'

Many years earlier, soon after her wedding, the accidental revelation of a signed letter of that sort had taken Oporna from heaven and dashed her violently to the ground.

But no, Oporna had not told anyone about that injury. She had taken the entire matter into her own hands.

It is by her arrangement that Srikumar has been following this routine for the past eighteen years: content, satisfied, grateful. It doesn't seem that his age is advancing, it doesn't seem that anyone thinks anything of it.

But the language of that letter is still a source of amusement for Oporna. Now and then she quotes from it, to vex her husband.

Srikumar stays quiet a minute or so longer, then says gravely:

'Do you believe that I could do anything that would truly hurt you, Oporna?'

'Now would you look at that, such nonsense in the middle of the night!'

'No, Oporna, don't brush the matter aside, tell me, really – '

Does the cast of Oporna's lips suddenly change? Why do they seem so soft, seem to tremble this way?

'That I would believe *that* – is that what you believe?'

'No. And that's why I don't worry, Oporna – but still, sometimes I wonder why you don't force me. Why you don't try to keep me completely for yourself. It's your right, after all.'

'What a nuisance! This is madness, really! Look, mister, to assert your right over a tree, do you have to uproot it entirely and bring it home with you? Is that the sensible thing to do? I don't have the all-consuming hunger that would make me claim everything. . . . But what's happening tonight? No sleep at all? The Brahmin cook's not coming tomorrow – you understand, mister? There's plenty of work.'

Meaning, drop the curtain over these matters. But Srikumar is restless this evening. He's unwilling to close the discussion so soon. Suddenly he says, 'My conduct is disrespectful towards you, it's not as though that hasn't occurred to me, Oporna, but it's your indulgence that drives the feeling away. But now there's a real need to make some kind of change.'

Oporna replies immediately, in a gentle fashion: 'Truly, I think so too. I think – this time when the tailor comes, instead of a panjabi for you I'll get him to make a few undershirts.'

Srikumar says in utter astonishment: 'What do you mean?'

'That'll be "some kind of change".'

'Ah! These jokes of yours again! Do you think my giving up Kanchon would be so – '

'Chhi!'

At Oporna's sharp admonition, Srikumar falls silent. Looking at his abashed countenance, Oporna laughs lightly. She says, in very easy tones: 'The other woman is the thorn in *my* path, I'll scatter sweets when it's removed, but why do *you* say something like that? Your "forever-sheltered" servant, isn't she?'

Sitting on a folded blanket in the bedroom, Shukumar was turning the pages of a book called *The First Step to Spiritual Self-Realization*, or some such long-and-wide name, and when Abha stepped inside the room, he asked right away, 'What was all that about asking the tutor to leave, I couldn't understand – '

'An act, just an act!' Abha purses her lips scornfully. She relates the evening's events in brief and says, 'A husband's bad habits can add up to a great achievement, *this* I've learned only after coming to this house.'

'Just thinking about it leaves me headless, the shame of it! What can I do, he's the older brother – I'm helpless! Gurudeb! Gurudeb!'

Shukumar spreads out the blanket and lies down. It's Sunday – most auspicious for the practice of austerity – and he won't sleep on the bed today.

But then – if Srikumar had not bared his own head to all the material storms of the household world and instead merely exercised his rights as an older brother and asked Shukumar to share the burden, who knows how helpless Shukumar might have felt then!

Even as she said 'I'm going, I'm going,' Nonda stayed a few more days. A nephew was to come for her. There was no sign of him. Nonda perforce began to make her own efforts. Now and then she would say: 'Listen, why can't you find a way to say goodbye to this pest?'

On every subject, Shukumar is merely impartial. He remains silent.

Srikumar says to Nonda, 'Why, you're not sinking in deep water, are you? That fellow didn't show up, why do you insist on going? Why don't you stay a few more days?'

On the other side, Abha sits in the pantry gnashing her teeth. She says to herself, Oh, indeed she'll stay! If such a wanton charmer stays unclaimed in the house, it's convenient for you, isn't it? If it were in my control, I'd have said goodbye with a broom, long ago!

The well of companionship has long dried up, there's nothing new to the topics of discussion. The young Nonda's sound health and spontaneous levity seem to spread poison in Abha's body. Nonda, too, not getting enough attention, doesn't stick quite so close to her. That too may be one reason she's getting anxious to leave. And moreover, she's heard that her younger sister-in-law is in poor health, and if she doesn't go there right away, who knows how much she'll have to hear about it in the future.

In the end, it is Oporna who broaches the subject one day.

She said, 'Thakurjhi is getting anxious – the day after tomorrow is Sunday – why don't you take her to Srirampur?'

'Who are you asking? Me?' Srikumar raises his head from his meal.

'That's crazy! Why would I ask you? I'm asking the Brahmin cook.'

'Oh, what a nuisance! So no one's coming to take her?'

'Did anyone show up? – Doesn't matter, take her there, she's getting anxious, poor thing.'

'All right. When? I mean, which train?' Srikumar asks the question innocently.

'Don't worry, you'll be back by the evening,' Oporna says, and suppresses a smile.

And over there, as soon as she sees this, Abha freezes in wordless astonishment.

What strange foolhardiness is this! Who gives Oporna this wealth of heedless foolhardiness?

Abha cannot even imagine letting her own husband go with Nonda on a train with no third person present. Where does Oporna find so much courage? Courage with which she's not afraid to send her husband into the tigress's cage, to leave him before the she-snake's outspread hood?

Oh, thank heaven Boro-Ginni didn't make this proposal to Shukumar! God did raise his head and smile on her!

Hai! Who could have known that in the end God would lower his raised head and commit such treachery with Abha! Or what was the need for him to throw Srikumar into a sudden fever in the middle of the night, that same Srikumar who never suffered even from a headache?

A plot! A conspiring God's conspiracy!

'Thakurpo, now it's up to you to go to Srirampur.'

Oporna makes this proposal to Shukumar after breaking the news of Srikumar's illness. As though it's nothing much at all. As though it's a simple matter, like dropping Shefali off at school. As though – oh! – if only Abha knew some mantra that would break and crush that simple faith of Oporna's!

Shukumar glances once at his wife's face and stammers: 'Me? How me? I mean, me, when – '

'What a nuisance! What "when"? The nine-o'clock train.'

The blood in Abha's heart turns to ice; the blood in her face turns to fire. The agitation does not remain hidden from her voice: 'How can he go, Didi? It's his Sunday!'

'That's fine, he can have his rice and daal early and take a later train. There's a train every hour to Srirampur.'

As though the train were the only problem, as though only the thought of the rice and daal made Abha so desperate.

'What's the need for that? Why not cancel the departure? Can't Nonda-di make do without leaving this very day? She's been here so long – will the Mahabharat be defiled if she stays a couple of days longer?'

Abha blurts this out in desperation – without looking at Oporna's mouth. Ignoring the slowly appearing smile. But where? Oporna isn't smiling. Rather, she's saying, astonished: 'O Ma, why're you making such a simple matter so complicated, Chhoto Bou? It's only a few hours! Thakurpo will be back in time for his evening prayers, and for his fruit and water. He won't suffer at all. We've sent them a letter, it won't look good if she doesn't go. What do you say, Thakurpo, does it look good?'

Thakurpo shakes his head to say either 'yes' or 'no', it isn't clear which.

And Abha? All her heartstrings want to call out, but what they want to say, she has no way of uttering, so she goes out of the room muttering under her breath.

Cannot the Lord raise his head again and smile on her? Cannot Shukumar too be struck down by a sudden fever this very instant? A hundred and four – five – even more? Or – an accident – can his foot not slip under the tap while he's taking his bath? So many times people become dizzy and fall down for no reason at all! No matter how – no matter what – any mishap? Will nothing happen? Are mishaps so hard to come by? . . . Then what recourse does Abha have?

Sunday vanishes somewhere with its fruit-and-water, its plain boiled-rice-and-ghee, all its show of prayer and ritual; and Abha cannot find any hope in it.

When she imagines the train compartment with no third person present, she feels like hitting her head against the wall and dying.

Who knows her husband better than she does?

Poddolota's Dream

পদ্মলতার স্বপ্ন

Poddolotar Shopno

The desire to go from her husband's house to her father's house once or twice: that desire, it's quite natural; it's only because she gets winded staying in the same place that a woman wants to come to her father's home.

To change the taste in her mouth, or to draw a breath of freedom.

If there's no father, she might go to her brother's house. But since there's no father, no brother, does that mean Poddolota will never set foot on the ground of Shonapolashi village even once more? Where she spent her entire childhood and youth?

Not only memories of happiness or peace or pride, even memories of sorrow and disgrace do indeed have their own appeal! After seven years, maybe Poddolota's secret desire to establish a reputation for herself cannot be suppressed any longer.

How astonished the residents of Shonapolashi will be when they see 'Podi', the daughter of the Brahmin cook at Jodu Lahiri's house, manifest herself as Poddolota! For seven years, day and night, seed by seed, Poddolota has fondly tended the mischievous desire to see that astonishment, indulged it in dreams of happiness. She's pictured those few days in colours and moods luminous, dazzling.

It's as though nothing else in life, no other place, holds any meaning for Poddolota; and so with much effort, after repeated pleas, she's taken a few days' vacation from her husband and come this once to Shonapolashi.

And her coming hasn't been in vain . . . there's no one who isn't astonished. . . . Not because she's come suddenly, after such a long time – they're astonished at her demeanour. Why astonished, they're almost overcome.

'Misfortune's leaf masking your destiny' – that well-known adage – was that the case for Poddolota? There's no doubt about it; it's a wartime economy, isn't it! There's no word like 'impossible' in the lexicon of this age, everything's possible. . . . For many people, the stormy winds of this war have blown away all the leaves that concealed their good fortune.

Even if you see a dung-collector turn into a queen overnight, you can believe it and still breathe a normal breath. So when Jodu Lahiri's Brahmin cook's daughter 'Podi' suddenly starts to chew gold for food, what's so surprising about that?

Now it only remains for them to be flooded with an overwhelming love for her.

If Poddolota's mild-as-a-cow, schoolmaster husband can climb the golden steps of a military contract to build a permanent paradise – then can't he find jobs for a few of the village's useless, dissipated lads, those pumpkins out of season? Or – can't Poddolota take up the burden of finding husbands for one or two helpless women? The Poddolota who had barely climbed down at the station before she started strewing money around. She's been here two days – and in that time everyone from Roton the guard to the priest at the Kali Bari has become voluble with hymns praising Poddolota's virtues. . . . It seems such a noble vision was never found in all the world.

It seems Poddolota's smile is wondrous, her remarks sweet, her conduct incomparable. That her qualities are without peer, ever since her childhood – who does not know that? . . . Isn't that why people all across the region loved this girl, lit up from within by her beauty and her virtue? That now people would fight over her – what was so strange about that?

Having come on the promise of staying only four days, the question of whose invitation to accept for which meal has become a problem for Poddolota. . . . And the Lahiri house is now bustling after a long time, there's no end to the people gathering there. Poddolota has received them with an open-hearted smile and substantial, rich hospitality, as though she herself were the mistress of the house.

With Jodu Lahiri's death, the power and predominance of the house had passed. Poddolota's coming has made its fame blossom again.

Today, too, after most people have left, Shottobala ties her hostess's gift of five rupees into her anchol and says with honey in her voice, quite melted by love for Poddolota: 'Tomorrow you'll have to come over and have a bit of fish and rice, Ma Podda-rani, I won't hear any excuses.'

'But Rai-jethima's already asked me, Shotu-pishi.' Demureness plays through Poddolota's voice. 'If I don't go, she'll be very hurt.'

'O Ma, who is she to me – Rai-jethi! Mukundo Rai's brother's wife, I suppose? All that's just flattery in the shape of an invitation! I'm telling you straight, yes.'

'The things you say, Shotu-pishima! What kind of person am I, that they'll flatter me! Chhi chhi! But she was insistent, that's why I'm saying it – '

'And we can't insist, can we, dearie? And I'll say this too, why should we have to insist, Ma, are you an outsider for us? My claim comes before anyone else's, I'll tell you that. Maybe you don't remember, but didn't your mother have such great respect and devotion for me?

"Shotu-thakurjhi!" she'd say, and go fainting away. Do all those ties of love need to be explained with words, Ma?'

But is it at all necessary to explain them with words?

After all, Poddolota ate this village's food and drank its water until she was sixteen.

Food that came with many reprimands, many insults.

Why should she forget? How much 'respect and devotion' her mother had for Shottobala's poisoned tongue – is her memory so weak, that she'll forget it so soon?

Poddolata does not grieve for her mother, but whenever she thinks of her, the ocean of her memory churns violently. Yes . . . on this very courtyard of the Lahiris' . . . a night of intense cold . . . the biting winter wind piercing every bone like a needle . . . a lean, gaunt widow . . . for twelve months her cough hasn't been cured. . . . Pulling the rough, unglazed fabric of her short anchol across her body in a useless effort to ward off the cold, she gathers together the ingredients for the following day's pujo,[1] and she coughs incessantly. It's as though the *khok-khok* of that cough still adheres to each wall bordering the courtyard, as though it only wants for a winter night to be far enough advanced for that cough to be heard again. . . . At her feet wanders a little girl . . . her winter clothes, too, are not adequate: she wears a long skirt of coarse cloth, studded and prickly with stitching, made from tiny pieces of fabric cast off by the granddaughters of Jodu Lahiri.

Even though her chest may be somewhat warm because she nestles against her mother's back, the knife-edge is sharp against her neck – cutting, cutting against her, it finally turns her numb. . . . Then she no longer feels the cold, only a twinge, a mild discomfort in parts of her body. . . . The greater pain is in her hands . . . as she splashes water on those two small hands, hands like pieces of ice, trying to help her mother's work along as best she can, suddenly her bent fingers become inert . . . and then her mother's labour is doubled. She presses her anchol to the hurricane lantern, then warms her daughter's hands and feet . . . then pulls her to her lap and rebukes her gently. 'Why do you wander about in the cold, child? Your mother has so much left to do . . . just because she's the cook, that doesn't mean she can stop when the cooking's done, is it for nothing that her young daughter is being fed her rice? Doesn't she need to do some of a servant's work as well?'

. . . So she urges her daughter to take shelter in her bed. But even to think of that spare, uncovered bed makes the poor girl's heart quake . . . as though someone's poured water on that oil-streaked pillow . . . how can she stay without the warmth of her mother's chest? . . . And besides, aren't all the world's ghosts-goblins and ogres-monsters gathered and waiting? – in every eerie corner of that bare-ribbed room with its layer of plaster fallen away?

Jodu Lahiri's ailing wife doesn't shift or stir, but it's a wonder how all the world's news shows up in the mirror of her thumbnail.[2] . . . When once or twice Poddolota's mother entices her daughter into bed with the lure of a lamp, right away Lahiri-ginni's broken, irritated voice comes from the second-floor window: 'O, you nawab's daughter, turn down the affection for your daughter a little, lamp-oil isn't free. . . . If they had any brains of their own, I wouldn't have to waste my breath. . . . It's very easy to keep two people in food and clothes, isn't it! There's hardly any household work to be done, and still this incessant buzzing of mother and daughter at all hours of the night. The way you do your work at midnight, for your convenience – Brahmin girl, do you know how much of my kerosene you burn in a month – have you ever added that up, dearie? But why should you feel sorry for another person's loss? It's what they say, isn't it – "I get a Brahmin's meal, I don't know its cost" – that's what you're like. . . . And I'm so weak now that I have to feed a crook like you.'

Once she starts talking, she doesn't want to stop.

By this time the lamp has died and attained nirvana. However overpowering the fear of ghosts-goblins may be, not so for Lahiri-ginni. . . .

And then, the memory of going back and forth to the pond with her mother on rainy days, splashing through the water, her legs smeared with mud up to her knees, is wrapped somehow in both happiness and sorrow. Some days she really enjoyed, but it was terrible when her mother's coughing grew worse, those days she wanted to spend all day with her among that torn bedding, she didn't need to eat, so what if she didn't eat for two or four days? . . . But saying there's no need doesn't make the need disappear – her mother makes even her little daughter understand that. . . .

She remembers another scene in the same surroundings . . . this house, this courtyard . . . but two other people . . . copper-coloured, slim arms and legs, a healthy young woman instead of that girl in the torn frock . . . only a sari isn't enough for modesty. . . . Much more distressing than warding off the cold is the useless effort to ward off shame with a sari that's short in both length and width. But she's the one who does all the work, shyly, of the entire household. There's no end to her loving reproaches of the emaciated widow. She scolds her mother to make her go to sleep early . . . she laughs and says: 'Why don't you want to go alone? Are you afraid? The ghosts will eat you?' . . .

How can her mother explain to this young woman that she's more afraid for her than she is of ghosts. Even normally, a widow's fatherless daughter growing up is an impudence, and on top of that there's her beauty! She walks around, and the mother watches entranced: – Yes, naming her Podda was right, her feet are two lotus blossoms. But how can she flourish this way? Can the food of neglect be so nourishing?

Whether Jodu Lahiri's wife gets angry or not, it's true. Her two granddaughters, suffering from malaria, have turned gaunt, like two black titmice, and before she's even fourteen, this girl is a sight! It might sound harsh, but she does give good advice, says: 'Oh, Podi, eat a little less rice, don't eat your fill just because it's someone else's money. Day by day you're growing into an elephant, and I can see your anxious mother's blood turning to water.'

'Podi' swallows all the insults and laughs with some difficulty. She says, 'Is there any blood left in Ma's body, Didima? It's all water.' And so if Lahiri-ginni had not turned five-mouthed and voluble and criticized this rude girl's audacity, people would have faulted *her* instead.

But it's not only Lahiri-ginni, no one in the neighbourhood passes up the opportunity to make their mouth happy.

. . . 'Podi's' beauty is an eyesore, her qualities annoying, her age the subject of much jealousy.

. . . 'Podi's' conduct is suspect – and her manner . . . but let that go – 'Podi' is dead now.

No one minds singing 'Poddolota's' praises.

Jodu Lahiri's wife spreads her cloudy gaze from cataract-heavy eyes and announces loudly, 'She's no mere girl, she's the image of Lokkhi, I've watched her since her childhood, there's no end to her virtues. Oh, the wretched woman's bad luck, she didn't see this. Your mother's gone, but we haven't died, Didi, come once every year, don't forget us and stay away. What's the difference between my Komli–Bimli and you?'

In her mind she knows there's a difference. Komola and Bimola won't even offer their Didima burnt muri[3] or ask after her, and Poddolota has just counted out three hundred rupees cash to meet Didima's expenses for her pilgrimage.

Getting an invitation from the Rai-house is a memorable event.

Not the one today, but the one on the pages of past history.

Mukundo Rai's mother observing some vow or other. Everyone from the Lahiri-house has been invited . . . and so 'Podi's' mother's come too, to toil; and in the midst of it all some serving lad sat Podi down as a Brahmin's daughter along with the invitees. The boy was none other than Murari, of the Shannal-house. And this had become the object of much slander, with signs, gestures, and hints by the neighbours. Plain-spoken Shottobala had reduced Podi's mother to tears and sniffles one day . . . if a green and growing boy and girl happen to meet on the way to the pond and start laughing and talking, what's left of decency?

Thank God it had only fallen to Shottobala's eye; if anyone else had seen her, getting that girl married would have become impossible – let someone dispute that!

. . . It wasn't impossible after all – that very month, with the help of many well-wishers, 'Podi' was married. The boy had passed his matric . . . a teacher in a junior school in some obscure village, in all he earned a salary of thirty rupees, but he had seventy rupees' worth of glorious future. But let that go, Podi's marriage is irrelevant here. The memory of the meal at the Rai-house has grown clear . . . she wasn't allowed to sit down to eat in the same line with everyone else, she was pulled up by the arm. . . . The suppressed storm of signs, gestures, and mocking laughter had swirled all around, until Mukundo Rai's older daughter Nibhanoni had suddenly stood up . . . and after all, her logic wasn't bad. Really, if a Brahmin cook's daughter can get the respect due to a Brahmin's daughter . . . then what stops a cockroach from being awarded the title of 'bird'?

As she climbed up the stairs to the courtyard on the second floor, she recalled this scene from about eight years ago. . . . Mukundo Rai's daughter-in-law's smiling welcome broke her reverie, 'Come, Thakurjhi, at least you remembered your brother's wife – you haven't come to visit us even once!'

'What can I do, Boudi, I've been here just three days, I've only been going from place to place, I haven't really met anyone properly, and I have only four days' holiday.'

'Now, that's nonsense, bapu, what sense does it make to come after so long and stay only four days? Write to that husband of yours, tell him he's enjoyed your company a long time, now let us enjoy it awhile. And then he's a businessman, involved in many matters, what's this "wife, wife" obsession of his?'

'See, that's exactly it – it's an affliction, that's why I can't come here. That man is quite insane.'

A light smile is always etched at the corner of Poddo's lips, like a faint sign of power and plenty –

After a few restless, eager moments the wife lays out the real question, she says: 'I suppose you can't bear too many ornaments on your body, Thakurjhi?'

The question is problematic indeed – the paucity of ornaments on Poddolota doesn't quite match the dignity of her position. Why this hasn't come up in the past three days, that's the real surprise! In the glow of her flowing silver, perhaps the lack of gold hasn't fallen to people's eyes.

All it takes to turn silver into gold is to reduce its weight, who doesn't know that?

Poddolota laughs a pleasant laugh of great satisfaction and says, 'See, that's just it, your nondai's snatched away my ornaments and driven me out.'

'Oh, it's as bad as death isn't it, Durga! Durga! Look at the way she talks.'

'What can I say, bhai, my husband has the notion that the village is home only to thieves, robbers, and good-for-nothings, if they see any ornaments they'll steal his wife and run. He says, "Take as much cash as you want, but ornaments on your body? Not a single one – ." It's only to preserve my ayot[4] that I keep a few on my arms, neck, ears.

Yes – what was I saying – is the weaver Giri still here, Boudi?'

'She certainly is, only the price of cloth's gone right up.'

'Oh, let that be, will I get about fifteen or twenty saris with nice borders?'

'About fif-teen – or twenty? How many will you wear at once?' The wife widens her eyes.

'Oh, it's just – they're not for me – I've come to visit you all after so long, shouldn't I give a sari in greeting?'

'But to everyone in the village!'

'Only by your blessings, Boudi!'

After this, can the meagreness of ornamentation seem suspect? Mukundo Rai's older bhaj seats Poddolata beside herself and watches over her meal with great care, and she expresses much sorrow over Poddolota's coming for such a short time to her father's village.

At least Poddolota's sorrow is gone.

She has done away with Jodu Lahiri's cook's daughter 'Podi' and established Poddolata in Shonapolashi village. Only – Murari.

Isn't there one small thorn that still remains?

The Murari who had once laughed a mocking laugh and said, 'Do you imagine I'll marry you? Right, hold on to that happy thought! My mother won't bring a kulo to welcome you home – she'll use it to chase me away.'[5]

Now she feels no shame in inquiring casually after Murari.

The question can be asked along with five others about the neighbourhood. 'Oh yes, Rai-jethima, what news of Murari-da? He's in the village, isn't he?'

Rai-jethi says with some sorrow: 'Hai hai, don't talk about that lad, Ma! He suffered until he was eaten up, isn't able to earn a paisa, now he's sitting around with his whole house pledged away. He's only long on words. His wife and children are just burnt skin and bones.'

So he's still long on words? Shouldn't Poddolota for once try using the medicine that'll stop those words?

Murari puts down the bowl of barley and, scowling, is about to ask his wife for a clove when Poddolota pushes open the courtyard gate and enters.

Even before Murari can make a smile blossom on his twisted face, Poddolota says with some surprise, 'What's the news? What were you eating – sago?'

Murari turns both his hands palm out and says, joking, 'Ha Gobindo! Sago! That's a dream of the past. Barley – pure "Mondol's Barley".'

'Are you sick?'

'Sick? Is there only one kind of sickness? Poverty, anxiety, fear of money-lenders, domestic disputes, spleen and liver disease, fever, dyspepsia – '

Poddolota says, scolding: 'All right, that's enough, no need to make the list any longer, where's your wife?'

'She must be somewhere around – '

'And Borda, Boro Boudi?'

'Them? They moved away long ago, right after Ma died.'

'And since then you've been in this condition!'

Murari glances at his gaunt body and says in a mocking tone: 'Why, is my condition so bad? Not everyone can have their finger swell up and become a banana plant!'[6]

Poddolota says sharply, 'No, not a banana plant but a sugarcane stem, I can see.'

'How sad,' Murari says, laughing again, 'that a cane doesn't leave a mark on rich people's thick skin.'

Poddolota doesn't let the witticism touch her; she sits down and says, 'So you won't ask me to sit – you're such a highly respected person – I'll have to sit down myself. Where are you, lady of the house, why don't you come out?'

The lady of the house is busy adjusting her graceless clothing. Truly she's as badly off as a battered old pot; it's difficult to come out and meet people on short notice. The boy and the girl are both disciples of Adam: some clothes must be arranged.

Poddolota understands this, so without calling out any more she keeps talking to Murari.

'I can see you're long on words, same as you always were, but what kind of state is the household in . . . what have you turned it into? The way the house looks, it makes me feel faint – '

'The house? Oh, what's the use getting attached to someone else's house?'

Poddolota asks as though she doesn't know: 'Someone else's house! Someone else's house, what do you mean?'

'The meaning's very simple – I'm up to my neck in debt, house and land mortgaged. Why, haven't you heard this tasty bit of news yet?'

'What a disaster – the house is mortgaged? What are you saying. Chhi chhi, you've spoiled the good name of your forefathers.' Poddolota seems to turn melancholy with grief and sorrow.

Murari laughs a little and says, 'Well, it's lucky I've spoilt it, at least you got the chance to lord it over me. But your high-and-mighty manner does make me laugh, Podi! What did Mukundo Rai's daughter say, "Even a cockroach has become a bird"? A fair comparison, wasn't it?'

Poddolota understands that this is a deliberate insult; maybe it's a retort to her own insult. Maybe this is the way it happens, when a sweet relationship turns bitter, it turns this bitter. Each side wants only to see the other humiliated.

But – no, it won't do for Poddolota to get angry.

She laughs and says, 'Your memory's quite sharp, Murari-da. At least it's good that one person in the village remembers "Podi" – after coming here I see everyone rushing to call me "Poddo, Poddo!" Anyway, give me all your news – '

'Us, and our news! Hai Modhushudon! Like they say, does a ghost have birthdays? You're the people with the news worth hearing. I hear you've become very rich, you're raining money with both hands? Good! Good!'

'You haven't seen my face yet, how did you get this news?'

'O Baba! The past three days, hymns to your greatness have eaten my ears away. Donating to public events, donating to the school, donating for a tube-well, donating to fix the Kali-temple courtyard – it's a Horir loot, really![7] I feel sad about your stupidity. Still, a reputation is worth something.'

Poddolota laughs it off and says, 'My burnt bad luck! How little I'm able to give, and to get a reputation! I haven't been able to do what I wanted – in my hurry I couldn't bring much at all – I had about a thousand with me, so I brought that, and my husband had given me about eight hundred to spend – that's all, and a hundred or two more in change, if that. And for this, a reputation! Bhuti-pishima's granddaughter can't get married for lack of money – I heard that, and my hand's itching – I'll just have to go back and send some.'

'How many lakhs has Obinash made, really? What contract did he get? Rice? Wheat? Cows and goats? Girls?'

The tip of Murari's thin nose seems to twist in aversion and mockery; a pointed smile sharpens the corners of his mouth.

But Poddolata hasn't come here to be defeated, she's come to gain victory. So she feigns a simple manner and says, 'Who knows, mister – and you're a fine one too – what business he's in, why do I need to know all that? All I need is to get the money when I want it. But for you, I won't be able to rest even if I die. You mortgaged the entire house, and what if you can't get it back? How much is it mortgaged for?'

'Five hundred. Why, are you going to pay it?'

'I am indeed, should you lose your home and land for such a small amount?' Poddolota becomes busy untying the knot at the end of her anchol.

'Podi, do you walk around with five or seven hundred rupees in your pocket nowadays?'

'What can I do, Murari-da, Lahiri-didima's reluctant to take on the responsibility of keeping even these few rupees. What I've brought stays in my anchol. Anyway, the money's for spending – all I need is the return fare.'

As she finishes counting out the five large notes one by one, Murari suddenly turns serious.

He says, his voice full: 'Look, "Podi", a cockroach turning into a bird is fine – but don't try to turn into the mighty Gorur bird all at once!'

'You can insult me as much as you want, but you'll have to take this, mister, I won't let you become landless for such a small amount of money.'

'But why should I take your money? So you've become a big person full of money. You can go brag about your money to your cousins and aunts and suchlike and buy their hearts with cash. Don't come to impress me with your fine ways.'

Saying this, Murari pushes the notes away and calls out angrily to his absent wife: 'I've been asking for a clove for so long – what's happened to it? Are you all dead?'

Murari's wife had, in the meantime, brought some decency to her clothing and was about to come out – but hearing the matter of the money, she had stopped and stayed in the green-room. At her husband's summons she appears on stage and says, annoyed, 'If I died I'd be relieved, I'd be free of your clutches. But will I be that lucky? Thakurjhi, you see his attitude in the little time you've been here?'

'Yes, I do see it. The man's gone mad. Take these few notes, Boudi, the land and the house must be saved.'

The wife has, of course, heard everything from start to finish – still, she casts a greedy glance before saying: 'Who would lend *him* money, Thakurjhi? Will he be able to repay it in this lifetime?'

'Stop it, you silly girl, what's all this about repaying it? I didn't give you a wedding gift, did I? Let me give it now, take it. And have you hidden the boy and girl in some iron chest somewhere? Haven't seen them even once.'

The wife pounces on the notes and ties them in her anchol. She calls out in an exultant voice, 'O ré Pushpo, Khoka, come and do your pronam[8] to your pishima.'

Murari's burning desire to communicate with his wife in signs and gestures comes to nothing, and he says harshly, 'Return the money, Chhoto Bou, I can't take it.'

But to take something already tied into her anchol and set it free – Chhoto Bou isn't that foolish. So she says in an endearing tone, 'Yes, I'll certainly return it; and maybe not today, but tomorrow, when you have to stand under the tree holding your children's hands, what then? Should I return it? Why, is Thakurjhi not one of our own? Won't you tell him, Thakurjhi?'

Meanwhile, Thakurjhi's stuffed two rupees into Pushpo's hands and is now searching for Khoka's hand.

No, really Poddolota has no regrets, no worries now. Nothing more to pray for in her whole life. She holds the contentment of utter success in her two hands.

Right at this time – Obinash, leaning on his arms, lying on the shaky cot in the small, pigeon-hole room in the damp dark, was writing a letter . . . such a long letter after only four days' loneliness? . . . But without a long letter, how will the poor man express his extreme anxiety? Even knowing that his wife will return the next day, he cannot refrain from writing the letter.

He writes: 'I'm completely ruined. The job I had applied for in Patna – there's no chance of getting that, not in this lifetime. . . . I had thought that if I could get this job, we'd be able to spend the rest of our lives in some kind of peace, but God is displeased with me.

... The money I needed for the security deposit, the two thousand rupees I got from selling all the land and the house, that money's lost.... As you know, out of fear of swindlers and such, I didn't put the money in the bank but hid the bag of money on the shelf where you keep the blankets – but how the thief's glance fell even there, that's astonishing!

'... I believe this is the work of someone with a grudge against the family ... what can I say to anyone now ... today I am utterly destroyed! I cannot see even a gleam of hope in the future, who knows, maybe this is my punishment for giving up my ancestral land.... I regret having agreed to let you go at this time – you are the household Lokkhi, if you'd been here, I would not have been reduced to this condition. Anyway, make arrangements to return as soon as possible. I no longer have the ability to go there ... I feel ashamed even to show you my face....'

Prisoner

বন্দিনী

Bondini

The thin mattress is about four cubits long, there isn't enough room to spread it out fully, about a handspan has to be kept folded.

It is a blessing that the Creator was smart enough to make the ancient human race smaller and smaller until they stood at three and a half cubits – if not for that, to fit one whole person into a five-cubit-by-four-cubit room – after giving shelter to an entire household's boxes, trunks, and everything broken and holey – would have involved no end of trouble with that person's arms and legs.

It's only because humans have become so small in size in this age that Charubala has been able to get her young son of twenty-three years to adjust to so many unadjustable things on this tiny piece of land.

The room is stuffy, the pillow torn, the mattress without a cover.

But blaming Charubala for all this won't do.

It is not Charubala's job to cover up all that is ugly in the household.

But, in this room, on that bed – how is it possible to sleep so much? Shonkor thinks, why does the desire remain unsated even after a whole night's uninterrupted sleep?

Still – he has to get up.

There's the tuition at seven o'clock – the office at nine. And in the intervals between, the daily demands of the household must be met.

Of course there is no hope of getting any work done by Taranath. The head of the house, Taranath, cannot be trusted enough to be given two annas in his hand. The thought of it leaves Shonkor headless with shame.

If any money falls into his hands, he immediately disappears for the entire morning or evening.

And then, with red-red eyes and the smell of ganja sticking to his body, he will come back home and start tormenting Charubala.

Not weak, not incompetent, but averse to work.

Insufferable!

Shonkor finds his father absolutely insufferable. In this tiny house built of narrow bricks on a few yards of land, Taranath seems an ugly misfit . . . like another symptom of a diseased household.

Thoughts deep in your soul are no sin –

Sometimes, looking at Charubala, Shonkor tries to think: that coarse, short, gaudy sari she wears, if its two faded borders were to be completely erased, how much worse would it be? . . . How much uglier could those two arms, roughened by repeated drudgery, look – if those two brass bangles, thinly plated with gold, were thrown away?

But the imagination doesn't want to advance in that direction.

So what if his appearance is bloodless – a ganja-smoker's appearance – Taranath's health is sound.

That's why Shonkor runs around, taking care of the work around the house, the office, the tuition, with an annoyed face and an acid temper.

He'll have to see his father's face as soon as he steps out of the house – this irksome thought breaks his sleep. . . .

Yes, that's exactly the way it is – even this early in the morning, Taranath sits on the kitchen porch with his legs dangling, pulling on a biri.

On that lean, sinewy face, the cunning of a fox.

This is Shonkor's father.

Pita hi poromom topoh: one's father is the ultimate object of one's tireless devotion.

He feels contempt for himself!

Father and son are not on speaking terms, more or less. Maybe Taranath asks a question, maybe Shonkor answers if he feels like it, doesn't answer if he doesn't feel like it.

The morning is greatly advanced.

Shonkor has thrown his shirt over his shoulders and is quickly washing his face when Charubala calls out from the kitchen, 'Shonku, don't run off, I'm pouring the tea – '

'Let it be, there's no time,' says Shonkor, trying to slip his head somehow into the shirt.

Taranath becomes officious, and along with a mouthful of smoke he disgorges this comment: 'The nawab-son wants eighteen annas' worth of sleep,[1] but for washing up and eating he has no time.'

Of course Shonkor has become inured to this kind of comment.

He pays it no heed.

He merely casts a contemptuous glance at his father and goes on with his task. Meanwhile Charubala has brought in the tea.

Having come in holding the cup, full of boiling-hot, blackish tea, in a fold of her anchol, she sets it in front of her son and says, 'Since it's so late, take the money with you, and on the way back get the groceries as well.'

Groceries!

The sky breaks and falls on Shonkor's head!

After teaching the boy and getting the groceries, it'll be nine by the time he finishes his bath. Even if he ignores the meal, surely he needs some time in hand for the path he must travel?

The path!

Path, meaning not just the distance of four or five miles between the house and the office building. 'Path' means many things.

Path means –

A measure of waiting, hard to bear, with every limb aching . . . the suffocating embrace of the poisonous air . . . a measure of dejection, an apathy to helpless capitulation at the hands of fortune.

Path means –

The squandering of some measure of life-force every day.

'If I live, I'll live', 'if I die, I'll die' – the daily leaving-and-returning, with this in his mind.

Shonkor says, in a burdened manner, 'Can't you make do for today?'

Charubala says, pleading, 'How can it be, baba? There aren't any potatoes at all.'

Meaning, they're definitely needed!

The groceries, the rations. The inviolable laws of the world, like birth and death.

In the middle of this exchange between mother and son, Taranath coughs a little, then clears his throat and says in a greedy voice: 'It's late in the morning, why bother him? Give me the bag, why don't you?'

As though the bag were the only thing needed to get the groceries.

It would have been fine not to offer any reply – Taranath himself does not expect a reply every time. Shonkor answered with only a twisted smile of contempt and mockery – but what has happened to Charubala all of a sudden!

Sizzling like eggplant dropped in hot oil, she screams out: 'You're not ashamed to say that? Wretched, shameless addict!'

Shonkor is startled.

Who said that? Was it Charubala?

His head and ears suddenly seem numb, dizzy.

It's true, contrary to her nature the quiet Charubala has recently grown sharp-tongued; the language she uses about Taranath often hurts the ear – for its lack of a mother's courtesy if not respect towards a father.

But even so –

Such crude, outright abuse?

Right from his childhood Taranath was poison in both his eyes, but – how wonderfully fond Shonkor was of his mother!

When Shonkor hadn't yet learnt to read well, Charubala would make him memorize nursery rhymes, poems, songs. When his mother taught him, laughing, with the earrings swinging from her ears, the book folded back in her hands, 'If my boy decides to go – he can fly right now, to where the parijat flowers grow' – he would feel he could really accomplish impossible things. . . . And the fragrance of some unseen parijat grove would pervade that innocent child's heart.

And then, when Taranath railed at her, not pausing even to draw breath, and Charubala cried, without saying a word, he thought – Ma's a princess in a fairy tale, imprisoned by this ogre! . . . Sad and helpless!

When he was bigger – when he was much-h bigger – he'd kill the ogre and rescue his mother. – And that terrible scene caught hold of his imagination.

Although the power of that scene has certainly faded as he's grown older, that terrible urge to rescue his mother seems to have become subtle and stayed in his mind. . . . He wants to keep his mother in a princess's luxury, but the poor fellow is helpless.

As soon as he passed his matric, he had to pack up his studies and get into a job – a thoroughly worthless job. . . .

He had to scrounge up tuition work; tuition, with his meagre knowledge. Teaching three small boys: or if not teaching them, force-feeding them their lessons.

Still – whenever he sees that his mother is unoccupied, like a child he lays his head in her lap and embarks on meaningless speech – about the kind of luxury he'll keep his mother in when he's rich.

As though his being rich is a certainty.

Mother and son!

One faction.

Taranath is alone, Taranath is in a separate chamber, his entry into their kingdom is forbidden.

But –

Recently, what lamentable changes have slowly taken place in Charubala.

Her health has broken down from her lifetime of hard labour; old age has left its stamp on her face.

Having dispelled with the need for blouse or chemise, all day she wanders around in a carelessly worn sari, labours endlessly, and keeps fighting with Taranath.

It's as though every instant she is astonished anew at Taranath's shamelessness. . . . Astonished, she says, 'A young boy works until his mouth bleeds, in order to get rice for this family' – how can Taranath lift that rice to his mouth? She says, 'However well or poorly he did it, at one time he did keep the household going, but now that the boy's learnt to bring in two paise, have his arms and legs become useless?'

Nowadays she makes him hear many such remarks, but today her manner was truly ugly!

Shonkor was about to make some remark and pass over the matter. But Charubala suddenly seems to have grown ferocious. And so, losing her common sense, she abuses Taranath as she pleases. . . . For a man who has his arms and legs and still lives as someone else's food-slave, she prescribes such a thing for his mouth, which – whatever else it may be – is not food.

However much he may abhor his father, still Shonkor cannot remain silent at the prescription of fire for his living father's mouth, so: 'What are you saying, Ma!' he scolds her, and at that Charubala seems to go utterly mad.

She makes an ugly, bitter remark about her husband and goes on speaking: 'What I'm saying is what needs to be said.' Of course she'll say it – a thousand times she'll say it. . . . The man who steals his son's money to buy drugs, not just fire for his mouth, but a rope around his neck too. . . . If there's a drop of self-respect or shame still in Taranath's body, he should go right away and buy a coil of rope for himself. . . . Charubala will get rid of the sindoor on her forehead and the shankhas[2] on both hands and breathe a sigh of eternal relief!

All this time Taranath sits with an unconcerned expression, dragging at his biri. Looking at him, there is no way to tell if his hearing is sound, but at this last remark he completely loses his patience.

He yells at Charubala, threatening: 'What, your words are bigger than your mouth can hold! . . . You know I can't control myself if I get angry!'

Charubala suddenly laughs an ugly laugh and says, 'Oh, I'm dying of fear! I'm so terrified, I'm going to faint! . . . I'll get rid of them in front of your face, what will you do to me?' She says this and immediately pulls off the two bangles – thin, quite worn away – and tosses them aside, then starts rubbing at the sindoor in the parting of her hair with her anchol, keeps rubbing at it . . .

Astonished, Shonkor stares at her!

He seems bereft of all his powers of understanding and feeling. . . .

What is he looking at? . . . What ugly play is being performed here?

His faculties awaken . . . when Charubala, holding that sindoor-smeared anchol to her forehead, slumps down on the floor, and . . . a red-coloured fluid trickles out through the gaps between her fingers.

Taranath's store of endurance is immense, but not endless.

If a heavy lump of coal can be found within arm's reach, will he not pick it up and hurl it at her?

When she is hit, it's strange how suddenly Charubala falls silent!

How pathetic, how helpless the way she sits on the floor!

Has that prisoner princess of twenty years ago returned after so long?

And so – has that childhood urge of Shonkor's returned to him?

And now he is bigger . . . much-h bigger – so why should he not fulfil that age-old desire?

A bewildered and stupefied Taranath suddenly feels a hard grip on his shoulder . . . and hears an enraged bellow, 'Get out . . . get out right now. . . . Not another instant here!'

Why did Taranath forget to become angry? . . . Because he couldn't understand the measure of his disgrace? . . . That's why he stammers like a fool and says, 'That's good, boy, well done! You've grown so smart! Can I ask – who are you to drive me out of the house? You're the owner, are you?'

Shonkor grinds his teeth together and says, 'What else, when it's me who counts out the house rent! I don't want to hear any more, you can find your own arrangements.'

Taranath seems to become more and more stupid; he says, in an even more puerile manner, 'Fine, fine! These arrangements can easily be found on the streets, can't they! . . . Where will I stay?'

'Why, you have so many friends at the ganja den, what's the

worry? They'd love to make room for you,' Shonkar says, and marches out.

Once he's out, he can't remember where he's supposed to go, so for some time he wanders around uncertainly, and then . . . when his glance suddenly falls upon the hands of a clock hanging in a shop, he quickly boards a moving tram.

After he reaches his office – that's when he remembers he's left Charubala in that condition!

Maybe Charubala, after sitting there a long time, has lain down right there, and the stream of fluid blood has dried and clotted on her cheek.

Had Shonkor gone insane? . . . Or why would he talk to Taranath like that . . . no matter what – he was his father still!

Somehow he stays until lunchtime and then asks for the rest of the day off. Servitude is a terrible thing.

If only the distance between the office and the house could be made to vanish with some mantra's magic!

But what's this?

What's all this happening at home?

Why are there several boxes and bedrolls gathered on the porch? Could Charubala find no other day to rearrange the house?

Has she fallen upon the house out of attachment to her unbathed, unfed son? Maybe she herself is unfed too –

In happiness and compassion, tears come to Shonkor's eyes!

Going in to look for his mother, he suddenly stops short . . . what's this happening in the kitchen?

With great enthusiasm Taranath is tying some pots and pans together, and Charubala, with a rag tied around her head as a dressing, is helping him.

'Ma! –'

At her son's cry, Charubala comes out with a hand pressed to her forehead.

In an easy, calm voice, she says: 'You've come back – that's good. I was wondering whom to leave the key with . . . the train's at four, you see.'

'Train? To where? . . .' That is all Shonkor can say.

Charubala replies in the same easy and calm voice: 'Where else? To the village! . . . Even if there's nothing else, there's at least the few bricks of the old family home!'

Shonkor spreads a helpless gaze at her and says, 'Why are you going?'

Charubala's words seem cut from ice: 'I'll have to go, baba! Better to leave with dignity before being pushed out by the neck! Where there is no respect for elders – how do I dare to stay there, tell me that? . . .'

What is Shonkor looking at, staring wordless at his mother's face?

Can he not recognize that rag-tied face? . . . Or is he trying to understand – at what opportunity did he swallow up the prisoner princess, leaving no trace – that terrible ogre?

Loss

লোকসান

Lokshan

Even before I got home, I heard the bad news on the train. It was the daily passenger Romesh Bagchi who told me, when he transferred from the neighbouring train into mine.

I've always noticed that Romesh Bagchi has a kind of enthusiasm for this sort of thing; the job of bearing the bad news is much to his liking. . . . But – is it only Romesh? Aren't most people like that? Who isn't eager to pour the news of my death into your ear? What can make a better subject for conversation and discussion than someone else's misfortune?

As soon as I entered the house, Ma, too, served up the same news. . . .

– Did you hear the news from Probodh-thakurpo's house, Orun? You heard? – Who told you?

– Romesh Bagchi.

– Romesh? Oh, he *would* know, he comes and goes every day. And you – you come home once a week, and in that time so many things happen! Oh, what a calamity this is! A lightning strike from a clear sky!

I said to her: – Really! It's unimaginable. A man like Probhash-da –

– It's just as you say! Was there another boy like him in the whole village? Lately he was earning a thousand rupees a month. And he was supposed to become the head of his office soon, and would've made fourteen-fifteen hundred – how can anyone lose a son like that! Oh, what a case of God's injustice! His greed for the sweetest offering on the prayer plate! Of course I shouldn't say this – may they live – Durga, Durga! – but there were two other boys, stupid and useless, weren't there? The mouths to feed remain – the hand that fed them is gone.

Unpleasant to hear, but it was certainly true.

In the family Probhash-da had been the only earning member to speak of.

Of course he lived very far away, in Meerut. He didn't come and go very often. Once in a while he would come during the Pujo holidays, leave his wife and son at his in-laws' in Kolkata, and visit here for a day or two. But be that as it may, the money order of large denomination that he sent at the beginning of every month was Probodh-kaka's only hope. And in this you'd have to say Probhash-da was the ideal son – never for any reason did he send it two rupees short or two days late.

And now that son was gone!

After much expression of grief and pain, Ma instructed me thus: – What had to happen has happened, now rest for a while and then go meet them once. Ah, it cracks your chest open to see the man!

Even though my chest hadn't cracked open, I was truly saddened, but at Ma's proposal I said timidly: Do I have to go? But – how can I show my face – that's what I'm wondering. . . . And what will I say?

– Listen to the boy, Ma said in utter astonishment, – what sin have you committed, that you can't show your face? If you can't go and say two kind words and give your relatives some consolation in their time of difficulty and grief, how can you call them your own?

When I heard about it, I had just put the pot on, but I dropped my work right from my hand and ran over there. . . . I'd never talked much with Probodh-thakurpo before, but at such a difficult time, can you sit with your mouth shut? I talked to him, offered a few words of consolation, for better or worse, and it was quite late when I got back. After studying so much and staying in Kolkata, why you're so tongue-tied, that's what I wonder.

I wonder why, too, but does that untie my tongue?

But would my mother let it be?

In the end she pushed me out, to go visit their neighbourhood.

Ah, really, I felt very sad seeing poor Probodh-kaka. Even though he was an uncle distant in relationship, we were close because we lived in the same village. Especially since along with Probhash-da's promotions at work, Probodh-kaka also seemed to get promotions in the community. And it wasn't as though pride hadn't touched him at all. Even though we deferred to him, the pride that came of an ignorant village elder's unexpected fortune was a subject for our discussion and enjoyment. . . . But let that be – today, all of Probodh-kaka's arrogance was broken, shattered. No need for deference today, I needed to run my hand over his back and offer him some compassion.

When he saw me, Kaka broke out into loud lamentation, then slowly began to talk about many things . . . what a son Probhash-da had been, what honour he'd had at work! It seemed his boss sat down and stood up at Probhash-da's word; he wrote poor English and gave his work to Probhash-da to revise. No one else in the office had Probhash-da's ability to carry on extended discussions in proper, flawless English. If he'd lived he'd have become some terrific Keshto-Bishtu – no doubt about it – we talked about all this and more.

The poor man had truly had a bright future.

Is there anyone with such a taste for cruel jokes as fate?

I was preparing to leave when suddenly I was startled by the sound of an intense, piercing cry. A Bengali man cannot err in recognizing the nature of such a scream – that endless cry! A frantic, unrestrained expression of profound grief.

First a sharp scream hit my eardrums. Then an anguished, inconsolable, pathetic lamentation poured forth, twisted my heart. . . . Extreme agony, and an unreasoning prayer for the very thing that would not happen, that could not happen, that was the one impossible thing in the Lord's kingdom. . . . The futile plea to the absent loved one, to come back 'just once more' – that interminable entreaty built from a store of pitiful words chosen out of the entire universe of words, wave after wave spreading out into the air and sky . . . it made all my nerve-strings quaver.

You could not mistake those words. –

But the words weren't coming from Probodh-kaka's house! They seemed to come from some distance away! –

Who else had had such a misfortune?

Whose heart lay not in her chest but with someone in some far country? Was there some woman with a fortunate daughter spending her days in untroubled content in her husband's home? Had a telegram come and uprooted the veins in that woman's chest? Torn out every connecting thread in her heart? Or was it a postcard that had announced the news that such a fortunate woman's happiness and pride now lay in the dust?

This seemed like some new grief.

With a panic-stricken glance I looked at Probodh-kaka, but what was this, he wasn't startled? Hadn't he heard that? Was that possible? Was he so overcome by his own grief that this hadn't even entered his ears to reach his mind?

Once again I raised my ears and tried to understand, but I could not recognize the voice. Who was it? Who?

I couldn't help asking the question – I asked almost unwittingly: – What's that?

Probodh-kaka smiled a despondent, apathetic smile and said: – What else! The screaming of New-Bride in that house! At least a woman can scream and shout and lighten her heart's burden.

At Probodh-kaka's words I fell from one darkness into a greater darkness. 'New-Bride', meaning New-Khuri – Probodh-kaka's step-brother's widow. Their homes and kitchens had been separate for a long time now. And New-Khuri was almost the same age as Probhash-da had been!

Was it entirely normal for her to utter these chest-splitting screams to lighten her heart's burden at Probhash-da's death? Of course Probodh-khurima[1] was gone, after many years of dealing with the world's aches and pains, and in her absence New-Khuri had taken on the responsibility for the household's rituals, its Lokkhi-Shoshti-Ghentu-Monosha, to keep its traditions alive. But even so – would she take on the burden of grieving for her son as well?

Maybe Probodh-kaka understood my state of darkness somewhat, and so he said, slowly shaking his head: – I see you haven't heard the news about that house?

– No, I haven't!

Probodh-kaka smiled a sorrowful smile and said: – You haven't? – But why would you? People can't bear to tell it – Shublo's gone too!

'Shublo'! Meaning Shubol!

That robust young boy! 'Gone' meaning what? Dead?

Stupefied, I was bereft of words. New-Khurima's only child! And was he a boy who should die? Of course he wasn't a diamond, or even the shiniest gem in the neighbourhood, the boy was utterly ignorant, and obstinate, but his physique was admirable! I'd seen him just this past Sunday – sitting at Kalitola talking with those neighbourhood rowdies. That substantial body, so great in length and breadth – that's evaporated like camphor?

I was silent a minute or two, then asked: – What happened?

– Nothing at all, just a day's fever. Didn't have time even to show a doctor or boddi. Wretched he might have been – whatever he was, he was New-Bride's only son – that's a very painful thing.

Probodh-kaka uttered these words with great melancholy and compassion, but still it seemed to me that a fine disregard lay concealed somewhere. As though there was no grief – only pity. As though it was enough just to show some pity for this brother's widow mourning her son. Her grief, the loss of her son, could not be compared to his own.

And it was true indeed – next to Probodh-kaka's immense loss, how much was New-Khurima's? Could they be compared? Is an ocean ever compared to a cow's hoofprint? . . . Probhash-da to Shublo? A boy who might never have been able to buy his mother a handful of rice!

I stood up slowly.

Probodh-kaka said: – Are you getting up? Come again, baba, this next Sunday. It gives me some peace to see you all. . . . Will you stop at that house too? Of course it's getting late. Or – tomorrow morning if you can. And what can you do anyway, I hear Bou-Ma's utterly inconsolable, no matter who goes to see her, she cries and screams and beats her breast and just carries on. It's how women are.

He did say 'it's how women are', but from the way he said it, it was clear that New-Khurima's behaviour was unreasonable, excessive. To go to such lengths for a boy like Shubol wasn't quite decorous.

Maybe Probodh-kaka's calculations were right. I did hear the same thing when I returned home!

All the way back I wondered how I would break this news to

Ma – how would I broach the matter? No matter what I decided – I blurted it out as soon as I walked into the house. I said – what's happening in our village, Ma? You know what else has happened in that neighbourhood? New-Khuri's –

Ma was not startled, she said calmly: – You're talking about Shubol?

– You've heard?

– How could I not hear it? Where would I hide, to not hear it? I sit in my house and hear everything. He died earlier. Shubol died at dawn on Tuesday, and the news of Probhash came the day before yesterday – Thursday morning.

I was quiet for a moment, then said: – Why didn't you tell me about this? I didn't go to see New-Khurima! It got late –

– See her! What good would it do! I haven't been able to see her either, it was Shoshti that day – all kinds of work, and the next day, what rain! I couldn't cross the threshold of the house, and the very next day that bolt of lightning struck Probodh-thakurpo's house!

It didn't feel good to hear that, and I think I said with some asperity: – But you dropped everything from your hand to go there – right away! And New-Khuri's house is not even fifty yards from there.

– All that's fine, but I rushed out leaving the whole world on Bou-Ma's shoulders! The mother of a young boy, made to work while her child was crying, how could I delay?'

As though it were the first time she'd 'left the whole world on Bou-Ma's shoulders'! As though 'to work while her child was crying' were an extremely rare occurrence.

– It would have been the right thing to go, I said gravely.

Needless to say, this gravity could not abash Ma even slightly. Her reply was disdainful: – Enough, you don't need to teach me what's right and what's wrong. . . . Let her calm down a little, I'll go one of these days. I've heard there's no let-up in her screaming, not even for a moment, these past five days. All the neighbourhood, the neighbourhood's five-people, have told her many times – to take a bath, to wash her face. But she won't listen – hard as a board. How long will you carry on this way? You can do it five days – six days – you can't do it six months, can you? So? And she can learn from watching others! What a prince your bhashur lost, but is he so agitated? Calm, steady, quiet. . . . If you act this other way, will people like it? And you have to depend on your neighbours, don't you? What do you have in this world? Goblin, monkey, whatever he was, whatever little you had, is gone now!

I said in a wounded manner: – He was New-Khurima's only child, Ma, even if he wasn't a raja or badshah it didn't hurt her soul any less. A mother's heart –

– That I know, Ma said, displeased. – You don't have to inform me of that. Still – I say this too, a son's a son only if he fulfils a son's duties. What hopes did New-Bou have of that boy? – Other than just putting the flame to her mouth when she died? Would he ever have been able to lift a handful of rice to his mother's mouth? . . . Of course the pain of the umbilical cord won't go away, but still there are degrees of loss. Think of Probodh-thakurpo's condition, why don't you? He lived like such a king lately, all because of Probhash's money. Every month he used to send four hundred, four hundred and fifty rupees, without anyone having to mention it. Can anything be compared to Thakurpo's loss?

I couldn't say anything more.

There wasn't anything to be said anyway. Really, if you didn't calculate the amount of loss but went by what your heart said – why would five-people stand for it? Why else was the word 'adikkheta', excessive fuss, created? . . . If you lost a necklace of beads and grieved as much as you would for a gold necklace, that might become a child, but for a creature living in the world, it's unbecoming – unforgivable.

Could an unemployed, vagabond lad ever be raised above 'a

thousand or twelve hundred' by mere screaming? No one measures the depth of your grief by how much you beat your breast.

I've never even dreamt of 'a thousand or twelve hundred'; if I could reach a hundred and seventy-five, I would be saved – that's the kind of notion I've had in my head. But I've never calculated my price! Never occurred to me.

I should ask Ma: – How much distress is seemly for that hundred and seventy-five? Where will the line be drawn?

But no, let it be!

What's the need to peek inside the green room? Our work has only to do with the illuminated stage. What's the profit in finding out once and for all, who has how much colour of their own, and whose thickly flowing hair is a rented wig!

Broken illusions – is that loss an easy thing?

Entering the Underworld

পাতাল প্রবেশ

Patal Probesh

Aroti sweats even on a cloudy day, standing in the doorway to the courtyard, behind Mejo-Jethi; she cannot bring herself to utter the word 'Mejo-Jethi'.

From the way Mejo-Ginni sits, head bent, completely absorbed in sorting a bunch of greens, there's little hope that she'll suddenly turn her head and look back.

How annoying these tasks are that Ma sends Aroti out on.

But she won't come herself! 'All perils upon my enemy's head.'

The fact that Aroti has to come and stand here for that same reason every time, to call out 'Mejo-Jethi', the fact that it will leave her headless with shame – *she* never thinks of that.

Aroti's Ma is utterly merciless.

Aroti is already offended by her mother's cruelty, and now her anger swells and falls on her father. What need is there for him to appear every so often at the house? Wherever he lives all twelve months, why, let him go live there the rest of his life. If he doesn't come, not once in seven births will Aroti ever yearn to see her father. Not a father, but a guest to be fed!

How Aroti and her mother manage to survive, he'll never bother to find out; he'll only put in an appearance now and then, to eat his king's meal. And her mother's another one! – she'll beg from relatives and neighbours to arrange that meal.

If the arrangements had been in Aroti's hands, she'd have shown them what the outcome would be of showing up anytime, without notice, landing with a thud at night in this world of two unprotected women, and asking for hot luchis and rice-and-ghee with cream on a whim! But that won't happen. Because Aroti's mother is the ideal Hindu woman, a shoti who has vowed to serve her husband.

A bitter indignation – at her mother, at her father, at her Mejo-Jethi, maybe at the whole world – gathers in her, this young woman of sixteen springs.

But how can I say that? Where's the 'spring'? Spring doesn't come so easy.

For the girl who gets nothing but water for breakfast,[1] to sustain herself from morning till noon, and whose only hope at lunchtime is a neighbour's squash or some edible root with rice, and who must then save part of that root or squash – as though it were the fanciest delicacy – so that she can have it with two brown rutis and call that dinner: wouldn't spring be ashamed to even glance at *her*?

The girl who has to master the mysterious skill of making do with only two saris for two years, morning and evening: can her age ever have the sweetness of sixteen? It's as though the bitter experience of a long life of forty-six years has come to settle firmly on the shoulders of this sixteen-year-old. The corners of her lips, the pupils of her eyes, are witnesses to that.

If indeed the age of sixteen has come to Aroti, then it is not to increase her mother's worries, but to increase her annoyance. 'A groom must be found' – such an impossible desire cannot find room even in the corners of her mother's mind. She is only annoyed at the thought that this girl, who a few days ago carried out her mother's orders without protest, if this girl now wants to stand fast against her commands, says 'I can't' and sits and stays quiet, what will happen with her in the future?

Why, just today, the girl was so reluctant to go to the neighbour's house to ask for a loan that she'd had to change her order to an entreaty. But really, she had won this time. An entreaty was stronger than an order. It could not be ignored.

And so Aroti has forgotten the earlier insults and come to stand near her distantly related jethi to ask for a loan – a loan that certainly could never be paid back. A loan like so many others that have not been repaid.

After sweating awhile and growing tired, Aroti coughs a fake cough to try and attract Jethi's attention, but it doesn't work.

Who knows, maybe this absent-mindedness of Mejo-Ginni's is a pretence! An outward expression of annoyance is not seeing something even when you do see it. Or what could be so captivating about the red spinach that Mejo-Ginni's gaze does not want to waver from it?

'Mejo-Jethima!'

The effectiveness of this indistinct utterance cannot be judged. Who knows if Aroti might not have turned away disappointed, but a sudden event forces Mejo-Ginni to turn her head. And Aroti has to move away from the doorway and enter the courtyard.

The man who, finding the doorway clear, rushes into the courtyard holds a fishing-rod in one hand, and in the other, two mrigel fish caught with that rod. They must be about three kilos each.

'Pishima, look at my morning's catch! I'll finish off all the fish in your pond in seven days, before I leave.'

Pishima glances sidelong at her niece once before she says to her brother's son: 'Does your Pishe-moshai have only one pond, Ronu?

And you're bragging about catching a couple of newborn fish!'

'From newborn to gigantic! ... What, it's Aroti! What news? Are you well? You've grown!'

It's not necessary to say that Aroti shrinks a little and doesn't reply. Mejo-Ginni says in an annoyed manner, 'You go home now, Aroti, I'm busy, Ronu's come – '

Before Aroti can say anything, Ronu raises an uproar: 'Oh, what a fuss! Why give me a bad name, bapu? How am I keeping you busy? ... No, no, Aroti, it's you who should keep your jethima busy, as much as you want, that's your permanent job. ... And is your mother well?'

Aroti gauges the rain of fire from Jethi's stare in her mind and somehow nods her head once. Ronu, or Ronojit, swings the fish in his hand and says, 'Where should I put these, Pishima?'

'Chhoto Bou's in the kitchen, go give them to her. I'll be there soon.'

As soon as Ronu leaves, Mejo-Ginni imports the blazing fire of her eyes into her voice and says, almost killing Aroti inside, 'So! I suppose your father's arrived?'

Of course Aroti is silent.

'There won't be any money! Go tell your mother.'

Even then Aroti stands there like a pillar. Ma has told her, 'If she doesn't give you any money, ask for some ghee and a few Nainital potatoes. Those Mejdi doesn't have to buy anyway.'

Mejo-Ginni's father's house is in Boddibati, her father's a potato trader, he often sends her potatoes by the sackful. ... But that doesn't mean that those potatoes should fall to the portion of Mejo-Ginni's good-for-nothing, distantly related daor. And the ghee Mejo-Ginni made herself.

'You're still standing here? Didn't I tell you, there won't be any money?'

Aroti becomes almost desperate and says, 'Not money, Ma said – a little ghee and potatoes – '

'Don't shoot the messenger' – Mejo-Ginni doesn't heed this principle.

She looks the girl over with a harsh glare from head to toe and then says in a bitter tone: 'Go tell your mother to cut down on the wifely devotion, Aroti. You can't lean on someone else's shoulders all twelve months. I can't put ghee on everyone's plate in my own house, should I always go giving to charity? Go tell her – there isn't any. When you can't even find the rice for the meal – why this whim about ghee!'

Aroti is no longer in any condition to even walk away, her eyes and face burn with shame and revulsion, things grow blurred all around. What humiliation! What humiliation! ... When she was younger, she did feel the shame, the hurt would bring tears to her eyes, but she didn't burn this way. This unbearable fire would not pervade all her consciousness.

And right at this time, with his slippers noisily slapping against the floor, Mejo-Korta makes his entrance upon the stage.

'What? What's going on here? Over there, the fish are all being cut up. I brought four fresh mourola, Shoshi already bought one seer of pona this morning, and now Ronu – '

Ginni interrupts her husband's words to say: 'So let my own household sink, the main thing is to keep all your relatives happy.'

'What's happened?'

'No, nothing's happened. Chhoto-Korta has graced us with his presence, so Chhoto-Ginni's ordered potatoes and ghee. And a few rupees would be even better.'

'There won't be any money! Where's the money! If there are any potatoes – you might as well give her a few of those. My dear brother can't earn a living, but he has the tastes of a prince. ... And where the fellow stays all twelve months – '

The remainder of his sentence is lost in the noise of his slippers.

Mejo-Ginni heads for the pantry in an annoyed frame of mind.

Maybe she's thinking as she walks, even the small stone bowls aren't really all that small! A bowl small enough for a spoon or two of ghee would've been good. A small amount looks bad in a large bowl. And the giver's shamelessness, rather than the taker's, is expressed this way.

On some other day Aroti might have remained standing there, she wouldn't have had the courage to walk away. Because she knows that Mejo-Jethi *would* give her something. And to leave without taking it would be unbearable audacity – how could the earlier insult to Aroti compare to the humiliation of *that*? It was nothing at all. Who is Aroti? Is she any kind of person?

Today she suddenly runs off. She can't bear to wait in hope for 'a few of those'. Who knows, maybe Ronu's presence has agitated her.

When Ronu was here last, Aroti was twelve. Considering her an absolute child, Ronojit had patted her back, shown her how to catch fish, praised her! That was all.

Still, the mere memory of that is valuable for Aroti.

Who even bothers to call out to her, talk to her?

Maybe people think, if they talk to her, she might ask them for something.

Aroti's mother has gone around asking everyone for everything, leaving themselves neither dignity nor good reputation.

Entering the house, Aroti rushes into the room like a storm and throws herself on the cot covered by a torn durrie.

It doesn't take long for this scene to fall to her mother's eyes, because she has been waiting hopefully for her daughter, open-mouthed. She comes and says, 'What happened? She didn't give you any, I suppose?'

Aroti sits up.

Ignoring her father's presence in the next room, she says in a loud voice, 'No! Why should people give you things every day? Don't you people feel any shame begging all twelve months? People who can't earn a living, how can they have a taste for ghee and potatoes and rice? Go tell Father, he shouldn't come anytime he wants, he shouldn't think he's bought our heads.'

'Oh, you evil-tongued girl, be quiet!' Her mother grows anxious. 'He'll hear you!'

'Let him hear, that's just as well. What's the need for all this quiet? Does he shelter our heads with his umbrella? He keeps us here in the hope of getting those few rupees from Mama – does he ever bother to find out how we eat, what we wear? Why should he hope that he'll come and find a meal all laid out for him like a guest? A man like that should put a rope around his neck.'

Trembling, Aroti lies down again.

Aroti's mother, too, is trembling.

In an enraged tone, she says, 'What did you say, you godless wretch? You're a daughter, and you talk about your father's death? Because he can't bring home any money, your father's not your father at all? Who doesn't need to spread their palm before their own people at one time or another? And that leaves you headless?'

'Yes it does!' . . . Aroti forgets the shame of her careless words of an instant earlier and shouts out again. 'I can't go from one neighbourhood to another begging for his sake, I can't do it any more. All right? And thank you too, Ma, you still care what he thinks.'

Aroti's mother is astonished, stupefied, she stays quiet for a minute or so, then says in a sombre voice, 'Fine! I've taken the pot of rice off the fire, let me go put a little of that in front of him and tell him, swallow these balls of rice, and after you've swallowed them, if you can't get hold of a bundle of rope, tie the end of your dhuti around your neck and go hang yourself from the roof-beam! Let your daughter's lowered head be held up high. . . . How much the man suffers, that he can't show his face in his own house – who can understand that? Fine, let him die, let him die. Dying is best for him.'

But look, can even these word-arrows abash Aroti today? She looks the way her mother went and lies there with her mouth clamped shut. No, she has no attachment to anyone anymore! Everyone's selfish. She has no mother –

Right then she hears her mother's voice in the neighbouring room. Shouts and angry words, lamentation – many different tunes at play. It's hard to understand who the target is! The daughter, or her father!

And right after that, an angry yet anxious voice: 'Don't go, I tell you – don't put down your rice and go! Oh, just eat me alive. You're still leaving? Fine, go. There's enough water left in the pond to drown one person. If you leave your rice and go, just wait and see what I do.'

'You'll die, isn't that it?' Aroti's father's voice is offended, angry, mocking. 'You're dead the way you are. The woman whose husband is so penniless and wretched, whose daughter is so learned, she's as good as dead! This is it for me. I won't come here any more. Just think you've been widowed. Who's out there?'

'It's me, sir, Chhoto-kaka-babu!'... Half pulling the ghomta[2] over her head, Mejo-Ginni's maidservant, Shoshi, steps forward. On the terrace she puts down a few large potatoes in a wicker basket, a little ghee in a small stone bowl, and a few pieces of fish wrapped in a leaf, and says in a honey-soaked voice: 'Ma sent these. Didi-moni had come – Ma's hands were full, there was a little delay, and Didi-moni couldn't bear to wait. She walked right back! Ma said, if there's time, Didi-moni could bring a bowl, she's cooking fish-bones and vegetables, she'll give her some. She can't send me over with a cooked dish, now can she?'

Maybe Chhoto-Korta thinks of his life in a Kolkata slum.

The people from whose hands he has to eat! Compared to them, Shoshi's a Bhotcharj from Bhatpara.[3]

He hides his rising glee and says, 'All right, all right, I'll go myself.

The girl's feeling dizzy after coming in from the sun, she's lying down. . . . I say – where are you – give me a bowl, won't you?'

In his unexpected joy at the prospect of fish-bones and vegetables, it seems he has forgotten the last scene of the previous act. So he doesn't need to maintain any consistency between that scene and the present scene.

And by then Chhoto-Ginni, too, is quite melted by this introduction to Mej-di's generosity. She understands that she should go herself. She needs to ask after her, to flatter her a little. It's clear that a misplaced word or two got the girl hot and she came away. Oh, bapu, does it do for us to show them our heat? And besides, as a person Mej-di isn't bad, it's only that sometimes her words seem a little haughty. And after all, those whom God has beaten, they do need to turn soft!

Instead of Mej-di, it is towards her maidservant that Chhoto-Ginni turns soft as butter. 'You go ahead, Shoshi, I'll come with a bowl.'

Shoshi smirks and walks out.

She knows these people's ways. Even before you can say 'Medho, will you have lunch?' they'll be saying, 'Where should I wash my hands afterwards?'

Wife and husband look at each other and break into a sudden smile.

One's manner suggests: . . . *Now* let's see you leaving for good!

The other's manner suggests: . . . Can't leave now, can I?

The happy faces of both seem to have the perfect smoothness of Nainital potatoes, the oily tenderness of fish and vegetables. Their shining faces seem to reflect the lamplight of Mejo-Ginni's kindness.

And over there, upstairs, the third, in revulsion and shame, instead of asking the earth to split in two and swallow her, only wants to pound her forehead against the edge of the cot and split it in two.

What ugly greed!

What a shameless display of covetousness! All her body seems to sizzle with revulsion.

Such are Aroti's mother and father! Maybe such shamelessness has never been seen before. . . . What can Aroti do? Should she not worry about it? . . . No, if a rope is to be put to a neck, it is Aroti herself who should do it. . . . Yes, she'll die, it is she who will die.

They can go around with a begging-bag hanging from their shoulders; let them be content with grains of people's mercy and lick their feet. She feels greater revulsion towards her mother than towards her father. As though Aroti had really hoped that today there would be some resolution. Some event would occur that would cause a separation for all time.

And this is the outcome.

Thinking about it, crying over it, hating it, after some time Aroti falls asleep. . . . And when her sleep breaks, she rises and sees that sunlight has filled the courtyard, and the house is quiet.

At first she doesn't remember anything, then she does.

Soon she feels the need to take a bath. Not with the water stored in the house, but in the pond. Her body burns.

But where have these people gone?

Ma and Baba?

As soon as she steps down into the courtyard, with a torn towel in her hand, she finds out where they are. In the kitchen. They can be seen through a chink in the broken boundary wall.

Baba has sat down to eat, Ma in front of him.

Aroti, having stopped, keeps standing there.

As though suddenly astonished.

Is her Baba so thin?

It's true he walks around all day in a torn fotua, but has Aroti never seen his bare torso? . . . Every rib seems to want to break free of its covering of skin. Even the bones of his shoulder poke out like twigs.

And the stare of hungering greed on his gaunt face seems to be aimed not at his own plate but at the metal bowl in his wife's hand.... Even though there's only a little of the vegetable left in it. It seems that it's only out of a sense of delicacy that he is unable to ask for it, but all his desire is strongly focused on that remnant.

And Ma!

Ma's face ... yes, even on that gaunt, wretched face, what is this picture of boundless satisfaction drawn on it – Aroti doesn't recognize this picture at all!

As she stares, a strange sympathy softens the tight muscles of Aroti's face.... Why her mother has sunk all her shame and revulsion and accepted this beggar's life, that question seems to be answered in that picture of satisfaction on her face.

Can such a smile still break out at the corners of Ma's lips? A joking smile, a smile of indulgence? Of affection and attachment? She says in a voice wrapped in that smile, 'What's the need for all this delicacy, babu, take this little bit. That conceited girl of yours won't eat any of this.'

She pours all the vegetable from the bowl onto her husband's plate.

'And you?' Chhoto-Korta asks, lifting his eyes shining with greed.

'Me? ... I've already eaten!'

'What? ... When?'

Chhoto-Ginni puts a hand over her mouth and laughs. 'Here, now! Along with you. If you eat, that fills me too – '

'O, ho ho! Now I see. But no, so much chochchori, it was first-class – a little for you all – '

'Ah, we eat home cooking all twelve months, you're the one who has to suffer that inedible hotel cooking.'

Untroubled love-talk.

That someone's witnessing this – they have no idea.

Suddenly Aroti feels a great desire to laugh.

Home cooking!

Really, what fine home-cooked dishes they eat.

'Are there any potatoes left? Any fish?'

Even after eating up to his neck, the hope for more hasn't waned. Inquiries are being made about the night's meal.

'There are two large potatoes. But no more fish. Two pieces were fried, and two are in this gravy.'

It's easy to see that three of the four have found a resting-place in the stomach of the one dining.

'The potatoes were pretty good. If only there had been a few pieces of rui with that, and cooked by your hand! Aha ha! Ages since I've had a kalia! Can't we arrange for two pieces of fish?'

'Who's where? Everyone's become a miser nowadays.'

The reply is gloomy.

'You're right. We never get a single invitation. Only that once, long ago, at the mukhe-bhat of Mejo-Ginnis's grandson, that was a good meal. That was the last one, wasn't it? How many years has it been?'

'Some years now.'

'That was the last time I had a good kalia. And the cooking was superb! Ah-ha! And that sour ilish? Do you remember that?'

The tone of his voice suggests the event took place just the previous night, the taste still clings to his tongue.

Suddenly Aroti is startled! Can she be angry with them? Hai Bhogoban!

Then where would she keep the thing called 'compassion'?

Chhoto-Korta has stood up.

In a flash Aroti walks off hurriedly towards the pond. It's past one-thirty or two in the afternoon: no sign of anyone on the path.

How strange! Ronojit sits there with his fishing-rod in this full sun, absorbed in his task.

'You've sat down to your fishing again?'

Ronojit is startled!

'You, at this time? For a bath is it?'

'Yes. Fell asleep at the wrong time.'

'Asleep? Wonderful!'

'Wonderful indeed. A wonderful nap at the wrong time is such fun – '

Has the sixteen years sloughed off the mantle of forty-six and expressed itself?

'Let it be, that pleasure suits only girls.'

'And what suits you – to give up eating and sleeping for your worship of fishing, right?'

The pond bank is deserted, and even the air seems to have stilled for its midday rest. And in this setting, Aroti cannot be brushed off as a mere child.

Still, Ronojit says in a serious manner: 'Where have I had any luck fishing? The last time I came, at least I got some help from a neighbourhood girl – '

'Why should any neighborhood girl – ' . . . A restless smile plays across an unwashed, unfed, graceless face. . . . 'Yes, I'd understand if there was hope of eating a hot piece of fried fish – '

'It's waiting to be eaten, I've caught one fellow, it's on a line in the water. Go fry it and eat it.'

'Wait, let me finish my bath. . . . But payment without any work?'

Have Aroti's eyes, too, like her father's, turned shiny with greed?

Greed for what?

Ronojit understands that there's no connection between that greed and her sixteen years, it's only a pretence! So he unties the fish and almost throws it, carelessly, near Aroti's feet and says: 'Payment? For a gift? Take it and eat it.'

His voice seems to have the bitterness of a failed hope.

But will Aroti bend to pick it up?

She's a spirited girl, Aroti!

Or will she stride off? Saying she has no need of a gift?

But how can she leave?

Through the chink in the boundary wall you could clearly see . . . a ribcage covered by thin skin . . . two hungry, covetous eyes . . . you could clearly see . . . a picture of boundless satisfaction drawn on a gaunt face.

What else can she do but bend?

Maybe –

Maybe she would not have been reluctant to bend even more. Ronojit has saved her.

Grieving for Oneself

নিজের জন্য শোক

Neejer Jonno Shok

In the middle of the night, still asleep, Obinash suddenly experiences a terrible discomfort. As if his breath will stop. An unfamiliar pain in his chest.

He wakes and feels his limbs wet with sweat, the pillow under his neck sodden wet. He tries to sit up but can't. He thinks it would be good to raise his head and turn the pillow over, but realizes he can't do it. He can't move his arms or legs, which are numb, stone-like.

About to go past his sixties, Obinash has seen much of life – this experience manifests itself as a swift question that runs a sharp-edged saw across every cell, every membrane, every nerve in his brain.

Am I having a stroke? This breath-stopping pain in my chest? This sweating, this numbness in my arms and legs – these are all signs of a stroke!

Unbalanced, panicking, Obinash tries to cry out someone's name – maybe his older son's, maybe his younger son's, maybe one of his granddaughters', or maybe even Shoilobala's! No, it can't be Shoilobala's, when has he ever called Shoilobala by name, how will it come to his lips? If it's not practised, it won't come even at the final hour. That's why the sages tell us to keep on rehearsing the Name.

Obinash has not practised that either, so he calls out some practised call. But whomever he might have called, that call doesn't reach anyone's ear: the call writhes and thrashes within; no sound comes out of his throat.

This must mean that Obinash has had an attack of palsy. A sudden attack, catching him completely unawares. The Obinash who was healthy, normal, relaxed, right until the time he lay down in bed – right up to the moment he fell asleep!

During the day he'd followed his daily routine without exception, and his body hadn't felt different in any way. He awoke at dawn and went out for a stroll in the park, and on his way back he stopped at the dairy to get milk for his younger grandson, having the cow milked in front of him and acquainting the milk-seller, as always, with his proper duty.

Certainly Obinash's younger son and his wife, his grandson's parents, have not asked him to do this. They rely on tinned milk. Obinash has taken on this responsibility of his own accord. He even carries the aluminium container with him on his walk. And proudly tells his granddaughters, I don't care if people laugh.

Anyway, today, too, he ate toast with his tea as soon as he came back home, and after finishing with the newspaper he had halua and some spiced potato with a second large cup of tea. It seems in his old age he feels hungrier in the mornings than he used to, but he's ashamed to say anything. So he notices it when he catches a sudden whiff of whatever's being prepared for his granddaughters' tiffins.

Obinash used to take ruti and torkari for his tiffin; his sons take luchi and mishti; his granddaughters can't wolf down the large luchis quickly at lunchtime, so they have to be given something easier to swallow, such as egg fritters, nimki, halua, spiced potatoes, and so on.

These airborne aromas float in from the kitchen and seem to make Obinash restless. Then he walks towards the inner rooms with his newspaper still in his hand. Have you heard the news? A wedding party killed in a bus accident near Motihari! . . . Or, voice raised, he says, Did you hear what happened? Yesterday, in a huge fire –

The target of this serving of news is of course Shoilobala. He cannot talk about the real news in the paper, politics and political machinations, with her, she has no time to worry her head about the country's problems. When prices go up, she's fired up in anger at the authorities, and if they come down somewhat, she's pleased. If she listens carefully to anything, it's to these reports of accidents and calamities. . . . So what's to be done, these topics have to be discussed. But sometimes when she's really in a hurry, Shoilobala says, Leave it babu, don't start telling me about all that, it makes me unhappy, and so early in the day too.

Obinash understands that the talk about unhappiness is an excuse; when she's busy she has no time even to listen to the news. He says, So that's why I say, it seems to have become an exceptional thing for people just to be able to survive – and then he potters about for a minute and says, What a fine smell! You're making halua, are you? . . . Are you frying potatoes? It smells as if you're frying eggs. What are you frying them in? Ghee or mustard oil? It smells very good.

Whether it's because of these hints or because of Shoilobala's consideration, with his second cup of tea Obinash receives a second breakfast. Today, too, he ate it with great relish.

In his mind Obinash sees pictures of the day's progression; he wants to find out if somewhere there was a sign of any weakness. But he can't see any.

After that he went to the market, as usual. That too is a repetition: his older son takes the servant to do the morning's shopping, but even so, after his sons leave for work, Obinash goes to the market once more to finish the job. He brings back something inedible and presents it proudly, it's something they don't even touch. . . . Banana stems, small greens, yam sprouts, tiny fish – people just don't eat these things. But if they don't eat it, why is it sold in the market! Anyway, if nobody eats it, Obinash will eat it by himself. Shoilobala, too, has now begun to insist that eating these results in acidity. That's all nonsense; it's just to ingratiate herself with their trend-following sons and daughters-in-law. Obinash doesn't care to ingratiate himself. In fact he made a point today of taking a large helping of unfashionable chochchori in front of his daughters-in-law.

Then he had biscuits with his tea in the evening; he performed his duty of bringing back his younger granddaughter from school; he went to the park with his younger grandson. The maid always goes to the park, pushing the perambulator; still, Obinash goes along. He cannot agree to leave it in the maid's hands. Even though his grandson's mother stifles her laugh and says, So many children go to the park with other people – whose grandfather comes along to guard them?

Let her say it; Obinash goes anyway, he went today too. And after that? What else – his sons came home one at a time, tea was made, he ate a little with them, as he usually did, and after talking for a while about this and that he finished his dinner and went to bed. And in all this, was there any sign of that deep pit into which the man called Obinash Shen has put his foot, into which he's sinking now?

Obinash tries to shout again, no sound escapes his throat. This means that the palsy has taken over his entire body. The demon hasn't even left him his tongue.

Pokkhaghat, palsy! Instead of using the common name for the disease, Obinash has taken this esoteric word from the pages of Ayurvedic science. This word is much more fearsome than 'paralysis', perhaps because it's so much harsher? But it seems necessary, to weigh the burden of his sorrow.

It's summer, but after a strong northwesterly breeze in the evening the air has turned quite cool, and because Obinash is susceptible to colds the window at his head is shut. The fan on the table in front of him turns gently, noiselessly. It's a narrow room, it couldn't really be counted a bedroom, so there's no ceiling fan, it's not really needed, if the other window's open the wind is strong enough to fly you away. Today, one panel of that window is shut.

Shoilobala took care of all this before going to bed. Of course she doesn't go very far, her dwelling place is in the very next room. This room is a small strip, the distance from the other is also very small, and between the two rooms the door stays open, with only a curtain hanging in the doorway. . . . Still, how immense this intervening distance.

When his older son's daughters grew up, Obinash lost a longtime habit and a prize possession: Shoilobala's being near him. He was forced to lose it for a petty reason: the girls' parents' share of the house was only one room, and apparently it wasn't proper to sleep with two grown-up girls in the same room, therefore to preserve propriety and decorum, one day Shoilobala herself made this arrangement.

Obinash was exiled from that very room in this ancient house in which he had had his phulshojja the first night of his marriage, and where he had spent all his days since. Shoilobala now sleeps in great comfort with her two granddaughters in the immense old-fashioned pair of beds that they received at their wedding, and Obinash in this narrow room, on a narrow cot.

When this arrangement was first discussed, it was a thunderbolt falling on his head, but Shoilobala had warned him earlier: Be very careful, don't say even one word about this, or there'll be no end to our shame. So Obinash kept his lips under lock and key, his sorrow pride anger mortification all stored away in his mind.

When his older son said, I think this room is actually better in a way, there's such a large window to the south, which you didn't have in the other room – Obinash lifted his newspaper and held it in front of his face.

And when his daughter-in-law pointed out, That room was always so cluttered, we didn't know it was such a beautiful room, if both the east and the south windows are open, the breeze lifts you away, isn't that right, Father? – then Obinash said, Bou-ma, when will the washerman be here?

Certainly Shoilobala understands, she understands in every bone the slightest difference in the way Obinash lets out his breath, but she doesn't show that she understands, she feigns a lack of perception. Still, Obinash tries now to make his final, grievous cry reach their ears, the ears of those who don't think it very necessary to heed what he has to say.

But it isn't reaching them. His utmost effort bears no fruit; his sweat gathers. In sorrow and pain he tries to cry out loudly, and then from his throat emerges a groaning noise, much like the wretched cry of some feral creature.

Now Obinash hears his older granddaughter's voice, Dida, oh Dida, Dadu's making such a strange sound.

This means that Shoilobala is still lost in blissful slumber, the noise hasn't reached her in the depths of her sleep. . . . Oh, Obinash is suffering his death throes at just a few hands' distance, and Shoilobala –

And then some kind of lump forms in his chest . . . that's just as well, if Shoilobala and her sons rise from their peaceful sleep in the morning to find Obinash's dead face. And as he articulates in his mind this terrible curse upon his wife and sons, a flush of water rolls down from his eyes.

But Obinash's curse doesn't take effect. The next instant, Shoilobala's just-woken voice cries out, O Ma what's this!

And then the curtain moves, Shoilobala's dishevelled form is seen beside it.

Obinash shuts his eyes. He has no wish to show Shoilobala his watery eyes. Obinash realizes, even with his eyes closed, that his two granddaughters have come into the room, and then the younger one runs out shouting, in a loud voice, Bapi Bapi, Kaku Kaku.

Obinash realizes that Shoilobala has sat down on a corner of his narrow cot and taken hold of his right wrist to feel his pulse. She's an Ayurvedic physician's daughter and has a keen, innate perception on matters of health – and she's very quick to use this knowledge. Whenever anyone falls ill, the first thing Shoilobala does is feel their pulse.

Obinash can feel that Shoilobala has lowered his hand carefully on the bed and is now pushing and shoving at him, calling loudly, Can you hear me? Oh, can you hear me? Where's the pain – can you hear me? Did you have a bad dream?

Obinash can open his eyes if he wants to, he has no paralysis of the eyelids, but he doesn't want to. He begins to enjoy that cry of distress. Can you hear me? Oh, do tell me what kind of pain it is? . . . And with that, Shoilobala's loving touch. But this dreamlike enjoyment doesn't last, both his sons enter the room. Even with his eyes shut Obinash can see that one has on a silk lungi, and the other his striped night-pajamas, and, stepping close to their father's bed and bending their faces down, they are calling loudly, Baba Baba. And then in a lower voice, What's going on?

He hears Shoilobala's reply, Don't know. Rinku pushed me awake, saying Dadu's making a strange sound, and I came and called to him, but I can't get any response.

But why is her voice changing this way? Why hasn't the lamentation burst forth in her voice? Even the distress of a moment ago is gone, her manner seems quite relaxed. That means she won't embarrass herself in front of her sons. So, anxiety for her husband is a matter of embarrassment for Shoilobala. Yes, that's true, Obinash has noticed this earlier as well.

The older son calls out again, but Obinash doesn't react. The boys broach the subject of a doctor.

Who knew that these two tiny leaves over the eyes could be such a screening rampart, behind which so much of oneself could be concealed.

With deep regret Obinash now realizes that the extreme pain in his chest has greatly abated, he thinks he might now be able to speak, he might be able to blow away their concern with a single breath, saying, Please, baba, there's no need to go out looking for a doctor-foctor in the middle of the night. Your father isn't going to die right this minute.

He thinks he might be able to speak, his condition has improved, but still Obinash doesn't try to speak, he lies there with his teeth clamped together and his eyes shut.

He is sure – and it is a dreadful awareness – that if he speaks up now he'll suddenly lower himself in their eyes, cheapen himself. No, he has no wish to cheapen himself right now. He'd rather lie there with his eyes shut and enjoy the situation, the doctor arriving and making his examination, calling to him, getting no response and indicating his suspicions with signs and gestures, it might be a cerebral haemorrhage, and giving the order: Keep him in bed. Absolute rest.

What then? His sons would no longer be able to remain so indifferent towards their father. And Shoilobala? It would be a fitting punishment for Shoilobala. It wouldn't do for her to live her life with all her energies, only coming once or twice into his room to turn the fan on or shut a window, and all for the sake of showing her concern, all mere lip-service to duty, before retiring with her granddaughters to sleep in her bed of comfort.

Obinash begins to wait for the doctor – from behind the shelter of his screening rampart. But his wait isn't successful. Obinash hears in Shoilobala's voice what he might have said himself, Let it be, Khoka, there's no need to rush out for a doctor right now.

The younger son says, Would that be right, not to call a doctor?

Yes. I think he's just had a bad dream and doesn't want to talk – nothing else. The pulse is fine. She's the daughter of a physician's house and doesn't shrink from displaying her pride in the fact. Oh, what shameless cruelty. What ruthlessness, just to maintain her influence over her sons.

His limbs burn with rage, a crop of words rises in his mind, I see your great arrogance! All at once you've become omniscient! The pulse is fine! And who on earth asked it to be fine. His eyes fill up again at his own misbehaving pulse. His eyes begin to smart from the salt water, but still he doesn't open them.

Shoilobala's careless-sounding voice is heard again, Turn up the fan, Rinku. And open the window wide. . . . Listen, can you hear me – will you drink some water?

Water! The sound of the word makes him eager, expectant in every straining nerve. He realizes that at this moment what he really needs is water. It won't do to keep his eyes shut any longer. Getting no response, they won't bring him any water – Let him be, there's no need to disturb him, he'll drink water when he wakes. Obinash opens his eyes.

The older son says, Baba, will you drink some water?

How many days has it been since Obinash last heard this tone of voice from his elder son? Soft with kindness, loving, compassionate. He nods his head, Yes. The older granddaughter quickly brings some water. This too is new, everyone knows; Dadu is usually Dida's business.

The younger son says, What happened all of a sudden? That tone, too, seems to float across a distance of many years.

Obinash turns his hands palm out and says, I don't know! All at once, somehow, I was a little –

And it occurs to him that he can move his hands normally. And he has been able to speak. Stealthily he tries to move his foot; it moves. That means all is well with the elderly gentleman called Obinash Shen.

The younger son says, Are you all right now? Or should the doctor be called?

Whether the doctor should be called is not a question to be put to the patient, and it hurts Obinash deeply. Once again his eyes well up, he shakes his head, No.

Then try and calm yourself and go to sleep. Don't sleep with your hands on your chest, sometimes that can cause this kind of thing.

Shoilobala rises from the edge of the bed and smoothes out the wrinkled bedsheet with her hand, and says easily, Khoka, why don't you get one of those pills you have, those digestive pills. I think it's indigestion of some kind –

It's only to be expected, Khoka says readily, I thought the same thing when I came in – he doesn't think about the fact that he's getting old, he should restrain himself a little in his eating and drinking. At least at night, it's better not to eat mangoes and such. It worries me sometimes, to watch him eat.

A violent earthquake shakes Obinash inside. His carefully moulded self-worth, founded in the pain of his hopes and longings, is reduced to dust. He has been cheapened, turned into an extremely small old man, the kind of old man who will eat without regard for the consequences and fall ill and suffer and cause others to suffer.

Shoilobala brings him a vest and says, Take off that sweaty vest. . . . Khoka, Budu, you all go back to sleep now.

Khoka yawns and says, What sleep! My sleep's ruined for the night.

Budu says, Yes, this ruckus in the middle of the night – my

stomach's starting to feel queasy too. I don't think I'm going to get any more sleep. He says all this, but still he walks off. He doesn't say: Since I can't sleep anyway, maybe I'll sit awhile with Father.

The granddaughters have left after watching him drink the water. Now there's only Shoilobala – and from her manner it's clear that she's preparing to leave as well.

Obinash says in an unconcerned voice, You're going too?

Shoilobala is somewhat abashed. No, it's just that Khoka seems to have forgotten the medicine. Let me get it, then I'll sit for a while.

You don't have to sit, why don't you sleep here?

Shoilobala looks at Obinash's two-and-three-quarters-foot-wide bed and says, her tone embarrassed, The things you say! – That bed of yours, wide as a field isn't it!

Surprising, just these few days ago Shoilobala and he had slept in the same bed, though it was the other, field-wide bed. In truth, some practices, once abandoned, cannot be resumed. One feels ashamed. In many matters: eating, dressing, sleeping.

Obinash says, Once on a train berth, the two of us wrapped ourselves in a single blanket –

Shoilobala says quickly, Stop it now, those days and these days, won't our granddaughters laugh if they see us? Let me see what Khoka's up to. – And Shoilobala stands up.

I don't want any medicine, Obinash says and turns on his side to lie facing the wall.

Perhaps Shoilobala sees this curse as a blessing. The boys have forgotten, now I'm reluctant to go and wake them up again. . . . After a moment Shoilobala turns down the table fan for no reason, then turns it up again, then quietly leaves the room.

Maybe the two granddaughters are awake, they might think the old couple are billing and cooing to each other. In youth, shame before one's elders; in old age, shame before the young.

As soon as Shoilobala leaves, once again Obinash feels his breath will stop. He sits up, then lies down again without changing his vest. And, lying down, he begins to pray – God, let Obinash have a stroke.

Not an attack of palsy, but the ultimate attack. So that his wife and sons can slap their palms against their foreheads and say – What a mistake we made last night, to call it heartburn and walk away!

Especially Shoilobala. In the morning, when she comes in to see him, to do her duty with Oh, how are you feeling?, and realizes that it's all over – her colourful sari, her bangles, her life's dues all cleared – what then?

Again he tries to find a fiendish delight in all this, and again it is useless. His eyes begin to water profusely, a slow stream of tears wets his pillow.

A man, Obinash by name, is lying dead, silent, alone in a room – Obinash's chest is bursting as he imagines this scene, as if he's watching the death of a close relative. He glances at the supine lifeless form and the tears surge up choking him but he keeps on praying for that friendless wordless wretched death, does Obinash Shen.

A Covering of Leaves

পত্রাবরণ

Potraboron

Shonibar, Saturday, is a day of celebration. On this day, smoke can be seen over the thatched roof of the kitchen even in the evening. Playing in the garden of the vacant Goshai house, Pitu sees the spiral of smoke, and it startles her.

Really, is it Saturday?

Thakuma did say so in the morning! Completely forgot. Brushing the dust from her hands, Pitu says, 'I can't play any more, bhai. I'm going home.'

'Don't go right now, Lokkhi-ti!' pleads her companion, Labonno. 'Play one more turn before you go.'

Pitu softens a little at her friend's plea and looks up at the sky. Considers whether it's possible to meet the request. No, it's already late afternoon, who knows when the sky poured its gold all around.

'Na, ré. Baba's coming today. I have to go, bhai.'

Labi pouts and says, 'Why do you act this way because Baba's coming, ré? Are you the only one whose father's coming? My father's coming today, too. Am I running off like you?'

Maybe Pitu can't find the answer to this question; she says, as though cornered, 'But your father's *old*.'

'Ei, you rude girl!' Labu glares at her: 'You called my father old? Is that how much sense you have? Isn't Baba your Jetha-moshai? Wait, let me go tell your mother.'

Even though Labu and Pitu are inseparable, neither of them is willing to overlook the other's offences! Of course, whether calling someone like Jetha-moshai old can be counted an offence, Pitu doesn't engage in debating that; she says, with a sorrowful face, 'Please don't tell her, bhai, I fall at your feet. I didn't know it was a mistake, I saw his hair had turned grey, so that's why – you won't tell, will you?'

Labi the Forgiving says in a reassuring voice, 'All right, fine, I won't tell. But in exchange you'll have to play another round.'

'It's gotten really late, ré. I have to wash my face and hands before Baba comes, and put on clean clothes.'

Labi breaks into a laugh and says, 'Baba-baba! It's like no one else has a baba. Only you have one. Baba's coming, I won't play, Baba's coming, I'll dress up – is Baba an honourable in-law?'

Even if there isn't any difference in age between Pitu and Labu, there is, needless to say, some difference in awareness. Pitu is embarrassed at her friend's jesting remark and says, 'Ba, why should he be an in-law? If I wear torn clothes, Baba will realize we're poor.'

It cannot be hoped that the fountain of Labu's laughter will remain suppressed after this. Almost drowning her friend in the fountain of her uncontrollable laughter, Labi says, panting, 'Oh, baba, what a simpleton you are! You're poor, and your baba's a very wealthy man, I suppose? It's only because your baba's poor that you're poor.'

Pitu says, her face red, 'Ish! Never! Baba's not poor. Go take a look. What clean clothes! How many things he brings home!'

Labi half-smiles and matches her tone: 'How much jewellery your mother wears!'

Labi's eight years old; that doesn't matter. Since she learnt to talk, she's learnt to talk far beyond her years, has Labi. Many girls learn, when their mothers and aunts aren't careful.

In this talk of jewellery lies Pitu's defeat. She says with hurt pride, 'Fine, fine, we're poor. Are you satisfied?'

'O baba, the girl's angry now. All right, baba, it was my mistake! You'll come to play tomorrow, right?'

'But Ma scolds me if I come!'

Pitu's mother doesn't like it when Pitu wanders around the fields and streets on a Sunday – Labi knows this, hence the question.

Of course Labi knows the answer too, and so she says immediately, 'That's the root of the problem. As soon as Sunday comes, it burns my bones.'

Pitu says, eyes wide, 'Sunday comes, and it burns your bones? . . . Don't you like it when your father comes?'

'No! Not at all. Does he come and make me king, tell me that? He only comes and talks to Ma, then runs off to his card games. The only thing I get is scoldings. He sees me and starts to scold! He stays in Calcutta, that's a relief!'

'My baba doesn't scold me.'

Pitu finds her stolen pride!

Labi doesn't strike a blow at her friend's pride in her father. She says solemnly, 'Yes. Ponkoj-kaka's a good man. All right, baba, you go home. Or else you'll get a mouthful from your ma.'

Eight-year-old Labi goes her way, in the manner of a middle-aged woman.

There's nothing to disbelieve about this. Those who are called 'girls' and ignored – very often, if you put your ear to one of their gatherings, you'll come to realize that they aren't suitable for ignoring.

In fact, girls like Pitu are the exception! She pushes the fence gate open like a thief and peeks in. No, there is no notice of Baba's arrival anywhere. So there's no need to worry, she can slip inside. All that's needed now is to splash her face with a couple of handfuls of water and change her clothes and drag the comb a couple of times through her hair. And after that Pitu is out of reach!

But the attempt to keep the matter of the bucket-and-dipper as noiseless as possible doesn't work. Even the tiny sound of the dipper being pushed into the water does not escape the ear of the person in the kitchen.

'Pitu.'

A tone of rebuke sounds forth from the room.

'Your game doesn't end, does it? Hurry up and wash your face. Your clothes are on the cot!' – That was all right – not too bad! Grateful Pitu finishes her task in an instant and goes and stands in the kitchen doorway. With a cheerful face, she says, 'What will you cook today, Thakuma?'

Thakuma lifts her head and says, smiling, 'You decide, it's your son who's coming.'

'Dhat!'

Pitu enters the room and squats on her heels. She says, her eyes wide in astonishment, 'Are you making kochuris, Ma?' – The reason for making kochuris is one for sweet bashfulness! A suppressed smile plays across Monoroma's face. It is Thakuma who answers: 'Han ré! Because your father really loves kochuris. Of course they eat a lot at their mess, there's nothing he could want for, but still, it's home cooking, that's what! Setting aside a little oil every day – '

Monoroma says, protesting in a low voice, 'Let that be, Ma. She's a child – she'll blurt it out to someone.'

Thakuma, covering her embarrassment, says quickly, 'My Pitu's not that kind of girl, she has a lot of sense. What do you say, Pitu?'

Pitu laughs a bashful laugh.

Monoroma says, 'Since they're being fried, go ahead and eat the two in your share!'

Her mouth waters, but Pitu tames her almost untamable desire and says, her manner dismissive, 'I'm not hungry right now. I'll eat with Baba.'

'You'll eat with him – and will you lick your fingers greedily when you're sitting in front of him?' Monoroma laughs.

No, no one's ready to forget the story of Pitu's carelessness that one day.

Pitu says, her face red, 'Ish! As if I do that every day! That was only once.'

Monoroma says with a smile, 'And what will you do today? Will you say, "What kind of thing is a kochuri, Thakuma? What does it taste like, Thakuma?" Isn't that right?'

Thakuma defends her embarrassed granddaughter. In a tone of mock reprimand, she tells her bou, 'You only want to provoke her! Is she so stupid? – Hunh! What will you say, ré, Pitu?'

Pitu says eagerly, with faith in this support, 'What will I say? I'll say, I eat kochuris free-quently, Thakuma makes them every other day. We eat so many kochuris we're sick of them, Baba, you go ahead, eat up!'

Monoroma laughs out loud and says, 'Oh, save us, you don't have to say all that! It's enough if you don't lick your fingers or your plate when you sit in front of him!'

Pitu casts her greedy glance here and there, to see if some choice edible might fall to her eyes, something unhoped-for in the golden opportunity of this celebration! Sometimes such things can be seen. Like the other day. Fresh coconut grated and heaped in a half-shell.

Pitu hadn't asked for any, had only said, 'What's that, Thakuma?' and that had been enough for Thakuma to pick up a lot of it and put it into Pitu's hand.

No, there's no fresh coconut today, the only things that can be eaten raw are some chickpeas soaking in a bowl.

'Why are you soaking the chickpeas, Thakuma?'

Monoroma says in a rebuking tone, 'To cook them, why else. If you're hungry, why don't you eat what you're supposed to eat, bapu?'

Thakuma understands her granddaughter.

She rebukes her bou. 'She didn't come here to tell you she was hungry, dearie! Why do you keep rushing her in everything? I'll cook the lau with the chickpeas, ré, Pitu. Labi's pishi came by and gave us half a lau from their plant. Quite tender. Your father loves ruti and lau ghonto. Here, chew on these for now.'

Thakuma picks up a couple of chickpeas and holds them out to her granddaughter.

But Pitu won't reach out so easily. Doesn't she have her dignity? She glances sidelong at her mother.

'That's enough, no need to be shy.' – Monoroma laughs out loud and picks up a pinch of salt. 'Take this, it'll taste better with salt.'

'Why in the kitchen? Go sit outside.'

This is a hint.

'Go sit outside' – what that means is 'Go keep an eye out.' To see Baba coming is in itself a great delight!

Once, Thakuma wasn't there, she'd gone to Tribeni to bathe in the Gonga, and both Pitu and her mother had kept watch from the fence gate, standing there an hour before he was to arrive.

'Baba! Baba! Baba! Baba's come, Baba!'

In the kitchen, Monoroma's chest starts thudding loudly. It's been eleven or twelve years since the wedding, but still it thuds.

Ponkoj enters, laughing and mimicking his daughter's words, 'Baba! Baba! Baba! . . . Look, babu, watch this magic, look at Pitu-rani's Baba. . . . Tickets four-four paise each, babu, tickets four-four paise each!' Ponkoj is this sort of jovial man. He laughs at everything.

Now Pitu no longer has the patience not to grab Baba from the back and hang on to him.

'Now her silliness begins.' Monoroma comes out and issues a quiet scolding. 'The man's arrived tired and hot, let him get a moment's peace?'

But Pitu's not afraid of her mother any more.

She's not, for two reasons. First, there's great help at hand – Baba's right there. And second, the hint of a smile that has lit up her mother's face and eyes hasn't escaped Pitu's glance.

As though it's all right to not be afraid of this mother.

Mohamaya's practice of cleanliness is well known in the neighbourhood. The water vessel cannot be touched while one is in one's railway clothes. Monoroma goes to the edge of the well and pours water for Ponkoj to wash his hands and face.

Ponkoj smiles a little and says in a low voice, 'There's no virtue in withholding the water that will slake my thirst and offering me water to wash my feet.'

Monoroma replies in the same way, 'That'll do now, that's enough. Now the girl's growing up, you should learn to watch what you say.'

'The girl? There's plenty of time before she grows up.' And Ponkoj gazes fondly at his daughter nearby.

'That's what makes it even worse! She might run off to ask Ma right now, "Thakuma, what does water to slake my thirst mean?"'

Both of them laugh out loud.

It's taking so long to wash his face . . . Pitu thinks. Monoroma says, 'You've brought a whole pile of things again? You seem to have made a hobby of spending unwisely. It's such a small household – tell me who eats so much here? We still have all the papor you brought last time, and you've brought papor again!'

Ponkoj says seriously, 'Well, if you all won't eat it, I won't bring any more!'

'Now look, what a fuss! How much will we eat? With so many vegetables and such, where's the chance to eat other things?'

'Who's giving you so much? You haven't made some arrangement with someone else, have you?'

Ponkoj keeps laughing!

'Now I think I *should* do that. How uncivilized you're becoming day by day. Unfit to live in a family.'

Mohamaya calls out loudly, 'O Ponkoj, are you done washing your face? These few kochuris are turning stale! Can't you wait until you've had a little food and water before you start telling your stories?'

'Are you happy now?' Monoroma says, and casts an angry sidelong look at her husband, then walks away with quick steps.

Ponkoj climbs up to the verandah and sits down to his tea and snacks.

The task of serving him food is in Mohamaya's own hands. She's not satisfied even if his wife serves him! Mohamaya certainly has nothing left to learn about their manners and ways! Maybe right while eating they'll set to laughing so much, the person eating won't know what he's eating, the person serving will forget to ask, 'Did you eat well?'

Mohamaya cannot bear such misuse of what was prepared with so much care, so much painstaking effort. She will sit next to him and serve him food, ask him how it is, will keep insisting that he have some more – then there's some satisfaction!

Mohamaya doesn't touch the fish, on Sundays there's fish, it's Monoroma who cooks it. Mohamaya stands and supervises the serving of it. Once Monoroma had forgotten to serve the sour kholsha curry, and for that offence Mohamaya had given her a good never-before-and-never-again. Ordinarily she's affectionate towards Bou, but not where her son is concerned.

Ponkoj settles himself comfortably, then says, 'Kochuris and chilli-potatoes? Like the Grand Hotel! Today's meal is absolutely kingly!'

Mohamaya, melting with affection, says, 'They're kochuris in name only! Our bad luck that the ghee ran out today, so I fried them in oil. If you eat them hot, they won't taste bad.'

'Won't taste bad?' Ponkoj takes a bite and says in a tone of utter satisfaction, 'Hunh! They taste better if they're fried in oil, Ma! Why, at our mess they burn pots of ghee in their cooking, but let me see how they can fry even one Grand kochuri like this! To tell the truth, Ma, for the past few days I've had a longing for some chickpea kochuris fried in oil.'

The tears in Mohamaya's eyes become unstoppable. She says with difficulty, 'O ré, it's not for nothing that the Shastros talk about a mother's heart! There's a saying, "The son calls out on this shore, the mother cries on that shore." The mother's heart cries from the far side of the river!'

And then there's no delay in the last few kochuris in the brass bowl falling on her son's plate.

Now it's Ponkoj's turn to get angry.

'Enough, enough! You piled on all of them? No, it's not possible to praise anything to you people! Am I supposed to eat all eight or nine of these now?'

'Why can't you? I'll make fewer rutis for dinner tonight!'

'And won't you all eat any? You could have saved at least a couple?'

'Bou-ma's share is inside, I've given Pitu hers, so for whom should I save any? Do I eat anything with chickpeas at night?'

Ponkoj says in a distressed manner, 'Chhi chhi! Then why did you make them today? Couldn't you have made them tomorrow morning?'

Mohamaya smiles affectionately and says, 'Listen to what he says! It's hardly any kind of delicacy, a couple of oil-fried kochuris! And those your Ma didn't eat, and this didn't happen, and that didn't happen – leave it alone! – Am I not eating? Bou-ma cooks for me every hour and half-hour. Why, only this morning she was saying, Ma, on Doshomi I'll feed you your fill of daal-puri. Cooking is an obsession with Bou-ma.'

'Yes! Who could have such good qualities if not your bou? Hey, Pitu, do you eat kochuris and daal-puri every day?'

'Every day.'

Pitu looks as though she's standing in the middle of a desert, bewildered. Where are those impossible things? . . . The one or two extra things that can be seen on a daily basis around the central rice or ruti are kochu greens, ol stalks, or those gifts of affection from their neighbours, lau or pumpkin. Baba brings potatoes, but almost all of those potatoes are kept aside for the next Saturday and Sunday. But that doesn't sadden Pitu. Shonibar and Robibar are days of celebration, even Pitu knows.

It doesn't take more than a second for all this to go through her mind. Pitu swallows and says, ' . . . Not every day, but we eat them free-quently.'

Innocent Pitu won't tell a lie, that's certain. Ponkoj says in delighted astonishment, 'Amazing! You all run this household so well on such little money, and look at our mess! Hunh!'

Mohamaya says in a suspicious tone, 'But you say the food you get is very good.'

'Oh, but the money's very good too, what even the three of you don't spend, I alone spend that much.'

'Oh, never mind, let that be. Young men, sweating from forehead to foot to earn a living, they need to eat well.'

Pitu says with great eagerness, 'But everything's so cheap here, Baba. It's not like your Calcutta! We eat so much! Why, Thakuma makes pyesh every day, and I think of you. Will you make pyesh again tomorrow, Thakuma?'

Mohamaya recalls the amount of sugar in the pantry and cannot commit herself. 'Let's see, if that rascally milkman delivers good milk, only then. I won't do it if the milk has water mixed in it!'

Ponkoj drains the glass of water and pulls the cup of tea towards himself. He says, 'I suppose he adds a lot of water?'

Maybe Mohamaya's conscience balks at criticizing the milkman outright. Because the milkman is not lacking in judgment. There are many colours of milk to be had from him.

If Mohamaya is the kind of customer who wants two and a half seers of milk for a rupee, what other colour can the milk be but a pale blue?

So Mohamaya evades her son's question and says, 'He will, as soon as I want some extra. All his customers are fixed. He doesn't have a chhotak of milk to spare. For such a country, to be in such a condition!'

After this there is a change of subject.

A discussion of the old days gets under way. Such discussion is the greatest happiness of a disappointed life without a present, without a future.

A race that is robbed of everything sings songs of its past pride; a person beset by want becomes absorbed in stories of past substance.

'Pitu. Take the paan.'

Monoroma's call comes from inside the room. She puts a couple of cones of paan in her daughter's hand and says in a tone of suppressed reproach, 'Pyesh-tyesh, who told you to make up all those stories?'

Pitu lowers her head guiltily.

Watching both Ma and Thakuma build palaces in space, she had thought, this game is lots of fun.

However, Monoroma doesn't find the strength for much reprimand for her daughter's falsehood. So she says in a forgiving tone, 'All right, go, give him the paan. And don't tell any made-up stories. Why don't you go study your lessons? Don't you need to get an education? And there's a fine man! That it's his duty to educate the girl, he has no idea.'

Education or burnt yams,[1] what's the difference?

What need does Pitu have for an education? Why, what wonderful stories she and Baba will tell each other, and to give that up for an education! Chhi!

It must be said that Ponkoj doesn't seem to have much interest in fulfilling his fatherly duties either. Father and daughter spin their stories.

And those stories, too, build palaces in space. It could be said that the title of their story session is 'When We're Very Rich.'

It's quite certain that they'll win a lot of money in the lottery, it's only the date that they don't know yet. But let that be, it's how the money will be spent that's the real issue. That's what father and daughter talk about.

Clothes and shoes, food and drink, toys and dolls, a silver pedestal in Thakuma's prayer-room, a golden fan over the idol's head, heaps of jewellery for Monoroma, a wristwatch and glasses for Ponkoj – father and daughter are agreed on all these things. There's a difference of opinion about only one thing.

Ponkoj wants all of them to move to Calcutta, but Pitu doesn't want that at all. This house, this village, Labi and her other friends and companions, the playroom crafted with such difficulty, with bricks taken from the the abandoned Goshai house, the swing tied to the amra tree in the courtyard – Pitu cannot even think of leaving all this and going away.

Ponkoj argues for his position by raising the matter of his office; Pitu cites the example of Bhotcharj-jetha's son. The son who's a doctor and has bought a car to travel to Calcutta twice a day, every day. When they're very rich, what will stop them from buying even a car!

In the middle of all this, Pitu blurts out: 'Baba, are you a poor man?'

Ponkoj is disconcerted for a moment . . . the next instant, he laughs out loud, *ha ha*, and says, 'Who said such a thing?'

With her father's laugh, Pitu finds some strength in her chest. So she says dismissively, 'Who else? That Labi!'

'Labi's a silly!'[2] After making this comment, Ponkoj slaps himself on the chest. 'There's no one in this village as rich as me, understand? No one.'

Pitu is a little surprised at such a pronouncement and stares at her father. It's hard to be completely convinced of this statement, but Baba's face, bright with laughter, seems to bear it out. And the laugh is somehow secretive too!

To dispel her doubts, Pitu says, 'But then why are your shoes torn?'

'Shoes!'

Even the tears in the shoes have fallen to the girl's eyes! Shoes cannot be made to look decent on the cheap, as clothes can.

And he had put the shoes under the front stoop, in the shadows.

But Ponkoj won't lose to his daughter in trading words, so he says, unperturbed, 'You're asking why the shoes are torn? When will I buy new shoes? Where is the time to go to the shop? As soon as it's Saturday, I'm over here. Shoni-Robi, two days gone. Other days, the office. When will I buy them? I'm going around with the money in my pocket.'

Pitu hears this and is amazed.

There's no time!

But there's so much time in the world! Endless, immeasurable! With the rising of day and the falling of night, on and on flows a ceaseless stream of time. The nights and days float away on that eternal wave. Bhotcharj-jetha wanders around from sunrise to sunset chewing his tobacco and smoking his huko. Choudhury-dadu sits twenty-four hours at the Chondi temple. Labi's pishi roams around the neighbourhood with a slice of lau or pumpkin on the pretext of making a gift of it. Nowhere is there any hurry or bustle. Everything is still. Everything is calm.

But poor Baba!

For lack of time, he's forced to walk around with money in his pocket and torn shoes on his feet.

It's as though these two have learnt a new and strange game of building with words. All of them are rapt in that game. It's difficult to say now who first invented the game. . . . Ponkoj? Mohamaya, Monoroma? No one remembers who. But no one will let the game be spoilt. If they do, then they will suddenly become poor. No longer will that poverty remain modestly veiled.

Then the secret of the ghee suddenly running out in Mohamaya's pantry will be revealed. Ponkoj's stories about the lack of time will end.

This is much better than that! . . . This web of sweet deceit!

And that's why Ponkoj easily continues, with great enthusiasm: 'Only my shoes? You know how much doesn't get done for lack of time? I'm going bald, I don't have the time to buy some good hair-oil. Your Ma is so good at knitting sweaters, and yet I can't buy any wool. And then there are so many things that you need. None of that's getting done . . . only for lack of time.'

Ponkoj feels no qualms lying even to a child. 'Lack of time' – is that a lie? Nothing's getting done, and it's only because of the lack of time.

Still, 'time' will arrive someday – that is Ponkoj's firm belief.

'Want', 'poverty' – it's as though these are merely a temporary condition. It will get better. When the time comes, then life will truly begin. Every scene of that life Ponkoj knows by heart.

Walking around with money in his pocket?

That's not a lie either. The pocket isn't in his trousers, it's in his mind. That's all.

Pitu, gladdened by her Baba's words, suddenly says, in a mocking tone: 'Labi's a silly!'

Ponkoj laughs out loud, *ho ho*. Drawn by the sound of that laughter, Monoroma comes and stands there.

The cooking is done, and Mohamaya, free from worry at last, has sat down to her evening prayers. Now Monoroma, too, somewhat relieved, can come and sit near her husband.

'Why all this laughter, tell me?'

Ponkoj says in a solemn manner, 'We do not say anything to those who don't sit with us. Ei, Pitu, be careful! Don't tell her why you're laughing.'

'Okay, so I'll sit. All right?'

Ponkoj's expression turns even more serious. 'Before that, you'll have to say why you're laughing. No one's told you any funny stories. You come and sit down, and you start laughing. What's the meaning of this?'

'Now where am I laughing? Oh, Pitu, am I laughing?' Monoroma tries to bring some gravity to her expression. Pitu stares at her mother's face. Monoroma has sat down directly before the brilliant flame of the hurricane lantern – on every line of her face, bent slightly forward, is the glow of that light.

But is this glow only that of the lantern's light? Pitu's often seen her mother's face with the lantern light on it. When she reads a book on the days Baba doesn't come, or when she sits down to teach

Pitu. That light only falls from the outside, it's not the light that rises up, radiating from within. This seems unknown, this seems unworldly.

Ponkoj looks at his daughter's astonished face and suppresses a laugh. 'Listen, Pitu's silly friend Labi says, Pitu's baba is poor. Isn't that worth laughing at?'

'Isn't it just!' Monoroma shines with dazzling light. 'What do you mean, poor? An emperor.'

'Ei, did you hear that, Pitu? Didn't I tell you? Didn't I tell you, there's no one richer than me in this village?'

Pitu stares at Baba's face. Amazing! It's an astonishing thing. On Baba's face, too, is that same brilliant light.

Pitu thinks, these ordinary words of theirs are not really ordinary. Certainly not their laughter. In every line of these jesting expressions so much else is hidden – so much lies beyond Pitu's grasp.

But still, how wonderful! How beautiful! . . . Suddenly happiness brings tears to Pitu's eyes.

If she could bring Labi here and show her this! If she saw them now, could she ever joke about Pitu's mother's lack of jewellery? Whether there were any ornaments or not – would Labi even think of that?

Brahma's Weapon

ব্রহ্মাস্ত্র

Brohmastro

That Ronobir would make such a proposal – Oshima could never have dreamt of such a thing! After remaining silent awhile, she says, 'Is that even possible?'

'Is it entirely impossible?' Ronobir says in a bitter tone touched with sarcasm. 'Why, will it leave you headless, the shame of it?'

'It's not a matter of shame. But there's been no meeting or contact for so long, and to show up suddenly with a proposal like that – '

Ronobir keeps the edge of bitterness in his voice, laughs out loud, *hah-hah*. 'Which married woman with a husband and children, keeping that world going, reports for duty to her first love every day, tell me that?'

'Stop it, don't talk like a barbarian.'

'Oh, but I was talking like an extremely civilized man before. Your sitting slantwise to it, that's what's annoying me! What's so damned impossible about it? . . . Something like that, when they're young – people don't forget that so easily, do they? In his youth Ghoshal-shaheb saw you with eyes of love, so if he can do you a favour now, he'll be more pleased than anything else.'

Oshima turns serious and says, 'Your knowledge of "something like that" seems very fresh, I can see that! But anyway, even if he's pleased, how can I be happy? Have you thought about my position?'

Ronobir says, as though utterly astonished, 'How much is there to think about? At this time the man has plenty of power – by, what do you call it, your "grace of God" – in his hands. He can easily get me a good job if he wants. All it takes is the asking! Why you'd lose all your honour just by asking him, that's hard to understand.'

'Even harder to *make* you understand.' Oshima arranges and rearranges, unnecessarily, the things on the table.

Ronobir's jaw muscles tighten, furrows appear on his brow. He says harshly, 'The man who has to flatter his own wife – his life is worthless!'

'Flatter? You're flattering me?' Oshima's face turns red.

'What else!' Ronobir says in a bitter, mocking voice. 'What I've been doing all this time, in our language it's called *khoshamod*, flattery.... You act as though I'm asking you to set fire to someone's house. It's nothing much at all... you and Ghoshal-shaheb have known each other a long time, it's easy for you to make the request, that's why I'm trying so hard.'

Easy.

A thin smile on Oshima's face – yes, a smile breaks out.

How easy!

After eleven years of no contact, to go on her own to Debobroto's house to see him, to appeal for a job for an unemployed husband – how easy! Easy maybe for Ronobir's people – maybe by their calculations! Debobroto was once a classmate of Oshima's, and there was a degree of intimacy between them – Ronobir knows this. That this classmate, through his own skills, now holds the goddess of fortune in his grasp – that news, too, Ronobir has gathered and brought home to Oshima.

Whenever he hears any report of Ghoshal and Company's prosperity, he comes and informs Oshima.

Oshima never expresses any curiosity; if anything, she expresses irritation: 'If it's prospered, it's prospered – does that mean he's bought my head with it?'

Ronobir wrinkles up his eyes, his whole face, to laugh, and replies, 'Oh, whatever it is, the relationship was very pleasant at one time, wasn't it? Now that he's some powerful Keshto-Bishtu, you'll be happy to hear it – that's why I'm telling you.'

But that was a different thing.

Now, this unreasonable demand of Ronobir's! Debobroto was a shareholder in a large corporation, Debobroto could give him a good job if he wished, therefore, go to him and make this humble entreaty, Take my husband, make him an employee, completely dependent on you. Because I'm facing hard times with my children.

Chhi chhi!

Oshima says in a steady voice, 'Everyone has different ideas of what's easy and what's hard. But let me ask *you*, will you be able to work under his direction, salute him every day?'

'Won't I? You're asking me if I'll be able to? Hunh!' Ronobir makes his face grumpy as an owl's and says, 'A beggar, and dignity! Besides, what's not-able-to about it? I've never gone to fight a duel with him, have I? He doesn't even know me.... I'm telling you, go to him as though you're doing it in secret! I'll put in an application the normal way, following the rules. All you have to do is go tell him my name-address and request "special consideration". That's all! One sly fox helps out another! Once it's done, who knows whom? Besides, he's one of the top bosses, what contact do they have with the punti fish?'

Her manner serious, Oshima says, 'And if he can't recognize me? It's normal for rich people to forget their poor friends! Suppose he can't even recognize me!'

Ronobir says with a smirk, 'Now that's just a debater's argument. He'll recognize you, you know that – and I know it too. Whoever's seen you once, can they ever forget you?'

Once more Oshima's face turns red. Still, she is not agitated. She says calmly, 'All right, suppose he recognizes me. But is there any guarantee he'll agree to the request? And then where will my face be?'

'Agree to the request – there's no guarantee?' Ronobir's smile grows a little more twisted. 'There *is* a guarantee! I know there is!'

Across all of Oshima's face, the sudden glow of fire!

It's clear she can no longer keep the agitation out of her voice. 'If you know so much, how can you dare to send me there?'

'Oh, come on, can't you understand a joke?' Once again Ronobir laughs out loud, *hah-hah*. Then he says, 'Can't you understand? *You*'re my strength, *you*'re my courage! Let the jokes be – because of this old friendship, Ghoshal-shaheb won't be able to refuse, that much is certain! At least if it were me, I couldn't!'

'Fine! That's all right, then! You people go ahead and understand whatever you like. I can't!'

'You can't? After so long you're telling me outright – you can't?'

'What can I do but tell you outright? What I'm not able to do – '

'Why *would* you be able to?' Ronobir almost grimaces at her. 'You'll lose the fine edge of your honour! Honour! Is there anything still left of honour? Can you see what's around you? Can you see what our household looks like? Can you see our children's condition?'

Oshima glances around once, distractedly. But who needs to look around again to see what the household looks like, or to understand their children's condition?

In a household penniless for some time, where the only earning member of the household has sat around idle for seventeen months, does the one who has to run that household, that world, need to look outward to understand its condition?

Still, Oshima looks, spreading her blank gaze. Then she turns that same blank gaze upon her husband and says, 'Don't I know it?'

'I see no evidence that you know! You're thinking only of your own honour, where are you thinking about the children's lives? Let's see, think how many days there's been no milk in the house? How many days – '

'Oh, stop!'

Ronobir had been thinking, After all, it's a woman's mind, wound her in the heart, that'll work, but when he hears Oshima's 'Oh, stop!' he loses faith in that approach.

So some other approach is necessary.

Ronobir now contorts his face – which has reflected several different emotions through all this – and says, 'Hunh! I see I'll have to suffer your scolding too! A jobless man's honour and respect! Fine, now I'll take up begging! Husband out on the footpath begging, the two children, with no food, will die one after the other, but so what? As long as the moharani's glory stays intact – that's all we need!'

Yes, now Ronobir has inflicted a fatal bite. Let's see how Oshima can object now! Ronobir glances sidelong at his wife's face. Tries to see what the response to his bite will be.

He can't quite understand it.

Anger insult grief pride – he can observe none of these reactions on that face. Only a kind of stony hardness! Not flushed with blood, not bloodless and pale, not ashen or wan, only a lifeless hardness!

'Fine, I'll go!'

Oshima says that and leaves the room.

That's done – now Ronobir needn't worry.

Now that Oshima's agreed, she won't waver from her decision. And if she goes, it'll work out – Ronobir's sure of that too.

Ronobir had not overlooked the flame that had first blazed up, *dhok!*, in Oshima's eyes at his proposal that she appeal to Ghoshal-shaheb on the pretext of their old 'friendship' for a job for her husband. . . . And he did not mistake the true nature of that flame – Ronobir wasn't such a fool either.

It is the fault of his decreed fate that Ronobir is in this condition today.

Otherwise, he is no less than Ghoshal-shaheb in his learning. Ghoshal, too, is an ordinary graduate.

Fate! Fate's writing on his forehead!

Casting their sidelong, envious glances at the wealthy – this is how the lazy and incompetent console themselves!

Not effort, not perseverance, not power of intellect, only 'fate'. . . . Apart from that, what other consolation is there?

All right, he would have to cool Oshima off some other time. Explain to her a little, explain that she's asking for a favour after such a long time, Ghoshal-shaheb will certainly be gratified by this. Ronobir does understand the male character, after all!

Daily life unbearable, kitchen and pantry yawning wide and empty, every day and night the sound of "there isn't any" rising up from their world: still, in their locked boxes their better clothes have not yet disappeared.

Ornaments and such go with ease – at the first footfalls of want they bid farewell, but saris and other clothes are more abiding things. Thus it is still possible to preserve some decorum while going out. Oshima went out quite well dressed. And when she returned –

She threw the vanity bag from her hand on the bed and sat down on one side of the bed. Without remembering that she should put away the silk sari she had on.

Ronobir sat silent in a cane chair near the window. Since sending her out, he had carried the burden of anxiety, suspense, distress, shame, and much else. As she made her preparations before leaving, Oshima had covered herself in such a hard, wordless veil that he hadn't had the courage to offer her any comfort.

After she left, he marshalled arguments in his favour to offer himself comfort. Had Ronobir himself always been this way? Was his sense of self-respect any less? What could he do? Scarcity destroys character.

Ronobir waited for a minute or two – to see if Oshima made any comment. No, a strange stillness! A minute seemed an hour. It could not be borne for long, this stillness. So after waiting only a minute or two, Ronobir turned his chair a little and spoke up abruptly. 'Did your doubts turn out right after all? Your wealthy friend couldn't recognize you?'

Oshima stood up. Faced Ronobir directly. The trace of a mocking smile in a corner of her mouth.

'What do you mean he couldn't recognize me? Whoever's seen me once, can they ever forget me?'

Ronobir looked Oshima over from head to foot, once. This aspect of Oshima was not new, only almost forgotten. How long had it been since he last saw Oshima's face with make-up on, smooth and polished, saw her shape in a silk sari in that style?

Was Ronobir happy seeing her this way?

If you're happy, do your eyes burn?

Ronobir ran his hand absently over his cheek, unshaven for two or four days, then smiled with some difficulty and said, 'Killing me with my own weapon? But what's the result of your expedition? What a face you've come back with!'

'So what else would I do?' Oshima brought a touch of contempt to her mouth and said, 'For a job worth two hundred and seventy-five rupees, should I double my face with delight – that's not possible!'

Two hundred and seventy-five!

A job worth two hundred and seventy-five rupees!

More than what Ronobir made in his old job! He had found it difficult to bring a smile to his face, now he found it difficult to hold back his smile.

'Is that right? Is that right? . . . Is that the truth, or are you joking?'

'Why do I need to make jokes?'

Greed and excitement burst out on Ronobir's face and eyes. Can there be a greater happiness than finding a job? The sum of money was indeed enough to rouse greed, but . . . it was true! It was true, somewhere, still, Oshima had such great value! Not only his eyes, he felt his entire body burn. . . . As though Ronobir had hoped it wouldn't happen. As though he would have been happier if it hadn't happened.

At worst, there would have been no milk in their house for some more time – at worst, the ribs on Khuku and Khoka's chest would have stood out sharper – at worst –

Yes, yes, many things would have happened – still, that wouldn't have humiliated Ronobir as much. . . . The urge that had been at the root of his pushing Oshima to go – it hadn't been the hope of a job working out, it had been the wish for the job *not* to work out.

Still, he'll have to talk about it.

He'll have to find out exactly how much wood and hay Oshima has had to burn. Maybe he can find some consolation in that.

'So you met him right away?'

'If I hadn't, would I be back so soon?'

'I was thinking – an old friend – he'd keep you a long time, wouldn't let you go easily!'

Oshima casts her gaze fully on Ronobir's darkening face and replies in a clear, sharp voice, 'It's natural to think that! An idle mind is whose workshop, that even a child knows.'

Suddenly Ronobir stands up from the chair and says in almost scolding tones, 'Always playing with words! What happened, can't you tell me straight?'

Even with this scolding, Oshima doesn't budge. Doesn't tremble.

She stands firm, says in a hard voice, taking her time, 'What happened that's worth talking about? I went, I told him, it worked out! He was gratified and gave me the appointment letter! The job starts tomorrow.'

'An appointment letter already! Starts tomorrow?' At last Ronobir seems to have found a way to express his rage. 'What's the work, what are the details, I don't know yet, I haven't considered whether it's suitable, and already an appointment letter? What if I don't go tomorrow!'

Suddenly Oshima laughs out loud, sharply!

A laugh that hasn't rung out in this house for many days, a laugh like that! It resounds off the walls of the house to the ceiling and bounces back, the tones of this instrument.

'Why do you need to go? I can go by myself. The office is in Dhormotola. I won't lose my way getting there.'

'Oh! So the job is yours?'

'What else? You wouldn't agree in the end – I knew that. So I didn't mention you, I talked about myself. . . . And why shouldn't I? All right, so I didn't graduate, but I did study until my final year, didn't I? I said – I'm sick of sitting around living off someone else's money, won't you give me a job? . . . And he said, "Right away, this instant, very gladly."'

Even if the listener's burnt-and-darkened face, burning more and more, turns to ash, why should Oshima let him go?

The woman who is forced to set fire to her own private, lonely world – why should she feel any compassion when she launches arrows of fire at another's?

Matchbox

দেশলাই বাক্স

Deshlai Baksho

I always compare women to matchboxes. Why? Because of the way matchboxes are – even though they have enough gunpowder to set a hundred Lankas aflame,[1] they sit around meek and innocent, in the kitchen, in the pantry, in the bedroom, here, there, anywhere – women, too, are exactly the same!

You want an example?

Then look carefully at that enormous three-storey house in front of us –

Sunday morning.

The dhopa[2] has come and is waiting.

Moments before handing over a heap of Ajit's dirty clothes to the dhopa, Nomita goes through the pockets one last time and discovers the letter.

A twisted, crumpled envelope with its mouth torn, and Nomita's name on the envelope.

A flame goes up *dopp!* in all of Nomita's nerves and veins. She drops the clothes in her hand and sits on the bed to open the letter. The first thing she looks at is the date: the letter must have come about three days earlier.

She turns over the envelope and matches the postmark to the date; that, too, bears the same witness.

Yes, the letter came three days ago.

Ajit had opened it and read it, then crumpled it and twisted it and dropped it into his pocket and left it there. He hadn't felt the need to mention it even once to Nomita.

The flame that had gone up *dopp!* now burns steadily, hissing, sounding its note on each of her mind's strings.

Because this is not a casual oversight; it's deliberate.

That's exactly how Ajit is.

Somehow he's gained possession of the key to the letter-box, fishing it through the gaps among the fifty-two hands of this joint family.[3] And whenever there's a letter with Nomita's name on the envelope, he opens and reads it first, and only then does he give it to her. It's possible that quite often he doesn't give it to her at all. At least that's the suspicion that has taken root, taken deep root, in Nomita's mind.

Even though, to this day, Ajit cannot truthfully claim that he's been able to discover any letter in the slightest degree suspicious.

Still – still – he won't give up this ugly habit of his.

– Not with Nomita's anger, not with her taking offence, not with bitter reproaches, her trying to shame him, sarcasm – not with anything.

If she mentions it, first he tries to laugh it away, and if laughter doesn't get him out of deep water, he scolds her.

She sits perfectly still for a minute and reads the letter through.

It's nothing much, a letter from Nomita's mother.

It's her standard speech – the good woman has once again placed on the record the news of her various hardships and complaints getting worse, misfortune upon misfortune, the ceiling of her room is cracked and the rain water falls through in ceaseless streams; if this is not immediately remedied, she will have to die crushed under the weight of a collapsed roof. Of course she does not dread that eventuality. Her daughter is a queen, her son-in-law high-minded, large-hearted. Therefore – etc., etc.

An indigent widow, without husband or son, she was successful in consigning her daughter to a wealthy family's house on the strength of looks alone. But the good lady has never stopped taking credit, at the slightest opportunity, for her skill in the matter. And she's been finding such opportunities all along.

Whenever Ajit sees a new letter from Nomita's mother, he smiles derisively and says, 'Why bother to read it? I'll go and fill out a money-order form.'

And Nomita's head hangs low with the shame and the insult of it. So, some time ago, out of anger and grief, Nomita told her mother not to write to her on postcards. She thought that from then on she'd try to send her a little money, whatever she could pull together, in secret. So – this was what came of sending letters in envelopes too.

Suddenly Nomita flames into rage at her mother.

Why, why does she keep on begging like this?

Why won't she let Nomita keep her self-respect, her dignity. No, this time she will write and tell her mother clearly: 'I can't do any more, don't hope for anything from me.'

Just then, Ajit steps into the room after his leisurely Sunday bath. Nomita's sharp indignation at the insult, simmering all this while, wants to dash itself violently against him.

Nomita roars out, 'When did this letter arrive?'

Ajit glances at her obliquely, estimating the magnitude of his error.

'Another handful of cash for this,' he had thought, and decided not to give the letter to Nomita; he was going to tear it up and throw it away. He'd made a big mistake.

Not that Ajit is going to feel abashed about that.

As though trying hard to remember, he says, 'Letter? What letter? Oho, yes yes! Indeed there was a letter from your mother. I just hadn't got around to giving it to you.'

'Why hadn't you got around to it? Why? Why? Answer me, why didn't you get around to it?'

'What a nuisance!' Ajit says. 'I'd forgotten – why else?'

'Liar!' Nomita hisses like a snake.

'Why are you saying whatever comes to your mouth? Don't people forget?'

'No they don't! Why did you open my letter?'

Ajit tries to scatter this charge to the winds. 'What if I opened it? My own wife's letter – '

'Be quiet, be quiet, I tell you. Why should you open my letters? Haven't I told you a thousand times not to?'

Ajit doesn't fear Nomita's anger, he fears a row. So he smiles an affected smile and says, 'If you're forbidding it then there's definitely something. Shouldn't I make sure that no one's passing you love letters in secret?'

'Stop it! What a common, vulgar man you are!'

After this it's not possible for Ajit to smile his fake smile any longer. Now he too picks up the poisoned knife. He says, 'Is that so! Those who whine day and night and hold out their palms to their son-in-law, they're the high-class people! A dung-picker's daughter becomes a queen, and so – '

'Shut up!' Nomita yells.

Their room's on the third floor, that's a blessing. Otherwise with that scream, everyone would have come to look.

'Shut up?' Ajit roars. 'What shut up? I'll damn well say it! I'll damn well open your letters. I'll do what I want, what I please. What will you do? Can you do anything?'

'I can't? I can't do anything?' Almost panting, Nomita pronounces each word clearly: 'You want to see if I can do anything?'

And immediately she does something astonishing. She grabs Ajit's matchbox that's lying near his cigarettes on the table, and *fssh!* she lights a matchstick and touches it to her sari.

Instantly it flares up – the fine anchol of a wealthy wife's sari.

The very next instant, Ajit shouts, 'Have you gone mad?' and jumps to her side and grabs the burning patch and slaps it between his hands and puts out the fire.

And – to tell the truth, now he's a little afraid. He looks fearfully at Nomita's face. Sees a fire burning there, bright, blazing red.

He doesn't have the courage to put out that fire by slapping it between his hands, so he tries to pour water on it. With great difficulty he attempts to speak normally. 'You lose all your common sense when you get angry, don't you? A woman, and such anger! Oof!'

Who knows what Nomita would have said next, for right then her niece Rini steps into the room.

She says in a shrill voice, 'So, Khuri-ma, how long will the dhopa have to wait? If you don't want to give him any of your clothes, at least tell him that!'

For a second or two Nomita remains still, perhaps trying to recall the dhopa's face, waiting for her downstairs, then she picks up the dirty clothes and starts sorting them. She says in a calm voice, 'Go tell him I'm coming. I'll bring the clothes.'

Nomita always speaks her mind, so no one attacks her outright, to her face, they only jab her with sharp words. Her second sister-in-law is almost exhausted with work this morning, and when she sees Nomita, she puts a twisted smile on her sweat-streaked face and says,

'Well, that's something, at least, you finally decided to come down! Baba! There's no good or bad time for you, you find the smallest excuse to go into your room and get cosy with your husband. The love-talk never gets old, does it?'

Nomita looks around once, to get a sense of the climate. She sees the hurly-burly of the morning, sees the forest of people on either side. Her voice must not tremble. So she too smiles a small smile and says in an extremely soft voice, 'Oh, it's nothing like that! You should come and peek in sometime. Our talk is all angry talk, do you know?'

Mejo-ginni laughs *Hoo-hoo* and says, 'Stop it, Naw-ginni, don't cover up the forbidden fish on your plate with your pious spinach. We haven't been raised on donkey grass. Why do we need to peek in? What you're showing us right in front of our eyes, twenty-four hours a day – '

Nomita laughs a laugh that brings an attractive flush to her white face. After laughing that laugh, she says, 'Go on. You say the naughtiest things!'

The busy Boro-ginni runs up. 'Have you chopped the vegetables yet? Or are you just telling stories?' And suddenly she stops and starts. 'What's that? What's this unlucky thing, Naw-ginni? How did you burn your anchol like that?'

Nomita starts as well, but only for a moment. Then she folds the anchol back quickly and says, laughing, 'Oh, don't remind me! It's exactly what you keep warning me about. I didn't listen, and see what happened! I used my anchol to lift a hot pot of water off the stove – and that did it.'

Nomita pulls the basket of potatoes towards herself and sits down to peel them, and in her mind she keeps thinking about how she might secretly send her mother a few rupees. She can't really write to her: 'I can't do any more, don't hope for anything from me.'

Back there, the entire village knows Nomita is a queen – Nomita's husband is high-minded, large-hearted.

This – this is precisely why I compare women to matchboxes. Even when they have the means within themselves to set off many raging fires, they never flare up and burn away the mask of men's high-mindedness, their large-heartedness. They don't burn up their own colourful shells.

They won't burn them – and the men know this too.

That's why they leave them scattered so carelessly in the kitchen, in the pantry, in the bedroom, here, there, anywhere.

And quite without fear, they put them in their pockets.

The Scheme of Things

কাঠামো

Kathamo

Keshob Rai first heard the news from Neelkontho. He heard it, and it left him speechless.

Yes, after he heard it, at first his condition didn't even permit anger. What came was astonishment. Witnessing New-ginni's audacity, at first Keshob Rai in his extreme shock lost the power of speech, and then he exploded in rage. He said, 'Is that so! That rascally woman, relying on that dried-up, hunchbacked brother of hers, has come to put her hand in the cobra's hole? Fine, I too am Raghob Rai's son Keshob Rai.'

In fact, the person to whom Keshob Rai had applied the refined adjective of 'rascally', that New-ginni was by law a quite venerable elder of Keshob Rai's. The woman was his father Raghob Rai's second wife, Kodom. The fact was that in his old age Raghob Rai, having accepted an invitation to attend a granddaughter's wedding, had gone and married a friend's mother-and-father-less, landed-on-his-shoulder-from-nowhere niece, and had brought her without notice and presented her at the house! This downfall occurred eighteen years after the loss of his wife.

His son Keshob now had four or five boys and girls.

Kodom was about fifteen or sixteen years younger than Keshob.

For one thing, there was this unthinkable and unbearable marriage. On top of that, it was rumoured that Kodom's father was from a family much inferior to Raghob Rai's people. So Keshob was never willing to grant the respect appropriate to this achievement of his father's old age! In Keshob's world, Kodom's position was comparable to that of the countryside Bagdi[1] woman whom his grandfather Madhob Rai used to look upon with favour.

But the problem was this, Raghob Rai had brought her and fully installed her in the inner quarters of the house. And so his wrath and hate were even greater.

Maybe if Kodom had been of a gentle, yielding nature, had considered her flying-in-and-taking-over a wrongful entry, had been abashed, had treated Keshob's wife with love and respect as for a mother-in-law, over the course of time Keshob's mind might have grown somewhat softer. But what happened was the opposite.

Until the age of twenty-five, in her mama's house, Kodom had digested the rice of many reprimands in silence, waiting for her day to arrive. And she had agreed at one word to marry an old man with five grandsons and granddaughters only in the hope of establishing herself. And apart from that, her mami, at the time she sent her niece to her husband's home, had given her, instead of such insubstantial stuff as jewellery and clothes, some substantial advice.

Following that advice, this Oshto-mongola bride,[2] Kodom, had frowned at the maidservants and cooks of the house, the sheltered and the favoured there, and said, 'Why do you all call me "New-bou, New-bou"? Am I the bride of this household?'

Disconcerted, the cook had said, 'Should I call you "New-bouma" then?'

'Why, why would you call me New-bouma either? I heard you

have been here a long time! Keshob's mother – I mean, Babu's first wife – what did you call her?'2

Wide-eyed, the cook had said, 'Her? Everyone used to call her "Ginni-ma".'

'Fine, then you will call me "New-ginni-ma".'

It is unnecessary to add that this juicy bit of news became juicier and grew exaggerated and spread across the entire household. And then, although 'Notun-ginni, Notun-ginni' was uttered as a taunt, it became permanent in the end. But the word 'Ma' nobody would consent to add, except when speaking to her face to face!

Let that be, Kodom didn't gain or lose anything by it.

She easily addressed Keshob by his name and called his wife 'Bou-ma' and thus established her position. Keshob had never in his life conversed directly with Kodom, but one day Keshob's wife said to her mother-in-law, some five or seven years her junior, 'He's so much older than you, and you call him by name – don't you feel ashamed?'

Kodom pouted and replied, 'Ashamed – what for? I'm taking such a grown man's father by the ear and making him stand and sit; and should I be ashamed of calling his son by name!'

The wife had fled to hide her blood-red ears and save herself.

It is unnecessary to say that it didn't take Kodom very long to tie the household keys to her anchol. And from her conduct it was evident that she had first outfitted herself with both spear *and* sword, and only then had she stepped onto the battlefield.

But all this happened seven or eight years earlier.

Now things were different.

It's been about two years since Raghob Rai's death, and so Kodom's moon of good fortune too has set. Keshob's wife has set about recovering her lost pride, and Keshob has been thinking of arranging a monthly allowance for Kodom and sending her to her cousin's house along with her five-year-old son. And at such a time, this news! He heard it, and his mind suffered as though with the agony of sea-nettles!

On behalf of her minor son, Kodom had initiated litigation for the division of property. An eight-anna share along with Keshob Rai![3]

Hearing about this eight-anna share for that cold-in-the-nose, enlarged-spleen-in-the-abdomen, amulet-on-the-arm, tiger's-claw-around-the-neck, rickets-stricken boy, Keshob Rai sputtered like an eggplant in hot oil and, burning with anger, said, 'Is that so! I had thought I'd give her something every month. I won't give her a single paisa. Let's see New-ginni's mettle. I'll prove in court that that marriage of Raghob Rai's was no marriage at all – just a makeshift ceremony. What sort of marriage is it? Is there any witness from this family? Did a priest from our house go there? Was there a final viewing? Did anyone hear about it in advance? Nothing! That son is Raghob Rai's illegitimate son!'

Keshob's wife said curiously, 'But New-ginni has lived in this house for all this time – what reason will you give for that?'

Keshob Rai said in a negligent manner, 'Fooh! Plenty of men commit these follies during their lives. They bring daughters of Haris and Bagdis and install them in their homes – at least she's a Bamun![4] Not everyone can be a flawless moon like your husband, can they?'

Melted by the charm of that flawless moon, his wife laughed a grateful laugh and said, 'Han go, so it'll be proved in court, they really have no rights or claims?'

'Of course! Even if she's a Bamun, what class of Bamuns are they? Acharji[5] Bamuns! Do we have anything to do with them? There you are – I have this proof right in my hand. And I have a whole village-full of witnesses, also in my hand.'

Keshob Rai's clan was seven-generations-famous as litigants. And so Keshob had burnt in anger at this sky-defying audacity of Kodom's;

he hadn't died of fear. But the times had changed; now, it seemed, the law always favoured the weak.

Gradually it became evident that the negligent ease with which Keshob Rai had thought he would render the suit ineffective – it wasn't turning out exactly that way. Rather, the case kept getting worse for him; the situation grew more and more tangled.

And on the other side of the house, Kodom's cousin, his shala, and a crony of the shala's had set up a permanent seat in the household. It seemed this man was a newly graduated lawyer. And their eating and drinking, their merriment and hilarity was enough to turn the people on this side cross-eyed. Their howls of laughter would burst the eardrums of the people over here. The house had not been divided, it was true, but when Raghob Rai was dying, the cooking-pots had been separated, and the closed panels of the doors and windows were made to serve, as far as possible, as a fence.

Often nowadays after coming back from the court-house, Keshob would take to his bed. Going back and forth in the heat gave him a severe headache, he said.

His wife comes running and asks, 'Han go, what happened?'

Keshob Rai says gravely, 'You won't understand.'

'Aha, I can understand winning and losing, can't I? Who's losing, who's winning?'

'It's not possible to understand that before the final verdict is announced! The judge is a master moralist, that's the problem. All our paths would be clear if only that godforsaken scoundrel caught cholera and died.'

Keshob Rai says this and sits up.

It's not necessary to add that this godforsaken scoundrel is none other than Kodom's five-year-old son Maniklal. Even though he is the son of Keshob's extremely revered progenitor, Keshob Rai does not use anything other than the aforesaid civilized adjective in reference to him. For Kodom it was a woman's edition of the same.

Apart from those, no other words would ever come to his lips when talking about them.

Keshob's wife, a mother of children herself, shudders in her mind once and says without saying them the words 'Shaat, shaat'.[6] Then she asks aloud, with a displeased expression, 'Why talk of dying and living when we're talking about who wins or loses the case?'

'Why? Why, how would you understand why? It's not your father's estate, is it! It's not you who has to stand in court as your high head's being lowered.'

'But you said that they had no lawful claims?'

'Certainly they don't!' – With blood-red eyes Keshob Rai paces the room.

His wife says fearfully, 'The lawyers and barristers won't understand what's lawful and what's not?'

'No! They won't!' Keshob Rai scolds her. 'Don't try to talk about what you don't understand. . . . Oh! Now I'm thinking, when that puppy was born, why didn't I just get hold of the midwife and feed him some salt and kill him?'

As long as there's breath, there's hope!

Whether it's for a patient, or for a case.

When the patient is about to die, people run far and wide to fetch doctors, and when the case is about to die, they run far and wide to get lawyers and barristers. The local Goari lawyer isn't enough any more, now Keshob Rai is having lawyers brought in from Calcutta. But no one offers much hope. The marriage of Kodom and Raghob Rai has been proved lawful, and the full sixteen annas of the court's compassion appears to be directed at the powerless widow and the minor child.

It is unnecessary to add that there has been no lapse on the part of Kodom in trying to attract that compassion. The day she has to appear in court, she washes her hair with soda, picks out a partly soiled, borderless sari to wear, and makes the expression on her face as tired and troubled as it is possible to make it.

As long as there's breath – that was the basis on which Keshob Rai had gone to seek the counsel of a man very learned in the law; he returned by the one-thirty train. His mind and mood as bitter as they could be.

It had been drizzling *tipi-tipi* since dawn; the sky remained covered with clouds. Alighting at the station, he saw that the rain had merely paused, the sky looked the same. Since he hadn't said which train he would return on, there was no car ready for him at the station; he thought, the hell with it, no use hiring a car, let me walk. Maybe he made this decision because at this moment he didn't care for company or speech.

Keshob Rai left the main road and took the crooked street that ran along Ghosh's pond, not because it was a short cut but for its lack of people. He was walking along absorbed in his thoughts, when suddenly he glanced not too far away, and his two eyes climbed up on his forehead: who was that wandering right along the edge of the pond? Wasn't it Gopla? What was this? What did these people think? On this day – they'd left the boy by himself and were sitting unconcerned! 'These people', meaning, in fact, Keshob's wife. Gopla or Gopal was Keshob's youngest son. And why had he come so far from the house?

Keshob moves quickly forward to catch hold of the boy. But he comes to a stop and his entire body seems to shudder in a convulsion of hatred!

It's as though he's seen a fistful of worms!

Not Gopal; Manik!

Manik is gathering green tamarind pods blown down by the wind. He doesn't pay the slightest heed to anyone on the path.

Along with hatred, a fire of malice burns up every part of Keshob's body. This – this is his adversary! His eight-anna sharer! A bitter, bitter enemy from a past life! Keshob Rai remembers that he hasn't seen the boy for quite some time. Meaning, he hasn't been able to see the boy. Out of fear, Kodom has kept the boy removed from the view of her greatest enemy. Maybe word of Keshob's going to Calcutta today has reached them, hence this freedom for Manik. And apart from that, another reason: Kodom has gone to make a fire-offering to Ma Anondomoyee and to promise a sacrifice if she should win the case. If that fire can be kept burning for three days and three nights, then victory is certain.

Keshob Rai, however, does not know this.

He only sees that the boy has sprung free – who knows how – of his mother's custody and landed up here!

A cold in the nose, enlarged spleen in the abdomen, amulet on the arm, tiger's claw around the neck.

Suddenly an awful, murderous desire catches hold of Keshob Rai! Against all laws, against civilization, against humanity – a terrible desire! . . . He wishes to pierce that tiger's-claw-dangling, thin-as-a-sparrow neck and tear it apart.

Half a minute's work!

In only half a minute his worst enemy can be destroyed!

Keshob Rai looked all four ways. It seemed the uncomfortable atmosphere of the cloudy afternoon had pushed everyone across the land into their houses and kept them there. There wasn't the slightest sign of anyone on the path. Even ordinarily, this path had few travellers; now it was completely deserted. Keshob gnashes his teeth, his hands with their ten nails seem to become restless. The desire in those hands, which grows indomitable, is the desire to twist and wrench that wizened, ugly body and fling it into the water of the pond.

This is his opportunity!

Who will know?

If he should mash that worm, crush it, fling it hard into the water of the pond, then return to Calcutta by the next train? There, if he can spend the night with some trustworthy relative on the pretext of having some work – the fort is won!

Many people know that he left here by the early-morning train. He was at the lawyer's house until noon, so that is a solid piece of evidence. If he can only find a direct witness from the evening until the end of the night, it will be proven that from this morning until the next morning Keshob Rai was away from Keshto-nogor.

Who can then bring a charge of murder against Keshob Rai?

Keshob Rai looks at the 'godforsaken scoundrel's' neck. It can only be compared to a sparrow's. He also looks at his own tong-like fingers. Not even half a minute – perhaps a few seconds!

That stupid fool of a boy now stands gaping at the pond and sucking on a tamarind pod!

Keshob Rai moves forward, one foot at a time.

The scenes that will follow float through his mind one after the other.

Kodom is crying, beating her breast, tearing the hair from her head. Now, with all her big talk at an end, she's going and boarding the train with her cousin in silence!

If her minor son himself has picked his potatoes and gone, on whose claim can she persevere with the case?

Imagining that pride-smashed, defeated expression on Kodom's face, Keshob's feelings surge up with delight. Soundlessly he advances two feet more.

But suddenly like a blaze of lightning something occurs to him. The marks left by strangling are ruinous marks! It is from those marks that the police fellows trace the criminal in the end! Compared to that, pushing him into the water of the pond would be –

Right, right!

This is best! The wretched boy is standing right at the edge, just a little push from behind, that's all . . . so light, there won't even be a sound. And even if there is, who will know?

There can be no other explanation for this than drowning in the pond out of carelessness! . . . Excellent.

Keshob Rai keeps moving forward. Closer, yet closer. Quick breaths follow one another. His chest rises and falls! . . . Who knows what someone on the point of murder looks like! Who knows what terrifying aspect Keshob has attained! Who knows if some inarticulate sound has escaped his lips! Suddenly Manik turns his face away from the pond and stands facing this way – and as soon as he sees this figure of Jomraj[7] he grows numb and begins to move backwards!

One foot, two feet! Right up to the edge of the pond.

Truly he fears his dada like Jom.

And Keshob here?

He thrills in every pore of his body!

He won't have to face the charge of murder. The boy himself is making Keshob's task easier! Two or three feet more!

If he just yells and gives him a fright, that will be enough! Finished!

No – no need even to shout.

The breeze might carry to an enemy!

It's enough to make his eyes round. If he sees Keshob's round, angry eyes, Manik becomes confused. It's a tried technique!

Opening his two eyes wide, like flaming kiln-holes, and even wider, Keshob keeps moving forward, and fearfully the boy, too, keeps moving back, one foot after another.

A muddy chunk of the bank, wet from all the rain, breaks off, and immediately with a sudden jerk Keshob pulls the boy away and lands a slap *thash* on his cheek and roars out a furious scolding: 'Where the hell are you going, you scoundrel? Do you want to die!'

Grief

শোক

Shok

About to step out onto the footpath, on the point of leaving for the office: and in front of him stands the postman, letter and magazine in hand. Now holding the two things in his already occupied hands, Shoktipodo is forced to turn indoors again. He'll have to give them to Protibha. No need to look at the magazine, it is obviously *Chhaya-Chhobi*.[1] A film magazine dear to Protibha's heart. Comes regularly, Wednesday after Wednesday.

The letter, too, is for Protibha. A few lines written on a postcard.

A postcard from Bordhoman. Protibha's father's house.

He wouldn't read a letter at a busy time like this, but still, as he walks, his eyes move by themselves over the few black lines, and right away Shoktipodo's two eyes seem to turn to stone. With those two unblinking stone eyes Shoktipodo reads the letter once again, and once again! No, there's no room for doubt any more. Concise, exact, and unambiguous, this news. Written in Protibha's kaka's clear hand!

Protibha's mother is dead.

Kaka hasn't considered sending a telegram; he's informed her in this letter: 'Last night your respected mother left for her heavenly home. That she would cut off her attachment to us after only a few days of fever – we never even dreamt of that. We are all terribly stricken with grief. Dada is gone, Boudi has also left us, now you are our only source of consolation. Therefore, please come immediately and provide us some comfort.'

Shoktipodo doesn't have the strength to read the two lines of blessing that follow; he stands there a couple of minutes, unable to decide what his duty is. While he is in this state, images, like scenes from a film, float up one after another in his mind. Not scenes he's viewed before, but scenes he can imagine. The difficulty he'll face if he tells Protibha about this heartbreaking letter now – and the scenes that will follow.

It's not necessary to add that the news of his mother-in-law's death from malaria hasn't caused Shoktipodo any terrible grief, but the poor man's insides dry up when he thinks of what Protibha, whose mother is her heart and her life, might do when she hears this news.

The thought that first raises its head is the thought of his office. Going to the office is finished for today! But by a turn of misfortune, today is the first of the month. And the irksome rule at Shoktipodo's office is that if by chance anyone is absent on the first of the month, he will not get his salary until the seventh! As soon as he recalls this, a chilling current flows down his spine.

And besides – coping with Protibha!

Protibha's nature, and when he adds her mother-grief to that: the poor man's heart turns to ice.

Protibha's mother-grief!

And on top of that, such a sudden shock!

Imagining an unprecedented storm, the man who could not determine his duty suddenly decides it.

No, not now. Let it be covered up for now!

Going and telling her suddenly this way is impossible.

Much better to move silently away now, stealthily. When he comes back, what has to happen will happen. But he can just say, I was in a hurry – but O ré baba! Has Shoktipodo gone mad! He went hurriedly to his office after getting the news of Protibha's mother's death – will he have to tell her that?

That's impossible!

So then?

Then should he put it in his pocket and take it with him? As though, getting it on his way out, he stuffed it into his pocket without reading it and left, and only after coming home, when he was taking his clothes off – no! That too would be difficult.

Seeing that the letter was from Bordhoman, then forgetting about it and working all day at his office, unconcerned – is that a forgivable offence either?

Hasn't Pratibha been worried because no letter has arrived for several days now?

As he thinks it over, a stroke of brilliance plays across his mind like a flash of lightning! This is it! Why didn't this occur to him before! It's true – is there any proof that the postman delivered the letter into Shoktipodo's hands?

Why, very often he drops the mail in from the outside, slipping it through the window. He would have done it today, but for the fact that he saw Shoktipodo! Hai hai! Why didn't Shoktipodo step out for the office a minute earlier? Then he wouldn't have to endure any of this anxiety!

Let it be! Shoktipodo will drop it in from the outside, through the window.

Shoktipodo thinks it over again before carrying out his plan. No, that won't be right. So many familiar people in the neighbourhood

– someone might see him. What will they think? It is better to leave it under the window from the inside!

With noiseless steps Shoktipodo comes and stands, ears erect, near the living room. This is the room into which the postman drops the mail.

Where is Protibha?

Certainly in the kitchen. He can hear the sound of a ladle stirring. He can smell the inviting aroma of fish being fried. So she won't come this way soon.

Slowly he places the magazine and the letter on the window-sill. Let the letter sit on top of the magazine! Yes, that's right! Otherwise, as soon as she sees the *Chhaya-Chhobi* she'll forget the whole universe – will she even look to see if anything lies below?

Let the letter sit on top. Bearing the writing on its chest. Let Protibha get the bad news herself. Let Shoktipodo be free of the onerous duty of bearing ill tidings! Let the severe storm of crying and wailing take place behind Shoktipodo's back. When Shoktipodo returns, surely Protibha will have regained her balance to some degree.

But it doesn't take more than a few seconds to think all this. Because thought is swifter than wind.

Shoktipodo lays the letter on the *Chhaya-Chhobi* packet and goes out of the house as silently as he came. And as soon as he is out, he fills his chest-cage with a deep draw of free air.

Ah! How light he feels!

That is a brilliant idea that came to him.

But when he reaches his office, this feeling of lightness no longer remains! A sense of guilt, rather, hangs heavy on his mind. Time and again he thinks, if Protibha cries and carries on and lets her limbs fall limp, what will the boy's plight be?

Maybe there won't be any milk for the poor boy all day long!

Many times he thinks of returning home early, but what is the justification for that either? Why did he come back early? Therefore he will have to pass the day with his eyes and ears shut.

What he's done, there's no way to change that now.

Having put away the fried fish on a high shelf and completed the one or two other remaining tasks in the kitchen, Protibha comes this way. Her mind is restless, it's been a long time since Shoktipodo left, but the outer door has not yet been shut! Still, it's a relief that the boy isn't crying! As soon as she bolts the door and enters the living room, her eyes fall on the letter and the magazine packet on the window-sill. . . . Oh, has the *Chhaya-Chhobi* arrived? This week they are supposed to publish three interviews with three eminent actresses.

When did it come?

When Shoktipodo was getting dressed to go out, it hadn't come until then!

And here, the letter from Bordhoman has come too! But why is it written in Kaka's hand? Apart from the usual letter on Bijoya Doshomi, Kaka never . . . surely Ma is well?

Anxiety is swifter than wind, for everyone.

She thinks all this even as she stretches out her hand. And Protibha picks it up and runs her eyes over it and becomes still and sits down on the dusty floor!

What is this! What news is this!

What message is this that this three-paisa postcard has borne to her? Ma is gone? Protibha's Ma is gone? And this news of her going has arrived by means of this extremely ordinary letter two lines long?

Is the news of Protibha's mother-loss of as little value as a trivial communication about good or poor health? And did Protibha have to learn the news in such strange circumstances? She has to learn when she is alone that her mother is gone! Why didn't the letter come ten minutes earlier? Then Shoktipodo would have been there.

There would have been a witness to gauge the terrible measure of Protibha's grief. If Shoktipodo had been there – right then he would have run with the grief-stricken, maddened Protibha to Howrah station.

No, if there was no time to catch the train, Protibha wouldn't even have agreed to wait for one, she would have wanted to rush like a madwoman by taxi. . . . And Shoktipodo would certainly not have protested.

Shoktipodo is not such a heartless man that he would be miserly at a time of such great sorrow for Protibha! Protibha would have got off the taxi and thrown herself immediately on the ground near her mother's bed, and her kaka and khuri and pishima would have run to come and console her! The people of the neighbourhood would have come. How afflicted Protibha was at losing her mother, everyone in the neighbourhood would have known!

But what has happened? One aspect of grief – grief's grandeur – has been completely extinguished! So much so, that to scream out just once and start crying – she can't find inspiration enough even for that! Alone at home, can anyone cry out like that?

What grown-ups cannot do, youngsters can with ease. So, suddenly, with an uncontrolled scream, the ten-month-old Khokon churns up the entire neighbourhood. He was playing by himself in the room – what has suddenly happened?

In a house with no one else in it, on hearing such a scream from her son, what else can she do but run to him? Even if she's just heard the news of her mother's death, she must go.

It's only a large black ant!

It has caught the end of a small, tender toe in a dreadful bite. For a ten-month-old boy, this black ant is the equal of a scorpion. To make the boy forget the pain, she has to forget her mother-grief. And when the boy forgets somewhat, a burnt smell pervading the house startles her, reminding her that in order to save some work in the evening, she had put some chickpea daal on the dying stove in the morning. Fine, so that's the end of the daal. Even a dying stove picks its time to get its revenge.

Let the daal go, but it won't do if the pot holding the daal gets burnt. Protibha bought it just the other day, in exchange for as many as four old saris.

Carrying the child in her arms, Protibha lifts down the pot and puts up the chain on the kitchen door, then comes and sits near the letter. Once more she picks it up in her hand. As though reading it again might lead her to discover something else. As though suddenly she'll see that all this time she's been reading it wrong.

But no, there's no chance of any mistake anywhere.

Protibha's Ma is really gone. Even if she runs to that house in Bordhoman and wanders about searching everywhere, Protibha will not see her again. Her Baba died in her distant childhood, and she can't remember him at all; Ma's been her everything.

So – it's happened like this!

The first grief of Protibha's life, and the most fundamental grief, has made its appearance in this lukewarm manner.

And then Protibha will have to get up again soon, when the maidservant comes, and when the goat's-milk vendor comes. She'll have to talk to them. At least she'll have to tell the maidservant about the terrible event that has occurred in her life. She'll have to say it herself. If she doesn't, she'll have to act normal, like a normal person, and then – what will the maidservant say afterwards? And after she hears of such a momentous, such a dreadful thing, she'll certainly come to express her compassion at Protibha's grief. And maybe, finding an opportunity, melting with closeness, she'll come and run her hand over her employer's head or body. Insufferable! Insufferable! Besides, Shoktipodo will see that even after getting the news of her mother's death, Protibha has stood up, has walked – has fed the boy milk.

Having stopped crying, the boy, finding himself in his mother's lap, has gone to sleep; and Protibha sits motionless with the sleeping boy in her lap.

The day rolls on . . . it's three o'clock – the sound of the goat's-milk vendor's bell is heard.

Protibha makes a firm decision and stands up.

Yes, at what time the postman came and delivered the letter, Protibha doesn't know! She was occupied with the crying of the ant-bitten child. The child cried the whole day. And so Protibha hasn't had the respite even to glance at the rooms or windows or doors. And witness to that: the *Chhaya-Chhobi* packet hasn't been opened. Protibha puts the magazine and the letter on the window-sill in exactly the way the postman dropped them, then gets up; she takes a small glass and opens the door for the goat's-milk vendor. After taking the milk and putting it away in its place, she looks at the two objects once again and stops short: the letter near the magazine? No, let the letter lie concealed beneath the book! Was it possible that it wouldn't have fallen to her glance even once during her comings and goings? And if she saw the letter, Protibha ought to have read it eagerly, since she's been worried because no letter from Bordhoman had come for some time.

Chhaya-Chhobi? Let that be!

If that's lying there – it stays there. Someone whose son is crying all day and driving her crazy, does she have the time to sit with a film magazine?

It seems that the rice laid out by Protibha in the kitchen is still lying there. The maidservant has come and is shouting about it. But what could Protibha have done? With her headache, she hasn't been able to lift her head all day! How could she have eaten? The maidservant should take the rice home for her boys.

In the usual way, the stove is lit. Preparations begin for cooking the evening meal! Shoktipodo loves whole potol fries and small pieces of fried potato along with hot luchis. Let that be the meal. Because nothing has happened to Protibha. Protibha's fine.

Shoktipodo comes near the door of the house and stops short.

Are there any sounds of crying?

Keeping his ears erect for a while, for no particular reason he starts thinking he can hear something. Then he realizes his mistake. . . . So what's happened? Surely she hasn't gone off to Bordhoman alone in her agitated state? . . . No, if that were the case, how could the door be shut from the inside? But why is it so still? Has she fainted then?

Who knows, maybe Protibha has fainted and is lying there, maybe the child has fallen down and cracked his head open. Chhi chhi, how thoughtless Shoktipodo was in the morning!

Gently he shakes the ring on the door, then somewhat more firmly, then even more loudly. . . . Now the door is opened. And the person to open it is Protibha herself.

In an ordinary, natural voice she asks, 'You're so late today?'

Late!

Yes, it is a little late, Shoktipodo has taken some time to gather his courage before entering the house.

What answer he might make, Shoktipodo himself cannot figure out, but by then Protibha has moved on to another subject.

'Do you know what happened today? You had just gone out, and I was coming from the kitchen, about to shut the door, when suddenly Khokon let out a horrible scream. I went running – What happened? What happened? O Ma, what do I see – a terrible black ant has bitten him and is latched on to his toe. I couldn't pull it off easily. A little blood even came out! And after that, the boy didn't stop crying! No rest all day. I became really impatient. Why, just take a look at the house, look, a broom hasn't touched the floors all day, I haven't even tied my hair, what a bothersome state of affairs! – Now Babu's playing a little, at last!'

But the confused Shoktipodo's gaze is not directed at the child. That gaze is stuck like glue to the window-sill! So Shoktipodo's stratagem was in vain?

Is it still lying there? In exactly the same condition?

But this is only the magazine – where is the letter?

Where the letter is, that investigation cannot be undertaken now. Not even the ploy of seeing it suddenly and picking it up will work. The subject under deliberation now is the great trouble that had befallen them in the shape of the boy's ant-bite. And so he is forced to take the boy in his arms, has to wash his hands and face quickly. Because Protibha is warning him that the hot luchis are turning cold. She says that if he doesn't eat a lot of them, she won't spare him!

Afterwards, maybe he can pick up the letter and magazine absent-mindedly, to see what the postman dropped off when no one was looking. But of course when Protibha can't see him.

But where is the letter?

He looks this way and that for the letter, but only after he lifts the magazine does he realize where the letter is.

Astonishing! With his own hands he left the letter on top, did Shoktipodo. Nobody's hand has touched it, so how has it found shelter beneath the magazine? And what is this on the corner of the card? This distinct stain?

It will not do to spend any more time researching this.

Taking the letter in his hand, Shoktipodo has to stand as though thunderstruck and pronounce in a stuttering voice: 'Ogo, are you listening! What's this? What is this gibberish that your kaka's written?'

Protibha hears him and comes and stands there, easy expression, slow pace. A question with ordinary curiosity: 'Is there a letter from Bordhoman? Has Kaka written? Suddenly such a big favour from Kaka. What's he written? O ki, why are you quiet? Tell me what he's written, won't you? Ogo?'

As though Protibha's forgotten that she's not illiterate.

Shoktipodo sits down on the floor, puts a hand to his head, and says tearfully, 'What he's written, I just can't believe it! Ah! Is this possible?'

Her manner anxious, Protibha sits down on the floor and moans as though stricken: 'Tell me clearly, won't you – what's happened? I can't understand anything! Did something happen to my mother?'

Shoktipodo says in a melancholy voice, 'Yes, Protibha, Ma – she has left us and gone!'

A deep sigh falls from Shoktipodo, shaking all his ribs.

And Protibha cries out with a chest-splitting scream that splits the skies: 'Ogo, what's this you're telling me! What's this thing you've told me? What's this bolt of lightning from a clear sky!'

And right after the scream – Protibha leans over in a faint! But why wouldn't she? She's truly been in a faint all day. And, as he splashes her face with cold water from the water pot, Shoktipodo wonders: But really, how did the position of the letter change? And why is there, on one corner of the card, such a distinct print of a turmeric-coated thumb!

Bird Palace

পঙ্খীমহল

Ponkhi-Mohol

Not a moyur-ponkhi boat, with its peacock shape, but a moyur-ponkhi bedstead.

Rare black ebony wood inlaid with glittering ivory work in each of the peacock's feathers – this is an antique bedstead. Exquisite in conception, impeccable in craftsmanship. As though it's not a bedstead but a moyur-ponkhi boat poised to push its way upstream against the current.

In the bird's lap, a bed as soft as butter. Spring mattress, satin bedspread, velvet pillows fringed with silk. A footstool encased in silver and tooled brass. Above the head of the bedstead, a rope-drawn fan with a silken fringe.

The room is unique, amazing.

A long hall in white marble, at its extreme end a raised platform like a theatre stage. The platform is about three hand-spans high and eight hand-spans wide, spanning the room from one wall to the other, and the moyur-ponkhi bedstead is set on it. At two corners of the platform are two enormous brass lampstands, each bearing a five-branched candelabrum like a poncho-prodeep,[3] covered with lampshades of coloured glass. Near the head of the bedstead is a teapoy of Kashmiri lattice-work; on it stands a flower-vase of Italian porcelain.

Even now the gardener's wife has a standing order for a bouquet of fresh flowers every day.

The three or four steps, at this end and at that end, for climbing from the low floor of the room up to the platform, are also of white marble, with a black border of vines on them. Intact, flawless even today. But if you sat down to calculate the age of this palace you would have to skip over this century and cast your eyes at the middle of the previous century.

Even though built with the wealth and power of the British, there was still, in this region near Mukshudabad, evidence of the luxurious nawabi taste. As soon as some money came into people's hands, their only wish was 'to play the nawab until I'm sated'. Even though the light had suddenly flashed in the soul of Calcutta, at the time the other regions were still asleep.

The founder of this line, Gobindoram, had made the money and was gone; the fame and power was his son Shadhonram's. And since then, for three–four generations, they've been chewing the cud of wealth and aristocracy.

That the world is moving forward, that the earth has emerged from its screened palanquin and is rushing about the skies – it seems this news has reached them, but it hasn't quite. The earth still revolves here day and night in the lingering nawabi fashion, turns over and over in the smoky memories of the high tide of British rule.

So much rain so many storms lightning-strikes earthquakes have taken place in the country since then, but they don't seem conscious of any of that.

Outside – a secret restlessness, a great fear has arisen in the outer offices, on the waves of such news as 'Zamindari will be abolished',

'The title "raja" will be reduced to dust', but the inner sanctums are still calm. There this news is not believable.

In the inner rooms, the undaunted hearts know that no matter how much agitation there is anywhere else, it will not enter here to buffet them. Morning or evening, their lotions and oils in their silver bowls will not be exhausted. They know, when they sit down to dress their hair, if some strands of silver hair suddenly peer forth from among the teeth of the gold-plated comb, that is the ultimate bad news.

Shoroma was seated motionless on the low square stone chouki in the middle of the 'Moyur-Ponkhi Room', having chased away for the moment the servant woman who was doing her hair, but not because of such bad news as silver hair.

But what then was the bad news?

On the contrary, the servant woman who had borne the news to her – Shoroma had given her a reward of ten rupees on a new bronze plate.

Maybe Shoroma was sitting still with her gaze on the portrait in front of her. High on the facing wall was hung a three-colour, full-length portrait of Queen Victoria, set in a broad gold frame. On the other walls, scenes of the English countryside, similarly three-coloured. It was just that everything was dull, on everything there was a grey, shadowy layer of time.

Three colossal doors, on whose wooden faces were set velvet curtains tied with silk cords – the curtains were faded and worm-eaten.

All in all, it was as though a stale fragment of a Mughal harem, covered by a cavelike dark, lay in the midst of this 'Ponkhi-Palace'.

Even so, this room, this palace, this novel and amazing bedstead, set on the three-hands-high platform – with what immense strength these ever-familiar ingredients of ease, luxury, and indulgence have taken root in the heart-land of Shobhonram's wife Shoroma!

It must be said here that the name 'Shoroma' has been searched out and taken from the pages of history. Once she was 'Bou-rani', now 'Rani-ma'. Married at the age of ten, now she's in the house of forty. Never in her life has she gone to stay at her father's house; for thirty years she's been bound to this room by the snake's noose[2] of countless habits. Each perfumed, conjugally warmed breath of almost every night for thirty years has dissolved into these carved stone walls, these latticed windows, these household decorations of silk satin glass brass.

Unlike Shoroma's mother-in-law and *her* mother-in-law, Shoroma has never had to pass a night alone in the butter-soft furnishings of that moyur-ponkhi bedstead.

It's debatable whether there has ever been anyone in the family as fortunate in her husband as Shoroma. Why only husband-fortune, Shoroma's son-fortune is no less either. One son, equalling a hundred.

A face like the moon, qualities to be admired, famed for his erudition. Which, apparently, was a new import for this family. And Shoroma has found a beautiful bride. Worthy of her son.

Not the daughter of a noble house. Let her not be; after all, Shoroma herself came from a middle-class home. Had come to a house without a housewife, her shashuri wasn't around, and she had taken on all the duties and responsibilities of a housewife since that age of ten. And she had received the honour due to a housewife too, since her girlhood.

Shoroma's daughter-in-law is still without responsibilities, still a creature of the 'New Palace'.

She's there – she's still there, a resident of the New Palace.

Maybe Shoroma does pronounce the words once in her mind. 'She won't stay there any more.'

The chains of a strange custom still bind this family. Today those chains weigh heavily on Shoroma's heart and consciousness, like a grindstone. They are set heavy on her! But who has set them there? Who will punish her if she doesn't follow the custom?

Motionless, Shoroma was considering this very question, and after considering it she breathed out, No, it cannot be. It is Shoroma's civilized nature and her sense of honour that will force her to follow this cruel custom of the ages. She will have to follow the custom, *will* have to give up this Ponkhi-Palace and this moyur-ponkhi bedstead.

The custom of the family is that as soon as a grandson is born, the rani will have to give up this palace; the right to this palace will be born anew, to the new mother.

But is that the only thing?

Does the cruelty end there?

To protect the dignity of the grandfather and the grandmother, Rani-ma will have to live alone, and Raja-babu in the outer palace. The chains of this tradition are still unbreakable in Gobindoram's family. And today Shoroma is the sacrifice to that ritual. A servant woman from the New Palace has come and given her the first intimation of that extreme punishment, the servant woman to whom Shoroma gave a reward of ten rupees on a new bronze plate.

Rising from the stone chouki, Shoroma pushes aside the velvet curtain and stands in the verandah on the western side. It's a verandah, true, but nowhere does the outside world even beckon. The buildings surround a central courtyard, and opposite the verandah, on the other side is another verandah and a series of rooms.

Still, as she comes and stands in this west-facing verandah, a flash of golden light from the declining afternoon hits Shoroma's face. Shoroma feels it, and seems overwhelmed.

Shoroma is about to cross forty, yet how wonderfully graceful, how delicately lovely she still is! In the cast of her face, in the cut of her chin, in the lines of her lips is a young woman's tenderness. The tips of her fingers are still flawless, plump, like champa buds; her two feet are soft as tender mango leaves.

As a fragment of the middle ages still remains in the midst of the Moyur-Ponkhi Palace, perhaps in the same way the moonlight of physical grace still remains in Shoroma's body. It's as though this moonlight has forgotten to say goodbye. Perhaps it hasn't even found the respite to remember, to remember and become aware and rise to leave.

After the night, the morning has come; a servant woman has brought water in a small silver basin and, on a brass plate with a raised rim, the perfumed appurtenances for washing one's face; and after that has come the proshad of fruit, sweets, chhana, and sugar from the prayer-house. Then the servant woman has brought all the various things necessary for a bath, and after the bath Shoroma has worn a sari and blouse of fine cotton, and after trying on a few others, she's worn a slender necklace and light bangles. With her light, clean appearance she has gone to inspect the kitchen and the prayer-house, the guest rooms and the New Palace; and then she has fanned her husband with a silk-fringed sandalwood fan as he ate his meal. And with a similar fan the servant women have fanned Shoroma during her own meal.

In the evening, again, the servant woman has come for about two hours with lotions and oils in their silver bowls, the gold-plated comb and every kind of perfume bottle, the gold sindoor-box and kumkum in its gold case. Merely doing the toilette is not enough; every day she praises Shoroma's fall of soft silky hair, her graceful body, its posture, the softness of her skin, the brightness of her complexion. Then again, changing her jewellery for new jewellery, again waiting on a corner of the moyur-ponkhi bedstead in throbbing expectation. Age is stopped, stopped is the moonlight of charm and grace.

The responsibilities of the Rani-ma have been met – in every rhythm of this alaap[3] in slow tempo. They are not like housewives in middle-class homes; when the weight of responsibility falls on their shoulders, it doesn't break their necks; with their champa-bud fingers they take up their obligations and duties with care.

And so the servant woman comes and gives word of a grandson's arrival.

Shoroma exhales and comes away from the verandah. She must go and see her daughter-in-law once. She does see her once every day, but still, today she must go once more, in a somewhat ceremonial way – once more than usual, contrary to her custom.

Shobhonram's outside work, deliberations, and conferences have all gained importance, and frequently there is an infringement of fixed customs. That is why nowadays Shoroma has to wait even after the beaters have struck ten on the courthouse clock.

Shobhonram completes his nighttime meal in the care of the cookhouse staff, so all that remains for Shoroma are many mounds of lonely, motionless, cold time. Before late evening, her son will come and see her, calculating the hours and minutes, her son's wife will come at dinnertime. And who else after that?

The new bride's experience of waiting still remains, at the edge of forty.

Eight rings from his ten fingers and thumbs, Shobhonram takes off one by one and keeps on the small silver plate on the Kashmiri table, and after this, waiting for him is a crimped Shimle dhuti and an undershirt of fine silk, and waiting for him is a bottle of attar.

And also waiting is a soft body.

From behind a coloured shade shines a candle's gentle flame.

'Because it's late, the lady is piqued, isn't she?'

Shobhonram smiles gently. Shobhonram's age is forty-five years, yet his body has the build of a youth's.

'Who says I'm piqued?' – Shoroma sits up from her reclining pose.

'Should some outsider say it? Your face, eyes, lips are saying it.'

'You've learned to read nothing. Your reading is wrong.'

'Why should I believe that? I can see it myself. Your face, eyes, lips are brimming over with hurt feelings.'

'Is there nothing other than hurt feelings in this world?'

'Certainly there is, but I'm wondering what.'

Changing his dhuti, Shobhonram steps up on the footstool encased in silver and tooled brass and sits down on the butter-soft appointments in the bird's lap.

The rope-drawn fan swings a little wider.

The sleepy-eyed boy outside understands the hints of the slightest noise.

Shoroma lifts up a hand slightly and says, 'They can brim over with delight too.'

Shobhonram is concerned about many outside matters, and so he does not have much passion for jokes and jests. Still, he laughs, says, 'What has happened to cause such sudden delight?'

'Something has happened, a lot has happened.' – Suddenly Shoroma laughs out loud in an unnatural fashion. There must be some extremely bad news.

The laugh disconcerts Shobhonram. He says, 'Tell me what the matter is, won't you?'

Five years older than Shoroma is Shobhonram, but sometimes he seems naive compared to Shoroma.

'Matter! Matter!' – Again Shoroma laughs out loud. 'You'll have a grandson, that's what.'

'Hanh!' – Shobhonram, startled, sits up straight.

'O Ma, why are you so surprised?'

Shoroma's laughter doesn't seem to want to stop.

Shobhonram stays quiet for a moment and then says, 'How old is Kumar's[4] wife?'

'Eighteen.'

And so what else can be said? At that age, their son in Shoroma's lap was three years old.

'You have an accurate report?'

'I do indeed. That's not a mistake you make.'

Shobhonram feels somewhat helpless. As though he cannot quite grasp Shoroma.

The chain of custom that binds Gobindoram's family line, that custom is not unknown to Shobhonram. And so the news that should have delighted him in the extreme, that news makes him feel strangely empty.

After staying quiet a while longer, Shobhonram makes a sound like a distressed laugh and says, 'So then our term is over?'

Shobhonram's voice sounds extremely doleful.

For the past few hours Shoroma has been thinking exactly this, but who knows what happens – this helpless, distressed laugh and this doleful, plaintive tone from Shobhonram makes her explode, *doppl*, like gunpowder. In a sharp voice she says, 'Our term is over – what do you mean?'

Shobhonram says in an even more dejected manner, 'What else do I mean! You know everything.'

'I do, but I won't obey.'

Maybe Shoroma makes this resolution in the moment she utters it, but still she announces it in a tone of firm resolve. 'Those old, rotting customs of your family – I'll blow them away.'

Hot wax melts and drips within the coloured glass, and in that illumination the moonlight of physical beauty has become the high tide of beauty. In this illusory radiance, no decay can be seen anywhere in the room, no shadowy stamp of time can be seen.

Suddenly Shobhonram presses a soft hand between his own and says in a choked voice, 'Is that possible?'

Shoroma replies in a careless manner, 'What's not possible about it? There are so many changes in your outer world, why shouldn't something happen in this inner world of mine?'

'But – .' Shobhonram releases her hand. 'Is that really possible?'

'Stay silent, and watch whether it's possible or not.' – Shoroma lies down in a pose of sweet languor and says, 'The New Palace isn't all that bad either. It'll be fine if we make some new arrangements.'

Shobhonram presses down the satin pillow under his elbow and watches this pose of sweet languor, then speaks up like a child. 'Won't Kumar mind?'

'What should he mind!' – Shoroma cups a hand over her eyes to shade them from the light and says, 'I did not deprive anyone to take possession – I entered this room a newly married bride, and I'll leave this room to go to the Gonga directly.'

Shoroma had entered a home without a mother-in-law and had claimed the Ponkhi-Palace at once – this is what Shoroma is alluding to.

Shobhonram remains silent for some time and then says, 'Does Bou-ma know about all these rules and customs?'

Shoroma says in a manner even more careless than before, 'She might know. And even if she doesn't, there's no lack of well-wishers to inform her.'

With the palm of his ringless hand, Shobhonram presses gently down, then with a little more weight, on the body of the woman lying next to him. 'So those are your arrangements. But what about mine? I'll have to go and stay in that outer palace?'

'Yes, you will.' – A bejewelled hand comes and falls on his hand. 'All I'm concerned about is how I can guard this Moyur-Ponkhi.'

The resolution has been announced, but still there is the deception of a false hope. The news could be wrong, and so much else could happen. Shoroma shivers mentally once and lets a secret, heartening hope grow in her mind.

Who knows what might happen. In a first pregnancy, there can be so many obstacles and dangers, so many unexpected turns!

But the froth of Shoroma's secret hope gradually congeals, gradually the day draws closer without any obstacles making their appearance. In the end Shoroma stills her divided mind.

Really, why this!

Why should this insignificant ritual, this invisible prohibition pull such a noose around their necks! And why, too, should she secretly wish harm to a person not yet arrived! No, this is much better. This is much better. To take this custom and toss it carelessly aside.

A man who has taken his leave of the earth a hundred years ago – what right does he have to etch a line of prohibition on this earth of today? What right to etch that line of division between two lives?

No, Shoroma will not accept this.

She will not give up the Ponkhi-Palace.

Earlier, Shobhonram had been in a dilemma, riven by doubt, hesitant. With Shoroma's brave words his manner changes. Now he believes himself gratified. What was not possible for Shobhonram himself, Shoroma has made possible – would this not make him grateful!

The only shame would be in meeting Kumar face to face. Indeed, Shobhonram is an exception in this family lineage. A family that took pride in the tradition of father and son sitting down together for a drink of wine – should Shobhonram, a man of that lineage, be ashamed before his son because of such a trifling matter?

The brides of this house do not go to their fathers' homes.

Kumar's wife, too, has not gone; she is here.

A slowness in her movements, in her speech.

In the meantime, the entire palace has grown voluble in criticizing Shoroma. Of course the critics are distant relatives who stay nearby, dependents and servant men and women, but their tongues are no less venomous. Shoroma gives no sign of moving from the Ponkhi-Palace – what can be more shameless than that?

Kumar's wife takes refuge in the sick-room, and then the criticism, too, comes closer to her ear. Shoroma, though, is unperturbed. At the time of her grandson's birth, she 'breaks the treasury' to distribute wealth, gives fat pronami gifts to all elders and worthies, sends pujo offerings to every temple.

She gives a bejewelled necklace from her own bridal days to see the face of her grandson, makes Shobhonram give a necklace of guineas. There should be no omissions, no shortcoming anywhere. Maybe the lustre of this faultless devotion to duty will hide the history of that slight weakness.

But still it does not remain hidden.

People's cruelty casts glances at other's weaknesses, seeking an opening.

Shobhonram's widowed sister, living in a holy city, returns to her father's house after a very long time to see the face of her nephew's son. To see the newest rivulet of the stream of Gobindoram's family lineage.

That day, Shethera Pujo[5] is being celebrated for the newborn.

Borodamohini takes Shoroma along to the Bou-Palace, gives a gold necklace to see her grandson's face, and after speaking of this and that suddenly says, 'Now, Bou-rani, I didn't see any painters in the Ponkhi-Palace?'

For Borodamohini, Shoroma is still 'Bou-rani'. At her nonodini's question, Shoroma's face turns white for an instant, then becomes red. Still, she glances sidelong at her daughter-in-law, Shulokkhona, and answers in an easy manner, 'Oh, it was painted just a few years ago.'

'Listen to that!' Borodamohini puts a hand to her cheek. 'We've always had the custom of having the palace painted before the new bride enters it with her new son; the ponkhi bedstead is varnished and polished, the bulbs in the chandelier are changed – are you going to change all that? It's only a few days before Rani-bouma enters the Ponkhi-Palace.'

The young cast of Shoroma's face suddenly looks very hard, a flash of lightning runs along the lines of her lips, she is about to say something, but it remains unsaid.

On the back of Borodamohini's comment, Shulokkhona, less adept at matters of etiquette, speaks out abruptly. 'Save us, Pishima, I have no use for that Ponkhi-Palace of yours. Baba! Just the sight of it suffocates me – it's not a house, it's a cremation ground. That New Palace of yours is much better. I'll be fine there.'

Who knows what happened and by what means, who knows which musical instrument had its strings pulled too tight, who knows which string broke and twanged loose, but right away, with that hard expression on her face Shoroma says in a voice sharp as poison, 'This household's rules and customs will not run by your fancies and whims, Rani-bouma. As soon as the Shoshti Pujo is over on the twenty-first, you'll have to enter the Ponkhi-Palace. There's no need for any repairs, it's in very good condition.'

The new wife is benumbed by this sudden poison-arrow of Shoroma's. She looks confusedly at her shashuri's face, then says in a whisper, 'When I see that palace, I feel afraid.'

'You feel afraid now, but the fear will break.' Shoroma says this and rises and leaves the room.

At night, the astonished, despondent, distressed Shobhonram says in a weak voice, 'But you kept saying all this time – '

'What did I keep saying – is that a fact?' Shoroma says in a callous, detached voice. 'You're old enough now, don't you understand a joke?'

Her chest is bursting indeed, all the nerves and veins of her eyes want to burst, still she must remain hard. That rash act of a moment's impatience: the rest of her life, Shoroma will have to bear its effects. After that moment, there can be no stratagem to control the queenship of the Ponkhi-Palace. The art and skill of so many days, the deceit, the false pretence of blowing away the merciless truth without even looking – all of it has crumbled at a moment's carelessness!

But what will Shoroma do?

When the fire burns, does it consider whose house it should burn?

The heaven for which Shoroma could easily have emptied out all the gold in her treasure chest, the heaven that Shoroma was prepared to sink all her honour and pride to preserve, the heaven that is Shoroma's all – if someone should express such extreme scorn and careless irreverence towards that heaven, doesn't the blood in the head boil up in an instant?

How humble, how small, how greedy do those disdainful words of another make one feel!

Shoroma herself has been destroyed, but that other woman – she too has been taught a lesson.

Shadowsun

ছায়াসূর্য

Chhayashurjo

There are two girls in our house, and about the two of them everyone – at home and outside, relatives and mere acquaintances – keeps saying the same thing. They say, 'Aha – their virtues match their looks!'

But this is said with two opposite connotations. That there's the difference of sky and netherworld between the two.

The two girls are my own bhaijhis.

Not born of two mothers; born from the same mother's womb. And I hear there's only thirteen months between younger and older. It is certainly astonishing that the Lord would have been replaced in such a short period of time, but it is also impossible to believe that the same Lord made both of them. Maybe the real Lord had been on vacation at the time, and someone unskilled had taken on the workload temporarily.

My Mej-di said, 'The bottles and bottles of tonic that you drank after the birth of the older girl, Boro-bou, I think they were an extract of coal tar. That younger daughter of yours grew bigger and bigger rolling around in that solution.'

Younger, 'chhoto,' daughter is the right term, because many years have passed since their births, and no one else has appeared to turn that 'chhoto' into 'mejo', second-oldest. Mej-di says, 'Looking at her, no one's had the courage to come after.'

The naming of Boro-boudi's daughters was also a praiseworthy contribution by Mej-di. The older's name is Mollika,[1] the younger's Ghentu.[2]

Named after the names of flowers.

By count of years, it's true that Ghentu's the younger, but she's the one who looks older. Ghentu, with the intelligence to match her looks, Ghentu of the long arms and legs, wide bones, square shoulders. And in the square cast of her face there wasn't the slightest measure of feminine sweetness.

If she didn't have a headful of hair like Rokkhe-Kali, people would have thought Ghentu a boy dressed up as a girl.

Next to that hard, capable, sturdy frame of hers, Mollika's pink, delightfully soft, small body seemed almost like an English doll's. Mollika's eyes were large, nose sharp, lips slender. Only her cheeks were somewhat full, but that fullness seemed to have the air of aristocracy. In Mollika's shape and appearance, in her manner and speech, the nobility of our family was clearly revealed.

Even if not as much as Mollika, our aunts and sisters were almost all beauties.

Even those from outside, meaning our boudis, were none of them bad. In this Aryan[3] family Ghentu seemed the one un-Aryan.

From childhood, sitting on beds and stools twenty arm-lengths from dust and dirt, Mollika would play at setting up the dollhouse and arranging dolls, and Ghentu's business was with the dust and the dirt. All morning, in the fallow land littered with refuse behind the house, Ghentu would play tipcat, climb up to the third-storey rooftop in the blazing sunshine to fly a kite, go down to the street in the evening to play marbles with the neighbourhood's pumpkins-out-of-season boys.

Scoldings, beatings, locking-in-rooms, not-feedings – no punishment was enough to tame Ghentu. Boro-boudi would lose heart and take up sweet talk; she would say, 'Why do you wander about playing on the streets like a ruffian, Ma, do play indoors, you two sisters together.'

Hearing this, Ghentu would turn out her lower lip scornfully and say, 'Play with Didi! What does Didi know about playing?'

On the other side, Mollika would furrow her brow and say, 'Play with Ghenti? Save us!'

This was when they were quite young.

After she entered school Ghentu's self-willed sportiveness diminished somewhat, but could it be stopped completely? During recesses and holidays she would make up the arrears. At school there were new complaints every day. Ghentu was eating alu-kabli while sitting in class! Ghentu had talked back rudely to Didimoni's face!

And besides that, losing her book, not preparing her lesson, sitting with her fingers in her ears when Didimoni scolded her, et cetera – Ghentu's done all kinds of things.

Mollika would return and say, her pink face all red, 'I won't study in the same school with her. Her uncivilized behaviour leaves me headless with shame.'

This being left headless of Mollika's was corroborated by everyone else, but really it wasn't easy to separate the two sisters quickly in two different places. Changing schools involved no mean difficulty. So at first efforts were made to change Ghentu by various methods: penalties, discipline, flattery, enticement.

In the end, everyone admitted defeat.

But by then Mollika's accusations too came to an end. She passed her exams and went beyond the school's boundaries, and Ghentu, after spending two–three years in every class and saying 'I don't like school', came home and applied her mind closely to swallowing storybooks whole.

Therefore, who wouldn't use two different tunes in their comments on the two sisters? Who possesses what sort of beauty, what kinds of virtues, is obvious from the commentator's manner of speech!

Every task of Mollika's is beautifully carried out, with an artist's touch. The needlework that she does with those champa-bud-like fingers of hers, surpasses even machine work in its finesse; the pictures of Hor-Parboti, wedding scenes, landscape and scenery that are hung on the walls of the house, she has copied with brush and paint and paper and pencil so skilfully that if they are placed side by side, it isn't clear which is the real one and which the fake.

And Ghentu?

It's doubtful if Ghentu's sewed a single stitch in her life. Never does she come even close to finesse. One day when she was ridiculed in relation to her didi's painting, she turned out her lip in disrespect, in that way of hers, and said, 'Ohh, making a picture is such an achievement! Sitting and filling in Radhika's eyebrows by the numbers – that's painting, is it!'

And right away she grabbed her didi's brush and paint and paper and pencil and *khosh-khosh* drew a bull! The bull was nothing other than a pose with lowered head, about to charge!

And about that pose there was no little mockery and joking in the house. Some said, 'That's a sign of the way she thinks,' . . . some said, 'That's the innermost essence of Ghentu's heart,' . . . some said, 'That's a picture of Ghentu's soul!' Only Bor-da said, 'Tear up the picture, Baba, otherwise whenever it falls to my eyes, it seems Jom's creature is charging at me.'

Mollika sharpened the pencil again, and threw away the paintbrush. Because after Ghentu had used them once, both had become completely worn.

Mollika was not a girl to scream and shout or scold or express her anger. Whatever annoyance she expressed was by the slightest wrinkle of her eyebrow. Even that wrinkle she made smooth, and said to her sister in a gentle voice, 'Don't come into my room any more.'

Mollika had been given not a bedroom, but a study of her own, because in this house she was the first girl to go to college. Everyone looked at her with honour and deference in their glance. It was a small room, but smart and tidy. Mollika had decorated it to her taste. She stayed there most of the time.

At her didi's prohibition, Ghentu spoke out, answering in her un-Aryan voice, 'Who wants to come into your owl's hole? I just wanted to show you what painting means.'

Ghentu makes these kinds of remarks to everyone. Even for us, the elders, she doesn't produce any very Aryan voice. But I won't deny that the girl loves me. Yes, loves me, nothing more than that. To admire or respect someone isn't written in her horoscope.

It's because Ghentu shows me some regard that Boro-boudi sometimes comes and attacks me. 'So the girl will ruin herself just this way? And none of you will be able to reform her. You write so many books, and as a kaka you can't set a stubborn girl straight?'

I must say I don't know what the connection is between writing books and setting a girl straight, but Boro-boudi brings up the matter of my writing books at many random moments.

I laugh and say, 'I write books, I write some fake stories about some fake people. To take God's true writing and write it in a fake mould, I don't have that kind of pen in my hand, Boudi!'

Boudi gets angry and says, 'You only talk in this twisted way! And those two dadas of yours, they're shoulder snakes.[4] Boro, mejo, both are the same. Once they sit down to their cards, they forget everything. And when can I talk about all this? Here's a grown-up girl, running around with all the neighbourhood boys, going off to play carrom, flying kites at all hours, or else sweeping the neighbourhood clean to find storybooks and swallow them – what'll become of this girl? And on top of that, such an avatar of beauty – how will she get married?'

Whether she would get married, meaning whether it was possible to get her married, is a subject about which I myself have the gravest doubts, but still I console Boudi for the moment. 'Aré baba, you're the ones who say that marriage is a matter of destiny!'

'That's for people, not for zoo animals.'

A little later I catch her. 'Ei, zoo animal! Where are you going?'

Ghentu, trying to loosen my grip, says, 'To learn the tabla!'

To learn the tabla!

My eyes climb up to my forehead. 'You're going to learn the tabla. Are you really completely insane?'

Ghentu says spiritedly, 'Why, no one else plays the tabla except the insane?'

'Should a girl play the tabla?'

'So what should a girl do, tell me? Only cry like a cat, *pirring pirring*, like Didi does?'

I hadn't known it, but I understand that Mollika must have taken up some stringed instrument. I say, 'Whatever she does, she does at home, she doesn't go roaming around the neighbourhood like you. Whose house are you going to?'

'Pintu's folks' house.'

'Pintu's folks' house!' To tell the truth, when I hear that, like Boudi I grow worried too. I scold her. 'Why do you need to go to that no-good boy's house?'

'What do you mean, no-good? What no-good thing has he done to you?'

'What would he do to me? Night and day he sits on the porch and puffs away at a cigarette.'

'Cigarette!' Ghentu laughs out loud, *hee-hee*. 'The sieve mocks the needle's hole! Which one of you doesn't puff away at cigarettes? Your fingers have calluses from holding all those cigarettes!'

'Our age, and his age?' I say, getting angry.

Ghentu stops laughing and says, 'That means you're even more no-good. What a foolish, innocent youngster is doing, you're doing the same thing, and you're learned, intelligent, grown-up elders!'

Which saint can help getting incensed at such a face-to-face attack? I grow irate and say, 'Your learning the tabla won't do.'

'Fine, I won't go,' Ghentu says, and sits down hard on my new suitcase, which is kept on a stool. Doesn't even argue, doesn't even disobey me.

There's a problem with this. Because in such situations, the good bits of advice don't work. But it's necessary to make them work. So I say in a somewhat softer tone, 'Have you ever heard of a gentleman's daughter going to slap at a tabla?'

'I said I won't go – ,' Ghentu blazes up, ' – so why this subject again?'

'You won't go today, but you'll go tomorrow – right?'

'All right, I'll never go,' says Ghentu, swinging her legs.

Ghentu, and sensitive – this is an unprecedented business. My heart yields a little. I say in an even softer tone, 'Why are you getting angry?'

'Angry? Not at all. Why would I get angry?'

'Because I said don't go?'

'Oh, that tabla thing? Nonsense! Would I have listened just because you said no? I don't even like it all that much. It's only because I was wondering what to do.'

'Why – why're you wondering what to do? What do all the other girls do? What does your didi do?'

'They're learned people, they study for their exams.'

I say eagerly, 'Fine, why don't you do that too? Study with a tutor, take the exams. If you're ready to study, I'll make the arrangements.'

'Save us! Modhushudon.' She raises her hands to her forehead.

'So you'll remain a tree monkey like this? Your mother says you won't be able to get married.'

Suddenly on her un-Aryan face Ghentu brings up a somewhat Aryan smile. She smiles and says, 'Wait and see if I do.'

Now it's my turn to calculate the danger hidden behind those words.

What does this smile signify? Is some wily fellow playing with this foolish girl? Deceiving her, tempting her with marriage –

I catch hold of her braid. I say, 'It won't do to get up and run, tell me what that means.'

'What do you mean, means?'

'Who's going to marry a Rokkhe-Kali like you, let's hear?'

'I said you'll see.'

'You won't tell me his name?'

'All right, babu, all right, I'll bring him here one day. But you can't go around announcing it all over the house. He's very shy.'

She begins to swing her legs.

Truly, I grew anxious.

What an unexpected occurrence!

It wasn't Mollika but Ghentu who had gone and fallen in love!

But my supposition about Mollika, too, was wrong. Mollika wouldn't do anything as atrocious as falling in love. Mollika was civilized, Mollika was well-mannered, Mollika was noble. Mollika knew that as soon as she passed her B.A., the most worthy groom on the market would be found and brought for her. First the ceremony of seeing the girl, then the final formal viewing, the giving and getting of the traditional gifts, the body turmeric, the tying of knots, et cetera – her marriage would take place through absolutely the proper channels. Mollika would wear a thick garland of jasmine flowers around her neck and she would open her closed eyes following the barber's instructions and cast the auspicious glance at the auspicious moment on the auspicious day. Then she would take her virgin heart from the iron safe where it had been kept so long and give it into the hands of its lawful claimant.

Mollika wasn't so impatient – nor so greedy – that she would break her heart before marriage. I understood all this later, observing Mollika.

I saw that two instructors came to that small room of Mollika's thrice a week – one for her studies, one for her music. Young men, not at all bad to look at. But not even by mistake did Mollika ever lift her eyes and look at them.

She sat and received her education in perfect solemnity; if she had any questions, she would ask one or two in a soft, gentle voice. It's difficult to say whether she understood that the pair of eyes in front were looking slack-jawed at that pink face of hers.

Indeed, Mollika is worthy of honour, worthy of respect, worthy of praise. I can understand Mollika.

But Ghentu?

It's getting almost impossible to understand her. Where is the femininity within her, that she'll fall in love with a boy! And besides, who in the world is so pitiable that he'll even lift his eyes to look at her!

No, it must certainly be some worthless boy from her kite-flying or tabla-pounding gangs! How could the girl be saved now?

One day I seize her again.

I say, 'Here, you said you'd catch some monkey or gibbon and bring him over to show me – you didn't bring him?'

Ghentu says, somewhat sadly, 'No, he's ill.'

'Ill? What kind of illness?'

'What do I know. He says he has fever.'

Now this girl has created a major problem! Where she goes, what she does, who knows, baba! I say, 'Have you told your Ma?'

'Ma! What should I tell Ma?'

'All this. About this boy – '

Ghentu abandons her sadness and becomes suddenly inflamed. She says, 'Aha-ha, you just this moment dropped from paradise, didn't you! You don't know anything about the world, do you! If I tell her, your Boudi will feed me hard-boiled sweets!'

I grow serious and say, 'But this hiding and stealing around isn't good, Ghentu! And besides, those aren't your habits either.'

Ghentu becomes sad again. She says, 'It's not for nothing that my habits have changed this way. It's because he pleaded at my hands and feet. He said, if the people in the house find out, they won't let you come out any more. He said, when this illness is cured, I'll take you and run away and get married.'

I'm amazed more than it's possible to be amazed. No words come quickly to my mouth. Then I say in a disappointed voice, 'You'll run away and get married! Chhi chhi, Ghentu, you're a girl of our house, how can you say an abominable thing like that?'

Ghentu says in an unyielding voice, 'So what else will I do? If I don't run away, will you all let me marry him? Won't your prestige be damaged?'

I say gravely, 'That means you're friendly with a boy who will damage our prestige?'

'What wouldn't damage your prestige? If another wax doll like Didi had been born instead of me, that would have been good for you.'

It's my turn to be startled once more.

I'd thought she'd be envious of her sister, at least that was natural, but no – scorn! Does she consider Mollika inferior to herself? Should I laugh or cry!

But no, right now I had a duty, it wouldn't do to stray from my objective. I say, 'Tell me what his name is, or give me his address.'

'I'll tell you, baba, I'll tell you. If I tell, it's you I'll tell. But let me go now. I have to go get medicine from the pharmacy.'

'Medicine from the pharmacy! You'll go?'

'If I don't go, who'll bring it? How many servants does he have, let's hear?' Ghentu says this and springs away from me and leaves. Without letting me get ready. It occurs to me later that maybe I ought to have followed her. I should have observed what she was running around doing. But by then she had gone. God alone knew when and how Ghentu would smear ink on the face of our high lineage. Could that ink be obscured by Mollika's brilliance?

Who knows if it would have been obscured or not, but because of Mollika's brilliance our house suddenly begins to bustle! Truly we have had great hopes of Mollika, but this seems beyond our hopes.

An engineer son of Mejo-boudi's cousin, working somewhere in England or America, with some job that pays a terrifyingly fat salary, he has come back for three months to get married, and has asked for Mollika as his bride! And right after the wedding he will take his newly married bride and go away across the ocean.

Truly everyone in the house is so delighted we don't know what to do. She is the first girl in our family to go to college, but an in-laws' house across the ocean, such a rare girl is the first in our father's line, in our mother's line, in all our lines.

Preparations for such a rare wedding are not easy. Time and again the boundaries of our financial condition are crossed to make arrangements suitable to this bridegroom's glory. Maybe Bor-da does carp a little about the expenses, but he is floated away like a bit of straw in the ocean of Mej-da's and the women's powerfully flowing arguments.

Mej-di is a rich man's wife, she says haughtily, 'If there's no money,

I'll lend it to you. But it won't do to act as though this is some ordinary middle-class bridegroom.'

Right from Mollika's birth I've been hearing, we won't need a paisa for her wedding, they'll just take her away. . . . But it turned out that Mollika's wedding cost as much cash as it would take to get four girls across.

Bor-da says, 'And there's still another one, a Rokkhe-Kali hanging around my neck! It's her I'm anxious about.'

That comment is floated away on Mej-di's mocking laugh. Mej-di offers up the idiom 'neither will seven maunds of oil be burnt, nor will Radha dance'[5] and rolls over in laughter.

I don't hear anything in the house that is not related to shopping. That sport goes on ceaselessly. It goes on in the entire family. Mejo-boudi never enters into other people's affairs, but this time she too is interested. She's written to some people and had a Benarasi sent for the girl from Benaras, cloth for a suit for the groom from Kashmir.

In all this hobnobbing we've quite forgotten Ghentu. Whether she is at home, whether she's not, whether she eats or doesn't eat – no one pays any attention at all. Suddenly one day Ghentu comes and stands in the limelight.

The day before the wedding!

A terrible uproar arises in the house!

It seems that about a hundred rupees cannot be found in Mejo-boudi's purse. The money was Bor-da's, but Mejo-boudi had come back from the market and kept it with her. On a table in her own room.

Every layer of the world and the seven underworlds is turned upside down.

Simply because twenty-two or twenty-five thousand rupees are being spent on the girl's wedding, it isn't as though those hundred rupees can be waved away with 'it's gone, let it go'. After searching all places possible and impossible, the servants and workers are stopped. With his forceful cross-examination Mej-da sets about making them forget their fathers' names, and right at that time, with long strides, Ghentu makes her appearance from somewhere.

Her face dry, eyes sunken, her normally unkempt hair even more unkempt. The uncomely Ghentu seems the avatar of ugliness.

None of us acknowledges her presence or looks at her. What connection does she have, after all, to the house? Never do we take any notice of her, and she too never takes any notice of us. But today she herself comes and stands in the middle of our proceedings.

She says, 'What's going on here?'

Boro-boudi speaks out in a sharp tone, 'Here, the girl has appeared like the Kali of the burning-ground! Where were you all this time?'

'At the burning-ground!' she says and, turning her face towards me, asks, 'What, you're not telling me?'

I tell her what's happened.

Ghentu says in a calm voice contrary to her nature, 'How much money?'

'One hundred! A whole hundred rupees from Mejo-boudi's – '

Ghentu says in the same calm manner, 'There's no need to throw them out. I took the money from Mejo-kakima's table.'

A thunderbolt seems to strike the house.

'You took the money!'

'You!'

'You took it, and all this time we – '

Boro-boudi shouts out in a cutting voice, 'Why did you take so much money?'

'I won't tell.'

'Won't tell? Won't tell?' Boudi is enraged. 'The more I stay quiet, the greater your excesses become? Wicked, uncivilized girl! In the end you turned into a thief?'

Suddenly Ghentu wrinkles her brow like Mollika and says, 'That money is Baba's.'

'Ba! Ba! An excellent argument!' her Mejo-kaka says. 'It's Baba's money, so you can take it without asking?'

Ghentu ignores her Mejo-kaka completely and says, looking at Bor-da, 'If I were a good daughter of yours, Baba, then you would've had to spend money on my wedding! Just consider it gone from the same account.'

Once again a thunderbolt strikes the house! To say such a thing to her father's face! Chhi chhi, how shameless! How harsh, how distasteful!

Boro-boudi almost dances up and says, 'So it's okay to act that way? Hand over the money, I'm telling you!'

'There isn't any! It's been spent.'

'It's been spent! So much money, it's been spent! What did you do with all that money?'

'I'm telling you I won't tell.'

Mej-da says sarcastically, 'Fine, if it's inconvenient to tell, don't tell. But when you took it, it would have been a great favour to let us know! Then all these people wouldn't have been turned into thieves.'

Suddenly Ghentu laughs a quite un-Aryan laugh with that dry-as-wood face of hers. Then she says, 'I thought no one would notice if one pot's worth of water remained in the ocean or was removed. You all are spending twenty, twenty-five thousand for a glass case for a wax doll, and so a hundred rupees – '

With long strides Ghentu walks away into another room.

And in this room a storm of contempt begins to blow. Oh! What jealousy! What jealousy!

Didi's marrying well, there's going to be much pomp and ceremony at Didi's wedding, so out of jealousy she's completely lost all common sense!

But what did Ghentu do with all that money?

By unanimous opinion it is resolved that she must have secretly bought a sari or some jewellery.

Boro-boudi says with sharp distress, 'I'd thought that from the saris and jewellery Mollika's received, I'd give her some too. But no, I won't give her any. Chhi chhi, I'm so ashamed I want to put a rope around my neck! Such a lowering of one's head in front of the servants!'

And after all this time Mollika says only one thing, in a gentle, smooth voice, 'And still she acts as though she's not greedy for anything in the world.'

But even if everyone agrees that she is greedy, I am not able to.

Although I don't have the courage to admit it clearly and support her, I can't deny it either: compared to my older niece, that flawless creation of the expert Lord, it is this strange younger one, created by the unskilled Lord, that I love more.

And so, after the storm blows over, I go up to her and say, 'I haven't come to scold you, only to ask if someone has deceived you and taken the money.'

She lifts her sunken eyes to me and says, 'No.'

I stay quiet for a while, then say, 'I suppose you spent it for that boy's illness?'

Ghentu lowers her eyes and turns her face towards the window, then says in a very calm voice, with her head still turned, 'No, I didn't get it then. It was just today – ! I had to give it to his friends for the wood to burn and the other things they needed. Ten rupees for just some flowers and such – '

In my life I've had to face many distressing events; it was my conceit that shame never made me drop my eyes.

That conceit is destroyed.

With some pain, I say, 'Why didn't you tell me earlier, Ghentu?'

I think Ghentu is somewhat startled. Then she turns her head and says, 'I thought I would. But you all were so busy with wedding matters, I didn't find you alone even once. If only I'd got this money before! If I'd got it, maybe I would have been able to save him!'

Looking at her face, I cannot offer the spiritual truth that longevity cannot be bought with money. I keep my head lowered, trying to control my shame.

Ghentu is quiet for a while, then perhaps she smiles and says, 'Let it be, Chhot-ka, don't feel bad. In fact, it turned out well. You're all saved, otherwise I would have married a boy from a laundry shop and lowered your high heads, wouldn't I!'

Looking at her face with that unnatural smile drawn on it, I think, the one I've thought foolish, all this time – is that really true?

Earth Sky

আকাশমাটি

Akashmati[1]

The stomach of the bag was near bursting point, but Rojoni forced it shut with his body weight as he tugged at the zipper and closed the bag.

Rojoni Dhor, the famous Borua Tea Company's not-so-famous employee.

Almost all of whose life has been spent in this sparsely inhabited forest-shaded countryside settlement in the Assam valley! Wood-and-bamboo huts spaced far apart give this the title of 'village'. When Rojoni first arrived here, it was almost a jungle. By the grace of the company, there is now electric lighting, and a road to the city fit for motor vehicles. The company's built a shed over a large swath of land, to clean and sort and pack tea.

The shed and all the rest of it were built in front of Rojoni's eyes. It began with only a handful of thatched huts; at that time, when you went walking, a glossy fat black snake might slide over your foot, and ten days in a month you'd have to lie in bed with blood dysentery. And much else happened that was not in the least favourable to living there. But still, Rojoni Dhor had stuck on, the way a slender tree will endure many gusts and storms and stick on.

The day that mother-and-father-less Rojoni suffered a beating at his kaka's hands for some trivial reason and ran away from home in disgust and sorrow, he had been no more than thirteen or fourteen. It is unnecessary to add that his schooling came to an end at that time. How Rojoni – wandering recklessly on foot and travelling ticketless on trains with no clear destination – came to be the packing-master of this Borua Tea Company, that history is like a fiction. But Rojoni did not become detached from the life of his home village; he did not let himself become detached. As soon as he grew into a man, meaning he was able to gather the money to pay his fare to Calcutta, he came and presented himself right at his kaka's house in Sheoraphuli.

There's a mystery!

The place he had left vowing 'I'll never enter here in my life again', he entered there first of all, upon first becoming an earning man. There was no one there he could feel inwardly drawn to. But why that home-leaving youth's inner soul decided to come back to strike its head against that many-miles-distant, crumbling-plaster brick wall, who knows!

But many years had passed when Rojoni came and stood at the door to that broken house again: from thirteen he had arrived at twenty-three.

When the formerly lost and aimless Rojoni, face dry and grey with dust, khaki shirt and pants deprived of a washerman's beatings, made his dramatic appearance without notice, the person who had beaten him earlier was gone to the land of the eternally lost.

His khuri had opened the door. His khuri, in a plain, borderless sari. At first, both had been surprised and had stepped back two feet. She hadn't recognized him. Then Rojoni collapsed in the courtyard and howled and cried – for the dead Oboni Dhor; and in the end it was his khuri who consoled him and helped him stand up.

Rojoni had to leave after staying only about ten days, because the company allowed him only those few days of vacation every year. But even after he left, Rojoni didn't really leave, every month he sent his khuri a money order for five rupees and thus kept himself established in that broken house in Sheoraphuli.

But all this happened a long time ago.

After that Rojoni has come back many times. His khuri has treated him with love and affection, and she has married him off to a distant niece of hers and made a family man of her nephew. She pleaded repeatedly with him to leave Assam and find a job in Bangla-desh,[2] and in the end she died one day.

After getting that letter, Rojoni cried for his khuri also, sitting in that low room shadowed by wood and bamboo. But he wasn't able to fulfil his khuri's plea – he couldn't find a job in Bangla-desh. There, only those ten days a year.

For that, Rojoni counts the days for ten months. Ten nights before coming, he can't sleep. This middle-aged Rojoni, the hairs on whose head have all yielded their lives to his bald pate, and the hairs on whose chest frequently laugh a white laugh – he too experiences a youngster's great excitement at the thought of coming home.

In the meantime, there have been the usual four or so children born to Rojoni, and the two boys have found jobs for themselves. The older daughter is married. And at the time of her marriage, Rojoni had, as an exception to his usual practice, taken leave at a different time of the year and come to attend. He told his wife, 'It's nothing else, you're a resourceful woman, I know you could have arranged the wedding very efficiently, but – I hear giving away your daughter in marriage carries as much virtue as giving away the whole world, so I came.'

His wife, Shurobala, said in sharp rebuke, 'Only for that?'

Rojoni laughed in an embarrassed fashion and said, 'Aha, don't you see, it's you who's doing everything.'

That was true. Shurobala had done everything. Had sat in the middle of that broken heap in Sheoraphuli and raised four boys and girls, had separated out her share of the house and kitchen from her distant brother-in-law after asserting her familial claim, had settled on a groom for her daughter, and by lending some money on interest had even got two paisas in her hand.

How could she not?

Whom else could she lean on, apart from herself? In all her life she hadn't found even a bunch of straw to lean on. At first, every time Rojoni came, Shurobala would insist that he take her back with him, the nights of togetherness were frequently tarnished with tiffs and sulks and tears, but where could Rojoni take his young wife, take his newborn child? Was that a place you could take anyone?

The impatient Rojoni tried repeatedly to explain that to the inconsolable Shurobala. He described the terrible surroundings of the place and how he was able to stay there only because he was a man – and gained a little self-satisfaction from telling her that.

Gradually that inconsolable sorrow has lessened, has been extinguished; since her khur-shashuri died, she's been won over by her independence and the savour of her household world. Among her rice and grains, her cows and calves, her plants, her ducks and her fish, she is the paramount ruler and, it can be said, is thoroughly satisfied.

It's also a matter of special satisfaction to be able to show this achievement of hers to her annual visitor, Rojoni. The household of her khur-shoshur's son had been a battered pot scraped bare; and the reason why Rojoni Dhor's household world had done so well – surely Shurobala was at the root of that? Rojoni had spent most of his life away from home, and yet the way she had built up the household wasn't bad at all. The expert manner in which she handled the responsibilities of that world – the two sons had not grown up illiterate, the two daughters had not grown up brazen, she had not had to rely on anyone else's money or strength even for a day – was that any small achievement?

Rojoni comes and is enchanted, is astonished, is also a little abashed.

He does send money, it's true, sends it regularly, but how much money is that? It cannot yield so much prosperity; that has come by virtue of Shurobala's industrious nature, her keen intelligence, and her boundless ability to work.

So what can he do anyway?

The dice of Rojoni's life have fallen thus, and he moves his pieces accordingly. But still . . . even though he is a little abashed, how pleasing are those days when he receives hospitality in his own home! They seem to reach out and draw Rojoni in with a thousand arms.

And so for ten nights before coming, Rojoni cannot sleep. In the middle of the night he climbs down the steps from his wooden platform house and wanders a little, *thock-thock*ing with his stick. The powerful lure of a spotless bed, a soft pillow, and a face marked by a household's ordeals beckon to him and make him restless.

Those ten days of the year Rojoni sleeps on a proper bed, and here? Ram be praised, is this any kind of bed?

A cheap Manipuri khesh and a pillow covered in oil-spotted ticking – that is all. Until the day they wear thin and finally rip, they are not dipped in water nor hung out in the sun.

And the food?

Better not to talk about that either.

A pot is hung from a nail in the wooden wall, on it the black soot of a lifetime spent on a wood fire; it descends once at the end of the day, and rice and chicken are boiled together with a mixture of salt, red pepper, and turmeric powder, and that's it. There are no cooking duties at night. The lorry driver Boshir Sheikh makes rutis, and there is an arrangement to share with him.

If he doesn't have the energy, he can only fast.

This is life!

In this manner Rojoni Dhor has reached the age of fifty-eight years.

And so it's not possible to wait even until the morning of his vacation. As soon as his work hours are over, that very night he sets out. It's bothersome to take five different bags; that one canvas bag is Rojoni's all. It contains everything. But then, what is there that he can call his own? A couple of vests, a pair of pajamas or a lungi, that is all. What fills the stomach of the bag to bursting point is packets of tea. Along with the vacation, as a bonus he gets five pounds of tea. And from here and there he collects another two or three pounds. And on top of that are the oranges from the tree that Rojoni's planted with his own hands.

Just because the place is Assam, that's no reason to think that the oranges are top quality, but there's this advantage, the tree does bear fruit all year round. And so even for these Pujo holidays Rojoni takes oranges – sour and small – from the tree.

With the bag in his hand Rojoni peers into Boshir's hut. 'Boshir, for ten days your rutis can take a break.'

Boshir smiles a cheekful, toothless smile and says, 'Go, Shahab, come back refreshed after eating rice and fish curry made by your wife's hand.'

Rojoni leaves.

Boshir sighs.

There's no way for him to return to his land. There, three summonses in his name are waiting. Rojoni's shape vanishes from view; Boshir thinks, his two sons are supposed to have come of age. Who knows if his own son is living or if he's died.

Rojoni knows the story of Boshir's life. He knows he's an absconding criminal, but still he doesn't dislike him. Rather, he feels compassion. He thinks, aha, the man wanders around during the holidays. Can't go home even once. Isn't able to taste heavenly contentment.

Rojoni has heaven in his fist.

Rojoni opened that fist.

He lowered the bag near the door and rattled the door-ring and called out, 'Anyone there?'

And then, heaven's throne!

The older son runs to get sweets, the younger son sits down to cut open a green coconut, the younger daughter starts fanning him, the married, older daughter, who is here on the occasion of the Pujo, she goes to stuff wood into the dying clay oven. And Shurobala, with her face that has a household's experience marked on it, smiles a sweet smile, and says, 'Same as always, no letter before you arrive!'

Rojoni laughs an overwhelmed laugh and says, 'I'm coming to my own house, what's the need to write about that?'

'Aha! Now that you're here unexpectedly, you'll have to eat rice with burnt brinjal. I never know for sure – '

It's true.

Even though it's ten days on the calendar, the lunar dates aren't the same every time.[3]

Having sat down to eat, the emperor Rojoni smiles another overwhelmed smile.

He says, 'Now look, you tried to scare me with talk of rice and burnt brinjal – but what's all this here? I can see you've arranged a feast for a great occasion, all in one hour!'

The statement, though an exaggeration, isn't altogether a lie; within an hour the efficient and industrious Shurobala, with the help of her elder daughter, has served rice along with five dishes. Certainly it's not merely the expertness of her limbs; there's the expertness of her brain as well. I think that's primary. Lighting the wood in two ovens on two sides, and putting spinach and vegetables in with the rice, Shurobala has cooked a dish with those boiled vegetables and arranged them on the plate. Along with that she's given him the cream from the household cow's milk, and ghee from that cream, pressed mango preserves, champa bananas, and pickled jujubes and lemons. The eggs of Shurobala's pet duck have made up for the lack of fish.

Such kingly arrangements, apparently without any preparation.

Rojoni wants to show all this to Boshir Sheikh. And he doesn't consider himself any less than the emperor of the world.

As usual, towards the evening the neighbours come to visit him in ones and twos. Relatively elderly neighbours. The younger ones are too proud. They don't come to visit him on their own. They believe that the one who comes from outside, it is *his* duty to visit them.

The elders' curiosity is stronger than their pride, so they come and make an occasion of it. They say, 'So, Rojoni, what have you decided?'

Rojoni is startled and says, 'Anh, what are you saying?'

'I'm saying, your younger son too has learnt to bring two paisas into the home, the older son does so already, why should you remain in that godforsaken place any longer? Now come and stay in your village, do your household duties!'

The proposal seems like a sweet dream to Rojoni. He looks in all four directions. Lately Shurobala has had the house cleaned and repaired; there are pictures of gods and deities and great personages on every wall, a white sheet is laid out on the cot. On this cot, propping himself on a pillow, Rojoni sits and talks with five gentlemen. At this time, in the evening. When Rojoni usually returns from work and sits dozing. And because he doesn't feel like making tea, half the time he doesn't drink any.

The fragrance of newly bloomed shiulis seems to pervade everything. The leaves of the neem tree in the courtyard rustle in the breeze. At the edge of the terrace the gentle moon of the shukla fifth[4] has drawn a line of light, and this sky and breeze, tree and earth, even the wall of Ma's room seem to spread an enchanting web of love and plead with Rojoni, 'Stay, stay!'

Suddenly he thinks, it's true, really, what need does Rojoni have to leave this paradise and go? What need does he have to remain in that distant, foreign land? Here he'll get his coarse rice and clothes by the grace of his sons. Why else do people pray for their sons to grow up?

At the thought of coarse rice and clothes, suddenly Rojoni wants to laugh. He recalls the appearance of that eternally soot-faced pot of his, hanging from the nail on the wall.

Coarse rice and clothes!

Aha, what fine stuff he lives on, on his own!

He nods and says, 'That's what I'm thinking, why not, really? Now that the Lord's helped them stand on their own – '

The older son commutes to work every day. Right then he comes home from the station. Hearing the end of the conversation, he says, 'We've decided too that Baba won't be allowed to leave any more – '

Won't let you go!

Won't let you go!

The sky, the air, the water, the earth, the people, all are calling out, 'Won't let you go.'

At night Shurobala too says the same thing.

'I'm not letting you go any more.'

The boys are grown up, one daughter's married, but still Shurobala breaks with her sense of delicacy and comes to sleep in his room. The heart that's starved for three hundred and fifty-five days is unable to sit with food before it and boast of self-restraint. And apart from that, when can she talk about things except at night?

During the day, for one thing there's no end to her work, and on top of that all the people of the village overflow with love, saying

'Rojoni', 'Rojoni'. And Rojoni cannot but reciprocate. He loses all sense of time and keeps on talking. And when he says goodbye, he wraps some tea-leaves in paper and gives it to them. The tea, collected from here and there, is put to good use this way. He stays honest in his own judgement. He's not drinking it himself, is he!

Shurobala says, 'You handed it out to the whole village and finished it, now I suppose there's none left in the house?'

Rojoni laughs out loud. 'I haven't touched the five packets of your share, dear. Drink as much as you want.'

Neither of them goes anywhere near polished or witty language, the conversation is extremely simple and not oblique in any way, but still there are these gestures within it. Shurobala says with her eyes, 'Aha, am I saying that only for myself?'

At night, too, Shurobala uses the same language. 'Aha, as if I'm saying it only for myself. I'm saying, look at yourself, you've remained in the jungle all your life, you've never known what worldly contentment means – don't you think I feel bad about that?'

Rojoni lies on that white bedsheet, on a soft pillow, with one hand resting on Shurobala; the gusts from the fringed fan in Shurobala's hand come and play on his face and head; Rojoni's eternally deprived inner soul, now heartened, stares hopefully at Rojoni's face. Rojoni says, 'Na, I've decided I won't go anymore.'

'Joy guru, hé Ma Kali, Baba Bishshonath!' Shurobala presses her two palms together and touches her hands to her forehead and says, 'You've saved me! I've prayed to my guru night and day that good sense may prevail on you. I said, "Hé guru, let there be no stain on your name."'

Rojoni takes Shurobala's two hands – hard as wood from all her labours – and says, in as kind a tone as is possible for him, 'Why do you say good sense, my good bou, do you think I stay there because I want to, in that worthless place not fit for humans, far from my home and village, my father's homestead and my motherland? I didn't learn to read and write enough to work in an office, whatever I got – '

Shurobala, too, brings as much affection into her voice as she can and says, 'Aha, don't you think I know that? That's why I didn't say anything all this time. But now that God has granted you some good days – '

That is true! God has granted him some good days! Granted him good days!

Rojoni, too, melts with gratitude at God's infinite kindness.

Now Rojoni is free! A bird with its wings unbound! Get up as late as I want, bathe, eat whenever I want – is there any greater happiness in the world?

When he gets up in the morning, the earth seems a hundred times as bright. Honey spills down from the breeze! Freedom's melody sounds through the sky, in the air, in the body and mind! What contentment! What delight! Never again in his life will Rojoni have to pluck down that grimy black pot from its nail in the wooden wall, he won't have to puff at the smoky fire. Won't have to peek and peer into Boshir's haunt whenever he's hungry and sleepy, won't have to call out, 'Where are you, Boshir Mian, is it done?'

This house, this courtyard, that bin of grain, that cow in its shed, these sons and daughters, this wife, all Rojoni's. Rojoni is the overlord of all this. Hungry and deprived all his life, Rojoni Dhor can now partake of all this, at length and at ease.

Rojoni can now give that zippered bag to Shurobala for her use. He won't have to stuff his vests and lungi, his coat and clothes into it while furtively wiping the tears from his eyes.

Yes, stuffing them in: while going back from here, too, he has to stuff. The bag is loaded with Shurobala's loving gifts. Afterwards, Rojoni's heart grows sad as he eats those sweetened rice narus, pressed-rice sweets, mango preserves, coconut chhaba-cakes; he thinks his life is utterly detestable.

Today, too, Rojoni feels a sense of hatred as he thinks about that past left behind and its circumstances.

The man who stands in front of Boshir Sheikh's hut wearing a dirty lungi and tearing pieces from a ruti and eating it with onion gravy from a bowl held in his palm – is that Rojoni? Oboni Dhor's nephew, the current head of the Dhor household, Rojoni Dhor?

This is the man for whom a pujo has been conducted at the temple, that he might stay in this house awhile, and for whom arrangements are being made for a sweet-offering on the next Kojagori[5] day. Is Rojoni so precious? The packing-master of the Borua Tea Company, the inglorious Rojoni Dhor! And he had not known of this value of his.

The boys are successful, and the credit for that is Shurobala's, it's true, but they were all prepared, with the ceremonial offerings ready in their hearts, to serve Rojoni!

The older son, Debu, says every day, 'Baba's worked so hard all these years, now I want to give him a little relief.' Where will Rojoni put the weight of this relief, its contentment?

He proclaims it from neighbourhood to neighbourhood: 'This time, bhai, I've beaten my job with a broom. It's enough; no more. Just look at the way Rojoni Dhor's spent this long life of his. If you'd seen it, you'd have said, yes, he's truly a brave man.'

On their golden wings the birds of the days fly on.

'Baba, the resignation letter – .' The older son reminds him morning and evening.

'Yes, yes.' – In the end Rojoni comes out with the truth of the matter. 'You can understand how learned and capable I am, baba, and whatever little I used to know, I've stirred it up and swallowed it down. If you can, maybe a draft – '

Oh ho, that's right, isn't it!

His son writes it out neatly, with the right words. Rojoni's body has broken down completely from having lived so long in an unhealthy place, and so he truly wishes to spend the rest of his life in his own village, in his own household. Therefore, could the company do Rojoni this great kindness and relieve him of his work. At the end of the letter he mentions the company's benevolence, generosity, munificence, etc., along with asking forgiveness for his own ingratitude, and sets down his closing salutations.

Even after listening to it twice Rojoni is astonished and fascinated. 'Read it again, let me hear it one more time?'

Rojoni's quiet, polite, and virtuous son reads it again, slowly.

Tears of joy come to Rojoni's eyes. He signs his name with carefully formed letters and says, 'Yes, this is the virtue of knowledge! How good was that language! The snake died, and the stick didn't break. The company got its flattery, and yet – ogo, did you hear the letter?'

Shurobala smiles gently and says, 'I don't have to hear it. Who gave your learned son the idea anyway?'

Rojoni stares open-mouthed at the originator of the idea.

Putting the letter in his pocket, Debu sets out for the station; it's better to drop it off at a large post-office in Calcutta, it'll get there quicker. Without his having done anything much, the days of vacation are drawing to an end. The letter should reach them before Rojoni's appointed date of return.

The younger son says, 'Let's see if the company lets you go now!'

Rojoni says in an obstinate voice, 'What do you mean they won't let me go? Am I a bought servant? Or is it a tyrant's kingdom? What if my body can't keep up any more? What if I myself don't want to be a slave forever? Now that God has given me a few days – '

In her mind Shurobala acknowledges her part in the 'given days' and says quickly, 'Here, come have some tea.'

'I just had some.'

'That's fine, now you're a retired householder, you can do what you want,' Shurobala says and smiles that special smile.

But Shurobala doesn't seem to have made the tea all that well. It's bitter somehow. He doesn't feel like drinking all of it. Has to push it aside. The whistle of the train can be heard from the house; at the sound, the agitated Rojoni thinks, the train's leaving, I hope the letter hasn't fallen out of Debu's pocket? . . . That would be a disaster! The letter won't reach, and Rojoni won't reach either. . . . Maybe it hasn't fallen from his pocket, but letters do get stolen sometimes? What if that happens?

He could have gone to the station with Debu, warned him to be more careful.

As the afternoon grows long, Rojoni's anxiety about the letter grows along with it. What if it doesn't reach? The company would see that his vacation was over, yet Dhor-babu hadn't returned. Ish, that would be extremely shameful!

The anxiety in his mind spills out.

Shurobala says, 'Why are you driving yourself crazy? He said he'd drop it off at the main post office.'

But if a man's already gone completely crazy, what recourse does he have?

Towards evening, the measure of his anxiety grows so strong that Rojoni cannot even swallow the green-coconut water. He lets his body go limp, when he speaks his voice quivers, and in the end, with that quivering voice he says it right out:

'Look, I've thought it over, it's not right to resign by just dashing off a letter. I should really go there once – '

'Go there once!'

Shurobala stands still like a lightning-struck tree and says, 'Where will you go?'

'Where else? Where I spent all my days!' Rojoni says in a vexed tone. 'The idea was wrong, really. A long-time employer, and to come away like this, without seeing them, without explaining to them – no, chhi chhi! That was very bad.'

Shurobala, too, knows how to be vexed.

She too says in a bitter voice, 'But you're not leaving right away, are you? Let Debu come back. See what he says.'

Debu'll come back, what he'll say – if he waits in hope for that, will the train stand still for him? At this childish remark of Shurobala's Rojoni smiles a slightly mocking smile and says, 'Is the train my servant? Hand me my clothes, will you – o ré Kajol, see where my bag is – '

Kajol brings in the bag and says with a hand to her cheek, 'Baba, are you crazy?'

'Just look at that! Why should I be crazy?' Rojoni pulls open the zipper of the bag.

Shurobala says in a voice of thunder, 'You can't go until Debu comes back.'

The next instant Rojoni flares up.

It seems as though these people are plotting to get him into trouble. And Rojoni may be stupid, but he's not so stupid that anyone can make him do whatever they want. So he says in an angry voice, 'Debu's not my guardian.'

The stomach of the bag is slack, unfastened.

The zipper is easy to pull; Rojoni stands up and says, 'So then I'm leaving, explain it to Debu when he comes. Just five or six days to go there and come back, that's all – '

Shurobala does not speak. Kajol says, 'But there's a long time before the train leaves, and to go this way, without eating anything – '

'Eating's not a problem! Eating's not a problem – !' The impatient Rojoni says quickly, 'I've fasted so many times, this is nothing, I'll eat at Shealdah station. You're saying there's a long time, but from here I have to go to Howrah, and then from there to Shealdah.'

Whichever way he gets there, Rojoni sits down in the train and seems to sigh in relief! Oh, he'd got away just in time! If Debu had come back –

Baba, with what ties they'd been tying him, with their temptations and wheedling! How lucky!

These fields and docks, these houses and homes, the station, the cinema halls that had spread a hundred thousand arms these past few days and embraced Rojoni and held him, their arms have grown loose. Rojoni thinks, astonished, what spell had they cast to make such a fool of him, to get him so entranced by such an illusory plan, that he would put his signature on such a dreadful document.

To think that Rojoni would never go back again to that platform house on a field in the Assam valley, that he wouldn't wander around in that vast, dense, green jungle – nothing could be more illusory than that, he thinks.

Let that be; maybe he would reach before the letter did. As soon as he got there, he would inquire at the post office, and if indeed the letter had arrived, he would go to the owners and fall at their hands and feet and say, 'Sir, that rascal younger son of fine forged my signature to play this prank on me.'

And in Sheoraphuli?

Rojoni doesn't worry about that.

Even if Rojoni doesn't have the knowledge to make a draft of a company letter, he doesn't need to be taught the language other letters are written in.

He'll only write and tell them, the company's not at all willing to let him go, the owners are falling at his hands and feet. It seems their business cannot go on without Rojoni Dhor. And so he is forced to take the yoke upon his shoulders again. He feels bad that he wasn't able to see anyone before he left –

Now at least he's free for another year!

This World

এই পৃথিবী

Ei Prithibi

When the call 'Doctor-babu, Doctor-babu' comes at midnight, the people in the doctor's household are not thrilled and delighted – even if no one else knows this fact, they know it very well. It's not enough that behind the call is the faint presence of money.

Hearing such a call, the doctor's mother can burn with anger, can easily say, 'Enemies, all enemies! They won't let my child live.'

The doctor's wife can easily say, about the patient, 'Couldn't find any other time to die except in the middle of the night!'

And the doctor's daughter can go up to the caller and wrinkle her brow and say, 'Baba isn't well, he just lay down, how can I call him now, tell me?'

Can say all this, even ignoring the possibility of the clink of money.

But in a case where there's no such possibility at all?

Then?

What level does the heat of irritation, the meter of anger reach?

Looking at the face of Srimoti Durgaboti, Doctor Boshak's wife, at least, one feels that a meter won't suffice, the thermometer will burst.

But she'll have to suppress this powerful rage and sit quietly; she can't utter the slightest cheep. Because this midnight's destroyer-of-the-peace is Doctor Boshak's heart's friend Shudhakanto's elder son, Shukanto.

Shukanto doesn't call him Doctor-babu, he calls him Kaka-babu.

But does he call only once or twice?

No, otherwise hearing 'Kaka-babu' wouldn't make Durga's bones burn this way. This is almost a casual, daily event.

Shudhakanto's wife has a heart ailment, suddenly at any time she's at the point of death, and generally it's in the middle of the night that she's at that point. Therefore Shukanto has to come running sleepy-eyed, and he has to shout from under the window, 'Kaka-babu! Kaka-babu!'

It's true he doesn't have to run very far; the doctor's house is only five or six houses away from Shudhakanto Shen's. The Shudhakanto who is the doctor's childhood friend.

As soon as he hears 'Kaka-babu', the doctor sits up. Because his sleep is easily broken. And Durga's sleep is no deep sleep either. She too wakes up. Doctor Boshak says, 'Someone seems to be calling – '

Durga says, 'No one new! Your Shudha's son. I suppose his wife's death is again imminent. Astonishing, hard as wood, her life-force! Doesn't ever die!'

The doctor says in an angry voice, 'Why? Will you benefit from her death? If she stays alive, does that plough up your ripe paddy-field?'

'You can't say it doesn't. Look, she attacks you regardless of day or night – '

'She has, and she will. Everyone will attack the doctor-babu!'

'Maybe you're a saint, joy and sadness don't matter to you. But this daily destruction of my sleep is making me ill – '

'Your Baba should have thought of that when he picked a doctor bridegroom. Astonishing, they say women are affectionate, caring. If Shudha's wife dies, what'll happen to their household, have you ever thought about that?'

Still Durga doesn't budge.

She grows desperate. So she descends to argument even as she sees the doctor rushing down the stairs. She follows behind and says, 'How is she even alive? She's dead already. What use is she to the household?'

The doctor's answer to this cannot be heard; he goes down swiftly.

The doctor's mother bawls out from her room, 'Bou-ma, o Bou-ma, did Noni go out again?'

Durga says in an annoyed tone, 'He did.'

'Aha, this kills me, he just lay down – who now, from where – '

'Who else and from where else? Shudha-babu's boy.'

'That's what I thought. What can I say, Bou-ma, if I say anything you all will think, the old woman's a schemer. But this wife of Shudha's, she's a drama! A full twelve annas[1] of that ailment of hers is for show! . . . Just this morning I was coming back from my bath in the Gonga, I see she's called the vendor and is standing at the door haggling to buy fabric for clothes. What could have happened now in such a short time!'

'Ask your son what happened.' Durga says this and goes to her room and lies down.

And the doctor's sixteen-year-old daughter, lying in bed, stays awake and thinks, Certainly Baba must have had a special something for that wife of Shudha-jetha's when he was young. Or else why is he so drawn to her!

Whatever that girl, precocious from reading novels, may think, that isn't the fact of the matter. Shudhakanto is a childhood friend of Noni-doctor's, dear as his life. Shudha's wife's being ill is the same as his own wife's being ill. As though if Shudhakanto's wife died, Noni-doctor's world would break down.

Ever since Noni Boshak graduated as a doctor, he's been the fixed doctor for Shudhakanto's household. Shudha's father suffered and suffered and died; one sister suffered for five years before she recovered. The boys and girls suffered all twelve months of the year when they were younger. And Noni-doctor has suffered the burden of everyone's suffering.

Earlier, Shudhakanto used to come himself; now grown up, the older son has taken the weight of the father's work upon his own shoulders.

But of course the grown-up son cannot take on the weight of the doctor's work! So even though Noni is almost the same age as Shudhakanto, he has to take on the role of a young man.

Even at midnight he has to walk the distance past five houses in a minute.

When Doctor Boshak returned that night, it was almost dawn.

Durga had been thinking, so today the final hour has really arrived. She felt some fear too. Today I came right out and said very plainly – she should die! She was dying anyway, and she will die, but now I seem to share the responsibility for it!

The doctor returned towards the end of the night.

The doctor's mother called out in a broken-sounding voice, 'Bou-ma, o Bou-ma, did Noni come back?'

Bou-ma didn't respond.

Bou-ma lay feigning sleep. Right then she didn't have the courage to face her husband.

But it didn't take long for her fear to break.

She could hear her shashuri's son's reply.

'Yes, I'm just coming in – '

'So how is she? Making a huge fuss?'

'No – oh, the usual, you know – .' The doctor's voice was dull, tired. 'You know how anxious Shudha is, don't you? Gradually it seems to be turning into a mania. If he sees just a little something, he gets agitated, makes a big commotion – '

Durga thinks it's nothing else, just 'when the reasons are lacking, you have to keep on talking'. All his wife's ailments have exhausted the poor man, and so now he needs to make a big show.

She stands her ears up again; her shashuri is saying, 'So, why did you turn the night into dawn before coming back, baba? You could have slept an hour or two?'

'Oh, don't ask!' The doctor's voice grows even more dull and tired. '"I won't live, I'll die right now" – and weeping and wailing – '

'Go, go, at least lie down a little, go – ,' Ma says, and maybe she herself resorts to the bed again, to do that very same thing.

Durga doesn't utter a word or make a sound. Durga is quite unconscious in her sleep.

Durga thinks, Now one day I'll make him swear upon my head, he won't go at night any more. A friend's wife will cry 'I'm dying' and let loose a stream of self-indulgent weeping and wailing, and he has to stay up night after night and kill himself?

But all this anger and acrimony of Durga's isn't much use. Because on this subject, Noni-doctor is firm, immovable.

Even if they don't call him about her excessive illness, on his comings and goings he often stops at his friend's door. Whether Shudhakanto is at home or not, he calls out, 'Shudha, are you in?'

One of the boys or girls comes out, and Noni-doctor says, 'How's your mother, ré?'

Maybe they say, 'A little better.'

Maybe they say, 'About the same.'

The doctor comes back home. And he thinks, 'Maybe if this medicine takes hold – '

He thinks, 'No, I should change the medicine.'

When he returns, Durga says, 'Have the flower-offerings been made at the goddess's feet?'

The doctor laughs and says, 'How jealous women are!'

Durga says, 'If anyone hears about Shudha-babu's wife's illness, her condition, and the history of her treatment, they'll never think of you as a doctor again. A doctor who's kept a patient hanging for eleven years, how is he a doctor?'

The doctor laughs.

He says, 'If the patient paid me by the visit, then people would say I'd deliberately kept her hanging. For a doctor, a heart patient is as good as a landed estate!'

Durga says in her mind, 'If you were paid by the visit, your friend's family would have recovered long ago.'

She doesn't say it out loud.

The smiling doctor, he'll think his friend and his friend's family have been insulted and quickly turn solemn.

This is the doctor's one weakness.

No one in his household can stand to look with their two eyes at this affectation of illness by Shudhakanto's wife – this the doctor knows. And so if any remarks about them seem to go a little this way or that, he decides they've been insulted.

And the fact is, he's a doctor, he understands that a full twelve annas of the illness is exaggeration, and that's what he tries his utmost to defend.

And over there, Shudhakanto's wife is always extremely sensitive!

If the doctor is called in the morning and he comes not in the morning but a little later, she'll be so offended and angry that at first she won't even talk to him straight.

Then she starts. 'This miserable woman, this curse on the world, she doesn't ever die! The doctor's given up in disgust, and still she wants to live!'

Noni-doctor has to offer solace. Meaning, he has to change the medication.

But certainly Shudhakanto is not ungrateful.

Whenever they meet, he says, 'You were there, that's the only reason your boudi can still share in the earth's light and air.'

Noni-doctor laughs and slaps his friend on the back and says, 'Enough, that's plenty of your smart remarks.'

Shudhakanto's boys say, 'What would have happened if Kaka-babu hadn't been there!'

The doctor laughs and says, 'Tell me, what would have happened? The ocean would have risen up to the sky, and the mountains would sink down into the underworld?'

Shudhakanto's girls say, 'As long as Kaka-babu's around, it doesn't seem like there's anything like sickness or grief in the world – '

The doctor laughs out loud and says, 'It's those two things that we deal with, that's why we sprinkle some earth on them[2] and keep them covered up.'

But what the girls say is no great exaggeration. Improving the climate of the patient's home is a major remedy – this is a principle in which Noni-doctor believes.

That's why he takes the burden into his own hands of lightening the climate with entertaining conversation.

And he's successful too.

A man clever in speech, jolly by nature, with entertaining conversation he truly does lighten the heavy air of the patient's home.

This morning, too, he sat in that house chitchatting for almost an hour. At that time Mrs Shen had rolled over in laughter at his speech and gestures. . . .

And suddenly this very night –

Yes, at night Shukanto's anxious, overwhelmed voice comes and throws itself at the doctor's door: 'Kaka-babu! Kaka-babu!'

Not in the middle of the night, but early in the night.

Doctor Boshak has not returned yet. He's sent word that he'll be very late, a patient might or might not live!

For one thing, everyone's heard that it'll be very late before he returns, and now on top of that, this annoying ever-familiar call for that spoilt-rotten patient.

Durga herself comes down.

She says, 'What's happened now?'

'She's about to go, she seems in very bad shape,' the agitated Shukanto says. 'Please send him as soon as he comes. Before he takes off his shoes – '

It goes without saying that Durga loses her patience.

Or else she's come down after losing her patience.

So she says in a sharp tone, 'Is your mother's life the only life there is? No one else's life is a life in the universe?'

Hit by so many arrows of 'life' at once, Shukanto is perhaps disconcerted and says, 'What are you saying?'

'I'm saying, is the patient the only one who needs to be saved? Is there no need for the doctor to survive? The man went out at such an early hour of the morning, and he still isn't back. There's no eating, there's no drinking for him, and now you're telling me to send him even before he takes his shoes off! – There's such a thing as compassion, isn't there?'

This time Shukanto makes no mistake in understanding. He isn't disconcerted either. He says calmly, 'I come here only because I'm helpless, Kakima! If you see Ma's condition – '

Today the doctor isn't home.

Today Durga has found the matter in her grasp. So even that statement doesn't embarrass her. She says in a dry voice, 'What's there to be so helpless about? Are there no other doctors in the universe? Your Kaka-babu hasn't been able to cure the patient in all this time – '

Shukanto doesn't listen to the end of that. With the question of whether there were any other doctors in the universe, he's sprung away and landed on the street.

It wasn't as though Durga didn't feel some fear. Still, she hardened her mind and thought, All right! If they get a little angry, that's fine. We'll be saved.

That they were truly angered, that was evident after only a little while. When Doctor Boshak was returning home after killing a patient and signing his death certificate.

It was one o'clock at night then.

It wasn't Shudhakanto who came to call, it wasn't any of his children, it was a household servant.

Maybe it was at seeing the servant's being sent, or maybe it was fatigue after a long tug-of-war between Jom[3] and man, after which he had to admit defeat at the hands of Jom; the doctor said in an aggrieved voice, 'What a bother you are! Now it's Ma's excesses again? Go tell them, Kaka-babu just came back, he's very *tired*[4] – ah, tired – he can't come now, he'll come in the morning.'

The servant went away.

He went without saying anything at all.

And right then Noni-doctor thought, Damn it, it would've been better not to send him back! I should have gone and looked at her while I had these clothes on.

But now he couldn't go. Durga was standing there and had heard everything.

And besides, his body really seemed to be breaking down.

That foolish doctor, that Noni-doctor who was so utterly ignorant about the world, had he thought then that his ordinary 'body breaking down' would lead to the breaking down of the dream mansion he'd built over the course of his entire life? That it would crumble into dust?

He hadn't thought of that.

But it did.

The doctor's eternal 'Shudha' was somehow transformed into poison by the chemistry of that one failing!

When Noni-doctor ran to that house the next morning, before even the light of dawn had bloomed, Shudhakanto didn't come down from the second storey. Nor did the oldest son, Shukanto. The oldest daughter, Shubochona, came down and, with a heavy face, said in a bitter voice, 'Ma has taken a sleeping medicine and is asleep – now there's no need!'

A sleeping medicine!

The doctor fell from the sky.

There was no sleeping medicine that he had prescribed for her. Without knowing, without understanding, what sleeping medicine had Shudha gone and fed her – a heart patient!

The peculiar nature of Shubochona's manner of speech didn't strike the doctor's ear; he said, concerned, 'Now where did he find a sleeping medicine? What medicine did he suddenly go and give her?'

Even before he had finished, Shubochona raised her eyebrows and said, 'Where else would he find the medicine – the doctor himself came and gave it. Doctor Pal had come, he gave the medicine.'

Gopalchondro Pal was the doctor at the neighbourhood dispensary; everyone laughed at his name. They said, 'Gopal Pal, gorur pal – '[5]

That was why Noni-doctor couldn't help expressing his irritation. 'Ah, your Baba couldn't wait two hours. Who went and called that Pal?'

Shubochona answered in a sweet voice, 'It was only because we were helpless that we had to call him, Kaka-babu, after all, it's not possible to let a patient die in front of your eyes without medicine!

. . . And he looked over everything and said, "All the treatment that's been done so far, it's all wrong."'

He burned in rage from head to foot.

The doctor didn't know about the Durga-caused episode. He thought that the one failing of the previous night was the only reason for this, and in his mind he roared out. In particular, he burned with indignation at the rude manner in which the girl – who had always said 'Kaka-babu' and rolled over in sheer delight – served out the news.

In an angry voice he said, 'I'm gratified to hear it! Call your father, let's see!'

Shubochona remained standing still and said in an unconcerned voice, 'How can I call Baba now? After staying up all night, he's just lain down for a bit, *tired*, at the end of the night!'

No, certainly after this the doctor didn't stand there any more. He came away from the door of his childhood friend. . . .

After this, that door was closed to Noni-doctor's face. And what was the need to keep it open anyway? After only three or four visits with a fee attached, Doctor Pal had cured this patient of eleven years!

And no longer does Shudhakanto-wife reach the point of death at the slightest opportunity.

And so when they meet on the street (and that happens often), Shudhakanto's boys pretend they don't recognize Kaka-babu and walk away, and the girls, if their eyes happen to meet his, turn their eyes away and laugh excessively and walk away talking to one another.

And Shudhakanto says 'There you are, coming back from work?' or some such thing, quickly, and moves away.

And?

And – it's heard: 'Because she was a "free patient" Noni-doctor treated his friend's wife with such little regard that for ages this human being lay there a human in name only. . . . Why, baba, look, right after her treatment changed hands, Shen-ginni came around and recovered fine! . . . Closing your eyes and ears and shoving any old medicine at your patient, is that called treating someone? In fact, the patient was on the point of dying because of this poor treatment. It's only because she was granted a long life – '

Like the mosquito-borne malaria, like the housefly-borne cholera, like the virus-borne cold, this neighbourhood's flock-of-women-borne news arrives in the inner quarters of Noni-doctor's house.

Durga wants to say to her husband, 'You weren't able to cure Shudha-babu's wife's illness, but she's cured your lifelong disease, hasn't she – with such powerful medicine? Surely you've recognized the world now?'

She can't say this.

Maybe it's because she sees what her husband's face looks like that she can't tell him. Even if the doctor says so, she's not really made of stone, is she?

Glass Beads Diamonds

কাঁচ পুঁতি হীরে

Kanch Punti Hiray

Dipok stopped the car at some distance from the wedding-house. Then he said in a smiling voice, 'So you'll walk from here?'

Shomita, too, says, smiling, 'That's what I've decided. You, sitting in the car, on display in front of the house – does that look good?'

Dipok says in a dry voice, 'Who says it's good? I can't find anything good in this strange notion of yours. What sense is there in seeking out insults! What a dangerous situation you can land yourself in, you have no idea – '

Shomita forces some strength into her voice and says, 'I'm going prepared for all kinds of situations.'

That much is true.

Shomita has come to this wedding-house today prepared, indeed, to face a terrific storm. But why? Shomita would not be able to answer that question. She doesn't have the answer to it herself. But what a notion suddenly descended on her the other day, when she saw the invitation letter on the table at a friend's house! Her friend's name and address on a friendly invitation – that seemed to swallow up Shomita.

'So they're coming to Calcutta to get their daughter married,' Shomita said after returning home.

Dipok made an unsmiling joke. 'Well, if it's utterly impossible on this earth for two people to have the same name, then we have to assume they are.'

'Ba, only two people, I suppose?' Shomita said in a tone of argument. 'The bride's name, the bride's father's name, grandfather's name, the name of the town – everything would match?'

'Then they don't, I suppose,' Dipok said. 'But the address?'

'Oho, that's a rented wedding-house. Don't you remember, your Oshit-babu's niece was married in that house. Didn't you see the address?'

'Is that so! Amazing! You remember the address?'

Shomita said, 'Women have much better memories than men.'

'That's certainly true. But they're not inviting *me* to your former bhashur's daughter's wedding feast, so it's not as though I should stop eating at home?' Saying this, Dipok draws the curtain on the subject and goes and sits at the table.

Draws the curtain on the subject for the moment.

But was he able to draw the curtain on Shomita's agitated mind?

It was as though Shomita's mind remained overcast with those few lines of the invitation letter that whole day. And the next day she abruptly raised the matter with Dipok. 'The girl loved me so much – she would call me "Kaki, Kaki". What if we send some sort of present without giving our names?'

Dipok stared at her for a while and said, 'Certainly if we send it, she will indeed have the gift, but she won't know it was her much-loved Kaki who sent it. Because you're not giving your name! So she won't think of it.'

There was some logic in that. Shomita fell silent.

But she didn't remain silent for long.

She walked around and came back and said, 'That's what you say! But if I put my name on it, will they accept it? I'm sure they'll return it.'

'That would be natural,' said Dipok.

Shomita said, as though she were making a great joke, 'Better to go ourselves and drop it off, what do you think? Would they return it to our face?'

Dipok stared at that joke-making face for several moments, then said, 'They could even throw it at our face and shut the door in our face too.'

Shomita laughed even louder and said, 'You're getting so alarmed, you seem to think I'm really going?'

'What's to stop me from thinking that? Aha, your so-beloved kaki!'

'She – my kaki?' Shomita grows angry.

'Something like that,' Dipok said. Then he said in an extremely kind tone, 'Fine, if you want to, get a nice sari and send it to her. If you give the address of the wedding-house at the sari shop, they'll send it themselves. When is the wedding to be? The day after tomorrow, right? You could go to the shop tomorrow.'

No, Dipok couldn't think any further than this.

But Shomita was thinking many things.

The next two days, Shomita could not rest even for an instant, making all kinds of plans.

In the end, this decision. To go uninvited, bearing the gift.

She hadn't mentioned it to Dipok until the previous day. She had only gone to the shop earlier that day. And instead of getting a sari, Shomita had bought some jewellery. A set of imitation jewellery.

But it's the fake jewellery that has the greater sparkle. So, when she opened the box and showed it to Dipok, Dipok's eyes were dazzled. Who would say that in that variety of colours, there were no diamonds, no pearls, no rubies, no emeralds – that everything was glass and beads.

Still, Dipok creased his brow and said, 'You'll give this fake stuff?'

Shomita lifted her eyes and cast an extremely suggestive look at him. 'So what? I'm still the same me.'

Then suddenly she said in a normal voice, 'Do you know what? In her childhood the girl used to love these glass and bead ornaments very much. I would joke and say, when you get married, I'll give you so-o-o many glass bangles, bead necklaces and silver earrings. I remembered this when I went out to buy the sari, so I bought these.'

'That's fine, then,' said Dipok.

To tell the truth, he wasn't particularly enthusiastic about this new excitement of Shomita's. Even husbands in truly settled marriages get restless when they see that their wives have not forgotten the worlds they knew earlier: they grow agitated, thinking that their share is diminishing or that the boundaries of their rights are shrinking; and he was in no marriage! He had no boundaries to his rights.

And so Dipok only said, 'That's fine, then.'

But he didn't know then that Shomita would turn the joke into reality, and that he would be the one to take her there.

Shomita had not raised the matter all day the previous day, she'd only shown him the fake set of jewellery and put it away. She raised it the morning of the wedding-day.

She said, 'I was going to say something. But should I be afraid and say it, or say it unafraid?'

Dipok started. His eyes turned red. Still, he said with a laugh, 'When did the question of being afraid come up?'

'It didn't. I mean – .' Shomita laughed a little too much and said, 'But not being afraid is itself the most frightening thing! Anyway, I'll go ahead and say it, I was going to say, the wedding-house is nearby, won't you be able to go along?'

Dipok had suspected something of the kind. But still he feigned not understanding. He said, 'Sending the gift by my hand, will that look really – you know?'

Shomita smiled an abashed smile and said, 'Aha, who's asking you to carry the gift? I was talking about taking me – I don't feel brave enough to go alone.'

Dipok turned solemn and said, 'You're going, is that a firm decision?'

'Firm, infirm, what difference does that make? I just feel like it,' said Shomita.

'How can you say "just feel like it"? Does anyone ever do something so daring just because they feel like it? But I was going to say, is there really any need to do this?'

'Now look at that!' Shomita floated the conversation into a gentler stream. 'The word *need* doesn't mean anything here. I was thinking, that little girl's getting married – who knows how big she's grown! Anyway, if you have an objection – then let it be.'

Dipok turned his face towards the wall and said, 'I have no objection. But I'm wondering if they'll let you in.'

'Aha, I'll go in with some group in the wedding-party – .' Shomita finished up the matter as though she were making a small joke. 'Who stops anyone? They say so many times even pickpockets take advantage of wedding crowds to get in.'

Then, in the evening, this expedition.

Dipok will sit in the car around the corner, Shomita will walk a little distance –

She'll have to stay inside for a little while. If he parks right outside the gate, Dipok will feel uncomfortable.

Holding the jewellery case firmly, Shomita gets down from the car.

Dipok gets down too. He is a little surprised when he sees the box in her hand. He thinks, yesterday I saw three or four small boxes, today I'm seeing one huge box.

He doesn't say anything; he looks at Shomita. Her clothes are plain, her beauty flawless. In an ordinary fine-spun, red-bordered Tangail sari she seems extremely well-dressed.

Dipok stares steadily at her, then says, 'I'm afraid.'

'You're afraid? What are you afraid of?'

'What if they grab you and keep you? Stop you? Don't let you come back? I don't have any claim on you, after all!'

Shomita says in a bloodless voice, 'Right, that's going to happen! Grab me and keep me! I'm not even sure they won't rush at me and throw me out by the neck!'

'Shomita, think about it now. There's still time to reconsider. If you really – '

Shomita smiles gently. 'What is there to think so much about? Hunh! I'll say Joy Ma Kali and jump right in!'

'Go ahead!' Dipok sighs and says, 'I'll stay here, then. I can see that you're thinking, Akla cholo ré[1] – with whatever strength and support you get from that jewellery set in your hand.'

'Jewellery set!' Shomita starts, then adjusts her hold on the box and says, 'O ma, what jewellery set? Didn't I say everything was merely fake? I took the case from that good set of mine and put everything in that, so they wouldn't catch on. And they'll never catch on! They'll think, why wouldn't she give this, now that she's a rich man's wife – '

Dipok looks at her for an instant and says, 'What's the use trying to fool them?'

Does Shomita tremble a little? Does Shomita look the other way when she speaks?

Maybe she trembles, maybe she looks the other way when she says, 'Now the main thing is to keep one's dignity, to make one's face large.'

Dipok suddenly breaks into a laugh and says, 'Look at this, we've sat down to calculate profits and losses now, standing on the road at this momentous time! Go on in, I think there's a group of women getting out of that car, jump into the fray along with them.'

Shomita moves forward. Dipok keeps staring at her with a gaze of extreme curiosity.

Indeed, Shomita goes into the wedding-house close behind that group. And as soon as she enters, a powerful churning inside her seems to want to push her out into the street.

What is this I've done, what have I done! Shomita's innermost spirit seems to cry out *hai hai* in a kind of detached anxiety. What ghost was this that got hold of me! Was I insane! With a brave face I said to Dipok, 'I'm going prepared for all kinds of situations', but if someone says as soon as I climb up the stairs, 'Who are you? Why are you here? Who gave you permission to come here? Do you have none of that thing called shame?' –

What answer will I give then?

If they say, 'Go throw that gift of yours in the garbage dump' – what will I do? she begins to think. Still she keeps climbing up the stairs, like a mechanical doll.

And when Shomita comes down the stairs, what else is she but a mechanical doll?

She comes down, goes out through the gate, walks up to the car and climbs in as though on the energy of a wound-up spring.

Dipok says, 'What happened? Fulfilled your wish?'

Shomita doesn't speak, only waves her hand to signal for the car to leave.

Dipok doesn't speak any more. He looks at that insult-wounded face and restrains himself. Even if you suffer because of your own faults, suffering is still suffering. She must be given time to settle. She must be given time to calm down.

Slowly he lets the car move forward.

But had someone really insulted Shomita? Had someone raised up a mighty storm of hatred and disdain and thrown her out by the neck? For which her heart had been thirsting these eight-nine years?

No, Shomita had not found the water for her thirst. No one had inflicted a sharp insult on her. Even as an uninvited guest she had been given the hospitable reception due an invitee. Familiar and unfamiliar had all behaved politely towards her. Even the bride's kaka.

Whom she had met while leaving, in the hallway downstairs.

When she climbed up the stairs, the bride's mother, in a brand-new taant sari with a red border a hand and a half wide, was coming forward with a smile on her face. Noticing a woman in front of her, she said in a delighted voice, 'There you are – Mejo-boudi, able to come at last! Baba, how unsociable! Didn't come at all to the gae-holud![2] Asked you so many times!'

Mejo-boudi, loudly trying to offer an explanation for her absence, moved forward and behind her went two-three others.

Suddenly, for an instant, Shomita came face to face with the bride's mother.

Shomita's former brother-in-law's wife.

But perhaps only for an instant.

In the next moment, the woman feigned a terrible impatience and cried out, 'Here! O Bou-ma, where did you go? People are coming, look after them.'

And along with her hand-and-a-half-wide-red-bordered sari she vanished.

But Bou-ma came.

Even the mechanical doll thought of something. She thought, Bou-ma! That means Debu is married! Amazing! How fast the days run away!

Perhaps Bou-ma didn't know anyone at all very well. So she said in a gentle, polite voice, 'Please come!'

Some words indeed emerged from Shomita's mouth. She said, 'And the bride?'

'Here, in this room.'

Bou-ma, showing her the way, took her to that room, the room where Phulu, queen for a night, was seated in thoroughly splendid fashion.

Did Phulu flinch when she saw Shomita?

Was she startled – for which Shomita had arranged her words in advance! She had decided she'd say, Ki ré, it seems like you just saw a ghost? But not a ghost, a she-ghost! Then she would add more words on the back of Phulu's words. Many words. After all, it's to spread her words around that she's come. She'll go speak her words to anyone and everyone. Meaningless, disconnected.

Those words will go from this ear to that ear, from here to there.

And then to that place. Where those very meaningless, disconnected words will become connected and bear the suggestion of meaning.

But Phulu didn't flinch.

Phulu looked at her first as at a stranger, then with a foolish, confused glance.

That clever, artful, jolly girl had become so foolish!

Of course she would! Like her mother! Like all the people of the house! But was Shomita herself able to display any intelligence? She too didn't say anything, just held the box out like a fool, without even removing the lid.

Had Phulu's foolish air touched her body too?

Some other girl was seated next to her. Perhaps a friend of the bride's. Curiously she opened the box and held it out in front of the bride, with the flash of a beatific smile on her face.

And immediately, on the bride's face, too, a piece of that beatific smile broke out.

A signal passed between the eyes of the two friends, and that signal meant: Ish! How superb, how beautiful! Who knows how much it must have cost!

Shomita, sweating, asked, 'Do you like it?'

Phulu smiled gently and nodded.

But was there no one else in the room?

Certainly there was; the whole room was full of women. They glittered in their finery and fragrance, in their gems and their glory. They had formed groups of two or four and, engrossed, were setting off fountains of stories.

They wouldn't run up greedily and sit down to look at the jewellery.

They'd look. They'd look later. Now they merely glanced at it sidelong, briefly. That was how everyone was looking. Jotting down in their mental account-book who had given what; they'd come and make their examination later.

But listen, where had those familiars of Shomita's gone? Mother-in-law, brother-in-law, sisters-in-law, their husbands, nephews-nieces?

It seemed there was some conspiracy on the inside, no one was going to come this way!

Will Shomita ask Phulu about their well-being? Or will Shomita just sit like a fool for all eternity, with her face towards the bride, her back to the door?

Familiar faces! Familiar faces! Where were those familiar faces?

Shomita's wish was fulfilled.

Shomita's nonod came in to call the women to dinner. She went up to everyone and said, 'Come, please come.' It was her turn to come up to Shomita.

She stopped short and stood still.

Looked into Phulu's eyes. Then said to Shomita, as if she were a complete stranger, 'Please come, dinner's been laid out.'

Please come! Shomita's voice was choked. But still she said, with some difficulty, 'I won't eat anything.'

Astonishing! That nonod of hers was the same age as Shomita, yet *her* voice wasn't choked. She spoke in a clear voice.

No, she didn't say this: 'Who invited you, ré? I suppose it was that shameless Chhor-da? But I say bravo to you – with what face did you dare enter this wedding-house teeming with people?' That was her style of oratory, after all.

But now she abandoned that manner. She said, 'O ma, why won't you eat? Are you unwell? That's all right; you'll have some mishti, won't you? . . . O Bou-ma, bring a plate to this room with – '

The room emptied out. The women left hastily in search of their banana-leaf dinner plates.

The next moment, Bou-ma came in bearing an earthen plate with about eight or ten sweets on it.

Now Shomita was able to laugh.

She laughed aloud and said, 'Can a person eat so many sweets?'

Bou-ma didn't say, 'What can a person not do? And do you act according to the standards of what people can and cannot do?'

Bou-ma only said, 'Do eat what you can.'

'I won't be able to eat at all,' said Shomita.

But why? Was Shomita hoping that many people would gather around to discuss her not-eating? Would they beg and beseech her? But Shomita had been intelligent at one time. How did she suddenly become so foolish? But Bou-ma didn't go and call anyone. Bou-ma stood there silently.

Shomita leaned on her courage.

Shomita asked, 'Are you Debu's wife?'

Bou-ma nodded her head.

'How long have you been married?'

'Two years.'

Shomita felt as though the girl were a wooden doll. She spoke again. 'Take the plate away; why should it lie there and go to waste?'

Bou-ma took the plate and went away.

Phulu said in a low voice, 'Won't you eat anything?'

Yes, even Phulu used the formal 'apni' with Shomita.

Shomita laughed enough to tear the veins in her chest. She laughed and said, 'Why should I eat? Did you invite me to your wedding?'

Phulu lowered her head.

'I'll leave now,' Shomita said, getting up.

Phulu, looking this way and that, made as though to offer a nomoshkar, but did not. She was confused. Phulu's mother entered the room. She said in an impersonal tone, 'At a wedding-house you must eat something sweet.'

Shomita cleared her throat and said, 'Let it be, today.' Then Shomita bent down to touch her feet.

Saying 'Let it be, let it be', she moved away.

Shomita came down the stairs.

She went to cross the hallway.

The hallway in which the bride's kaka was sitting, trying to repair a broken table fan, even in a wedding-house.

Astonishing! Even now he hadn't given up that old obsession of his.

That meant that in his world there had been no change in anything anywhere.

That Shomita herself, too, still sought out wool patterns to knit – she didn't think of that.

Shomita could have stopped short while crossing the hallway, but she wasn't able to. She kept moving forward like a mechanical doll.

The bride's uncle didn't say anything, only pulled at the wires and cords that had been spread out, and moved them away, lest they get tangled in Shomita's feet.

Shomita observed this caution, and a fire lit up in her head. She spoke up in a sharp voice. 'What's all this?'

The bride's uncle said in a polite, gentle tone, 'Nothing in particular. The fan was slightly damaged, so – '

With as respectful a tone as should be used with an invited guest – that was how the bride's uncle spoke.

No rage, no hatred, an ordinary gaze. And then the bride's uncle withdrew that gaze.

Turned his attention to his work. As though at that moment he had no concerns other than the work. That meant he was disavowing the person called Shomita, telling her this: we have not remembered you. And not your hateful, ugly behaviour either. Shomita felt an urge to pounce on that man. To take a fistful of his hair and shake it and say, 'Why? Why? What was the harm in remembering that much?'

It wasn't possible to pounce on him. So Shomita spoke in a suppressed, angry voice. 'Why is the wedding being conducted in Calcutta? What crime did Munger commit?'

The bride's kaka didn't insult Shomita by not answering; after close inspection he twisted two fine wires together, and as he did so, he spoke in a detached voice, as though he were answering the wall, 'The groom's side decreed it!'

Shomita said in a more suppressed, sharper voice, 'No one asked me to come, still I came – you won't ask why?'

The bride's kaka said in the same manner, as he held the wire and adroitly wrapped some black tape around it, 'What's there to ask? Phulu was very dear to you – you must have heard that she was getting married. You felt like seeing her – '

'Oh right! Kindness! High-mindedness!' Shomita jerked away and came out. Like a doll with a wound-up spring.

Everyone's showing their kindness to Shomita!

Ignoring all shame and decency, Shomita's run here out of attachment to Phulu. And so no one's said anything, out of pity.

Maybe they thought, let it go; a house like this, where something's going on, so many beggars show up this way!

They thought of Shomita as a pitiful beggar!

Will Shomita shout and cry out, 'I don't have such cheap sentiments! I haven't come for Phulu.'

After a long time Dipok says, 'Didn't I say, going there to be insulted, and for nothing! What a notion you had!'

Shomita suddenly wakes from a bed of ashes.[3] She says with some heat, 'Who told you I was insulted? Everyone behaved decently enough with me.'

Dipok smiles gently and says, 'But that's a bigger insult.'

Shomita clutches his shoulder hard, shakes him. She says in a sharp voice, 'What does that mean?'

'Mean?' Dipok laughs and says, 'Meaning, the entire expedition was wasted. What you wanted didn't happen.'

'What did I want, let's hear?' Shomita's manner turns even sharper.

And Dipok's, calmer. 'You know what you wanted. You'll be angry if I say it.' He moves his shoulder away from her hand.

Suddenly Shomita laughs and claps her hands together. She says, 'You've caught it exactly! Oh, what a brain you have! You can read clearly what's in people's minds. . . . I'd gone to fight with them, why didn't they invite me to their daughter's wedding! But it didn't work. They didn't fight. They saw that gift and were scared. They couldn't catch that it was only a fake! They've never seen anything like it, you see! They saw the glass-beads-brass and thought it was diamonds-pearls-gold and were charmed, they believed it, that's why they gave me their respect. They completely forgot to insult me. What fun! What fun!'

Shomita claps her hands again, like someone excited and garrulous. 'I fooled them, how completely I fooled them, you saw it, didn't you!'

Dipok smiles a mysterious smile and says, 'I really did. I saw it from beginning to end.'

To Be Unable to Be Able

পারা না পারা

Para Na Para

A sharp voice could be heard barking out the command from above: 'Please get off the bus, please get off right now.'

Very polite indeed, it must be said; if he'd wanted he could have said, 'Get off the bus, you bastards.' Instead of that, 'please get off.'

The crowded busload of people scrambled to get off. The group of the unfortunates forced to stand was larger than that of the fortunate ones who had a seat; now, suddenly the dice of fortune were turned. It was those unfortunates who were able to get off first, pell-mell; the fortunates, even with pushing and shoving, became passengers on the last ferry.

But nobody had fallen as far behind as Tribhubon Chokroborty. The bus was like an empty matchbox with all its sticks gone, and still Tribhubon was making a great effort, with his rheumatic knees.

The voice above could be heard once more, 'Did Dadu[1] suddenly decide to dance the twist?' And the next instant, a voice of thunder, 'Fooling around, are you? Get off this minute!'

Tribhubon climbed down, and looked around speechless. In just these two minutes or so, that whole busload of people had vanished like magic. The street yawned empty.

Now what had to happen would happen.

Tribhubon didn't look back. He forgot the pain in his knees and moved forward quickly. At every footstep he felt a wrench, but where did he feel that wrench? Only in his knees? Or somewhere else as well?

In the condition that Tribhubon's body was in, it had become almost impossible to ride the buses and trams to work, pushing through the crowds that way. He shouldn't have been able to do it, but being able and being unable depend only on the circumstances. Tribhubon's cousin's wife, grieving for her dead father, had not been able to get out of bed for three months; after the child in her lap died, Tribhubon's wife got up to cook for the older boys and girls the very next day.

No, being able being unable is nothing.

Or else would Tribhubon, unconscious of which direction he was headed in, right or wrong, be able to run half a mile down the road? – The Tribhubon who says 'Baap-ré, Ma-ré' whenever he has to stand up or sit down?

Running aimlessly, Tribhubon ends up entering an alleyway, then sits, panting, on the scuffed porch of a crumbling building.

He's forgotten about his knees a long time ago, he has a terrible discomfort in his chest. As though it's leaping *torak torak*. If this jumping doesn't stop, it won't be possible to go any farther.

But is his chest doing this only because he's been running? Not because of that voice above? That voice is terribly familiar to Tribhubon. Familiar to every atom and molecule of his body, familiar to his blood his marrow his being his heart and life his thoughts his soul, to everything.

But suddenly now it seems terribly unfamiliar. It is because of this terrifying imbalance between familiar and unfamiliar that Tribhubon is panting this way.

A man comes out from inside the house, asks the question in a tense voice: 'Who is it?'

There's really no reason to make his voice so tense; still, he does. Maybe it's only because the instrument that produces the melody of the entire world is strung so taut that every person is so tense.

'What's going on here?' says the tense voice.

Tribhubon says, 'Nothing. Resting a bit.'

'Why are you panting so much? Don't have some kind of heart trouble, do you?'

'No, no! Just a little pain in the knees – .' Tribhubon's tongue has dried up and retreated into his throat; he pulls it out and says, 'Running away so quickly – '

The man says in a suspicious voice, 'Why, what was the need to run away quickly? Saw the police van and got scared?'

Police van!

Tribhubon says, astonished, 'But I didn't see a police van anywhere.'

'What do you mean you didn't see one? From the roof I could see a police van making its rounds all this time, and the people on the street running around. How long have you been sitting here?'

A voice thoroughly prickly with suspicion.

How long? Tribhubon looks at him confused.

How long has he been sitting here? An eternity? . . . I suppose he's lost all sense of time, wondering, wondering how the sound had reached him of a curly-haired-wax-doll child's sweet babble?

Tribhubon stands up.

Pressing his chest.

Now the man says, 'You've certainly got some problem with your heart, mister, let's see you get out quickly, catch a rickshaw and get yourself to a doctor, don't get us in trouble, an outsider dying in this neighbourhood.'

Tribhubon was going to say, 'There's no death for a man like me, bhai,' – but he can't say it. *Dum, dum*, three or four sounds are heard one after the other. Not the sound of fireworks, the sound of bullets. Familiar. Can be heard any time, even sitting at home.

The man says, 'That's done it. They're shooting. Go, mister, go away.'

He says that and goes inside the house himself and bangs the door shut.

He'll have to take a rickshaw . . . thinks Tribhubon, even if he has no money.

But where's a rickshaw? An empty one?

One or two fall to his eye, running out of breath with their mounted passengers. Why are they running so hard? Not only the vehicles, even the people on the street seem to be running. People here running there, people there running here.

Tribhubon isn't able to run, he doesn't seem able even to walk. It feels as though someone's pulling at his feet from behind. . . . Not someone, some people. Their comments have tied a rope around Tribhubon from the back and are pulling at him. They're trying to plant him to the ground.

But the comments aren't new at all, they've been heard so many times. These remarks are made all the time.

What else can I say. The fruits of an evil mind. He was running away after setting fire to the bus, and the police came and started shooting. What usually happens: when the bus was being burnt, those gods weren't around; even the tips of their mustaches couldn't be seen. They made an appearance only when everything was over. . . . The body? There it is, lying over there; arrangements are being made to remove it. Have you seen it? I saw it, I did, a young boy, fair, bright skin, a black mole on his cheek, a lightly bearded face. . . . Sure, there would be a beard. . . .

Which way will Tribhubon run?

Right? Left? Forward? Back?

But hot waves of fire come rushing out from all four directions. And rushing out is a fair, bright-skinned, black-mole-cheeked young boy. And he comes rushing here and suddenly stumbles and reaches out and falls on his face in front of Tribhubon.

Which way will Tribhubon run to evade his hand?

Without thought or reflection, Tribhubon begins to run one way. If someone who knew Tribhubon had seen him, they would have said, 'The man's rheumatism is just an obsession. It seems he has rheumatism in the knees. If that were so, this wonderful fellow wouldn't be able to run like this.'

But who knows Tribhubon in this place? Everyone, everything is unknown. The streets, the houses, the shops, the people on the street.

Who knows how much time passes before Tribhubon is able to find an empty rickshaw! He climbs on and sits and gives the name of a street.

After a long time Tribhubon seems to see a few familiar sights, houses, shops, streets. But why is everything so hazy? Can there be a fog at this time? Still, Tribhubon climbs down in front of a familiar house, and, strange, he counts out the fare, too, and gives it to the rickshaw-wala.

And right after that, that pain in his knees bites him with its teeth, not only in his knees but in his whole body.

Now he is really unable to drag his foot forward; he calls out in such a distorted voice, 'Bishu!'

Tribhubon's older son, Bishshobhubon, is taking the M.A. exam this year, he was studying in the outer room, he comes out quickly.

He starts and says, 'Baba! What's the matter? What happened? It's so late – you didn't fall down somewhere, did you?'

Tribhubon says in answer to all these questions, 'Take my hand.'

Tribhubon's tone of voice, too, seems unfamiliar to his son. How did this broken, hoarse voice find its way into Baba's windpipe and take shelter there?

Tribhubon suddenly sees a light in front of him and says, 'Yes, I fell.'

'When? Where?'

Tribhubon's wife comes out from the kitchen, says, 'You fell in the street? How?'

'Getting off the bus – .' Tribhubon says, groaning, 'I can't move my knees.'

Wife son daughter all fall forward at Tribhubon's knees. The girl, Ruby, a class-nine student, speaks up. 'I could tell right away, when I saw Baba getting off the rickshaw, something's happened, or else, would Baba spend money on a rickshaw?'

'You stop now – all the girl can do is make smart remarks. . . . Han go, you didn't break any bones, did you?'

'Who knows,' says Tribhubon.

Son wife daughter all together take Tribhubon to the cot in the bedroom and set him up there. Everything's on the same floor, there's no particular inconvenience.

Bishu moves the cloth off his baba's legs and examines them minutely, then gives his opinion, No, it isn't scraped or anything. It would have been a problem if it had been scraped, the dust on the street has tetanus germs.

The bones?

No, no bones have been broken, it seems, if one was broken, would he have been able to drag himself upright and bring himself home?

Fine, that's all right then, it'll get better with some hot-water compresses and some iodine-fiodine.

But where has Tribhubon been all this time?

He was supposed to be back from his office by six or six-thirty at most, he was off at four-thirty, and the delay was only because of the buses. Otherwise Tribhubon never went this way or that, coming back from his office.

Tribhulon snarls out his answer to the question.

What a strange question, where else could he have been? It was only because he wasn't able to get up and come away that he sat down on the porch of a house beside the street.

Tribhubon's wife says in an extremely sorrowful and surprised voice, 'Han go, so no one on the street helped you?'

'Help? Who would go and help whom?' Tribhubon suddenly starts scolding again. 'Why does anyone need to do that?'

'Need, what other need?' Tribhubon's wife speaks of an earlier age. 'Humanity's need, its duty. A man trips and falls down, and no one will turn to look? Won't they help him up and get him on a car and send him home? If you really think about it, they should really take him to the doctor.'

Why has Tribhubon suddenly taken to scolding so much? The wife who is caressing his aching body with such affection, he's started scolding her? 'Oh! Should take him to the doctor! Should get him on a car! Who came and told you all this in your ear?'

'Who's going to come and tell me? This is what people have always said.' Tribhubon's wife says somewhat angrily, 'I'm only saying what the right thing to do is. If someone falls down in front of you, won't anyone help him up? Is there no such thing as humanity?'

If someone falls down in front of you!

Tribhubon keeps running again, keeps running aimlessly, because chasing Tribhubon from the right the left front and back is a running man, running so he can stumble and fall on his face in front of Tribhubon.

Tribhubon tries with all his strength to stop running, he comes to a stop, sits leaning on a pillow in his room, then he scolds again: 'Humanity! Do you still remember how to spell it? Now don't keep talking such nonsense.'

Such an insult, in front of an M.A.-studying son! Now who's going to caress his aching body with her hand? Tribhubon's wife jerks away and says, 'Wonderful! Look, Bishu, I've been so anxious for such a long time now, pacing in and out, and Babu comes back like a military man! As though it's me who pushed him off the bus. . . . What, are you able to get up and wash your hands and face? Or should I bring some water in a basin right here?'

It's not at all new for Tribhubon to wash his face and hands from a basin placed in the room; sometimes that does happen.

He suddenly flares up, says, 'No! No need for such luxury! I'm going.'

With his towel on his shoulder, Tribhubon walks off towards the bathroom. Ruby says, 'Baba's walking fine, he wasn't hurt much.'

Bishshobhubon sees that too; he laughs a little and says, 'After getting late for some reason or other, Baba's made up a story.'

Bishsho's mother speaks up. 'All right, so at least that's an end to worrying about one person, now when will this other person come back – only he knows, and God knows.'

This other person is Bishobhubon's mother's younger son, Joybhubon. He has to give his Part I, but whether he goes to college regularly or whether he goes at all, no one in the house knows. His activities are completely unregulated.

Now Bishsho looks at the clock from King Mandhata's[2] time that's hung on the wall, subtracts fifteen minutes for its running fast, and says in a scornful voice, 'Joy, come back at this time? Rest assured it'll be another hour or so yet.'

'What a treasure I held in my womb!' Tribhubon's wife, Komola, says in soliloquy. 'A rowdy, a gang-leader even before his milk teeth fell out. Forget scoldings and such, there isn't any chance to even say anything reasonable to him. . . . And now after he emerges from the bathroom it'll be time to sing a poem in praise of Joy. On one side his stomach's burning, on the other side he doesn't want to sit down to eat if Joy's not back, and the bitterness of all that falls upon me. For me it's a conch-saw.[3] Here, you're a boy too, you grew up together, and yet – '

'Everyone's not the same, I have no guts – leave me out of it – '

Bishshobhubon says this and goes to sit down to his studies again.

Komola calls Ruby and tells her to set out the places for dinner. Ruby lays out two faded seat-mats, pours two glasses of water, says, 'I shouldn't set a place for Chhor-da?'

'Let it be.'

After saying this, Komola stretches her neck and takes a look at the street through the window. No, there's no such satisfaction. Komola will indeed have to listen to that song of praise. If he'd come back by now, all the fuss would have blown over.

Tribhubon returns wearing a wet towel and says, 'Ruby, do get me an old dhuti, I'll put it on and lie down, I've taken off those dusty clothes.'

Ruby goes and circles this way and that, then comes back and says, 'I can't see a dhuti, Baba, shall I bring you the lungi?'

'That's fine.'

Komola comes from the kitchen carrying the plate with the rutis and vegetables arranged on it and places it in front of the seat. She says, 'The girl's got her eye on the sky, can't see a thing – I'll wash my hands and get it.'

'Let it be, it's done – .' Tribhubon says in a hoarse-sounding voice, 'You served my food already? I'm going to bed.'

'You're going to bed!' Komola looks at her husband sharply. It did seem as though the falling down was a made-up story. But what has happened? She jerks back and asks the same question again, 'What do you mean? Why? What's happened to you?'

Suddenly Tribhubon's arms and legs turn to ice with some terrible fear. Why is Komola's gaze so sharp? An engine seems to be running in the middle of Tribhubon's chest – why does her gaze want to fall there? Tribhubon will remove himself from that eye. He sits down *jhop* on the seat-mat and says sulkily, 'No one's ever allowed not to feel hungry. A fine oppression!'

He begins to tear large chunks from a ruti and stuff them into his mouth, as though he is angry.

This means that the troublesome song of praise is postponed for now. That's fine in a way, Komola thinks; scoldings on a full stomach are less sharp than on a burning stomach.

She stretches her neck and looks out through the window once more; the street is silent and empty. Nowadays it's no longer the way it used to be, when the street lights stayed lit even at midnight. Now, even before it is nine at night, the street has the appearance of midnight.

But that one young boy, out somewhere –

She takes hold of herself and shouts out, 'Bishu, come and eat.'

Bishu gets up and comes.

He sees that Baba has sat down to eat, and is somewhat relieved. If Baba had been sitting with his arms folded instead of eating, Bishu would have had to obey and sit down to eat. He says, 'Let it be, I'll eat a little later.'

Tribhubon raises his neck and looks at the clock, then says, 'Why? Why will you eat later? Isn't it nighttime already?'

'The clock runs fifteen minutes fast,' Bishu says in a detached voice. 'Let me study a little more, let Joy get back.'

'What?'

Tribhubon seems to explode suddenly.

'No, no, there's no need to sit and wait for anybody. Eat up, all of you.'

'All of you', meaning Komola too.

The sound of Tribhubon's voice seems unnaturally harsh to Komola. His manner is unnaturally agitated. That means his anger has climbed to the absolutely highest scale.

But Tribhubon's meal is almost at an end, and the courage in Komola's chest has increased too. As long as the man hasn't eaten, there is the fear that he will suddenly blurt out, 'Damn it, I won't eat!'

It's not a little trouble that Komola has because of Joy.

'If it gets really late, I'll eat –,' says Komola, and as usual she brings a couple of rutis and some jaggery for Tribhubon's plate at the end of the meal.

But Tribhubon suddenly seems to have forgotten that daily ritual. 'Who asked for anything more?' he shouts, and pushes the plate away.

Bishsho was headed back to his studies, but at that sudden shout of Baba's he is forced to stop and stand still.

This time he speaks up a little more firmly. 'Some days Joy comes back much later than this – why are you making such a fuss today?'

'Making a fuss – .' Tribhubon, perhaps frightened by his son's scolding, is extinguished. In a downcast voice, he says, 'When did I make a fuss? Fine, I'll eat –,' and pulls the plate back towards himself again and leans his head almost over the plate and tears large pieces off the rutis and begins to stuff them into his mouth like some uncouth person – this man called Tribhubon Chokroborty.

The man who, at one time, had been quite refined and had therefore, to maintain the spirit of his own grand, traditional name, named his sons Bishshobhubon and Joybhubon.

Not Guilty

বেকসুর

Bekoshur

'Who called me from behind? Who called me back!'

Boloram Shaha turned and looked back. But where? He couldn't see anyone. Although he had heard clearly – 'Shaha-moshai! Shaha-moshai!'

Because it was late, Boloram had tied the laces of his keds tightly and was striding along with forceful footsteps; now he was startled. He had a shop that sold floral-ornamented bell-metal kitchenware in the Khagra bazaar, a business three generations old. It's about two miles from his house; Boloram goes back and forth on foot. On his way back, if it's cloudy or raining and someone says, 'Why don't you take a cycle rickshaw, Shaha-moshai, such a long way' – Boloram Shaha takes the umbrella from under his arm and opens it over his head and says, 'When there were no rickshaws, Obhiram Shaha and Horiram Shaha had to go this long way from house to shop and back. Now at least there's a paved street, at that time there was only an unpaved street.'

After Boloram strides thudding away, someone else remarks,

'Telling him was just wasting your mouth, I know he won't listen! Just as stubborn as his father.'

Even though after the introduction of stainless-steel pots and pans the fame of the shop has declined somewhat, the business has not declined. There are still plenty of old-fashioned people in the region! And apart from that, now a wave of another fashion has hit. To decorate their houses in an urban, up-to-date manner, people are buying pots and pans, tumblers, bowls, plates, and gewgaws of flowery bell-metal in various designs. And apart from that, foreign tourists, too, see the array of pots and pans and are charmed, and they buy bowls, lotus-flower plates, wave-bordered tumblers, ornamented boxes. . . . These standard names have floated down the stream of the ages by means of their unchanging appearance.

As soon as he goes and sits in the shop, Boloram's mind and body seem to find contentment. Maybe he feels his father and grandfather caressing him gently.

But the man was very ill-tempered by nature. Nobody could remember ever hearing a sweet word from his mouth. But a genuine, unadulterated man! Still, in secret people called him 'Snarling Boloram'!

As soon as he heard the call from behind, Boloram spoke out in his snarling voice, 'Who called me from behind? Who called me back!'

After he spoke, his eyes fell on three or four rowdy-looking boys coming from the direction of his house. That meant they had gone to his house and not found him there, heard that he had just left, and so the rascals had chased him and were calling him from behind.

Boloram looked at the boys with a hard stare; they didn't look familiar. What did these lovable fellows intend? Some contribution? Everyone thought Boloram was a money tree. And so now which god or goddess's pujo was it?

Boloram thought all this in an instant, he had slowed his pace somewhat, but he hadn't stopped walking. . . .

So what if there was no pujo listed in the almanac, it was enough to set up a neighbourhood pujo for Rokkhe-kali, and on that pretext they would create a noisy show. But if they did more than just pound the drums, if they organized a jatra[1] performance, that wouldn't be bad. He could tell Phuli about the occasion and try to bring her here for a while. The girl hadn't come for a long time. Her shrewish shashuri-ma did her best not to let her bou come to her father's house. . . . Why would she, for then she would have to do all the work herself. Aha, that Phuli of Boloram's, fallen into the hands of this shashuri with a mania for cleanliness, now had chilblains from having her hands and feet in water all the time. Five or six years she's been married – and no child yet.

How thoughts can turn into worries!

But the boys kept yelling – 'Shaha-moshai, please wait a bit – Shaha-moshai, a little slower.'

Still, in the midst of all that, his thoughts slipped along.

At last the boys did catch up with Boloram.

'There's something we need to tell you – .' A boy with his hair hanging down swallowed and said, ' – Something important – '

Boloram said in a contemptuous voice, 'What could you all have to tell me that's important? . . . I've set out on my walk, and now this calling-from-behind nuisance. Go away, come back later.'

Now all the boys spoke up at the same time. 'It's not for us, sir, it's your own, uh, a house you know, a terrible disaster, that's why we spent the coins from our own money-belt and came running here to tell you.'

Terrible disaster!

Boloram was somewhat disconcerted. 'Disaster – meaning what?'

'Yes, sir, like we said, a terrible disaster.'

Boloram looked all of them over from head to toe and frowned. 'Where have you come from?'

'Sire, from Keshtonogor.'

Keshtonogor! Meaning, Phuli's in-laws' place!

Boloram's chest trembled with an unknown fear! . . . But what kind of disaster was it, that no one from the house was able to come and let him know, that they sent some smart-mouth boys instead.

Boloram tried to keep control over himself, said, 'What's happened? Have robbers come and looted everything?'

'Sir, what difference would that make? Everything of Kundu-moshai's is in the bank or in his business. What does he keep at home?'

'Would you tell me straight out what's happened, instead of limping along this way, bapu? I don't have the time to stand and natter with you. Whatever you have to say, say it double-quick.'

'Double-quick? Oh!'

The boy with the shock of hair suddenly came forward as though about to rush him ferociously and said, 'Isn't your daughter's in-laws' home in Keshtonogor?'

'Who's saying it's not?'

'She's the daughter-in-law of Shoshi Kundu of Anondomoyeetola, isn't she?'

The middle of Boloram's chest goes *dhopash-dhopash*. What are these boys trying to say? That Shoshi Kundu is dead? Still, he makes himself strong and says, 'Yes, indeed! What of it?'

'Nothing else – your daughter was murdered last night, that's what we came to tell you.'

A victor's smile seemed to break out on the boy's face. . . . Now see how you like that! We poor fellows, even though we may not have spent the coins from our money-belts, maybe we came ticketless, we did come running here, killing ourselves, to tell you about your disaster, and you rascal, you, with your nose high, you told us scornfully, I don't have time to listen to your nonsense. Nuisance! Come back later! Are you happy now?

The ground is shifting from under Boloram's feet, in front of Boloram's eyes is an unbounded pall of smoke! . . . And even in the middle of that, Boloram thinks, speechless, That's right! Why did my thoughts suddenly take me to Phuli when I first saw these boys! Why did I get that sharp twinge in my heart about not having seen the girl for so long? . . . So can this impossible thing be true!

The next instant, Boloram Shaha steeled himself with an effort and said, 'Impossible! Are you mad! Why would someone's daughter be murdered, for nothing, out of the blue? Who would come and kill her? . . . Shoshi Kundu says she brings good fortune, thinks her a Lokkhi.[2] Right after his son's marriage, his business started booming. He says with a hundred mouths that Bou's bringing them good fortune! Shashuri-ma doesn't let Bou come to her father's house, that's because of her own selfishness! So what self-interest would she fulfil by murdering her bou? And the groom? Leave him out of it. I hear he doesn't come near his father's business, he's busy with his cards and dice, his songs and music, his socializing. . . . Sending this obscene news must be a cunning ploy by some enemy.'

Shoshi Kundu might have some enemies. Boloram knows the man is a truly honest person. But even honest people may have enemies, there's no lack of wicked people on this earth. Kundu-moshai has flourished day by day in both his jaggery business and his cloth business! . . . It was natural for his enemies to burn! . . .

The boys are watching –

The man didn't cry out in lamentation, didn't beat his chest, wasn't even terribly agitated – what did that mean? Astonished, the boys looked at one another's faces. . . . As soon as he heard, the man seemed to turn hard as wood, as though he'd had an electric shock! What could be the matter! Didn't he believe them?

That was exactly right.

Boloram ran his eyes over them again and said, 'I suppose you boys are from Kundu-moshai's relatives' houses? . . .'

They said angrily, 'Not relatives or anything, we're from the neighbourhood. . . . Saw the murder happen right in front of our eyes. We know it's your only daughter, so out of a sense of duty we came to give you the news! Now if you want to believe it or not, that's up to you. . . .'

Now Boloram sat down.

Although not right on the street, but on the porch of a neighbouring house. He said in a somewhat detached manner, 'You saw it in front of your eyes? Who killed her?'

'Sir, what can I tell you! Your jamai Shorot.'

The groom's appearance floated up in front of Boloram's eyes. Built like a roly-poly Naru-gopal,[3] his face too somewhat Gopal-like. Curly hair, arranged like rolls of wool above his forehead. The colour of his skin like fresh-cream kheer. . . . At the time of the wedding, people had seen the groom and found him praiseworthy. . . . That boy who looked like a cream doll? Impossible!

Boloram tried to reinvigorate himself again. He said, 'You stood and watched the man kill his wife? Did he cut her with a cleaver, or with a knife or some such – '

Apart from the shock-haired boy, the others stood quietly with sulky faces, fuming with anger inside. They had thought the man would recognize their sense of duty, be gratified, and offer them his thanks, he would be agitated and want to come running right away with them; but no, he seemed to be trying to twist their words to prove them wrong.

The shock-haired one had a somewhat cooler head. He said, 'If you talk like this, there's nothing more for us to say. But since we've taken the trouble to come running from Keshtonogor to Khagra, before we leave we'll tell you what really happened. I don't know if you know this, but lately Shorot Kundu had developed an addiction to liquor and bhang and other such virtues, it would be midnight before he came home. And every day there would be harsh words with his father. . . . But let that be – in the summer, nearly every house has its cots laid out on the rooftop. We too have the same arrangement. . . . We are in the house right next door to the Kundus. The heat's gone down and we're just about to fall asleep, and suddenly there's screaming and shouting on the Kundus' roof, a drunk's voice, and then right next to the parapet there's some kind of scuffle between two people. The words, "Ah, ah, he's killing me" in a woman's voice, and right after that the sound of something heavy falling, *doom*, from the second-storey roof. . . . And right then, Shorot's mother's sudden scream, "O Ma, what is this calamity" – that was all, the very next moment, absolute silence! . . . The whole affair took place within a few seconds. . . . We set out by the dawn train to give you the news. . . . We know they'll hide the truth, they'll say, she was sleeping on the rooftop, and she was so sleepy when she tried to come down the stairs that she put her foot into an opening in the broken parapet wall. . . . At the end of the night, that was what Shoshi Kundu's wife was saying, and beating her chest!

'Anyway, we should go. We have to return by the eleven-thirty train. . . . I had thought that with this sudden bad news you might – uh, if you became very disturbed, we would take you to the station right away. But it seems like you don't even believe us. . . . Come, let's go. In this Koli Jug[4] we shouldn't try and do anyone any favours.'

They set off walking.

The leader of the group came back a couple of steps. He said, 'The next train is at five-thirty in the evening. It'll be night by the time it reaches there. By then the dead body will be done away with. . . . Tell us if you want to go. We'll all be with you.'

Seeing their eagerness, Boloram Shaha's wilted mind began to harden again with suspicion. . . . There were so many kinds of swindlers and villains in the world. So many stories were heard about suddenly telling someone that a 'disaster' had befallen a near relative and taking them away and putting them in danger. . . .

Stealthily Boloram's hand touched the wad of money at his waist. Today some tradespeople were supposed to come to his shop to deliver goods, and he had with him four and a half thousand rupees in cash. . . . Had the lads found out about this somehow?

Boloram could not decide what he should do. On the one hand, there was a violent agitation in his chest, the world was turning dark, and on the other hand there was the fog of suspicion.

'You're not coming, are you? Fine.'

The boys started walking again.

When they'd gone just a little way ahead, Bolorom raised a hand and shouted, 'O Baba-ra, wait a little. . . . Listen – '

It was the shock-haired one who came.

Suddenly Boloram grabbed his hand and started crying, bawling. 'In the name of religion, do you swear you're telling the truth? Is it really true that my daughter's been murdered?'

'What would we gain by telling a lie?'

'Then let me come with you. I need to see Ma – one last time – '

Boloram stopped for a moment. He said, 'If one of you could go and tell them at my house, Baba. There's my old mother and widowed sister in the house. If I'm not home in time, they'll be very anxious. Tell them he's going to Ranaghat on some special work, they shouldn't worry if he's not able to return.'

One boy set off running.

Boloram hired three cycle rickshaws to go to the station. . . . No, no need to take anyone with him, jostling against the money at his waist.

Oh! What a bewildering situation!

God! Let those boys going ahead in those rickshaws be swindlers and liars. Let them be boys from the house of Shoshi Kundu's enemies. . . . He says he lives next door, but he's saying 'Shoshi Kundu, Shorot

Kundu'! Is it ever like that in the villages and marketplaces? They always call people by some term of kinship. . . . Even if they're not close, they always say 'dada' or 'kaka'.

No, these people are schemers.

God, let that be the truth.

But they won't be able to trick Boloram Shaha. . . . It's true he's been suddenly distressed and is going along with them, but they won't be able to do anything. . . . I was feeling uneasy about the girl, that's why I was even more ready to set out. Hé Ma Anondomoyee Kali! Let me go and find my Phuli all right. On the way back I'll make you an offering of sugar and sweets.

Boloram feels the money-pack gently with his hand, then hardens his mind again.

In the two rickshaws ahead, the four boys are going along. If they were swindlers, with some scheme in mind, wouldn't they have tried to escape somehow? . . . Once we reach the station, can they stick a knife in me and grab my money? . . . Or after boarding the train, with a thousand people all around, at high noon?

And after they reached Keshtonogor, too, they couldn't confuse Boloram Shaha and take him off somewhere. . . . He's gone back and forth from Keshtonogor all his life. And apart from that, in the few years since he married off his daughter, he's been coming and going countless times, bearing a pot of sweets, a basket of mangoes, pickles made by Thakuma, pressed mango preserves. There are so many people there who recognize me.

So?

How would they dare to make up a story and bring me all this way for nothing?

Boloram Shaha moves forward, ceaselessly pondering these contradictory thoughts. Sometimes his mind becomes somewhat firmer, and then again that mind crumbles.

That remark of Shoshanko's in the market the other day comes to mind:

'What's happening these days, Boloram-da? Every time I open the paper I find another story of some bou's murder. . . . In the city bazaars, in respectable homes, these incidents always seem to keep increasing. Murdering your bou is the latest fashion nowadays – doesn't it seem that way?'

Who had given ear to his friend Shoshanko's remark that day? Now it came to mind.

Certainly the boys would not have bought tickets before climbing on the train, but when Boloram offered the money for five tickets, they didn't dare to pocket the money for themselves.

As soon as the train pulled in and stopped at Goari, Boloram seemed astonished. How strange! Everything was exactly the way it had been before. Utterly unchanged. . . . Even the picture of the meditating Mohadeb torn from a calendar, with a garland of dried flowers around it, in the paan-shop in front, which he had seen earlier, was still hanging in exactly the same way, with a garland of dried marigolds around it. People came and went with their luggage in exactly the same way. As though he'd just seen it all this very minute. . . .

If he cast his eye over there, he could see the cycle-rickshaw stand, and above the bell on each cycle fluttered a blue nylon flower the way it had fluttered before, with not a thing out of place anywhere. . . . And those godless smart-mouth boys, they said – Yes! They said the whole universe had turned upside down.

Those absolute scoundrels!

And without glancing at them again, Boloram Shaha strode thudding away to the rickshaw stand . . . climbed up on one and sat down.

Said, 'Anondomoyeetola!'

'Are you going there first, Shaha-moshai?'

That wretched shock-haired fellow had made sure to follow him.

Boloram almost grimaced at him. 'Now what?'

'I was just saying – wouldn't it be better to go this way first? If you hurried, you could still find the court open. Start the case right away, and then – '

Hearing this, Snarling Boloram's face grew menacing. He said, 'I see I've landed in the clutches of a fine obstinate fellow. What's your intention? If someone tells me "A crow's taken your ear", will I run after the crow without putting a hand to my ear first? Go, go! Don't harass me this way any more!'

He settled himself in the rickshaw and said, 'Drive on. Anondomoyeetola.'

After going a little distance the rickshaw-wala spoke up. 'Anondomoyeetola? Whose house?'

Boloram's ire hadn't dissipated yet; he said in a still-angry voice, 'Why don't you keep going, Bapu? I'll show you which house it is. . . .'

'It's not that – '

The man said, pedalling, 'Last night there was an accident at a house in Anondomoyeetola, that's why I'm asking.'

The inside of angry Boloram's chest turned to ice. His voice choked shut.

Still, he said with difficulty, 'What happened?'

The man said eagerly, 'Sir, some people say it was carelessness, some say it was murder. . . . But, Babu, I think it must be the second. . . . It's become a custom to murder the bou of the house. . . .'

As though from a great distance, a faint voice came floating, 'Whose house?'

'Sir, that jaggery-businessman Shoshi Kundu? . . . He's also got a cloth shop in Anondomoyeetola. . . . What happened, Babu? Do you know him?'

Boloram Shaha had slumped over, but suddenly he controlled himself and roared out, 'Yes, I know him, I know him very well! Drive faster. Today I won't let them go without planting them all in the same hole.'

At the street corner near Shoshi Kundu's house there was still a small knot of people. A little while earlier the police had taken away the dead body, and they had taken away both father and son, Shoshi and Shorot.... Nearby, some people were lamenting this heartbreaking occurrence, and some were making fun of it.... Probably the number in the latter group was larger....

Shoshi Kundu's arrogance had grown huge. Lately he'd begun to view the world as his own earthen saucer.... And that godless son had suddenly lost all sense. Always drunk and dazed. That day, what a scandal he created in a drunken fit at Baganpara!... And no matter how many lies his father tells to make their case, it won't stick. Now it's life in jail for both of them, father and son! What do you say, hey? Their pride will die a little – and who's that getting off the rickshaw at Kundu's door? Isn't that Shorot's shoshur? ... So he's got the news?

Who gave him the news?

Aha, is there any lack of enemies in the neighbourhood?

As Boloram settled the rickshaw fare and looked this way and that, everyone melted away. No need to stay, baba. What if he questions them? What if he says, You all are witnesses, right? Save us.... Everyone wants the guilty to be punished, but no one's willing to go to court and bear witness....

The front of the house was deserted.

The door locked from the inside.

With a warrior's challenge Boloram shook the door. The whole house clattered. From inside a woman's faint voice asked, ' – Who is it?'

Not only faint, but also fearful.

'Open the door! I am Boloram Shaha of Khagra.'

The door opened slowly.

The old domestic Kanai's Ma stepped to one side.... As soon as she saw Boloram enter, the woman who would open the door and immediately shout out, all aflutter, O Bou-didi, Look, see who's come! Baba! Talu-moshai! I suppose there was no pot larger than this in your Khagra bazaar? ... Your daughter loves chhana-boras,[5] and you know that.

Today there was none of that fluttering. She stood to one side like a thief.

A little while earlier the man had slumped over in the rickshaw, now he gave a tiger's roar.... True, he had no weapon in his hand, only the umbrella that was a permanent fixture under his arm. Raising that high, Boloram entered the passageway and kept shouting, 'Where? Where is that scoundrel, that monster? Come out. Come, let me kill you and hang for it.... Come out, I say, you devil you pig you villain you drunkard.'

Boloram went from room to room, door to door, filling the house with threats and noise.

Kanai's Ma said in an undertone, 'But they've taken both father and son to the police station. They took the dead body, and them too –'

'Took them to the police station? Ish! Now they've slipped out of my hands. Didn't even give me the satisfaction of killing the scoundrel and dying for it.... All right, if I don't hang the murderer on the gallows, then – what? Have they taken the ginni of the house to the police station as well?'

'No, they didn't take Ma. They asked her some questions and let her go.'

Boloram raised his voice and said, 'Fine, the police have let you go, let them, Boloram Shaha won't let you go.... Call your Ginni. Boloram

Shaha will make her spend time in jail too, that's his straight answer. If you have the courage, come out. I want to know, after bringing someone's else daughter home, – oh!'

At Boloram's roar, Shoshi Kundu's wife came out of a room. . . . She wore a half-soiled sari with a thin red-lined border, and on her wrists a shankha, red ruli, iron bangle, and a pair of thick gold bangles. Face covered by her anchol. She came out and almost immediately stumbled and fell near Boloram's feet, then cried out in a subdued voice, 'No, I don't have the courage, Byai-moshai! I don't have the courage to show you my face. You gave your everything in this world, your gem, your motherless daughter into my hands. I couldn't hold on to her any more, Byai-moshai! He completely finished off that golden Lokkhi bou of the house – that monkey, that godless burden of my own womb! . . .'

'Ma!'

Kanai's Ma spoke up in an aggrieved voice, 'Why are you saying all this nonsense? Bou-didi was sleeping alone on the rooftop, and when she was coming down, sleepy-eyed, she didn't look, she thought it was the staircase doorway but stepped into a gap in the broken wall and fell down – that's what happened!'

'Stop. Stop telling your made-up and practised stories!' Kundu-ginni, crying, burst out sharply. 'Is Byai-moshai a fool? That he'll believe whatever you tell him? Byai-moshai's judgement is far better than any lawyer or barrister's. . . . Won't he find out what's the truth and what's lies? Now the life-wand and death-wand[6] for me are in his hands!'

'Hunh!'

Boloram Shaha was silent for a moment, then said, 'Your judgement isn't far behind either, Byan – No! Why Byan now? What kind of Byan now? . . . Only Kundu-ginni. Now you understand this, I'm not going to give up until I finish off that scoundrel, that pig. . . . My harmless, decent, motherless girl – '

Boloram's throat became choked, but still he raised his voice and said, 'Slapped seven times, and not a whimper. And a girl like *that*, he – will I let him go? Take his skin off and – '

Kundu-ginni removed the anchol from her face. She almost lay down prone and wailed out loud in a choked voice, 'I know, Dada, there's no punishment to fit his crime, his father was going to grab him and take him to the police station right then. He said, "You're a stain on this family, the Lokkhi of my house, the Lokkhi of my business, you killed this Durga-like bou! Come, let me arrange to have you hanged from the gallows. . . ." He stopped only after he saw my face. You too, take a look at me, Dada! After four daughters, that little one! Save him, please! My life and death are in your hands!'

'What are you trying to say?' Boloram Shaha roared out. 'Why all this explaining to me? Will Boloram Shaha go to court and give false testimony?'

Kundu-ginni's anchol fell completely off her face, she lifted her two eyes – as red as koromchas[7] from crying – and said, 'Nothing false, Dada – you can say, I don't believe Shorot can do something like that.'

'Is that so! Is that so! Is that what Boloram Shaha will say! My daughter, so full of life – '

He stopped.

Kundu-ginni wailed out loud again. 'Don't I understand that, Byai-moshai – '

'Don't! No more Byai-fyai.'

Kundu-ginni swallowed and said, 'Isn't it clawing at my heart? The bou of my household. If she stepped an inch out of the house, this world stopped moving. But that shameful monkey didn't do anything knowingly, Dada, he only did it because of his drinking. Don't they say – the wickedness of liquor! A gang of wicked cronies and friends got him addicted and turned him inhuman – '

'Stop! Stop!' Boloram snarled out, 'Don't come pleading the case for your boy, your stain on the family. If you stick your hand in the fire, it *will* burn, the fire doesn't do it knowing or unknowing, understand? The punishment for murder is hanging, that's my straight answer, Kundu-ginni. I'll go tomorrow and slap on a case, I'll fight till the end.'

Kundu-ginni!

Kanai's Ma, too, heard this and was startled. The man's manner of speech wasn't that gentle, it was true, but still he had always spoken with respect. . . . Had addressed her as Byan or Thakrun. . . . When pressed to eat more, he would say, The food is yours, Byan-thakrun, but the stomach is mine. . . .

Or after eating too much, he would say, You fed Byai enough for his stomach to burst, now who's going to be responsible for sewing up the wretched Boloram's stomach?

His voice was harsh, but there was no rudeness in his words.

The phrase 'Kundu-ginni' seemed to be a cuff on the ear.

Still, the woman swallowed the insult, lifted her two veiny hands and said in a 'falling-at-his-feet' tone, 'So will getting my son hanged get you back your daughter, Dada! Think of a mother's burning heart and – '

Boloram was pacing around, thudding; on hearing this he stopped and said in a cruel voice, 'Oh! Boloram Shaha will think of that and turn "yes" into "no" in court, is that so? . . . Who's looking at *his* burning heart, tell me that?'

Kundu-ginni now wilted completely. She pulled the cloth over her head and said in a calm voice, 'Don't think I'm not. I was only thinking, there's no remedy now, she won't come back. . . . Let it be, do what is just. . . . But I'm saying, you've come here all hot and tired, shall I cut a green coconut for you?'

Boloram Shaha's hectoring seemed to have lost some of its energy now, but at this he flared up again. 'What? Cut a green coconut for me? Boloram Shaha sit in this home and drink its water? . . . Boloram will drink from a green coconut the day when – I hang that murderer from the gallows.'

He opened the door-bolt with a clang and stomped out.

But why did Boloram Shaha take a rickshaw and turn towards the station? Hadn't he decided to go to the morgue? To see his Phuli for the last time?

No, no, Boloram didn't want to see the broken, monstrous Phuli. Let his Phuli remain whole in his mind.

After that, reports of the 'Phuleshshori Kundu Killing' case in every newspaper . . . 'Kundu Father and Son' keep on rotting in custody, aren't set free on bail. Many people of the neighbourhood have made known their readiness to give eyewitness testimony.

Particularly that shock-haired boy and his group . . . the son of a shala of Shoshi Kundu's relatives. Reared in his pishi's house . . . Shoshi Kundu always calls him an unwanted adoption, thinks him poison to both eyes, can never stand his coming to his house and looking in and calling 'Boudi, Boudi'. . . . Or rather, he never could.

And apart from that, because of Shorot's virtues, the number of people opposed to them in the neighbourhood was greater.

Nevertheless, the Phuleshshori case didn't take long to be resolved.

The accused, instead of hanging from the gallows, was found not guilty and set free to come out patting himself on the chest.

The case was saved by the prime witness Boloram Shaha's unimaginable testimony. . . . Although he had brought the case himself.

But –

Having come to the court to give testimony, he raised his voice and said, 'What can I do, Sir! My only child, motherless since her infancy – I suddenly heard of her accidental death, and I couldn't keep my head straight. Who could, Your Honour? Could you, if you were in a situation like that? . . . Wouldn't you run right up and bring a case?'

An uproar arose in the courtroom, the lawyer scolded him, but still Boloram spoke in his broken, harsh-sounding voice, 'Later I remembered her lifelong ailment. Now out of a sense of duty and my good judgment I'm telling you about it – and so – give me whatever legal punishment is prescribed for harassing the court. Boloram Shaha will lay his head down and take it. . . .'

But what was that ailment? That childhood ailment of Phuleshshori Kundu's? . . . Nothing else – losing her sense of direction when very sleepy. . . . Right from her girlhood, if she had to get up at night, how many times had Phuleshshori thought the wall to be the door and raised a bump on her forehead; or thinking the loosely shut door was the wall and leaning on it, had pushed against it and stumbled and fallen to the floor; or had confused the locations of the room's cot and bedding, clothes-rail, and chest of drawers, had tried to turn on the light and hit herself – all this!

Indeed the people of the house made fun of this disease of hers: who knew that this trivial ailment, fodder for laughter, would become the cause of Phuleshshori's death!

If it had been any other witness, it was doubtful whether this testimony could have withstood 'His Honour's' examination, but the man was the deceased Phuleshshori Kundu's father himself!

And therefore, the fact that Shoshi Kundu's son Shorot Kundu would be found not guilty and set free to walk around patting himself on the chest – what was so strange about that?

First and Last

প্রথম ও শেষ

Prothom O Shesh

Not half a day or a day, but a full four and a half years.

Yes, exactly.

Even in his painful state – breath stopped by that pressure on his collar – Probir calculated in his head: exactly four years six months.

But after four years and six months, the fact that Probir and Onadi would come face to face suddenly at twelve midnight in the waiting room of a railway station, and that the very next moment Onadi would pounce on Probir and grab hold of his shirt collar – that had not been among even his most intolerable imaginings.

If Probir had not seen Onadi in such a clear, sharp light, maybe he would have thought him a robber or hoodlum and yelled out. But now there was no reason for him to yell out. Because Probir had sat down directly facing the entrance to the waiting room, and on the wall behind Probir was that sign of the railway company's generosity, a high-wattage lamp.

Yes, even if first-class passengers nowadays were deprived of many facilities and conveniences, the first-class waiting rooms still bore some witness to their former grandeur.

But let that be; as soon as Onadi entered the room, Probir saw him clearly, making no mistake.

A frontier station far from Bengal. The last train had arrived at eleven, and now everything was still all around. If you saw it, you wouldn't believe that only an hour earlier a thunderous clamour had filled the place. Now it seemed as though an inert corpse lay there awaiting cremation.

The bustle would commence again at the end of the night.

The engine, having slept all night, would be stuffed with water and coal; its mechanisms would be examined to see if anything had been impaired. The guard would toil, the stationmaster would toil, the pointsman would toil, the gang of coolies and sweepers would toil, and then the whistle would be blown.

All these people who were lying around with their heads tucked in somehow, of the same family as their luggage, huddled here and there in the waiting room, or on the open platform – even among them the consciousness of life would awaken. As soon as the night ended, each would rush towards their destination. Some would go and catch buses to travel in different directions; some would go to the airport with the intention of travelling even farther.

The newly swept and swabbed railcar cabins would fill up again with new luggage and new people.

But all that could not be comprehended now.

Now everything was still, perfectly silent, lifeless. Only Probir had been sitting awake, because he had a lot of cash with him. He had to go to Srinagar on business-related work; right at dawn he'd have to get up and rush to the airport. But where had Onadi been all this time? He had come by the same train!

Astonishing, they were on the same train, Onadi and Probir! And yet they didn't see each other even once. Who knew why! Probir had to climb down and wander around the platform on two separate occasions. An agent of their company was supposed to come and meet him at Jallandar and Amritsar, that was the arrangement. Otherwise Probir could have taken the plane – then he wouldn't have had to risk carrying so much cash and sitting there sleepless.

But if he hadn't had to!

If Probir had chosen to travel by plane, as he'd done before!

Then at least this terrible, dramatic moment would never have manifested itself in this drama. Then two strong men would not have been finished forever.

Probir would have gone about Probir's pursuits, Onadi would have gone on doing Onadi's tasks, many more years would have passed like the past four and a half years – perhaps all the years of their lives – without the two seeing each other's faces. Although at one time it was almost certain, like the rules of the sun and the moon, that they would come face to face at least once by the end of the day, every day. The married, contented, fat-salaried man of the house Onadi, and the hostel-dwelling jobless vagabond bachelor Probir.

Onadi didn't go to Probir's mess all that often, it was Probir who was the perennial guest in Onadi's household of contentment. Of course, seeing the gleaming-and-shining Probir of today, wearing his expensive shoes, his valuable watch and glasses, and his costly woollen suit, it was difficult to recognize the poet Probir of those days, wearing that open-collared, half-soiled panjabi with an extremely ordinary pair of slippers on his feet, but Onadi didn't err even for an instant in recognizing him. And the instant that he recognized him, in that very instant the memory of that terrible night four and a half years earlier rose up like a recent experience and bit Onadi. And Onadi, writhing with the fire of that bite, lost his compass and grabbed Probir's collar.

Freeing himself with a jerk, Probir said, with the angry rumble of a suppressed shout, 'Onadi-da!'

Astonishing! That old salutation came to his mouth even at this intolerable moment?

Onadi reached out with his hand to press down on his collar again and said, teeth pressed down on teeth, 'Don't! Forget about trying to bring back that old relationship – now it's time to call on your god.'

Probir's large and robust body bucked away and slipped out of Onadi's hand once more, then Probir put a hand in his pocket and said in a terrible voice, 'You too might need to call upon God, Onadi-da. I'm carrying a lot of our company's money with me, and to ensure its safety I even have a weapon in my pocket.'

Onadi, panting, sat down in the cane easy-chair nearby and said in a tone of hatred, contempt, and ferocity, 'Where's Korobi?'

Korobi!

Probir was jolted as though struck by lightning. 'What did you say? Where's Korobi? You're asking this question, *you*'re asking *me*?'

Onadi stood up again. 'Which other devil should I ask?'

Probir suddenly became still and said, 'You don't have news of Korobi?'

Onadi sat down again. This one was shaking, the other one was panting.

'Those who can take someone else's wife from her family and run away – such acting comes naturally to them!' Onadi said in a bitter voice. Like the bitter voice in which he used to say to Korobi, four or five years ago, 'The woman who has lost herself in love for another man – such acting comes naturally to her!'

Yes, Onadi had suspected Korobi right from the beginning. From the day Korobi said, when the marriage was very young, 'That's Probir Rai! How astonishing! What fun!'

'Why fun?' Onadi had said, quickly furrowing his brow.

'Ba, isn't it fun, he's such a friend of yours, and I hear he's a kind of distant cousin as well, so we'll see him pretty often. I'll be able to see him, talk to him, if I want I'll be able to read his fresh writings even before he sends them to print – isn't that fun? If my friends hear, their mouths will fall open.'

'Is that so. That "him", I mean that Srijukto Probir-babu – I suppose he's almost the same as Robi-babu?' Onadi said with a sarcastic smile.

The new bride, young, brimming over with amorous affection for her husband, couldn't catch this sudden change of tone. She said, 'Aha! I suppose you can't be a poet unless you're the same as Robindronath? Is everyone cast from the same mould? Probir Rai's a modern poet!'

'All the useless unfortunates who have no ability to write, but certainly have the urge to hold a pen, they become modern poets,' Onadi said, and dropped the curtain on the subject for the day. But the thorn that pricked him right in the middle of his chest, that didn't come out.

That a face lit up with the joy of being a newly married woman could be so distressing, Onadi hadn't known even a minute earlier.

But Onadi had truly loved Probir.

Whatever the slim thread of kinship was, even if he couldn't recall it exactly, this fellow-student from childhood, this devoted friend from childhood, had created a lake of deep affection in Onadi's rough desert heart, which lacked the sap of poetic sentiment. The enchanted, marvelling gaze of Onadi's new wife towards Probir did indeed plant a thorny branch in Onadi's heart, but right then that lake of pleasant affection did not dry up at all.

A strange mystery from the mysterious play of the mind! It was at Onadi's own urging that Probir took on the role of daily guest at Onadi's house.

Onadi didn't have too many people who could be called close relatives, and those who had come and gathered at the wedding had all slipped away right after the wedding like floodwaters after a flood, leaving only Onadi with his new wife Korobi. Therefore Onadi turned to Probir for relief, with an appeal to grant some company to the solitary.

'You can come to your Boudi and chat with her a little. The poor woman is always by herself. Especially in the evening. You know I don't return before eight or nine in the evening.'

'Office-loving people like you ought not to marry,' Probir said, laughing. 'You'll return at nine at night, and I'll sit and babble – I don't think that's going to make Boudi overflow with delight.'

'You don't, do you?' Onadi laughed. That this babbling could in the end take on the tune of billing and cooing – nothing at all surprising about that. 'But you know what it is?' Onadi dropped his voice to a deep bass and said, 'Your Boudi stays alone in a desolate house, and that Nogen, I mean that servant fellow, is here, you understand? And besides, there's a lot of jewellery and such, right? Your Boudi says that in the evenings, when the man hovers around the room on the pretext of work, she turns queasy. A mighty cowardly girl, I can see now.'

Probir protested forcefully. 'No, Onadi-da, in such a situation you can't call her mighty cowardly, not at all. Boudi's a new bride, in such a situation any woman would feel the same fear and unease.'

'Is that so?' A hard-looking smile broke out on Onadi's face. 'So your Boudi has thought long and hard and discovered a pretty natural-sounding excuse, what do you say?'

Probir found another meaning for this 'excuse' and thought, Korobi must certainly have told Onadi about her fear and feeling queasy and asked him to come home early. So he laughed and said, 'It's natural to find an excuse, but the reason can't be ignored either, Onadi-da. You could do one thing, though – remove the servant and keep a full-time maid for her.'

'Would you listen to that!' Onadi waved away Probir's suggestion like so much cigarette smoke. 'What work would a maid be able to do? The dishes and clothes, at most. Don't we need a man for the outside work? I can't do anything at all. And besides, the man is a complete expert. His cooking hand is so good, if I eat his mutton, ghee-rice, or fries and cutlets, I think I'm eating at a restaurant. People would do severe penance to get this kind of man – and not find one. Besides, he isn't a villain type of fellow. That fear of your Boudi's is quite baseless. The truth is, she wants someone there in the evenings.'

'Someone?' Probir laughed. 'To say that anyone would be enough – that would be misjudging Boudi, Onadi-da.'

Suddenly Onadi laughed out loud. 'Onadi Shen never makes a mistake in judgement, I tell you. But what's your objection now? What work can you have at that time? Writing poetry, right? You can do that sitting here. In fact, you'll get more inspiration.'

'No, I'm not dying to write poetry.' Probir laughed. 'What do you think poets are?'

The shadow of refusal that was peeking into the room of Probir's judgement, Probir wasn't able to hold up that shadow in front of this easy, innocent, generous soul of Onadi's. He was ashamed, was abashed!

Truly, how could he say, in front of that extremely affectionate, liberal soul, how can you trust me either? Am I any less frightening than that servant of yours?

He wasn't able to say that.

Thus Probir had to take the job of daily guest at Onadi's house.

But was it possible to fathom this strange mystery of Onadi's heart? At least Korobi hadn't fathomed it. She couldn't understand it at all: the Probir about whom there was such jealousy and such a lack of trust in Onadi's mind, why this affectionate welcome on Onadi's part for him? Why this daily invitation, why this pleading with him to have dinner every evening, on the pretext of first-class cooking by Nogen's hand?

How many times, after all, did they sit down at night to dine just two at the table? Three were fixed for dinner. Why? Why? Countless times Korobi asked the question of herself, of Onadi. Never did she find a satisfactory answer.

How could he answer – did he himself know why?

Maybe that servant-related fear was not quite baseless to him, maybe he thought, certainly Probir would not do any major harm, or maybe he really couldn't help giving the hostel-dwelling Probir a share in their good eating and drinking.

Who knew what it was.

To all appearances Onadi was a liberal, open-hearted, affectionate friend to Probir.

And whatever darkness there was in his mind was expressed to Korobi.

A twisted smile, an oblique utterance, bitterness and sarcasm – Korobi became almost accustomed to all these. She took all these as a kind of amusement for Onadi. In the beginning she was extremely vexed and thought she would tell Probir, behind Onadi's back, 'Don't come here any more.' But she wasn't able to utter this unthinkable sentence in front of this civilized, polite, polished man. And then – she stopped bothering! Let Onadi speak; saying this or that was his amusement.

But the situation took on a terrible aspect after Khoka was born. After seeing the boy's face Onadi suddenly seemed to go mad. One day he spoke out clearly: 'Why would a dark-skinned man like me have such a fair son?'

The implication was so abominable, so vulgar that Korobi seemed to turn to stone. Jealousy, bitterness, sarcasm with a woman's heart was one thing, this was something else. Should Korobi bear such a monstrous dishonour, merely because she was Onadi's wedded wife?

Still, with difficulty she controlled herself, and, not heeding the dishonour, Korobi said, 'Why, am I any less fair than Khoka?'

'Not only his complexion,' Onadi said, biting out the words, letting out a poison breath. 'His entire appearance is witness to your treachery.'

That day Korobi did tell Probir, 'Don't come here any more.' She said, 'There's no end to your friend's jealousy about you. He has this idea that I'm in love with you. Anyway, at least now I have a companion! From now on Khoka'll be able to protect me from all the world's storms and strains and loneliness. . . . What do you say, Khoka-babu?'

No, it wouldn't do to say it any more seriously than that.

It struck at one's self-respect.

Was Probir startled on hearing of his friend's jealousy?

No, Probir wasn't startled.

With his man's heart, Probir had felt Onadi's inner agony at every moment. He'd felt it, but he hadn't moved away. Hadn't moved away, because he hadn't been able to move away. He'd known and understood everything but had still taken advantage of Onadi's mask. Why should Probir have revealed his understanding when, if he didn't show up even one day, Onadi would send the servant around to ask why he hadn't come the previous day?

And really, Probir wasn't causing Onadi any injury! Only a few sweet smiles, a little easy conversation, some innocent companionship – that was all he wanted!

Probir was pure in his own judgement.

But the upheaval was caused by Korobi's caution.

Probir wasn't startled, he only said: 'There's no end to my jealousy about my friend either. Whenever I see him, I'm reminded of the example of the string of pearls around the monkey's neck. And I want to snatch the pearl necklace from his neck and run away.'

Probir wasn't startled, Korobi was.

Then she looked at him with a kind of fixed, unblinking gaze and smiled a strange smile and said, 'You only want! But you don't have the courage!'

'I do!' Suddenly Probir clasped one of her hands. 'Are you ready?'

Korobi laughed out loud, a regular giggling kind of laugh. 'Do women ever answer that question?'

Silently Probir looked at her face, coloured with laughter, for a while, then said slowly, 'I had come to give you all a piece of news today, suddenly I've had a bit of unsolicited mercy from the goddess of fortune, I might have to leave Calcutta in a few days.'

'So much the better,' Korobi said, laughing. 'It'll be easy to rescue Sheeta from the forest.'

Probir, even if he was a little ashamed at his earlier outburst of passion, wasn't subdued, so he smiled gently and said, 'Even if the comparison is the wrong way around.'

'Which is wrong and which is right,' Korobi said, smiling, 'who's Rabon, who's Ram, can we discover that so soon? But yes, it's clear that you don't like the brother-in-law Lokkhon's role.'

Probir said, in a serious manner, 'You can joke all you want, Korobi, but I'm telling the truth – whenever I see you at Onadi-da's side, that kind of desire rises up in my mind. I want to snatch you and run away, far away.'

'A pious desire, no doubt,' Korobi said, 'but it's only that all the bravery of today's brave men seems to dissolve in that "desire". My Khoka won't be like that – what do you say, ré?'

After that, only two or three days later, came that terrible night.

That was the day Probir was to go to Amritsar on work. In the morning, Probir received a strange letter by Nogen's hand – in Korobi's handwriting.

'I've found out what time your train is, I'll be at the station at the right time – do you have the courage to take me with you? You won't step back at the last minute, will you? There's still time to tell me.

You know women. They don't step off the ground until they have their foot firmly in the boat.'

This letter, sent by Nogen's hand, in an ordinary, open envelope! Probir examined the envelope, turning it over. Had it been open, or had it been opened?

But what was the answer to this letter?

He asked Nogen himself, in a bewildered manner, 'Did she ask for an answer?'

Nogen said, 'Why, no, she didn't.'

The night train.

The whole day passed in such an unnatural state! How dangerous even the most wished-for event in life can be, when it appears before us – this is probably proof of that!

What would Probir do now?

Would he really gather up the courage to welcome and accept that most wished-for event with wedding-garland in hand? Or would he run and dissuade Korobi from taking this morally injurious path, this path of complete destruction?

The sound of Korobi's laugh of the other day began to play in his chest.

'All the bravery of the brave men of this age seems to dissolve in "desire".'

Fine. Let it be. Probir would see what his fate was ready to give him. Marking the conclusion of a most unbearable jobless life, this opportunity had presented itself in an almost unsolicited manner, quite beyond his expectations. Now let him see if the colour of life's inner palace was changed.

What was Probir's fault?

Probir wasn't deliberately doing anything on his own.

Why should he be blamed with the sin of abducting his friend's wife and running away? All day Probir had done much explaining to his conscience!

But who had imagined that the last scene of that day's drama would be so strange, so terrible?

The time went by in counting the moments of waiting and in piercing the entire platform with the arrows of his stretched-neck gaze. The train left.

Bewildered, Probir looked around foolishly. Then he shook himself and walked forward to send a wire to his destination: 'Missed train, will depart at next opportunity.' Then he turned back and headed towards Onadi's house.

But why did Probir go there?

To this day Probir has not quite understood that. Has not understood what purpose he hoped to attain! He only remembers that he burnt with an immense insult, and in his mortification, with his grudge, he wanted to say four harsh words to Korobi.

So then all this was a cruel joke of Korobi's!

But what need did she have to cause such an upheaval for Probir, right at the time when the luckless man had suddenly seen a glimmer of light? Suppose Probir was not able to reach there at the appointed time and for that offence lose the job! What consolation would Korobi be able to offer him then?

Why did Korobi act this way? Had Probir made a mistake in judging the colour of Korobi's face? . . .

No, maybe this was what was called 'rich people's affections'.[1]

On the head of anger, Probir even thought that if Onadi was present at the house, he would draw open the curtain on their relationship in front of him. He'd show him Korobi's letter.

Maybe Korobi had laughed merrily with Onadi about those few words of Probir's, embellished with passion, the other day; maybe Onadi himself had told her to make him understand. Maybe the letter was written at Onadi's direction. Or else why had it come by

Nogen's hand, in an open envelope, that letter? Probir should have understood right then!

Lashing out mentally at his own stupidity all the while, Probir landed up at Onadi's house, God knows how.

But when he reached there and came face-to-face with the door, he turned to wood.

No, no sounds of crying or sobbing came from within the house. Nor any commotion, nor any crowd of people on the outside. Only, in the evening, the house seemed to stand utterly still with a black cloth already wrapped around it. And standing even more still was the servant Nogen, just beside the door. The door hung with its mouth open.

Probir, too, became somehow still and stood there a few moments, then said in an extremely calm manner, 'Is no one at home?'

No sound came from Nogen. I suppose he answered only with a shake of his head.

Probir hesitated a little, then said, 'Do you know where they've gone?'

Nogen suddenly spoke up, in an unnatural tone, rapidly: 'Babu has taken Khoka to the burning-ground, Ma left just this moment, I don't know where she's gone. Please don't ask me anything more, Kaka-babu.'

Maybe Probir didn't hear the last remark, so he suddenly screamed out, '*Where* has Babu taken Khoka?'

'I told you,' Nogen said in an exhausted voice. 'Please don't make me say it with my mouth again. Let me go now, please, all of you. After seeing what happens in this house – '

Still Probir's intellect failed him; still he screamed out, 'What happened to Khoka?'

'Don't know,' Nogen answered in a rough voice.

Suddenly Probir thought, all this is a story concocted by this man;

the fellow wanted to fool Probir and get rid of him. So he pushed him aside suddenly and went into the house.

But for how many seconds, even?

He came running out again as though chased by a ghost, and without looking this way or that, without saying a word, he rushed out, leaving the neighbourhood behind.

But still, had his merely leaving the neighbourhood gained him release from the hands of that dreadful scene? Has he gained it yet?

The entire house yawned empty, from bottom to top. And Korobi's bedroom was fully open to view. Even the panels of the armoire were parted. And, and, on the floor of the room a small side-pillow of Khoka's had rolled, and close to that pillow was a blackened line of blood!

From that day until now, so many changes have come to Probir's life, so many lands near and far has he roamed, and yet whenever he's alone that scene seems to bare its horrifying teeth and chase after him.

How many thousands of times that scene has terrified Probir in these past four and a half years, and how many thousands of times Probir has thought, Maybe then that letter of Korobi's that day wasn't a jest after all. Maybe as soon as Onadi found out – .

But look at what happened, how it happened!

Had Onadi gone mad at his wife's treachery and taken his own child and – ! But why kill his child and not his wife? So had he tried to strike Korobi, and this grievous thing had occurred accidentally? The infant was barely six or seven months old, and maybe with the slightest inattention – ! Or had Korobi herself taken this child, this thorn in her path – chhi chhi chhi! Probir had lashed himself, but still that suspicion had chased him around. Or else where did Korobi go? Or had Onadi, frantic for revenge, come back from the burning-ground and finished his half-completed deed? No no, was that possible either?

Maybe, calm after the storm, Korobi was running Onadi's world even today. . . .

When he tries to think about that, his entire body fills with the poison of hate; and yet, the thought that everything is ended – he doesn't want to think that either! That he might see Korobi just once, that Probir might ask her the question just once, 'Korobi, what happened? Korobi, why this cruelty on your part?'

In these four and a half years, Probir has come and gone from Calcutta many times, and roamed one end of the city to the other. Roaming around was his job. But nowhere, never has he seen Korobi even for an instant. Has found no trace of her!

No trace of Onadi either. Some other tenant is in Onadi's house now.

The question that Probir has asked a thousand times in a rock-hard voice, coming face-to-face with Onadi in his mind – today he has the chance really to stand face-to-face and ask that question. But he didn't think that Onadi too would ask him the same question.

Where is Korobi!

Does Onadi hope to get the answer to this question from Probir?

To him, Probir's astonishment is only acting!

Suddenly Probir catches hold of him with both hands and shakes him and says, 'It's even more natural for that devil who can kill his own child.'

All of a sudden Onadi becomes completely immobile.

His face looks like a dead man's. In a hopeless voice he says, 'So Korobi's said the same thing to you too! And you believed it too? But by God – no, I won't take God's name – if there's anything completely pure anywhere in the world, in the name of that, Probir, I did not kill the boy. Even if he wasn't my child, he was a tender infant, wasn't he? And I would – ? You tell me, Probir, am I a monster?'

But by then Probir has given him another shaking.

'Even if he wasn't your child – ! What does that mean? Have you gone insane, or are you drunk now?'

'It would have been fine if I'd gone insane, and if I could get drunk that would be fine too.' Onadi speaks with the same immobile eyes and slack face, in a hopeless tone. 'But none of that happened. The boy wasn't mine! I had understood that, and in the end Korobi clearly admitted it too. Admitted the boy was yours! But even then, believe me, Probir, an innocent infant like that, I – '

Now it's Probir's turn to feel hopeless. Surely Onadi has developed some mental illness. Yes, surely. So he says, hopelessly, 'I'm not able to understand anything you say, Onadi-da.'

But I suppose Onadi hasn't heard what Probir said at all, so he carries on from his previous remark and says, 'A cruel jest of the Lord's upon a man! He can't know whether his wife's child is his own or not! What can be a more terrible cruel jest of the Lord's upon a human than this? The day Korobi herself admitted it clearly, that day I was free of doubt. But still, believe me, Probir, even though night and day I was burning to death with suspicion, I didn't deliberately throw the boy from the bed. He rolled and fell himself, at a moment when I was inattentive. Oh, what a terrible sight!'

The picture of that dreadful evening floats up once again in Probir's mind!

Then he says slowly, 'But Korobi?'

'Don't keep on with your fake acting any more, Probir,' Onadi says in an extinguished voice, 'and I won't make any claim to Korobi any more. The day Korobi wrote that letter and went to you, from that day I've turned to stone. Only when I suddenly saw you on the platform after so long, I don't know what happened, all the blood in my body started to boil! I thought Korobi was with you, so for a long time – '

Probir, astonished, says in a quiet voice, 'You're chasing an enormous mistake, Onadi-da, and I'm running too. But what had Korobi written in that letter?'

All at once Onadi lifts up his attaché case and opens it, and from a secret compartment he takes out a folded piece of paper. He holds it out and says, 'The letter is right here with me, all my life it'll be with me. I couldn't destroy it! You know why?'

By then Probir has the letter in his hand.

Before he unfolds it he looks once at Onadi with a questioning gaze. And Onadi smiles a strange, distressed smile and says, 'This is the only letter I have of your Boudi's.' He says, 'It's the last one, it's the first one. After we were married she was always with me.'

But by then Probir has unfolded the letter and read it. He utters an inarticulate cry and says, 'You believed this letter? You read that meaning in this letter?'

'How can I mistake its meaning, what should I not believe?' Onadi says, in a bitter, mocking tone.

'Whether you should or shouldn't – look at my face,' Probir says in a firm, serious voice, 'look carefully, clearly, distinctly! Then tell me if you should not believe.'

Onadi looks. He looks and trembles.

The letter's lying on the table. Attesting to a terrible lie. This is written: 'Your suspicion is indeed right, what you've said for so long is right. Khoka is not your child.

'All right; maybe it wouldn't have been possible to keep him alive while living at your house, God protected me by giving me freedom so quickly. Having received the notice of this freedom, I am relieved; I can go to him who is Khoka's true father! Be happy; find peace!'

Onadi says, bewildered, 'Did I misunderstand, Probir? But what else can it be?'

'It can be many things, Onadi-da, only your suspicion isn't right. Why did you make such an enormous mistake, Onadi-da? Why did you think Korobi so vile? I'm telling you the truth – Korobi never came to me.'

'Never came!'

'No.'

'Then where is she?'

'I don't know. I think the God who's given her freedom, he alone knows.'

Probir too has a 'first and last' letter from Korobi, but he doesn't take it out.

Let it be, let one secret remain forever undiscovered!

That lack of discovery is itself Probir's peace, and his consolation.

The two of them are seated at two ends of the table, motionless. Suddenly Onadi stretches out his hand and clutches Probir's arm and cries out, howling, 'Believe me, Probir, that small child, I – '

'I believe it, Onadi-da.'

Probir holds that hand of Onadi's with his other hand, tightly. Then both of them sit there in silence, their heads bowed over the table. As though two newly grief-stricken people are sitting with lowered heads, touching the bier of someone extremely beloved of them.

Newly grief-stricken, indeed.

It's only now that Korobi's death has occurred!

All these days Korobi had been alive in both their worlds! Maybe as a traitor, maybe as a cruel jester – but still, she was alive! She didn't end this way.

And with Korobi as their support, they too had survived.

As soon as Korobi ended, they too ended. Now what else can they do but sit with lowered heads, touching the bier of the glorious newly dead?

Foolhardy

দুঃসাহসিক

Du-shahoshik

'Aré, are you the Otonu Rai who's newly returned from America? . . .' Partho-protim used the convenience of the buffet dinner to move forward past various people and come face to face with the person who was his target.

He said, 'The famous Otonu of Priyonath Mollick Road, isn't that right?'

Both had full plates of food in their hands, so their greetings took the form of a slight lowering of their heads. . . . Otonu had to lower his slightly more. He smiled and said, 'I can't say it's wrong. . . . I'm wandering about with this six-and-a-half-foot body wrapped in a cover called "Otonu". And of Priyonath Mollick Road too, certainly. But in what way did I become famous?'

'It's difficult to say, moshai, who becomes famous and in what way. Someone becomes famous by sticking a knife in someone else, and someone else by getting a knife stuck in them. . . . Anyway, now that your identity's been discovered, we've also determined that you're closely related to me. Therefore, at the end of the party I'm going to arrest you and take you away.'

Otonu couldn't quite understand who this gentleman was, my-dearing him this way. Still, he made an instinctive guess. But there was some doubt too – was it possible?

Still, he said with a smiling face, 'Since you consider me closely related, I hope you won't arrest me and take me to a police station. But now that you're taking me away – if I knew *where* I had to go, I would get a bit of light. The close relationship must be on both sides, surely.'

'No! No! Should one ever solve a mystery right at the beginning?'

'That means I have to be covered by this web of mystery and follow you like a blind man?'

'Good Lord! Even after staying over there so long, you still have such a good command of Bengali? That's terrific. . . . Do you still write poems and such?'

'I can see that you know a lot about me. Then it's possible you might know that too.'

'Certainly it's possible. From the way you talk it sounds like you write, and you publish as well. But you know what the trouble is? I don't really understand modern poems-shoems, so they don't come to my attention, or maybe I don't bring them to my attention. Anyway, I hope you won't run away. . . . I'll be back.'

Otonu laughed and said, 'Then I need to keep you under close surveillance. If I knew your name, I could ask someone in the crowd – By the way, what's the license plate on his car? . . . But I can put my powers of deduction to use and say, maybe the name is Partho-protim Mukherjee.'

'Correct.' Partho-protim laughed. 'It's been proved once again that poets have great intuition. License plate . . . but you won't have to look for it, since I'm walking around with handcuffs. But your plate's empty.'

'I've finished eating. . . .' Otonu smiled a little and lowered the plate onto the long side-table. An enormous hall, with long tables scattered here and there and heaped with food, and uniformed servers frequently supplying fresh, hot loads. The party was in full swing. . . . The chief of the firm had come from Bombay on an inspection tour, and this feast was in his honour.

Partho-protim went over to the other side and saw that Lolita-di was single-mindedly picking up roshogollas, squeezing out the syrup with her fingers, and collecting them on her plate. Stopping beside her, he said, 'Lolita-di, don't eat so many roshogollas, your figure will be ruined.'

'Ah, stop it! Don't you keep on at me like Choudhury. Hey, it looked like you were talking to Otonu!'

'What it looked like – that's exactly what it was. I started up a conversation.'

It was Lolita herself who had noticed Otonu a little while earlier and pointed him out to Partho-protim: 'Ei, ei Partho, that tall man. He's Otonu.' Because before this, Lolita herself had served up to Partho all sorts of facts regarding Otonu.

But now she wrinkled her nose and said, 'What did you go and start up a conversation with him for? . . . What if he takes this opportunity and says, Someday I'll come to your house.'

Partho-protim laughed.

'Oh, I told him myself, that I would grab him and take him with me in the car when I left.'

'Take him with you! Where?'

'To this worthless man's hut. Even if I'm wretched, at least I have a homestead, thanks to my ancestors.'

'I see you've learned to be modest like the sheths.[1] They're the ones who take you into a palace and say, a poor man's poor quarters. And baba, your ancestors' homestead is no less than a palace either. . . . But anyway, you offered to take him to your house?'

'I did indeed!'

'Amazing! Partho, are you insane!'

Partho-protim looked at the embarrassed face of his cousin by marriage and said, 'Why so?'

'You've heard about Sheema's past history from me, Partho!'

In the middle of her remark Lolita Choudhury lifted a roshogolla from the plate with a spoon and carefully put it into her mouth, saving her lipstick, and carefully bit into it, then said in a disappointed voice, 'And you're asking me why! . . . My didima used to say, "Dig a trench, and climb in with a crocodile." This is just the same.'

Partho-protim smiled a little. He looked at that agitated and – with one more roshogolla stuffed into it – swollen-cheeked face and said, 'The history's in the past. Isn't that right?'

Lolita said in a soft but strong voice, 'Look, Partho, don't do something childish trying to show your courage. You know that even if you think the fire's gone out, you shouldn't believe it too easily.'

It can be seen that Lolita Choudhury, wrapped in a wrapping of extremely modern dress and makeup, hasn't been able to come very far ahead of her didima. . . . Or at any rate she's collected quite a few suitable proverbs from her didima and kept them with her.

Partho looked at her short hair, her short blouse, her short stature, and her tight-sari-clad, almost comic form, and in his mind he laughed an amused laugh. But still he brought an extreme solemnity to his face. 'Now that's surprising! Why are you magnifying such a small matter? A class-friend of Sheema's, and besides, a neighbourhood familiar for such a long time, he's back from abroad after so long, think how happy she'll be to see him? If the poor woman hadn't been ill, she would have met him here today.'

Lolita finished off the remaining roshogolla and put the plate down, then cast her glance this way and that to see if anything new had arrived on the table. . . . No, nothing new could be seen. That Partho was standing in front of her again. Otherwise she could have picked up a last fish-fry. They were first-class. Afraid there might be an objection to her helping herself freely, poor Lolita had moved away from Choudhury. But here too there was trouble.

Combining the two annoyances, Lolita said, 'The class-friend had at one time become a bosom friend – if you know that and still want to be so magnanimous, go ahead, bhai. I have nothing to say. But I can't really praise your judgement. If Choudhury hears this, he too – '

Just then Lolita Choudhury's 'Choudhury' himself made his appearance. He said, 'What, are you still eating? No, you'll be the end of me!'

'Ah! Don't talk like a boor. Everyone has to be a starving saint because you're a gastric patient, right? Otonu's come, that's what Partho and I were talking about.'

'What's there to talk about? You introduced him to Partho, did you?'

'I didn't have to,' Lolita said in a disgusted voice. 'Partho didn't go anywhere near good manners – he went forward himself and started talking to him. A man who's spent so much time abroad – think how he must have laughed to himself.'

Partho said in guileless fashion, 'There's so much fodder for laughter all around us, Lolita-di, a little bit more won't be noticed.... Anyway, now the crowd's thinning out, let's cut and leave. All right, Lolita-di, ... all right, Choudhury-da ... may I? Let me see where the gentleman's wandering ...'

Lolita spoke up quickly. 'So it's true, you're really taking him home?'

'What a bother, why this true-or-false about such a little thing?'

Choudhury let his pipe hang loose from a corner of his mouth and said, 'What's this sudden argument about true and false?'

'No argument at all ...,' Lolita said in a scornful voice. 'To please his wife, Partho's taking her former class-friend to his house, and so I was saying – it's not an act of great good judgement – '

'What? That Otonu? Really? *Ha ha ha!* Partho, in your wife-love you've outdone even me.'

'You?' Lolita cast him a fiery glance from her kohl-drawn eyes and said, 'Where does the question of outdoing you come from? Anh, outdoing you! You must think before you speak, understand?'

Choudhury said, 'The fate of the ill-fated! . . . If you could dig up a class-friend or two, I'd show you. Anyway, you have to say Partho has a hard chest. All right, Partho, okay!'

Lolita, as she walked out behind her loose-limbed husband, said, puffing, 'You don't need a hard chest to play with fire. You need a little stupidity and some stubbornness.'

Choudhury swung his pipe around and said, 'So why are you getting so heated up? What do you have to get or give? We spend money to watch someone play with a snake, what's so bad if you can see that for free?'

Even after sitting down in the car Lolita kept the subject alive. She held a small battery-driven fan in front of her face and dried the sweat on her neck in its fluttering breeze. She said, 'Well, can you tell me what Partho's intention is? I didn't leave anything out when I told him their history. And yet – '

Choudhury kept the steering wheel firmly under control and, turning it slowly, said, 'Since you took that responsibility, there's no question of leaving anything out. On the contrary, the telling must have been quite elaborate, with a layer of colour added – '

'Colour! I added colour in telling him? You always insult me this way when you talk – what do you mean by it? Didn't they always run away from college and go strolling on Chandpal Ghat? . . . And on the way back from college, didn't they make the excuse of going to get books from the library and go off and start talking? Didn't Pishe-moshai suddenly one day see Sheema and Otonu going into the Metro cinema? Am I making all this up?'

'It's very possible you aren't. But what was the occasion to tell Partho all these details, that's what I'm wondering.'

'What other occasion – wasn't it right to make him a little careful? . . . An unsuspecting fellow – '

'And Sheema's your sister!'

'What of it? I've always been on the side of the truth.'

'That's true! . . .' Choudhury laughed. 'But yes, this childishness of Partho's *is* stupidity. Once you start pleasing the female race, how far you have to drag that out in the end, he doesn't know!'

'Don't suddenly start generalizing about the entire sex like a boor, I'm telling you. . . .'

'Oh, sorry! When I talk about the sex, you go into an ill temper. But this is true . . . this is really Partho's stupidity. I saw the man. I might have seen him before – I don't quite remember. I saw in his appearance that he'd recently lived abroad. But I can't blame your sister either. On the contrary, I'd praise her. Finding such a treasure, in her unclaimed state, and merely going as far as Chandpal Ghat and the Metro and stopping at that. She could have gone to hell if she wanted. Wouldn't have blamed her if she had.'

Lolita said in a harsh voice, 'Maybe now your shali will take up the unread part of *that* book.'

Right about then, in another car, the two men under discussion were making remarks from time to time. 'What I was saying, Mr Mukherjee – let it be for today, I'll come to your house another day.'

'But what's the problem today? Your driver will go home and let them know.'

'No, it's not that. I mean, you were saying Sheema was unwell today, and to bother her suddenly – '

Partho laughed. 'Maybe the bother will make her feel better. Don't worry, it's nothing major, just a very minor fever. A fever largely due to will power. Whenever she hears about a party or such, she develops a fever. She'll get it up to a hundred at least.'

Otonu laughed. 'Can the temperature be raised by will power?'

'Moshai, I know that it can. Women can do many such things that are outside our comprehension. And yet, when it's a wedding at a relative's house, I see her dancing her way there.'

Right away Otonu liked the man. The manner of his speech was so homely. Maybe only a man from an aristocratic house could be this way. One seemed to find a taste of freedom in such a natural manner of conversation.... After living so long abroad, this seemed to appeal to him even more. Otonu too was a man from a homely home.... Kaka, jetha, khuri, jethi, dadu, pishi, ma and baba of course – with all of them it was a traditional, large joint family.

Hearing 'dancing her way there', Otonu laughed and said, 'I can see nothing's changed after marriage. Earlier, too, I used to hear her say, if I hear about going to a wedding at a rich person's house I get a fever....'

He laughed a little more and said, 'Since you keep track of so much, you must also know that Sheema is a woman from our neighbourhood. Or I'm a man from Sheema's folks' neighbourhood.'

Partho said, 'Wait wait, let me see which side should be primary. You from their neighbourhood... or she from your neighbourhood. ... The problem's almost as complicated as the question of the oil and the container.'[2]

The car resounded with the laughter of two male voices. The voice of the car owner was undoubtedly the more powerful.

At the point of getting down from the car, Lolita said, 'I want the car tomorrow.'

Not an appeal, not a request, more like a command.

This was the way Lolita spoke.

Choudhury laughed to himself: 'Tomorrow! Can't bear any more delay!'... Of course he didn't laugh out loud. He said, 'Is it enough if you get the car? You don't want the wretched driver?'

'Oh! If I take him it'll be a test of my patience. No no, I know you. ... When you leave you'll give me your word that you'll come back early, then *phut*, you'll phone me, I can't come, suddenly, there's an important meeting.... You'll take a taxi tomorrow. Tell the people at the office that your car's gone to the "hospital".'

'Why should I lie for nothing? If I tell them it's being used by my wife, what's the harm in that?'

'No harm. They'll just know that there's only the one car to depend on. That I have nothing else.'

'Oh, that's certainly true! What a terrible thing. Fine, *I*'ll take a taxi. Whom you'll take as your charioteer, that I need to know...'

'No need for a charioteer. I'll drive myself!'

'Disaster! Don't let that notion into your head.'

Lolita became angry and said, 'Listen, why do you never give the car into my hands?'

The reply was brief.

'Fear.'

'Fear! Fear of what? Didn't I take lessons and learn to drive?'

'I'm not denying it. You certainly took lessons.'

'So? Don't I have a licence?'

'You do, and that's even more trouble.'

'Meaning?'

'Meaning? Licence means power in your chest. The courage to be reckless. And that's true for all things in life.... Quite obvious where a car is concerned.... No – car and wife, two necessary things in life, I can't lose them at the same time.'

'Lose, meaning?'

'The meaning's extremely simple. With the joy of having a license, there's the inclination to become reckless. And if you're able to crash it hard enough, both finished in the same instant. At this age it won't be possible to get either of those a second time.'

'Oh, that's the only reason? Ba, I'm only a "necessary thing" for you. Excellent! If you had the time to get another a second time, maybe you wouldn't care? Fine, I'll take a taxi.'

They'd parked the car in the garage and come into the house, but still the argument burned on.

Choudhury said in a tone of compromise, 'Aré baba, won't it do if I take you after I come back?'

'No. . . .' Lolita's obstinate reply. 'Going then means you'll start hurrying me no sooner than we sit down. Do you ever give me any time to sit with my limbs loose and chat?'

'Sit with your limbs loose and chat! O baba! Where will you go?'

Lolita, taking off her earrings and her necklace and putting them away, said in a harsh voice, 'I'm not obliged to give you an account of all my movements.'

'That you're certainly not. About what can I dare to make *that* claim? . . . But if I don't know the address, where should I go to collect you and bring you back – don't I have to think about that?'

'Oh!'

Lolita, having taken off and put away the outer layers of her fashionable clothing and walking around the room in her petticoat and brassiere, said, 'Who told you *you* have to bring me back?'

'Who's going to tell me? What will people think if I don't go? Maybe they'll decide you've quarrelled with me and left the house!'

'They'll think I'm so quarrelsome?'

'Aha, am I saying you're quarrelsome? People think things their own way, don't they? What if they think that? There's something called "prestige", isn't there?'

Lolita retorted immediately, 'I know, I know. Prestige! With that one weapon you all have held us in your fist. Completely snatched away the freedom to do what we want – oh!'

Choudhury now put away the pipe and lit a cigarette and said, 'Fine, now that you've caught that, there's no use making a fuss.... I'll try and come back early tomorrow.... But did you really need to go to Sheema's house tomorrow?'

Lolita furrowed her brow and said, 'I'm going to Sheema's house – when did I tell you that?'

The loose-limbed Choudhury twisted his arms and legs and stretched and said, 'If you have to explain everything to me, what did I learn from making house with you all these years?...'

And right after that he suddenly asked, after such a long time, 'So tell me, why didn't they get married?'

'Who?' Lolita was slightly startled, then said, 'Oh! Don't talk about it! Those country conservatives in Otonu's house! It was more or less settled in their minds. Then suddenly Otonu's thakurda saw their birth dates and straightaway sat slantwise to it. It seems Otonu was younger in age than Sheema.'

'Aré, is that so?'

'Aha, not much at all. Very slightly. But the old conservative was completely slantwise to it. He gave his decision: this could not happen. This was impossible.... If he'd been ten or twenty years older, it would certainly have been possible, but because he was just a year or two younger, it was completely – whatever. Two, two lives ruined because of a silly little prejudice!'

Lolita, having wrapped an everyday sari around herself by now, settled herself down.

'Ruined!'

Now Choudhury truly became somewhat serious. He said, 'I don't know about *two* lives. If you look at Sheema it doesn't look like her life's been ruined.'

'Is it possible to understand from the outside what's inside a woman's mind?' Lolita asked this somewhat philosophical question.

Lolita's husband said, 'That's true. It's certainly not possible. But to find a husband like Partho-protim, too, is a matter of considerable good luck for any woman.'

'But good luck isn't everything.' Lolita breathed out a deep breath, then yawned and said, 'The biggest thing in life is love.'

Choudhury, too, sighed to himself. He understood that now Lolita would take the helm of another boat. . . .

But even if he understood it, there was nothing to be done.

There are some people in the world who, when they see others relaxing a little, can't ever relax themselves. . . .

Once again Choudhury thought, Partho didn't need to go so far. Was it really only a desire to please his wife? Or to show his courage?

The subject of discussion, Otonu Rai, also kept thinking the same thing in the moving car. What *was* this about? Was the man foolish or noble? Or was it an attempt to show his courage and become a hero to his wife? Or was there some deeper motive?

But that thought didn't stand. Otonu was completely unable to bring into his mind such negative thoughts about this gentleman, the husband of his childhood friend. . . . There seemed to be an aura of transparency about the man.

The journey came to an end.

Partho slowed the car. It drew up in front of the house.

Lolita's earlier remark wasn't too much of an exaggeration.

Partho's house was almost a palace.

But there was no mark of modern style on it . . . only a traditional, old-fashioned, wealthy aristocratic style. An enormous gate, a spread of lawn in front, tall storeys. The amount of sky it occupied with only three floors, even five floors in the modern style wouldn't have reached that high. A car-verandah on the driveway, and behind that, rows of rooms. About eight windows in a row, with Venetian blinds.

A driveway from the gate, bisecting the lawn and ending at the portico, which the old occupants of the house were not willing to call anything other than a car-verandah. Partho-protim entered that car-verandah with its thick, arched columns and stopped the car.

An elderly man in a white dhuti and white fotua ran up and held the car door open! . . . Partho said, 'Srinath-da, ask Boikuntho to inform Boudi, a guest has arrived.'

Otonu let out a small sigh of relief. At least it wasn't 'Memshaheb', it was 'Boudi'. But what did 'guest' mean? Would he ask him to stay? Who knew what trouble he'd fallen into. The huge house was like a fort; if they locked him up in there, it was doubtful he could find his way out.

Otonu sighed again. Who knew where in this fort that slender, carefree girl, Sheema by name, was held prisoner.

Just recently, Otonu had seen mansions thirty and forty storeys tall, had seen brick upon brick and how insect-people fitted themselves into the small holes among these bricks and carried out their lives' journeys. Still, he had never felt they were panting in there.

At the foot of the stairs, there was another person of the same kind. Partho asked him, 'Boikuntho, how is Boudi?'

'Bimola said she is well, there's no fever.'

'All right. What did she eat?'

'That Viva. . . . And biscuits.'

The two of them began climbing up the stairs. Stone stairs, of sizeable length and breadth.

Otonu smiled a little. 'Mr Mukherjee, Sheema used to get a fever even visiting a rich person's house. . . . So now does she always have a fever?'

Sheema had been lying down; now, annoyed at the news of a guest, she'd come out from the bedroom and was sitting in the outer hall. Who'd come to bother her now.

Partho entered, and behind him Otonu.

Suddenly Sheema's face seemed to light up, *dopp!*, like a thousand-lamp chandelier. And then suddenly her face seemed to sink again into the shadows of a power cut. A little later the light burned bright again.

She stood up from the sofa, said, 'You! When did you get back?'

Otonu was unable to find anything to say. He said, 'Who stays in such a large house, ré?'

Partho-protim laughed. 'Such a greeting to a childhood friend after so long? No, you've upset all my notions about that other land. . . . Let me answer that: many people stay here. My kaka and his family, a couple of thakumas. But on my side here, only Sheema and me and all of them, Srinath, Boikuntho, Bimola, and company. All people from my baba's time. All right, why don't you both sit, I'll go take care of my bath.'

He left.

Sheema said, 'I couldn't even imagine that you'd come.'

'I couldn't either. Even after coming I'm still wondering if I've really come. . . . This coming here was really foolish, wasn't it?'

'Ba! Why should it be foolish? . . . Seeing you feels so good. You've become terrifically handsome after going abroad.'

'You've become terrific after getting married too. How's the husband?'

'You saw him yourself, didn't you?'

'I can't quite figure him out.'

'What are you thinking?'

'That's what I can't figure out. Noble? Or foolish? Or devilish? The question's made me think.'

'Just take the first one.'

'Of course, looking at you, that seems right.'

'You're still writing your poetry!'

'That I am.'

'I see it in *Desh*, here and there. Although I can't understand all of it.'

'When could you ever?'

'I used to try to understand it then, with your help. . . . But really, you didn't send me even one letter. You could have let me know you reached there.'

'How shameless could I be? You didn't write either.'

'Same story for me. How did you like that land?'

'Oh, hang it! Is there anything new to say? Everyone's written so much about it, it's done.'

'You'll go back again?'

'If I can't get a job or something here, I'll have to go back.'

'This time, get married and take your wife with you.'

'Thank you for the suggestion!'

'How did you get to meet him, ré?'

'If somebody wants to meet someone, you don't need to make arrangements.'

'You'll come again?'

'Are you crazy.'

Sheema lifted her eyes and said, 'You won't want to see me again?'

'Does every want have to be fulfilled?'

'Fine, don't come.'

When it was time to take his guest back, too, Partho said, 'Let me drive you there. How far can it be from our Chokrobera to your Priyo Mollick Road?'

'That's all right, I'll take a taxi.'

'What are you saying – I got rid of your car and brought you here, and now I should say "Go graze the field for your dinner" and leave you out on the street? At least the driver should go. . . . Anyway, you'll certainly have to come again. Today it was just a token visit. You didn't even drink a cup of coffee. I'll come and fetch you.'

Otonu stood up. He looked at Partho eye-to-eye with a firm gaze and said, 'Since you keep track of many things, you must certainly know this too, I've been the object of your wife's love.'

'Ba, don't I know? I know, and I assume that from now you'll be the object of my love too.'

Otonu said in an almost harsh voice, 'Do you really believe in these simple calculations in life?'

Partho said with steady eyes, 'What if I say I do!'

'That's the Lord's blessing on you. But can all calculations be made so simple and solved?'

Partho smiled a little and said, 'All right, let it be a little complicated. There's a kind of joy to sitting down and solving complicated problems too.'

'I don't know if what we're saying is normal. Forgive me, maybe it won't be possible for me to come again.'

'Is it fear?'

'More a lack of belief. The matter seems completely meaningless to me. Strange, too. Does anyone choose to invite their rival home?'

'Rival!'

An almost unworldly smile broke out on Partho-protim's face. He said, 'If that's what you really think, why don't you come down to a direct confrontation? Let's have a test of strength.'

Otonu couldn't understand at all what the man's intentions really were. . . . In an almost annoyed manner, he said, 'Is there some great need for a test?'

'Suppose there is, for me.' Partho-protim smiled in the same way and said, 'The bank passbook that I'm carrying around so carefully – I should know whether the bank itself is insolvent.'

The driver brought the car around.

Otonu left.

Sheema said, 'What were you talking about with him for such a long time?'

'Oh, questions of happiness and unhappiness.'

'What was the need to bring him home for no reason?'

'Ba, would he have come if I didn't bring him?'

'So what if he didn't come?'

Partho-protim said in a calm, serious voice, 'One shouldn't practise deception on oneself, Sheema. Otonu has come back to the country after so many years, everyone can meet him, even me, but you couldn't – wouldn't you have felt very bad about that? Now tell the truth.'

Sheema lifted her face and said, 'Is it even possible I wouldn't have? But why should you go taking a risk because of that? Why should you go calling this trouble upon yourself?' She, too, spoke out, in almost her cousin didi's voice, 'What do you get from playing with fire? Suppose I saw him and fell tumbling in love with him again, what will you do?'

The last part, though, was in a joking tone.

'What will I do? . . .' A strange smile broke out. Partho said, 'If I'm afraid even now of losing to that boy, and if I have to live always on my guard – it's much better to be defeated and die.'

The Ballpen with Its Refill Used Up

রিফিল ফুরিয়ে যাওয়া ডট্ পেন

Riphil Phuriye Jaoa Dotpen

The household world had moved in time to the right beat all morning. No sound had arisen from anywhere to interrupt the beat or disturb the calm.

Load shedding had not immobilized the water pump since the early morning (as it often did), the pot-scrubber Shudhahashini had not dived out of sight without notice early in the day (as on many days she dived), the gas burner in the kitchen had not, after accepting the tea-kettle upon its breast, suddenly given its answer (as it intermittently gave), and the constant unspoken cold war between Oshima and Onindita had not, for some trivial reason, turned spoken and heated up what was cold (as at any moment it did heat up).

This day, it could be called a cloudless morning. So much so that even before Porashor and Poromesh could grow impatient, the newspaper arrived, Tutun and Mithun's schoolbus came to the door and stopped at precisely the right time and took both – weighed down by the weight of books-notebooks-and-tiffin-boxes carefully arranged with a mother's love – into its lap and dashed away on its destined route!

And then, even before Porashor and Poromesh could ask for it to be hurried up, their rice had been served and was sitting on the table for them.

Suddenly in this easily moving wheel of the household world a creaking noise arose. And then it became a continuous rattle.

The matter came to light when Porashor and Poromesh were on the point of leaving for the office. Lilaboti had been missing from the house since the morning! It came to light because whenever her sons left for the office, Lilaboti – no matter where she was, no matter how important the work she was engaged in, or even if she was in a state of meditation in her prayer room – always made her appearance saying 'Durga Durga' and stood near the door.

Today she didn't.

Poromesh said, 'Where's Ma?'

'Ma?'

The bous looked this way and that.

'Where – can't see her!'

'What do you mean you can't see her? We've sat down to eat, did anyone tell her?'

'Shorno usually goes and tells her in the thakur-room.'[1]

Why such an uncaring remark? Porashor shouted out, 'Did she go tell her today? Ei, Shorno!'

Shorno's clear reply: she's just this moment arrived, back from the Mother Dairy and the milk depot. Did she know when the kaka-babus had sat down to eat?

'Go run and look in the pujo-room. Go tell her we're leaving!'

Poromesh said in an angry voice, 'Oh, this is a new thing of Ma's nowadays. Three hours of prayer! Go and see if she's gone into a trance.'

He'd just set his foot outside the door when Shorno came and gave the news: No, not in a trance. Thakuma's not in the thakur-room.

'Not in the thakur-room?'

'So? What's this now! Where? Not sitting in a corner of the pantry, is she? In the rice store-room? Have you looked on the rooftop, Shorno? Not digging up the roots of the flower plants in the rooftop garden, is she?'

'No baba no, she's not on the rooftop.'

'Still, go take another good look.'

With a sulky face Shorno went up, and with an even sulkier face she came down!

'I told you she's not on the rooftop.'

'Aré, has someone looked into the bedroom? Uh, she's not lying down unwell or something, is she?'

Shorno said heatedly, 'How can that be! Thakuma opened the door for Ma and me, like she does every day. And then she turned on the pump.'

'Then?'

'Then she went into the bathroom.'

'Then?'

'Then what do I know? Do I walk around with Thakuma? Don't I have work to do?'

And the bous? Oshima, Onindita?

But what do they know either? They say because of the pressure of work in the morning they can't see or hear anything at all. Getting the children ready and sending them to school, getting their tiffin boxes ready and sending those along with them. The rice for the babus before they leave for the office. Do they have time even to breathe? And then they should go and see what their shashuri is doing where and when?

Now the men's harsh questions, 'So you won't see or hear anything? You won't try to find out where a person's gone?'

And immediately, the wives' sharp response, 'Everyone in the house has a pair of eyes and a pair of ears!'

Their judgement impaired, out of anxiety?

They roared in their wives' faces, 'Are we supposed to look after that?'

'Why not? Because someone's a wife, is she like a thief caught in the act? – She goes and sits in the thakur-room from dawn!'

'That's right! But today that didn't happen.'

Onindita suddenly spoke up. 'Maybe she's gone bathing in the Gonga-Tonga.'

Shorno laughed out loud, *khuk-khuk*. 'What does "Tonga" mean, Chhot-kakima? Tonga!'

'Stop it. Be quiet!'

Porashor said, 'Why did you suddenly think of bathing in the Gonga, Chhoto-bouma? Is there some ceremony or such today?'

'That I don't know. But she does go sometimes!'

'Sometimes. Not very often. So she goes alone? Without telling anyone?'

'There's not much to tell! Whomever she finds nearby, she tells them and leaves. Maybe today she didn't find anyone nearby. And alone? No, that she never does, it's true. She goes with the women of the neighbourhood. Last evening I saw her standing at the window and chatting away with Dotto-ginni.'

Porashor has a government job. He couldn't wait around any more. He said, 'Shorno, go take a look in Dotto-babu's house – '

I've moved the investigation forward quite a long way, he thought, and hurried out, unconcerned.

Poromesh's job is semi-governmental, or it could even be called non-governmental, so he could afford to wait a little longer.

Rubbing his feet against the ground, he began his wait for Shorno's return.

Shorno said with the sulkiest face possible, 'She hasn't gone to that house. Dotto-buri was sitting inside sorting the greens! She said, O ma! When did we ever talk about bathing in the Gonga?'

All this time Oshima was finishing up the work in the kitchen. Today it was her turn! The days it's her turn, Oshima manages to finish up a lot of the evening's cooking and stuff it into the fridge.

But it was her hands she was working with, not her ears. Now she came out and said, 'So if you saw she wasn't in that house, why didn't you look in Tuntuni's and Gopal's folks' houses? Sometimes she goes to the temple or the jhulon-bari with their grandmothers too. Also with Tabu's pishi – '

Shorno flared up and said, 'Yes. I don't have any other work. So I should go around all morning looking for your shashuri like I'm looking for a lost cow.'

It's not as though, because she wears a frock, Shorno's flare-up is any less than Shudhahashini's.

At other times people laugh at her flare-ups, or they ignore them. But now every nerve of Lilaboti's younger son was stretched taut. Because his job wasn't governmental, was it entirely incidental? Dada had got away just fine.

And so now Poromesh didn't laugh when he heard that tiny flare-up, suddenly he set off a bomb.

'Quiet, rascal! Always talking back.'

Oshima thought that her brother-in-law set off a bomb with Shorno only as a pretext; his real target was someone else! Her head burned with anger.

Fine, it wasn't the right time now, she would get her own back later. What she would get later, she rehearsed in her mind now. Oh. Showing our temper, are we. Where you people's mother goes and when, does she tell us and go? At home she wanders around night and day with such a face, it seems she's been ordered to the gallows. But once she gets together with her friends –

Pulling her anchol quickly across her shoulders, putting her feet into her slippers, she said, 'All right, I'll go and look!'

Poromesh went to the neighbouring stationery shop and spent one rupee sixty cash to call his office and tell them he was stuck on some important work and would be a little late going in.

The shop, 'Diner Shathi',[2] is run by Orobindo. A friend of Poromesh's from his shorts-wearing days. But such a skinflint that, far from giving him a little discount on the cost of the call, he won't even let him pay later. The shameless fellow has even pasted a notice on a scrap of paper near the phone: 'First you pay, then you play.'

Insufferable! If he weren't in such a fix –

He returned and saw that Boudi had returned as well. She was saying to her younger ja, 'Went around to three houses. All the ginnis are sitting at home. Only the ginni of *this* house has vanished into the air, since the morning, without saying anything to anyone! Where would she go! As far as the rickshaw – that's her limit! Maybe – '

A glance at the clock set his head on fire.

In his mind Poromesh directed a sharp, indecorous remark at his equal-to-one's-mother senior-brother's-better-half; then he looked at his own wife and said in a displeased voice, 'Where all does Ma go alone?'

'Where else? Maybe to your Chhoto-mashi's house, or Ghontu-mama's house, or else Bubu-pishi's house.'

'Nowhere else?'

'I can't think of anywhere. It's not as though she tells us before she goes. When she's ready to leave, she tells whoever she sees in front of her, "I'm going out for a bit." But when she comes back, I see her telling seven stories, how this one's such an angel, how that one's so neat and tidy. How all the children in this one's house are the very avatars of every virtue! That's how we find out where she went.'

The bou went on speaking rapidly; Poromesh didn't pay much ear to the latter part of her remarks. If they had to pay much ear to all their bous' remarks, it would be hard for men to survive.

But hearing the first part, Poromesh seemed to find shore in a shoreless ocean. There were phones in two of those three houses, and the third was right next to the bus terminus.

He said, 'All right. I'll catch a rickshaw and go look in Bubu-pishi's house, then go to the office and phone the other two houses from there!'

He thought to himself, What more can be done at this time? He couldn't go to the thana and report it to the police. Maybe she'd come back the very moment Poromesh stepped out. Certainly something must have happened between her and the bous, and she felt bad and was sitting in someone's house. Of course it could be that; Boro-ginni was really something!

But no. Lilaboti wasn't sitting in anyone's house! Bubu-pishi said, 'O ma, what's this! Lila-boudi doesn't go anywhere alone! She hasn't even come here in a long time.'

Chhoto-mashi said, 'Why, no, last Sunday Mej-di did come for a little while. But she didn't stay long. She's always dying to get back to her household.'

Ghontu-mama said, 'Boudi? She hasn't come here in ages. What do you mean she can't be found since the morning? Does no one in the house know when she went out? That's a blessed house of yours! So does she go walking in the parks or to the temples? Some festival or some such – you don't know? Wonderful! Never mind, don't worry about it, she might have come back by now. Maybe I'll go over towards evening and take a look.'

Poromesh said in his mind, And you'll buy my head by doing so. He laid the phone down. And he thought, it's a bad mistake, I should have told them at home to let me know as soon as Ma came back. They know the office phone number. But will the bous think of it? In other matters Boro-ginni is quite proficient. But only when she needs something. . . . Right then the phone rang out.

'What? What's up? Has she returned? She hasn't? I'll go back and hear about it? I should inform Dada? But what's the matter? Hallo. Hallo. There, it's gone!'

And the situation at the house was such –

All the neighbourhood women at whose homes inquiries had been made in the morning, they started arriving one by one a little later, and each of them would put a palm to her cheek and carry on a cross-examination, Since exactly what time has Lilaboti not been seen? With whom was she last observed? Didn't she say anything to anyone before she left? Didn't even go up to the pujo-room in the morning? What could the matter be?

That this woman called Lilaboti would suddenly cause this upheaval and throw both her sons' wives into such an awkward situation – they're grumbling to themselves about this.

Still, Shorno was a lot of help in answering all this cross-examination. She had the eyewitness account! Therefore her role was paramount.

Shorno is Shudhahashini's daughter. She comes with her mother very early in the morning, works and eats and does the chores in this house all day long, and at night her mother comes and takes her away. They live nearby.

At first Shorno was unwavering in her proud role. But after having to answer the same questions time after time, now she was saying sulkily, 'I told you, she went into the bathroom, that's all I saw. Where she vanished after that I don't know. I thought she had gone up to the thakur-room on the third floor.... Yes, it's thakuma herself who opens the door for us in the early morning. She opens the pump-house lock as well.'

Right after the neighbourhood ginnis left, the neighbourhood pishi-shashuri, Bubu-pishi, arrived. And the narration commenced once more.

The bous bit their lips and said, 'It'll be blamed on us, no one else.

But when does she ever tell us before she goes anywhere?'

'Aha, but that's in the afternoon or evening sometimes, when she's free, she goes visiting for a little while! But what's this? Would anyone go out in the morning without even doing her pujo? What I say is – doesn't she even have tea in the morning?'

'Why wouldn't she? She has it when she comes down from the thakur-room. Not in our mlechchho[3] department, though. She makes it herself.'

'Hunh! I'll wait and see a while longer. Today, at home there's – '

Before they could hear what there was at Bubu-pishi's home that day, Mithun and Tutun's schoolbus horn was heard. Shorno ran to fulfil her duty. The burden of carrying back the bags of those two was Shorno's.

As soon as they entered, they were almost pounced upon! 'Ei, did you two see Dida early this morning before you left for school?'

Mithun's age is three and a half, Tutun's five. Hence the latter was the target.

'Dida? Why wouldn't we see her? I was getting late washing up, and when I knocked on the bathroom door, Dida came out in her wet clothes. She said, Baba! Such strength in that small hand!'

'Anh, is that so? And then?'

'Then what else? Bubu-pishi! When did you come?' He smiled a cheekful.

Even though Bubu is their father's pishi, they call her pishi too.

Bubu said, 'Oh, just a little earlier. Your dida can't be found since the morning, and when I heard – '

'Anh.' Tutun was startled. Then he said, 'Then Dida asked me for paper and pencil.'

'Asked you for paper and pencil?'

'Yes, she did. I said, "Where will I find paper now?" And, uh – '

Tutun recalled what had happened. 'Uh – Dida said, so give me one of your pencils. *Hee hee*. Dida calls a ballpen a pencil.'

'If she does, she does. Then? What did you do then?'

It seemed the knot of a thrilling mystery was being undone.

'Then I gave her a ballpen. Dida, *hee hee*, wrote something on a paper bag, then she got angry and said, What kind of useless pencil is this. I can't write with it! But is it my fault if the refill ran out right then? Anh!'

Hot waves of fire were coming out of the nostrils and eyes of Lilaboti's bous. That avatar of loose lips, that pishi-shashuri, had to be sitting there right at this time! There was a witness to the tangled web of mystery that Lilaboti had spun.

Bubu said, 'No no, what fault is it of yours? So whatever Dida wrote, what did she do with it?'

'That! That!'

Somewhat confused, Tutun rifled through the pockets of his shorts and said, 'Then Dida must have gone to drown herself in the Gonga.'

'Anh! What did you say? What does that mean? What does that mean? What do you mean when you say that?'

A flock of simultaneous questions: 'Why did you say that? Did she say anything to you? Speak up! Tell us quickly.'

Tutun swallowed in his dry throat and said, 'She said, Tutun, will you be very sad if I'm not around?'

'Anh! She said that? What did you say then?'

Tutun swallowed once more and said, 'I said, what should I be sad about? Do you ever tidy up my books or clothes or shoes? Do you make my tiffin for me?'

'You said that? Anh. You heartless, cruel, wretched boy!'

The word 'wretched' used for Tutun.

Tutun spoke up with a hero's valour, 'Did I tell a lie? Does Dida do all that? She only – sits in her pujo-room! And you call me wretched! Fine! Like Dida I'm going to – '

Tutun rummaged through the jungle of pieces of chalk, broken colour pencils, half-eaten Cadbury's,[4] half-sucked-dry chewing-gum wrapped in paper, and many other objects from his pocket, said 'Here, take it' and threw a crumpled, folded-and-refolded, twisted scrap of a brown-paper wrapper, and marched off inside still wearing his shoes.

Onindita ran to that skinflint Orobindo's shop.

The little that could be recovered from that letter without salutation, written in snipe's-beak-marks with a ballpen with its refill used up, on a piece of brown-paper bag sticky with chocolate, was that Lilaboti was going out. If she didn't return, no one should go out looking for her. Even if they did, they wouldn't find her. She –

'She what?' That had not been written.

Bubu sat down with her back against the wall and said, 'There's nothing more left to understand now!'

But she couldn't stay sitting there, her new jamai was supposed to come that day. She left.

Clutching that scrap of brown paper, even more ravaged from repeated attempts at decipherment, in his fist, Porashor said in a deep, solemn voice, 'I knew Ma would do something like this some day.'

Astonishing! Even at such a vile remark, not the slightest protest rose up on the stage. Not from Boro-ginni's sharp tongue, not from Chhoto-ginni's loud mouth, not even from Porashor's eternal adversary Poromesh – whose sole delight and addiction since early childhood was to refute his Dada's every opinion, whether it be East Bengal or Mohun Bagan, Congress or CPM, Nozrul-geeti or Otulproshadi, no matter what the subject – even he didn't say a word! The whole universe seemed to stand still at this moment.

That there would be no attempt to find her simply because Lilaboti had forbidden it, that was not possible, but still, at this moment no one was able to think of anything. The situation seemed to have settled like a chunk of rock, a millstone on people's chests.

From beneath that millstone, Poromesh could see two small boys, back from school, thudding and stomping around, and a smiling-faced bou in a colourful sari calling out, 'Come and eat now! Baba, baba! Don't you even get hungry – you just come home and get started on your mischief!'

He could see two shiny brass plates, each with a few rutis and some torkari. One boy said in a loud voice, 'Rutis every day, every day. Go, I won't eat.'

The bou said, cajoling, 'All right, baba, all right. I'll have porotas ready for you tomorrow. Eat this today.'

He could see one of the two boys standing at the kitchen door and shouting, 'Why do you always only sit here doing these rotten things? Come and tell me a story right now!'

The bou said, her face lit up, 'Just a little more. Only five minutes!'

Not the bou – Ma!

Astonishing, Ma was so beautiful, Ma's smile was so beautiful – how did Poromesh completely forget all that?

When Ma found a little time from her thousands of tasks and came and sat near him, how delighted the boy would be! As though for such a long time all his heart was filled with only his Ma.

So –

What happened after that, and when?

That splendid picture called 'Ma' wasn't floating in the mind of the man called Porashor. What kept floating up in Porashor's eyes was a thin, black form in a plain borderless sari.[5] She comes and stands by their dining table; no one looks at her. Not even Porashor. The form slowly goes away.

He saw again, a question being uttered by that form that was almost a shadow, and one bou flaring up. Porashor spoke up: There's plenty that's been cooked, Ma! Why did you have to come and stick your head in the middle of this? Can anyone eat any more at this time?

The shadow-form moved away.

She came and stood again near the door. Porashor said without looking at her, I'm leaving.

Then he heard, Durga Durga.

And when, how long ago, did Porashor last say 'Ma' on his own and say a few words to her? He couldn't recall. If Ma came to say something, he'd always given a dismissive answer.

Fear and discomfort anytime Ma came and stood nearby. I suppose Ma's going to say something imprudent, and right away some hood-raised woman serpent will hiss out.

But really, what did Ma say that was so bad?

Porashor started suddenly. I'm thinking about Ma in the past tense already? 'What did Ma say'! But nothing imprudent comes to mind at all. Yes, I do recall one particular day. Suddenly Ma said, How much weight you're losing day by day, Khoka! Your collarbones are showing! Why, ré?

That was all! Such a little thing!

What a disaster! What a calamity!

Oshima took the keys to the pantry (which used to be tied to Ma's anchol earlier; who knew when they had moved to Oshima's anchol) and threw them near Ma's feet and said, You can take over the household again from tomorrow. Take good care of your sons. Aha, their collarbones are sticking out from eating food from someone else's hand.

What trouble Ma had to go to, to move those keys back to Oshima's anchol. And it was Ma whom Porashor scolded at the time. He said, 'Always these foolish remarks!' . . . Without a word Ma had gone up, at an unaccustomed time, to her thakur-room.

No picture of a smiling, happy, glowing face floated in front of his eyes, this man called Porashor; only a dull, melancholy form moving along, casting its shadow. Not a face, only a form! When had he looked at her face, really! Not for ages. Still –

It was out of this melancholy that the deep, solemn words had arisen: 'I knew Ma would do something like this some day.'

Astonishing – now that it was becoming known, it seemed everyone had known it already. Quietly everyone told their husbands and wives: I knew!

One of them said, 'You're right! Sometimes Chhoto-ginni would say something harsh right to her face, and then you could see that with the hurt and insult she would certainly do something one day.'

Another one said, 'Dada's observation isn't incorrect, sometimes I've been afraid of the same thing too. The way Boro-ginni was gradually expanding her control! The person who built up this household with her own hands – to snatch away all her rights! She had to hesitate five times before even giving a handful of alms to a beggar. She had to ask, Bou-ma, which rice should I take? As though she was no one in this world, as though she was a stranger!'

Everyone knew, or why else would the five-year-old boy, too, on hearing the news of her disappearance, say first thing, 'Then Dida must have gone to drown herself in the Gonga!'

And Lilaboti's younger son?

The one who, because of his character, or because of the faults in his character, had neglected his mother in every matter and kept her in check – he was sitting with both his palms pressed to his forehead and thinking, What did Ma eat, what did she wear, did Ma ever fall ill – not once had he ever looked at any of this at all.

Hadn't Ma said one day, I have something to discuss with you, Porom!

Maybe Poromesh had replied: What, do you want something or what? Get a list ready. Had Ma given him that list? No! And the other day? Maybe there was some pujo or some such –

At this time Porashor came and said, 'I don't know anything about all this, Porom – what needs to be done, I can't even think of anything. Do we need to report this at the thana? Or maybe the radio, TV – ? Porom! I can't seem to get myself going. . . . Before you go, ask one of the bous for a description.'

'Description! What do you mean, description?'

'Aha, just things like how old, the complexion, how many feet and inches tall, any particular marks on the body, what she was wearing at the time she disappeared – '

'I have to get a description of Ma from the bous?' Poromesh's angry question.

But his dada's helpless reply, 'What else? Do you know all this? I don't seem to – '

'What else would she be wearing other than a plain borderless sari and chemise? And her complexion – '

The remark wasn't completed; a hubbub rose up somewhere! The two brothers left the room.

Lilaboti's story should have ended here.

At least that's what would have happened if it had fallen into the hands of a writer expert in the emotions!

A fundamental place of honour for the proud Lilaboti would have been forever established in the penitent hearts – oppressed by guilt and driven by the goad of conscience – of the four men and women of this household. But of course the history of that scrap of brown paper would have been concealed from their social world.

But Lilaboti's story does not fall into the skilled hands of a writer expert in the emotions. It falls into the hands of an inexpert, incapable, thick-headed writer lacking all sense of emotion. And so, when they heard the hubbub somewhere outside, the two anxious brothers, engaged in consultation, came out and saw their mother, having descended from a rickshaw, scolding the driver about the fare.

Seeing her sons, she said in a voice that had found shore in a shoreless ocean, 'Now look at this, the small distance from the Shambajar corner to here, what a fare he wants, such an outrage.'

In their mother's hands is a small, shindur-smeared wicker basket covered with a sal leaf and containing proshad, flowers, and bel leaves from her pujo!

And after that?

After that, what else! From the answers to repeated reproaches and reprimands, it was discovered that Lilaboti had always seen other ginnis impetuously going by themselves to visit Belur, Dokkhineshshor, Mayebari, Kalitola, but she herself had had to look to someone else all her life. And so she had thought, Let me try it once, get up my courage and see if I'm able to do it. And indeed she *was* able to, asking one person and another. Aha, how good it felt. She'd gone to Dokkhineshshor once before, such a long time ago.

'Oh! But why couldn't you tell someone before you left?'

Where was the time to go telling and talking? Suddenly the urge came upon her. And she'd heard that there was a bus that left from the Shambajar corner for Dokkhineshshor at six-thirty. She'd had to scramble to get there.

'Oh. But you had the time, didn't you, to leave a very artistic letter?'

'Artistic indeed. *Hee hee*. Artless, rather. What a ballpen your son handed me. It would have been better to write with a stick from a broom! I didn't even look at what I wrote.'

The two ladies of the opposing side said in unison, 'All fibs! Nothing else, a trick to frighten your sons and bous! Chhi!'

From a male voice came the soft utterance: 'It could be, really, that maybe in the end she herself was frightened and – '

What else could have happened? Most of the time, the story of the Lilabotis is written with a cheap ballpen with its refill used up.

Glossary*

Diacritical marks omitted from the text are shown here, to help with pronunciation.

a	a longer version of the unstressed vowel (the schwa sound) in English, such as the *a* in *organ*
ā	like the *a* in *father*, but shorter
ch	as in *chair*
chh	aspirated version of *ch*
d	very soft, dental
dh	aspirated version of *d*
đ	retroflex, a harder version of the *d* in *drag*
e	a shorter version of the *é* in the French *café*
é	like the *é* in *café*
ė	like the *a* in *hat*
i	between the *i* of *slip* and the *ee* of sleep
ñ	indicates the preceding vowel is nasalized
ŏ	slightly longer than the *o* in *cop*
ō	slightly shorter than the *o* in *cope* (a pure *o*, not a diphthong)

* Some of the definitions here and in the preceding notes have been adapted from *Samsad Bengali-English Dictionary*, 2nd ed., compiled by Late Sailendra Biswas M.A., edited by Sri Birendramohan Dasgupta M.A., revised by Sri Subodhchandra Sengupta M.A., Ph.D. (Sahitya Samsad, Calcutta, 1982).

ṛ retroflex, no English approximation; the tongue touches the palate and flicks forward
t very soft, dental
th aspirated version of *t*
ṭ retroflex, a harder version of the *t* in *trip*
ṭh aspirated version of *ṭ*
u between the *u* of *put* and the *oo* of *pool*

There are regional variations, so that ŏ, for example, may be pronounced ō, and vice versa.

For some words, especially names, the Bengali pronunciation is followed by the Hindi or Sanskrit, for example, *ãñchōl, anchal* and *Bishshōbhubŏn, Vishwabhuvan*, for the convenience of Hindi speakers. I have not indicated the Hindi pronunciation.

āhā, āhā-hā, āh-hā, āh-hā-hā: exclamations indicating sorrow, sympathy, impatience
ãñchōl, anchal: the free end of the sari
āpni: you (respectful)
āré: hey (exclamation)
ātōp: a kind of rice

bā! : excellent! wonderful! (also used sarcastically)
bābā: father; also used affectionately to address boys or men much younger than oneself
bābā!, bābā-bābā!: literally, father; an exclamation indicating exasperation
bābu, -bābu: gentleman; a suffix equivalent to Mister
bāchhā: dear child (affectionate or sarcastic)
Bāgdi: a backward Hindu caste
bāpu: father, 'Dad'
bhāi: brother; also used to address a companion (male or female)
bhāijhi: brother's daughter
bhāj: brother's wife
bhāshur: husband's older brother
bhŏgōbān, bhagwan: God

Bijŏyā Doshōmi, Vijay Dashami: the final day of the Durgā Pujō, celebrating the victory of good over evil
Bishshōbhubŏn, Vishwabhuvan
Bishshōnāth, Vishwanath
bōddi, baidya, vaid: a physician
Bŏlōrām, Balram
bŏṛ-, bŏṛō-: prefix indicating oldest
bŏṛdā: oldest older brother
bŏṛdi: oldest older sister
bŏṛō bōu, bŏṛō ginni: senior wife [in the household]
bŏṛō bōudi: oldest older brother's wife
bŏṛō ginni: senior wife [in the household]
bōu: wife
bōudi: older brother's wife
bōu-mā: son's wife, younger brother's wife
buṛi: old woman
buṛō: old man
byan (beān): a son's or daughter's mother-in-law or aunt-in-law

chhānā: a kind of cheese
chhi, chhi chhi: exclamation indicating reproach, condemnation, revulsion
chhōṛdā: youngest older brother
chhōt-kā: an affectionate form of chhōtō kaka
chhōtō bōu: junior wife [in the household]
chhōtō kākā, chhōtō kāku: father's youngest (younger) brother
chŏchchōri: a dry vegetable dish
Chōnḍi: a manifestation of the goddess Durga
Chŏkrōbōrty, Chakravarti
chōuki: a low stool

-dā: suffix indicating older brother (also used socially)
daal: lentils; daal-puri: fried unleavened bread with filling of cooked lentils
dādā: older brother
dādu: grandfather, 'Grandpa'
dālpuri: a fried snack

daōr: husband's younger brother
dhat!: exclamation indicating disbelief or disagreement
dhuti, dhoti: a large rectangular piece of cloth wrapped and knotted around the waist, and worn with pleats tucked in at the waist
-di: suffix indicating older sister (also used socially)
didā, didimā: mother's mother
didi: older sister
didimā: mother's mother
didimōni: older sister; also used for a female schoolteacher
Dipŏk, Dipak, Deepak
Dŏshōmi: the tenth day of a lunar fortnight
Durgā: the goddess, chief of the female deities, slayer of demons and presiding over posperity, victory, and fame of humankind
Durgā! Durgā!: an exclamation seeking the goddess's blessings

ei: hey, hey you

fōtuā: an upper-body garment similar to a shirt

ghāt: a dock, a pier
ghŏntō: an almost dry mixed-vegetable dish
Gōbindō, Govind
Gōbindōrām, Govindram
Gŏngā: the river Ganga
Gōpālchŏndrō, Gopalchandra
Gōrur: Garud, the mighty bird on which Vishnu rides
Gurudeb: spiritual master or guide; also a name for Rabindranāth Thākur

hāi Bhŏgōbān: 'Dear God'
hāi Mōdhushudŏn, etc.: similar to 'Dear God' (*see* Mōdhushudon)
hāi, hāi hāi: exclamation indicating sorrow or remorse
hañ: yes
hañ gō, ōgō: a phrase used to get someone's attention, usually addressed to an equal, for example, a spouse
Hāṛi: a backward Hindu caste

Hōrirām, Harirām
Hŏr-Pārbōti, Har and Parvati, Shiv and Parvati
hukō, hukkā: a hukkah
huñh!: exclamation indicating disagreement or annoyance

ilish: a kind of freshwater fish, the hilsa
ish: exclamation indicating surprise, sorrow, pain, etc.

jāmāi: groom, son-in-law
jā: husband's brother's wife
jėŧhā, jėŧhā-moshāi: father's older brother
jeŧhi, jeŧhimā: father's older brother's wife
joi (pronounced approximately 'joy') Mā Kāli: 'Victory to Mother Kali', a battle cry
Jŏm, Jŏmrāj, Yam, Yamraj: the god of Death, who rides a bull
jŏrdā, zardā: chewing-tobacco

Kājōl, Kajal
kākā, kākā-bābu: father's younger brother
kāki, kākimā: father's younger brother's wife
Kāli Bāṛi: a temple to the goddess Kali
kāliā: a rich curry with fish or meat
Keshŏb, Keshav
Keshŧō-Bishŧu: Krishna or Vishnu, that is, a rich or powerful person
khōkā: boy
khōlshe: a kind of fish
kheer: a rice dessert
khesh: a thin blanket
ki: what; ki ré: what's up? (a greeting, used for a familiar or a child)
khuri, khurimā: father's younger brother's wife
khur-shāshuri: father-in-law's younger brother's wife
khur-shōshur: father-in-law's younger brother
kōchu: an edible root
Kŏdōm, Kadam
kumkum: a decorative red paste applied to the forehead

Lābōnnō, Lavanya
lau: a kind of squash
Lilābōti, Lilavati
lōkkhi: a term of praise or endearment for a child
Lōkkhi, Lakshmi: the goddess Lokkhi, Lakshmi, the goddess of wealth and prosperity
luchi: a kind of puffed fried bread
lungi: a piece of cloth shorter than a dhuti, wrapped and knotted around the waist and falling to the feet

Mā Lōkkhi: same as Lōkkhi
mā: mother; also used affectionately to address girls or women much younger than oneself
māmā: mother's brother
māmi: mother's brother's wife
māshi, māshimā: mother's sister
maund: a unit of weight approximately equal to 37 kilograms
meshō, meshō-mŏshāi: mother's sister's husband
mej-: *see* mejō-
mejdi: second-oldest (older) sister
mejō-, mej-: prefix indicating second-oldest
mejō-bōudi: second-oldest (older) brother's wife
mejō-ginni: the second-oldest woman or wife of the house
mejō-jethi: father's second-oldest (older) brother's wife
mejō-kortā: the second-oldest man or husband of the house
mem-shāheb: mem-sahib, a form of address for a woman of high social standing (used by servants)
Mōdhushudŏn, Madhusudan: Vishnu
Mŏhādeb, Mahadev: Shiv
Mōllikā, Mallika
Mŏnōrŏmā, Manorama
-mŏshāi, mŏshāi: a suffix or term used to address a gentleman
mukhe bhāt: lit. rice in the mouth, a ceremony where a child is given solid food for the first time

nā: no
nŏmōshkār, namaskar: a respectful greeting
nŏndāi: husband's sister's husband
nŏnōd, nŏnōdini: husband's sister

ō bābā: an exclamation indicating apprehension, etc.
ō ki: lit. what's that?, an exclamation indicating surprise
ō mā: an exclamation indicating surprise, dismay, etc.
Ŏbhirām, Abhiram
Ōbināsh, Avinash
ōgō: *see* hañ gō
ōhō: an exclamation indicating impatience, etc.
ōl: an edible root vegetable
Ŏninditā, Anindita
Ŏrōbindō, Arvind
Ōrun, Arun
Ŏshimā, Aseema
Ŏshit, Ashit

paan (pān): the betel leaf dressed with lime paste, catechu, crushed betel nuts, and spices and folded into a cone, often eaten after meals
pānjābi: an upper garment for males, similar to a shirt but without a raised collar or cuffs
pāpōr, papad: a thin flat cake made of dal or rice
parijāt: a mythological never-fading heavenly flower or its plant
Phuleshshŏri, Phuleshwari
phulshojja: (lit.) a bed of flowers; a Hindu custom of newly married husband and wife sleeping on a bed strewn with flowers or flower petals after the wedding
pishe, pishe-mŏshāi: father's sister's husband
pishi, pishimā: father's sister
pishi-shāshuri: father-in-law's sister
Pŏddōlŏtā, Padmalata
Pŏnkŏj, Pankaj
Pŏrāshŏr, Parashar

Pŏrōmesh, Paramesh

pŏrōtā, paratha: a fried flat cake of unleavened flour, sometimes stuffed with potatoes, etc.

pŏtōl, parwal: a vegetable shaped like a small cucumber

Prōbhāsh, Prabhash

Prōbōdh, Prabodh

prōnāmi: a present or money given at the time of offering obeisance

prōshād, prasad: a food-offering made to a deity and eaten afterwards by the worshippers

Prōtibhā, Pratibha

pujō, puja: a worship ceremony and often also a social occasion

Pushpō, Pushpa

putrō-bōdhu: son's wife

pyesh: a sweet dish made from thickened milk, rice, and sugar

Rāghōb, Rāghav

ré: a form of address to a familiar or a child

Rŏjōni, Rajni

Rōkkhe-Kāli: a manifestation of the goddess Kāli

Rŏmesh, Ramesh

Rŏnōjit, Ranajit or Ranjit

rui: a freshwater fish

ruti, roti: a baked flat cake of unleavened flour

Shādhōnrām, Sadhanram

Shāhā, Saha

-shāheb, shāhab, sahib: a suffix indicating respect; a form of address for a gentleman

shālā, sala: wife's brother

shāli, sali: wife's sister

Shambajar: Shyam-bajar, -bazar, a commercial centre in north Calcutta

shāñkhā: a bangle made of a conch-shell

Shānnāl, Sanyal

shāshuri, shāshuri-mā: mother-in-law

Shāstrōs, Shastras: the scriptures

Sheāldāh, Sealdah: a Kolkata railway station
Shen, Sen
sher, seer: a measure of weight, about a kilogram
Shib, Shiv: one of the three principal Hindu gods
Shōktipŏdō, Shaktipada
Shōmitā, Shamita
Shŏnkōr, Shankar
Shŏrnō, Swarna
Shŏrōt, Sharat
Shōshi, Shashi
shōshthi: the sixth day of a lunar fortnight
Shōti, Sati: the wife of Shiv; a wife very devoted to her husband
Shōttōbālā, Satyabala
Shubŏl, Subal
Shubŏchōnā, Suvachana
Shudhākāntō, Sudhakant
Shukāntō, Sukant
Shulōkkhōnā, Sulakshana
shupuri: betel nut
Shurōbālā, Surbala
Srijuktō: a respectful title used for males
Srimōti, Shrimati: a title for a married woman

taañt (tāñt): a loom
thākurdā: father's father
thākumā, thākurmā: father's mother
thākurjhi: husband's sister
thākurpō: husband's younger brother
tŏrkāri: vegetables; a vegetable dish
Tribeni, Triveni
Tribhubōn, Tribhuvan
tumi: you (familiar)

Notes

Introduction

1 Unless noted otherwise, the remarks in this essay about Ashapurna Debi's work pertain specifically to her short stories.

2 According to Blanche Gelfant, this manner of fictional perspective, known as the 'ecological' type, corresponds to a framework whereby which literature about the city represents one of three distinctive narrative patterns. See Burton Pike, *The Image of the City in Modern Literature* (Princeton: Princeton UP 1981) 10.

3 Ujjal K. Mazumdar, preface, *Selected Stories by Ashapurna Debi* (Calcutta: Model Book House, 1984) 1. Translation mine.

4 Kalpana Bardhan, ed. and trans., *Of Women, Outcasts, Peasants, and Rebels: A Selection of Bengali Short Stories* (Berkeley: U California Press, 1990) 12.

5 Krishna Dutta and Andrew Robinson, introduction, *Noon in Calcutta: Short Stories from Bengal* (New York: Viking, 1992) xix.

6 Anima Bose, 'The Bengali Short Story', *Indian Literature* 26, 4 (1984): 51.

7 Paul Oliver, *Dwellings: The Home across the World* (Austin: U Texas P, 1987) 200.

8 Oliver 200.

9 Oliver 210.

10 Oliver 211.

11 Antoine Prost, introduction, *Riddles of Identity in Modern Times*, vol. 5 of *A History of Private Life*, ed. Antoine Prost and Gerard Vincent (Cambridge: Belknap, 1991) 3.

12 Mineke Schipper, ed., *Unheard Words: Women and Literature in Africa, the Arab World, the Caribbean and Latin America* (London: Allison, 1985) 129.

13 Rasik Bihari, 'An Appraisal of Ashapurna Debi's Trilogy', *Indian Literature* 27, 1 (1984): 35-54.

14 Author's preface, 'A Few Short Words about Short Stories', *Swanirbachita Shrestha Galpa* [A Collection of Self-Selected Stories], by Ashapurna Debi (Calcutta: Model, 1988).

15 Dutta and Robinson xxx.

16 Dutta and Robinson xxx.

17 Susie Tharu and K. Lalita, ed., *Women Writing in India: 600 B.C. to the Present*, vol. 1 (New York: Feminist Press, 1991) 476.

18 Tharu and Lalita 477.

19 Tharu and Lalita 476.

20 Tharu and Lalita 476.

21 Manisha Roy, *Bengali Women* (Chicago: U Chicago P, 1972) 57.

22 Note: 'Debi' is not a specific surname. Until the latter part of the twentieth century it was customary for married Bengali women not to be referred by either their maiden or married surname, but rather by the title 'Debi', which is a generic term equivalent to the English 'Mrs'. The surname of Ashapurna Debi's husband is Gupta.

23 Gayatri Spivak, *In Other Worlds: Essays in Cultural Politics* (New York: Routledge, 1987).

24 Bardhan 3.

25 Tharu and Lalita 235.

26 Bardhan 24.

27 Anima Bose, introduction, *A Bouquet of Modern Short Stories*, by Ashapurna Debi, trans. A. Bose (New Delhi: Pankaj, 1978) 11.

28 Gaston Bachelard, *The Poetics of Space*, trans. M. Jolas (Boston: Beacon, 1994) x.

29 Philippa Tristam, *Living Space in Fact and Fiction* (London: Routledge, 1989) 1.

30 Tristam 2.

31 Tristam 229.

32 Witold Rybczynski, *Home: A Short History of an Idea* (New York: Viking, 1986) 51.

33 Rybczynski 112.

34 B.C. Southam, ed., *Jane Austen: The Critical Heritage 1870–1940*, vol. 1 (London: Routledge, 1968) 3.

35 Southam, *Jane Austen: The Critical Heritage 1870–1940*, vol. 2 (London: Routledge, 1987) 39.

36 Cited in Sandra Gilbert and Susan Gubar, *The Madwoman in the Attic: The Woman Writer and the Nineteenth-Century Literary Imagination*. (New Haven: Yale UP, 1979) 107–8.

37 Southam vol. 2, 84.

38 Meenakshi Mukherjee, *Women Writers: Jane Austen* (New York: St. Martin's, 1991) 74.

39 Gilbert and Gubar 84.

40 See Polly Wynn Allen, *Building Domestic Liberty: Charlotte Perkins Gilman's Architectural Feminism* (Amherst: U Massachusetts P, 1988) 79.

41 Gilbert and Gubar 86.

42 Gilbert and Gubar 88.

43 Peter Berger, Brigitte Berger, and Hansfried Kellner, *The Homeless Mind: Modernization and Consciousness* (New York: Vintage, 1974) 65.

44 Berger et al. 186.

45 Berger et al. 187.

46 Chiara Saraceno, 'The Italian Family: Paradoxes of privacy', trans. Raymond Rosenthal, *Riddles of Identity in Modern Times* 473.

47 Meredith Borthwick, *The Changing Role of Women in Bengal, 1849–1905* (Princeton: Princeton UP, 1984).

48 Tristam 233.

49 Tristam 5.

50 Bettina Knapp, *Archetype, Architecture, and the Writer* (Bloomington: Indiana UP, 1986) vi.

51 This is an unforgivably brief summary of one of a complex of arguments, all brilliantly put forth in Lawrence Venuti's groundbreaking study *The Translator's Invisibility* (New York: Routledge, 1995). My own thoughts on the subject are laid out more fully in the introduction (in the hardcover version) to my translations of Nirmal Verma's short fiction, *Indian Errant* (New Delhi: Indialog, 2002).

52 In order to avoid an excess of diacritical marks in the text, I have used the same vowel, o, to represent two distinct vowel sounds in Bengali, the first slightly longer than the o in cop and the second a shorter version of the o in cope. In the name Poddolota, for example, the first and third os are the first kind, and the second the second. For additional help with pronunciation of Bengali names and terms, see the glossary.

53 I should point out that while I render these characters' names thus, I do not do the same for my own, which should under this scheme be spelt Proshenjeet, but in my English-speaking life I've lived with Prasenjit for so long that I find it difficult to change it now.

Oishorjo (Wealth)

1 Wealth; splendour; glory; majesty; divine grace. Usually pronounced Oish-shorjo, with a doubled consonant.

2 'Shib' (Shiv, Shiva, one of the three principal Hindu gods) is rhymed here with 'jeeb', creature.

Poddolotar Shopno (Poddolota's Dream)

1 Pujo, puja, a worship ceremony and, when conducted on a larger scale, often also a social occasion.

2 The magical power of seeing distant events reflected on the surface of one's fingernail; the range of one's knowledge.

3 Burnt puffed rice, given to the poor.

4 Ayot, mark(s) indicating that a woman's husband is alive.

5 Kulo, winnowing-tray. A new bride is welcomed into her new home with various objects placed on the tray.

6 That is, suddenly become rich.

7 'Horir loot', a scattering of candy to worshippers after prayers to Hori (Hari, Vishnu).

8 Pronam, the act of touching the feet of an older person, symbolically to take the dust from their feet and place it on one's own head.

Bondini (Prisoner)

1 That is, (since there were only sixteen annas to the rupee) more than all the hours in a day.

2 Shankha, a kind of bangle worn by married women.

Lokshan (Loss)

1 That is, Probodh-kaka's wife (now deceased)

Patal Probesh (Entering the Underworld)

1 There is a pun in the original: she gets nothing but drinking water (khabar jol) for a snack (jol-khabar).

2 Ghomta, an edge of the sari pulled over the head to indicate respect.

3 Bhotcharj, Bhattacharyya, a Brahmin surname; Bhatpara, a place known for its very respectable Brahmins.

Potraboron (A Covering of Leaves)

1 There is a rhyme here in the original: 'Lekhapora na kochupora'.

2 There is a rhyme here in the original: 'Labi na habi!' [habi=mute, stupid].

Deshlai Baksho (Matchbox)

1 A reference to the Ramayan and the story of Ram's army of monkeys setting fire to Ravan's island capital of Lanka.

2 Washerman (Hindi dhobi).

3 There is a pun in the original: '*ekannoborti poribarer bahannokhana hater phank theke*...' [italics added], that is, 'through the gaps among the fifty-two hands of the family that eats together', where part of the adjective 'ekannoborti' ('eating together', or joint) also means fifty-one.

Kathamo (The Scheme of Things)

1 A lowly Hindu caste.

2 Oshto-mongola, an early rite after a wedding; hence, an extremely new bride.

3 There were sixteen annas to the rupee.

4 Brahmon, Brahmin.

5 Acharjo, Acharya, a teacher of the scriptures.

6 Invoking the protection of the goddess Shosthi for the child.

7 Jomraj, Yamraj, the god of death.

Shok (Grief)

1 'Film'.

Ponkhi-Mohol (Bird Palace)

1 An oil-lamp designed for five wicks.
2 Nagpash, a mythological missile capable of producing snakes that bound the victim (as with a noose).
3 The introductory piece of a classical-music composition.
4 Son, prince.
5 A prayer ceremony carried out on the sixth night after the birth of a newborn for his or her well-being.

Chhayashurjo (Shadowsun)

1 A variety of jasmine.
2 A derogatory-sounding name; also a flower.
3 Arjo=Aryan [the English word comes from the Sanskrit], meaning venerable; senior; excellent; noble; civilized.
4 Snakes draped over the shoulder by some holy men: that is, for effect only, of no practical use.
5 That is, an impossible condition won't be met, and the desired result won't be achieved.

Akashmati (Earth Sky)

1 Akash: the sky, the heavens; mati: ground, soil, landed property
2 Bangla-desh: not Bangladesh but Bengal generally.
3 That is, he may arrive on a day that entails dietary restrictions.
4 That is, the fifth night of the waxing moon.
5 The day of the full moon in the months of Ashshin (Ashwin) and Kartik, mid-September to mid-November, when Lokkhi (Lakshmi) is worshipped.

Ei Prithibi (This World)

1 Previously, there were sixteen annas to the rupee; hence, three-fourths.

2 Quacks would use soil to treat some illnesses.

3 Jom, Yama, the god of Death.

4 Tired, the English word used in Bengali transliteration in the original.

5 Gorur pal, a cow-herd.

Kanch Punti Hiray (Glass Beads Diamonds)

1 A Rabindranath song, 'Do walk alone'.

2 The custom of applying turmeric paste to the bride or groom before the wedding ceremony.

3 That is, on a funeral pyre.

Para Na Para (To Be Unable to Be Able)

1 Grandfather, 'grandpa'.

2 A mythological king.

3 A saw used for cutting conch-shells, which cuts both ways: a dilemma.

Bekoshur (Not Guilty)

1 A form of theatre.

2 Lakshmi, the goddess of wealth and prosperity.

3 Naru-gopal, laru-gopal, an image of the child Krishna (Gopal) with a laru (a kind of sweet) in his hand.

4 Kali Yug, the present epoch of sin and vice.

5 A juicy dessert.

6 From Bengali fairy tales.

7 A sour fruit that turns crimson when ripe.

Prothom O Shesh (First and Last)

1 From the saying 'Boror piriti, balir bandh / khone hate dori, khone ke chand': Rich people's affections, a dam made of sand / one moment, hands bound with rope, the next moment, (as beloved as) the moon, that is, extremely unreliable or unpredictable.

Du-shahoshik (Foolhardy)

1 Also seths, rich merchants or bankers.

2 'Patradhar toilo' or 'toiladhar patro'?, that is, which is it: oil held in a container, or a container holding oil?

Riphil Phuriye Jaoa Dotpen (The Ballpen with Its Refill Used Up)

1 The room of the gods, that is, the prayer room.
2 'Daytime Companion'.
3 Mlechchho, mlechchha, non-Hindu or anti-Hindu; given to non-Hindu or unscriptural or evil practices; that is, impure.
4 A brand of chocolate.
5 That is, a widow's sari.